DISCARD

NATURAL HISTORY

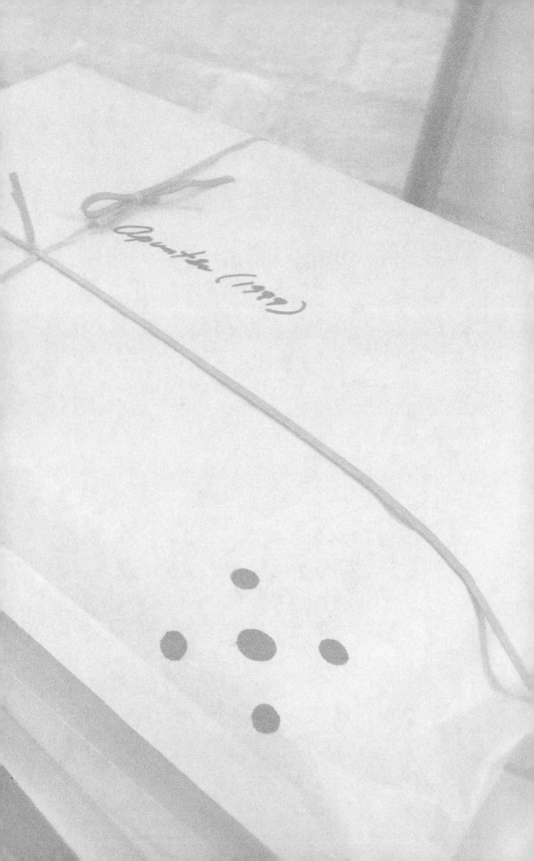

NATURAL HISTORY

CARLOS FONSECA

Translated from the Spanish by Megan McDowell

FARRAR, STRAUS AND GIROUX

New York

Farrar, Straus and Giroux
120 Broadway, New York 10271

Copyright © 2017 by Carlos Fonseca
Translation copyright © 2020 by Megan McDowell
All rights reserved
Printed in the United States of America
Originally published in Spanish in 2017 by Anagrama, Spain, as *Museo animal*
English translation published in the United States by Farrar, Straus and Giroux
First American edition, 2020

Library of Congress Control Number: 2020934828
ISBN: 978-0-374-21630-6

Our books may be purchased in bulk for promotional, educational, or business
use. Please contact your local bookseller or the Macmillan Corporate and
Premium Sales Department at 1-800-221-7945, extension 5442, or by e-mail at
MacmillanSpecialMarkets@macmillan.com.

www.fsgbooks.com
www.twitter.com/fsgbooks • www.facebook.com/fsgbooks

10 9 8 7 6 5 4 3 2 1

To Ricardo Piglia, for his incomparable generosity.

To Atalya and Rafael, as always.

We keep inventing folk tales of the end.

—Don DeLillo

The unknown is an abstraction; the known, a desert; but what is half-known, half-seen, is the perfect breeding ground for desire and hallucination.

—Juan José Saer

If we were to disappear, would the barbarians
spend their afternoons excavating our ruins?

—J. M. Coetzee, *Waiting for the Barbarians*

1

For years I remained faithful to a strange obsession. No sooner would someone start talking to me of beginnings than my mind would turn to the childhood memory of an old painter I used to watch on TV, who painted dozens of nearly identical landscapes. I'd flash on the image of that bearded old man, his solemn voice that could have been real or put-on, I never knew. On the heels of the image would come the moral, corny but efficient: the best way to avoid a new beginning was by imitating one that had come before. Inadvertently, I ended up taking that postcard wisdom to heart. The same way the old painter set to sketching yet another picture full of little trees and mountains, I would copy some other beginning stolen from my memory: a dribble of the ball, a first line that floated to the surface, an expression that would start a conversation. That repeated inauguration encompassed everything. For years, I thought that was the way to protect myself from the horrible anxiety that overcomes us all at the thought that we're doing something new. The old guy started painting another landscape, and I went on with my life, repeating it forward.

Maybe that's why tonight, when the package arrived past ten o'clock, I had the feeling that it wasn't something happening, but repeating. I heard a car pull up outside, looked out the window, and saw it all: the old, elegant green car; the driver taking something from the trunk; the curious faces of the teenagers who stopped on their bikes to watch. I understood immediately what it was about, but even so it took me a few minutes to answer the door. I decided instead to pour myself a drink, turn up the music a little, and wait until the last possible moment. Only when I felt that the driver was about to leave did I set the drink on the table, go downstairs, open the door, and confront what I'd been expecting: the familiar but now almost forgotten face of a man who handed me a package. I accepted it, hinted at a gesture of condolence, and closed the door on the attentive and slightly judgmental faces of the kids and one or another of their parents. Then came the sound of the engine roaring down the street, and my mind flashed on the distant image of that car making the same trip back to the city, only in the middle of the night and with me in it. I've relived everything as if it were seven years ago, not night but early morning, not a package but a phone call, and then I remembered the old painter and his landscapes. The strange thing, I told myself then, is this: in the beginning there's no sudden cut, no catastrophe or collapse, only a slight sense of repetition, a package that arrives just after ten, when no one is expecting it but one is still awake. Something that would have been more appropriate at eight arrives at ten, and suddenly the rules of the game are different and the onlookers' gazes have changed. Still, I accepted the package, felt its weight, and once inside I dropped it on the table. And like that, in the warm summer with the window open to the street that then really did seem empty, I started to think about that call that came seven years ago, just after five in the morning, an hour when no one expects their sleep to be interrupted. Then the package became heavy, real, a little bothersome, and I had no choice but to open it and face what I'd foreseen: a series of manila envelopes that would have been anonymous except that, on the last one, I saw a short note in her unmistakable handwriting. My suspicions confirmed, I've still not despaired. As Tancredo says, every dog will have his day.

Tancredo has his theories. He'll say, for example, that it was all a conspiracy, then take a sip of his dark beer and smile. For years now he's done nothing but criticize my decisions one by one, take them apart on the basis of humor and beer. Tancredo is my own little perplexity machine, my refutation device, not to say my friend. He tells me, for example, that accepting that call was unacceptable. Unacceptable not because I knew what was behind it but because I should have been asleep. Plus, he says, who was I to think I knew anything about that world? He says such things to me, then sips his beer, smiles, and tosses out another theory. I think, he says, that the key here is something else: they'll be back one day, and you'll realize this was all a big joke. A minor joke that grew and grew until no one had the courage to tell you it was a joke and you were left not knowing if the thing was tragedy or farce. He sees that I'm not interested in his theories and he changes tack. He knows I prefer anecdote to theory, and maybe that's why he asks, Do you know the story of William Howard?

I shake my head. With Tancredo you never know where he gets his stories, but there they are, always within reach, like a pack of cigarettes to be divvied up. And so he tells me the story of this William Howard, a gringo he met in the Caribbean. He tells me he met him on the street, when the guy approached him in rags, stinking and drunk, to ask him for money. Every day it was the same: he'd go up to Tancredo without recognizing him, and in his terrible Spanish he'd ask for alms. The thing is, Tancredo says, after a couple of months, this character started to fascinate me: Why was he there, how had he gotten there, why had he stayed? So I asked him for his story. You know what that scoundrel replied? He told me he'd come to that place because he collected islands. At first I thought it was a linguistic mistake, but then it became very clear that the man believed it all: he thought that islands were something you could collect, like coins or stamps. I always wondered who had ever convinced him of such nonsense. But there the guy was, in the middle of an island, and I had the feeling someone had forgotten to tell him the punch line of the joke. Tancredo smiles, slaps me on the back, and ends by telling me, Take it easy, the dog will have its day.

And so, when I discovered the newspaper obituary a week ago, I remembered Tancredo's words and the story of William Howard, island collector. I don't know why but the gringo's words came back to me, and suddenly the conviction grew that it was necessary to compile all the obituaries, printed and digital, absolutely all of them, as if they were islands. I started to gather them, one by one, with a collector's mania, until tonight, when I heard the car pull up and I knew what it was about. Since then, for a good hour now, I've been thinking about that first early-morning call, until a brief intuition began to hover over my stupor and forced me to confront the weight of evidence: the envelopes piled up like islands are making me think that, during all that time, she had a secret purpose for those notes. Tragedy or farce? For now I refuse to open those folders, which Tancredo swears hold nothing but a long practical joke.

Three manila envelopes, wrapped with a fine red cord tied in a bow, like a gift. Along with the envelopes, there's an obituary announcing the death, with that brief but pointed style they do so well: "Giovanna Luxembourg,

Designer, Dead at 40." Farther down there's a photo of her dressed in black with a little hat on her head, her eyes staring off into the distance. The obituary talks a bit about her work, mentions certain exhibitions, references an eternal legacy, and that's it. Regrets over a death at such an early age. A way of displaying a secret, I tell myself, or maybe of wrapping her in enigma. Stupidities of the press. The envelopes, however, are more real: they lie there, closed. Even without opening them, it's clear they contain a great volume of papers. Strange that they aren't numbered; it makes you think they've been compiled recently, without method. Something about the strange punctuality with which they've arrived in the car today suggests otherwise. Apart from that, the only distinctive thing at first sight is the little annotation that serves as an improvised title: *Notes (1999)*. And that's where I stop. I recognize her handwriting, the way the letters bump into each other and consume themselves until they're thin and indistinguishable. Then, when I move the title envelope over the others, I see a figure that seems to have been sketched in the corner of one in a moment of distraction.

It looks like a domino. No doubt about it, it looks like the five in dominoes, but it isn't. Now that I notice it, I think that doodle was put there

to remind me of how everything started. I linger again over the obituary: "Giovanna Luxembourg, Designer, Dead at 40." If Tancredo had been here, he wouldn't have missed a beat. He would have said, Note that your esteemed designer was only thirty-three, the age of Christ, when she sent for you. He would have stopped for a brief moment to rub that beard of his, which makes him somewhat resemble a dragon, or a Don Quijote with a good share of Sancho Panza, and he would have gone deeper into his nonsense. An apostle with no clear cause, he would have said, like the ones Napoleon met leaving Waterloo. They stuck with him and adored him, illiterates no one wanted anywhere, ignorant people who didn't yet know they were following a defeated Moses. He would have said that and he would have laughed, he would have told me more stories about islands and everything would have lightened up. But Tancredo isn't here, the clock is striking eleven, and the symbol that now reemerges is clearly recognizable: it's the quincunx that once so fascinated me. The obituary has reminded me that, in just a few months, I will also turn forty.

2

In my college years, when the plan was still that I would become a mathematician, a bearded friend with the aura of a false philosopher mentioned a text in passing, a text that had tried to demonstrate that behind every natural variation, behind any difference, a single pattern existed. A kind of primary form. For a while I forgot his comment, until two winters later when a different friend—my roommate, a terribly hygienic man who wouldn't travel without a bar of soap in his pocket—mentioned to me that a certain Thomas Browne, a melancholic man who was born and died in the baroque seventeenth century, had suggested in a posthumously published work that nature and culture came together in the repetition of a five-pointed shape called the quincunx. It reminded me of my first friend, his beard and his airs of a false prophet, and I headed for the library. It took me a while to find the book I was looking for. Someone had put it in the wrong place and it had ended up in the cartoon section—the librarian told me—alongside Mickey Mouse and Tom and Jerry, lost among Walt Disney's first sketches. So I went to the cartoon section and there, among those little drawings that have given so much fodder for conversation, I found an old edition of the book. The work in question was *The Garden of Cyrus*, originally published in 1658, twenty-four years before the author's death. My friend had been wrong: it was the author's last book before he died, not a posthumous publication. However, both of my friends had gotten one thing right: the idea of the prevalence of the quincunx pattern in nature as proof of divine design. On the cover I found the portrait of a small man with deeply large, red, and sad eyes; a pointed beard; and long hair. I remember thinking that Thomas Browne himself was a little like a blend of my two friends painted from memory. I didn't linger, though, over that impression. I paged quickly through the old edition until I found the shape. It was a kind of starfish, a geometrical butterfly that instantly awakened my interest. I picked up the book, checked it out with the librarian, and took it back to my dorm room. I remember how my roommate denied any resemblance to the melancholic Englishman.

Fifteen years later, after much reading and an unexpected career change, my obsession would end up producing a series of articles that I was more satisfied with than proud of. Among them, the least well-known was a history of the permutations of the pattern in tropical butterflies, a brief article called "Variations of the Quincunx Pattern and Its Uses for Tropical Lepidoptera," of which the British journal *The Lepidopterologist* had published a short excerpt under the more exotic title "The Quincunx and Its Tropical Repercussions." I remember that I started the article, solely on a whim, with a beautiful quote from Browne himself: "Gardens were before gardeners, and but some hours after the earth." Even today, when I read that article, I'm surprised to find that quote there, like a superfluous translation lost inside another one, necessary and relevant. For some reason I still haven't figured out, it was that little article that managed to catch the attention of a fashion designer whose name I knew in passing but of whose work I knew little. Even without opening them, I know: the three envelopes I now have in front of me are a kind of testament to a collaboration that started with a simple phone call.

3

The call had come at five. Usually I wouldn't have answered at such an early hour, but the night before I'd gone out drinking with friends and the heartburn had hit me right at four, leaving me prostrate in bed in a kind of doze that refused to decide between lucidity and sleep. Now I see it clearly: the call was just the excuse I needed to get up at that uncertain hour. But that's not important. The call had come at five, and on the fifth ring I answered, using that distinctive expression I had adopted in the face of the uncertainty that takes over the tongue abroad when the country speaks one language and your friends another: a kind of amorphous child of the North American *hello* and the Latin American *hola*, a flapping *alo alo* that had something of a desperate tortoise about it. In that strange language that's all of them precisely because it's none, I answered the phone on the fifth ring. A masculine voice confirmed my name in English and then, as though to give some indication of his intention, asked me, "Are you the author of 'The Quincunx and Its Tropical Repercussions'?" I replied that I was, that it was one of the texts I had published as a student, and I added that I no longer worked at the university, but at a small natural history museum in New Jersey. For a moment I felt that I had lost him, that the line was dead, but then I heard him again as though he were coming back from somewhere. The rest of the conversation flowed as if I were still sleeping: he told me about a project whose nature I didn't entirely grasp, he mentioned a name that somehow reminded me of a board game I used to play as a child, he talked about the importance of discretion given that we were dealing with a person of some public renown. In the early dawn I merely said yes, without knowing exactly what I was acceding to. I was possessed by a strange feeling of loss, a little like the one some people suffer on the open seas when they suddenly become aware that they've left behind all the equilibrium of solid land. I don't remember how the call ended, but I do remember that after the guy hung up, I sat there, unable to sleep but also not awake, an early-morning insomniac with last night's acid reflux in full force. I cooked some eggs with onion and started to search my computer for a copy of my old article, of which I remembered almost nothing. I read it once, twice, three times, while my mind played a movie of the past ten years of my life, a trajectory that many people would call a free fall toward failure, but that I had come to accept with a certain noble joy. I saw a thousand variations of the quincunx on Cuban butterflies, Costa Rican ones, Dominican, Puerto Rican, until there were no quincunxes or butterflies left, only my face as a fifteen-year-old boy, looking at a chalkboard covered in symbols. The sun was coming up, and I could see the white landscape out the window. It was winter.

I had recently stopped taking anxiety pills, and sometimes my reality seemed to jump a little. Nothing strange, no hallucinations or anything like that, just little slipups of perception that seemed more like appeals to lucidity than anything else. Something like that happened with the phone call. Not that I forgot it or rejected it, just that it stayed there, latent, and slipped through the cracks of life. During those weeks I ate in the same New Brunswick restaurants, had beers with Tancredo and my friends, went to the museum and returned home, all without mentioning the incident once. But without my realizing it, wheels were turning in my unconscious. What I did notice was the return of a certain interest in form, a perception of patterns. The return, so long delayed, of my interest in the quincunx. Maybe it was the many times I read the article with my gaze on something else, but suddenly the shape came at me from every direction: it was in an ashtray, in the marine fossils at the museum, beer bubbles, the configuration of passengers in the middle of the train station. It stubbornly appeared everywhere, it floated to the surface and then hid, only to emerge hours later in some other unexpected place. Just when I was starting to believe I was finally free of obsessions, one little phone call had made me haul up a forgotten passion. After a week it started to feel like a curse, like a weight that threatened to sink the raft of my everyday world. So I didn't wait—one afternoon I came home from the museum and started to look through the papers by the phone until I found one with a distracted scribble alongside a New York City number. I dialed it and the phone rang three times, but no one answered. I don't know why, but I thought that meant I'd written down the number wrong. Something in me associated that number with total authority: an all or nothing. So I didn't try again until two days later, after I read my article for the fifth time. The phone rang three times, and on the fourth, a masculine voice answered; it was similar to the one from the first morning but slightly different. I identified myself and mentioned the previous call, but, after a silence, he told me no one there knew what I was talking about. So I sat down to watch TV. Same stuff as always: earthquakes on the Chilean coast, polemics from corrupt politicians, absurd programs meant to bury boredom. When they called back, I was half-asleep, and for some reason I let the call go to voice mail, and that's how I heard her voice for the first time. It was a bit hoarse, and it sounded to me like it was fading.

4

So I could say that at first there is a voice that repeats on the machine: a hoarse voice that at times seems to wane but then rings out again. Then I see myself in a car (a green car like the one that stopped in the middle of my street today), crossing the snowy streets of that terrible winter, alternating lefts and rights, leaving New Brunswick without knowing exactly where I'm going, leaving the museum behind in the hope that the time has finally come to return to my ambitions. I remember passing abandoned factories familiar to anyone who's ever been to New Jersey, those snow-covered ruins, a small chapel peeking out through the white. I watch as two trains catch up and pass us. Then in the darkness I see little more than car headlights, the driver's face when he occasionally looks back in the rearview mirror, until suddenly that beautiful catastrophe of lights emerges: the city of New York as seen from New Jersey.

Sometimes I like to think that insomnia springs from a vision like that: a lucid and enormous vista that insomniacs can't forget. They close their eyes and see it there, a magnificent canvas full of tiny points that shiver like stars. I remember crossing the bridge and reaching that city I'd been to often, but that now grew like the sponge of my ambition—the way sea urchins or coral reefs grow, with measured patience—pursuing an obscure voice that now belonged to the entire city. I see myself there in the same car that pulled up at my house tonight. we cross a snow covered street and I feel the car turn right. Then I see an enormous, windowless building appear, and the car slows as the first cobblestones sound beneath us.

That first meeting was long, though it didn't seem so. It was night, more or less ten o'clock, when the car stopped on that cobblestone street that I would later come to know so well, between that terrible edifice with no windows and a luxury apartment building that had once been an industrial factory. I figure it must have been ten because I later understood that with her, everything had a strange punctuality, a certain precision that was not of a fixed schedule or the common sense determined by calendars.

Yes, it must have been ten because after that it was always ten, eleven at the latest, the kind of ambiguous hour when everyone is returning home for the night. I was greeted by a young woman whom for a second I confused with her, with the designer, but who I quickly realized was an assistant, one of many who would multiply almost anonymously, always a little on the margins, bothersome as they went about the strange labors of a glorified office worker. I introduced myself, and the next thing I knew we were walking through the halls of a building I would visit many times, but which, if I saw it again today, I would find foreign. It was marked by a desolate atmosphere, like an empty hotel or a forgotten factory; the doors were numbered inside. I remember I always had the feeling the doormen traded shifts with their brothers: the people who greeted me were always strangely similar, just a little different. I remember the assistant stopping at one of the doors and knocking with a lightness that bordered on fear. Then, when the door opened, I saw her for the first time: a woman in her youth, beautiful precisely because something in her refused to submit to another's gaze. I remember she introduced herself, but what caught my attention was a certain nervous tic, a way she had of pausing halfway through her sentences, as if she'd forgotten to mention something and in the middle of a phrase she wanted to back up, only to realize she had no choice but to finish. I think she was wearing a blue scarf, and I felt like I had seen her before. The rest of her clothes were entirely black, as I soon found out was her habit.

I remember it was still cold in the hallway, and she invited me in. We sat in the middle of the room, very far apart, me on a sofa I found extremely uncomfortable, her in a wooden chair. Out of shyness or distraction, I started to look at the picture that rose up behind her, an image made of rags soaked in oil paint, until I heard her start that strange and hallucinatory monologue that I still feel I'd heard somewhere else: she started by mentioning the eyes of the *Caligo brasiliensis*, the butterfly that has two dots on its wings that make it look like an owl. Then she went on to discuss the famous case of the praying mantis, how the insect plays at anonymity in the jungle's depths. I remember she mentioned something about rain in a tropical jungle, and then she stopped. She glanced distractedly at the painting, took out a little notebook, and started to sketch: butterflies, insects, marine figures, little doodles that barely communicated anything, but that she rushed to show me. Here are the *Calappae*, which look like rocks; here the *chlamydes*, they look like seeds; here the *moenas*, which looks like gravel: she said all of this with absolute seriousness, and then she started to laugh. I thought maybe it was all a bad joke, or maybe, worse, the monologue of a madwoman, but something in the tone of her voice made me think this was something else. Then, pointing to another drawing—a series of bell-shaped flowers I quickly recognized as Brazilian cholas—she finally got to the reason for her call.

"I'm tired," she told me, "of doing fashion collections. Before my time runs out, I want to do a collection *about* fashion. Not just fashion, but something more." Her finger, long and pale, pointed toward the notebook again. Something in her voice was left hanging in the air, and I thought back to the voice I'd heard weeks earlier on the machine, that first intuition that some part of her was being extinguished. Then we talked about more practical things, the city and the winter, my work at the museum and the quincunx, all that mundane fog that just then, at least, seemed disrupted. It must have been nearly two when I said my goodbyes. Somehow, almost four hours had passed. I remember that when I left, the driver told me he would take me home, but I refused on the pretext that I wanted to walk a bit. The snow, I told him, had warmed the streets a little.

I walked for several hours, a bit lost, while impressions from our conversation leapt up in my mind. Flashes, images of awkward moments, the echo of that laugh that seemed ever more ambiguous. I crossed the snowy streets unhurriedly, with the strange conviction that I was intuitively heading eastward, and soon the sun would appear and I could go home. I kept thinking about that hoarse voice I'd listened to with animal patience, and felt again the intuition that something in it was being extinguished. I passed Chinatown, then a strange street full of cats, and I remembered the odd way she had jumped right into the project with her sketches, and I almost convinced myself that all of it, the whole hallucinatory monologue, was copied from somewhere else. From a badly translated movie or some TV show. The strange thing was that when Giovanna spoke, something in her retreated, the way the original words in a foreign film retreat after they're dubbed over in another language. I was distracted from my speculation by the neon sign of a nightclub. Some kids were gathered in front of it. I realized there was still some life left in the night and thought maybe it was worth going into a bar and having a drink. It was the word "Bowery" that had drawn my attention to the sign. I knew the name the way I knew the whole city, the way one knows things from outside: through other people's stories, novels I'd read. I felt a newfound need to find out whether some ancestor of mine had been there, walked those same streets; I suddenly felt like that was the only thing that would give me the right to walk at those hours through unfamiliar neighborhoods. I remembered an expression that the designer had used that same night—"tropical animal"—and I thought that there wasn't much of the animal about my own tropics, and that she was wrong, I wasn't the right person for this project. Yes, thousands of Puerto Ricans had arrived in great waves of migration in the fifties and sixties, but my relationship with that generation was ambiguous and problematic. Perhaps that's why I'd decided to settle at the margins of the city, in odd little New Brunswick, with its bars full of veterans who looked at me sideways, with suspicion. My relationship with the town I lived in asked for something deeper, not a matter of second or third generation, since people always looked at me with profound distrust. Something told me I would be safe only if I had an ancestor who'd once walked those same streets in the nineteenth century. Then the root would be deep and strong and I could meet everything with a sense of right and inheritance. Somewhere I'd seen a photograph of the Bowery at the turn of the century: a crowd walked in the shadow of the first train lines, cobblestoned streets lined with storefronts inviting one to linger awhile—streets that invited one to vice. I imagined that precursor of mine amid the crowd, a man in a suit and hat— maybe the only ones he owned—laboring through those streets. Perhaps he felt the same sense of disquiet and confusion that now assaulted me, at the sight of how the old area of Manhattan vice had become, after a century, a timid shadow of itself. Perhaps in an attempt to forget the feeling of rootlessness that every photograph-inspired memory brings, I decided to go inside. Not the bar with the kids and the neon sign, but a quieter one I found a few steps farther on, down a set of stairs to a kind of hidden underground; on my way down, I passed a drunk couple playing at kisses.

———

There are places that give us the feeling of a mistake, and that bar was one of them. It was a Lebanese restaurant, full of hookahs and lit by a reddish light that gave it an air of false dawn. It must have been three in the morning when I pushed past the drunk couple on my way down the stairs, where the snow was starting to melt, and went inside. The place had a strange architecture that produced unexpected corners, where drunk young people were smoking and drinking wine at long wooden tables that would have been more at home in a rustic Italian restaurant than there, washed in the bar's tired alcoholic breath. More than anything I wished I had a book, something to occupy my hands and my leisure, anything, a cell phone or a blank page. I could have, at least, assumed the anonymity that things bestow on us as they occupy our hands, a seeming industriousness that would have neutralized the feeling of being alone, completely alone among groups finishing off their nights with laughter. I ordered a glass of red wine, and I started to observe the strange fauna. I was surprised by the subtle way the waiters maneuvered around tables, cool and diligent. There was something terribly silent about it all, considering it was a bar at last call. As though some kind of black hole had settled among the tables, ready to devour any excess noise.

Then I saw her.

She must have been sixty years old. Her hair was dyed red and she had the gaze of an obsessive. She was taking up an entire table, over which she'd spread out countless newspapers. The scene reminded me of old war movies, the part where the general meets with his colonels to plan the final ambush. Something about her seemed outsize, or measured on a different scale. I ordered another glass of wine and went back to watching her. The waiters moved around her with a strange calm. I came to think maybe she was the owner of the place, but was convinced otherwise by the thought that no bar owner would be awake at that hour. Her face showed traces of beauty, as if she'd once been lovely and today had to bear the weight of that initial beauty. Her movements were unhurried, but I managed to distinguish, within her fundamental calm, a seeming eagerness to devour everything at once. Then, through memory or intuition, as though to shake off that specter, I went back to thinking about Giovanna. She also had something of the mocking oracle about her, the Egyptian sphinx, the actress desperately seeking anonymity. Now that I thought about it, I noticed how odd it was, the naturalness with which she seemed to reject everything that was hers. Maybe it had been the shock of the first impression or how fast she'd launched into the project, but only now did I dwell on the designer's singularities. She had terribly blond hair, like Hollywood actresses in the fifties, and in the vibrant blue of her eyes I could discern a lie. I tried to imagine her in another key, with dark hair and brown eyes, but I couldn't. Everything had seemed normal when I'd been in her apartment, but now the idiosyncrasies leapt into view: the way she'd refused to speak English, preferring a Spanish of unclear provenance; the subtle though absolute lack of family photographs in the house; the way the conversation had seemed almost to have been planned in advance. I tried to imagine Giovanna old, but I only returned to the image of that newspaper reader who was now struggling with matters far removed from her task. Two drunk girls, curious about her like I was, had gone over to talk to her. The woman, clearly a bit neurotic, had reacted with gestures that verged on violence—gesticulations that could have escalated if not for the waiters, who asked the girls for discretion, and then the woman sank back into her reading. The theory that she was crazy felt disrespectful and superficial. As Tancredo says, we have to understand crazy people according to their own laws. Perhaps that was why I ordered yet another glass, and after so many, I thought that maybe she was right, that newspapers should be read in the wee hours of the morning, when the next day's news was about to arrive. When I looked at my watch, it was almost five. The sun would be out soon and I was far from home, far from New Brunswick and the museum, in a bar where a woman was obsessively reading newspapers at dawn. When I left the bar, two boys were fighting on the corner. I thought that the whole experience must have been a little like my false ancestor's.

In those weeks, I told only Tancredo the details of the peculiar scene I'd witnessed in the bar. Even today, part of me thinks I accepted the project just so I could go back there, to that bar of reddish rock and strange calm. Perhaps, I tell myself, this whole matter could be summed up as a childish fascination with the woman reading newspapers at dawn. The thing is, every time I tried to explain my fascination to Tancredo over beers, I felt myself falling short: the description failed me, my tone wasn't right, the words were rushed and ended up fading away before they reached their target. Tancredo, a little tired of so much ambiguity, tapped his cigarette into the ashtray and was quiet for a second, then pursed his lips and described a theory of his own. According to him, the Bowery bar was a little like what physicists call the "event horizon," the border around a black hole where the escape velocity is equal to the speed of light. Any phenomenon beyond that horizon would be imperceptible to an external observer, and vice versa. Like an ants' nest, Tancredo said, and for the first time I started to take a little pleasure in his crazy analogies. I remembered the stairs, and the neon sign of the nearby bar, the fight I'd seen on my way out. Later, when the project started to consume me, I thought how that borderline of ants could well describe, too, the strange, dead-end affair I'd gotten caught up in. But that was later. At first there was only that image of obsessive reading at dawn, and around it a routine of insomnia that repeated ad nauseam, until it left me exhausted over a beer across from Tancredo as he laid out his theories.

5

The calls usually came at three, always with different voices. The phone would ring, my coworkers at the museum would shoot me knowing looks, I'd leave my catalogs and go off to meet the usual: a soft-timbered voice informing me of the meeting's time and place. It all had an air of false secrecy, of illegality. I just happily, robotically accepted the routine. Later, around nine, the same greenish car would come by my apartment, and I'd go down the stairs with some anxiety, but willing to go along with whatever this was. In that first winter I remember seeing all the variations the snow can create on the same landscape: the thousand ways in which, as it melts, the snow paints that landscape—already ruinous—with allegories of war. After a few months the trip became so ordinary a ritual that I would sleep the whole way, only to rouse myself when I felt the first cobblestones under the tires. Then I would confront that building of a thousand faces, where I would hold long conversations with Giovanna on a thousand different subjects: a theory about the silhouettes of birds on the wing, the nature of color, mimesis and its animal origin, Latin American anthropology. Conversations that always ended up turning into extended monologues by Giovanna, in which I would catch phrases I thought I'd heard somewhere else. We talked about a thousand things, and her helpers moved discreetly around us, in a continuous activity that mimicked the hallucinatory atmosphere of that bar where the waiters moved with tact and grace as they tried not to bother the newspaper reader. Giovanna sketched in a small notebook with a red leather cover while I looked on and wondered where this was all going. Hours later, one of her helpers would see me to the door, with the excuse that the designer was tired. Then I would go out to roam the streets. I'd wander for a while before stopping, as always, at the neon sign in the Bowery, at the top of the stairs that led to the Lebanese bar where a sixty-year-old woman obsessively read newspapers. I would sit down, order a glass of wine, and start to soak in my surroundings: the drunk young people chasing kisses, the waiters who seemed ever more like Giovanna's helpers, and, in that ambiguous center that for Tancredo marked a borderline, the reader with her martial cartography of information.

I feared, in those first weeks, that I would be discovered in my fascination.

I feared that one day, the woman would stand up from her own fixation and see me there, staring at her. She seemed to have a different sense of space, however: as if, outside the newspapers, her reality was limited to her immediate surroundings. So I watched how night after night the drunk kids drew close enough to bother her. Only then, as though feeling an annoying insect, would she shake herself violently and rebuke them. One of the waiters would come to her rescue and shoo away the drunks, and then she would sink again into that cloud of information. I could watch her spend hours like that, until, at five o'clock, I took my leave and caught the train home.

I've just looked at the clock and it's almost one. Then I've thought how in those years, the image of reading in the middle of the bar came to be for me the reflected image of my own insomnia. I've thought a little about mirrors, and the strange feeling that overcomes a child when, in a moment of distraction, he relaxes his hand and sees his helium balloon fly through the air with inimitable lightness. I feel something of that inverted vertigo now, as I remember that year I spent immersed in a project whose logic escaped me, but over which I felt a certain growing sense of ownership. I felt, in a way, that my fictional ancestor was attending my steps, legitimizing them and lending them meaning.

Almost one, and the envelopes are still unopened. Outside, the street is empty; there's the occasional drunken shout, but in general, total calm reigns. I've walked around the room, a little bored, made a cup of coffee, and decided to turn on the fan. With a little white noise as background music, a cup of coffee to revitalize the early morning, everything hums along better. I look again at the envelopes and say to myself, "The dog will have his day." Then I open the computer again in search of anything that could distract me. After a while I find myself reading one of the obituaries. Another photo of Giovanna, this time on the runway in one of her last shows, and then a summary of her work. What catches my attention, however, is a piece of information I'd almost forgotten: in a brief phrase, the obituary mentions the terrible fear Giovanna felt in crowds. Just a line, but that fact jumps out at me unexpectedly alongside the image of the fragile designer in a crowded hall: the way she had of distancing herself from it all, creating her own space as if her life depended on it. Something in her expression tied her to the woman who read newspapers, something made her complicit in that sect of strangers who try to hide from their dreams in the middle of the night. She never mentioned her fear to me, but part of her would withdraw into hiding and I could see it clearly. Then I think it all makes a little sense. Her obsession with the mimetic tricks of the praying mantis, with thinking about fashion as an art of camouflage and hiding. Her hair dyed utterly blond and those false contact lenses through which she smiled shyly, like a person stepping backward. One didn't need to see her in the middle of a crowd to know that her place was elsewhere. As if, when everyone else had decided that fashion was an art of pageantry, she had proposed the opposite, to think about fashion as the art of anonymity in the jungle. I notice now that though we met in various places, of which the apartment in that industrial building was the first, the spaces tended to be enclosed, as if the city caused her a terrible dread. I notice now that in the many houses where we met, the furniture was arranged in such a way that she could disappear into it without any need for closeness. I take a sip of coffee, and the image of her shielding herself becomes so alive and real that for the first time tonight I feel a little sadness.

The envelopes are starting to tempt me.

It all started with the usual jokes, to later degenerate into realer possibilities: What if you sleep with her? Could it be that the quincunx has a crush? That maybe in secret, deep down, you love her? Tancredo's questions extended out over the table as unexplored possibilities. Giovanna was attractive, there was no doubt about that. Something in her false blue eyes forced one to care for her. But then, as soon as intimacy was insinuated, she cut all ties, and suddenly the distance was such that the very possibility of seeing her again came into doubt. She would disappear for months without leaving a message. Then I'd read in the newspapers that she was in London, Milan, Munich. Some part of me felt betrayed, and I again accepted my place at the museum, with my catalogs and beers, with the schoolkids who came through in noisy packs. Weeks passed and I would almost forget her and her project, except that I couldn't bring myself to give up on it so easily, especially when its nature still wasn't clear. "Tragedy or farce," Tancredo would say, and I knew I'd have to follow the plan to its final conclusions if I wanted to know the punch line. And the next week a call would come, and hours later I'd be back in the greenish car on my way to the city, in a new season, different weather, but willing to participate in the same enigma. For months I was saved by the idea that no matter how much time passed, I could always count on the fact that in a small bar in the city, hidden from everyone, a woman was reading newspapers. Constancy has its tricks, however, and the day it fails, a whole world seems to collapse.

Soon I found that Giovanna's terror of crowds was linked to another, greater fear: the terror of illness. It must have been spring when she told me. It had been an intense winter with a lot of snow and wind, and spring had arrived with a certain prophetic air. The call had come the previous day, at the usual hour but with different instructions: we would meet at noon at the designer's beach house. I remember how the next day I prepared a little backpack and waited with a beer in my hand, looking out the window at the dogs and their owners as they passed. Maybe because of the conversations I'd been having with Giovanna, that morning I found myself thinking how strange it was that there were no stray dogs in those North American cities. As a child I'd always been terribly frightened of them, those dogs that wandered the streets ungoverned by owners or laws, symbols of a latent violence that could lunge and bite at any moment. I would stay inside and watch them go by, happy to have a barred window in front of me. Modern cities, I thought, sublimate their violence with skyscrapers. Modern cities erase their borders with construction cranes. I was deep in these thoughts when I saw the car arrive. I gulped my beer, and when I went down I was met by the same driver's face. I debated mentioning my thoughts, but in the end I decided to keep quiet. We spent the next two hours in silence on the highway, me thinking about stray dogs and cities, dogs and islands, until nature started to win out over the landscape of ruin and I felt that something was approaching. A green sign placed the Hamptons ten miles away. Giovanna had mentioned the house to me during the winter. She'd inherited it at a very young age, and since then had spent long periods there every spring. I wanted to ask her about her parents, but something told me it was better to hold my tongue. And so, when I arrived, I confined myself to a cordial greeting and a discreet comment. Two hours later we were lying on the terrace in bathing suits, holding glasses of champagne, looking out at the waves, and talking about some small insects that play at cannibalism in the jungle. That was when she mentioned her fears. As a child, she said, she'd spent time in the tropics. She had traveled across islands, she'd been on coasts with clear water and intense downpours, she'd trekked through mountains and waterfalls. I wanted to stop her and ask for details, but I knew that when it came to

Giovanna, ambiguity was a decision. There, on an island, she'd fallen ill. An insect bit her and she spent torturous months sick in bed, hospitalized in a far-off country. I remember how she knit her brow as she told me details about her long stay in that tropical hospital, and how her speech seemed to shrink away in fear. I remembered the voice I'd heard months before on the answering machine, and I flashed again on the image of those dogs of my childhood.

Her convalescence had lasted two months, during which her only lifeline was a series of children's books that an old nurse read to her day and night. With my glass of champagne in hand, I imagined the contours of that scene: the little girl just ten years old, brown hair and black eyes—very different from the woman who now furrowed her fearful brow again—lost on a distant island, an unfamiliar language all around her. I listened to the story she was telling me and I could sense the absent silhouettes: the mother and father whose presence she should mention but didn't. I thought again about stopping her and asking about her parents, but her voice got ahead of me and I felt it would be disrespectful. The worst part, she told me, was the immobility. To lie there motionless like one of those camouflaged insects we could spend hours talking about.

Everything started to make more sense. Just then, Giovanna brusquely changed the subject and went back to our debate about mimetic cannibalism. "To devour oneself." I remember the words precisely because they didn't harmonize in the slightest with that sunny afternoon in the Hamptons, the ocean pounding all around us. I remember I kept thinking about the story of her hospitalization, but she went on with her theories. She outlined then what for a long time I considered the greatest expression of the whole joke turned farce: "The ideal thing," she told me, "would be to leave the runway pitch-black, have the models walk it completely naked in the dark. Not just darkness, but the girls walking the runway as they otherwise would, if they were wearing the full collection." She said these things and part of me wanted to hate her, to expose the farce, but that very same part refused to hate the ten-year-old girl she had been. I wanted to delve into the shadows of those months of convalescence. So I stayed there until the sun began to set and she invited me to spend the night, but I—maybe out of fear or modesty, maybe afraid of loving her— excused myself, saying I had a lot of work at the museum and I'd better get back to New Brunswick. Thinking about the story I'd just heard, though, I decided to head to the Bowery.

That night was different. I got to the Lebanese bar early and sat down to drink a glass of wine. The woman with the newspapers wasn't there, so I convinced myself I'd have to wait. Almost reflexively, as if I were filling a void, I called to one of the waiters and asked for a paper. After a moment they brought me one and I caught myself reading the art section. A short article about certain anonymous interventions by a British artist in various cities: graffiti in New York, installations in Berlin, large-scale conceptual art in London. The artist's identity was unknown but his signature was unmistakable. I thought of Giovanna, of Duchamp's signatures, and about the story of convalescence I'd heard that afternoon. Somehow that thought led me to a different childhood story: I remembered the vague pleasure I always felt on long afternoons spent fishing. My father and I used to go. He would guide us to some rocks on the coast where he'd start the routine, which was so precise: set the bait, the weights, fling back the rod and cast it. Then watch how the bobber floated there, in that suspended time of another world, a world of patience not so different from insomnia. Feel the flection of the tide on the line, make a game of distinguishing the force of a fish from that of the waves. Between one glass of wine and another, I thought how there was a line that ran through it all, convalescence, midnight newspapers, and those long afternoons spent fishing. A certain inverted gravity. I ordered another glass, and another. I tried, inadvertently, to rid my mind of the image of young Giovanna lying in bed, listening to stories in another language, terribly alone on that anonymous island. I thought about Tancredo and the story of William Howard, the island collector. I thought about that house in the Hamptons, the inheritance Giovanna had mentioned, and I told myself that the whole farce was about family. That it was all a subtle way to justify so much opulence. But there was Giovanna's face, its distant presence, her unease and her fear. There was something real behind that apparent solitude. That was when the lady of the newspapers came in, accompanied this time by a small man dressed in black, with a long-sleeved collarless shirt that lent him a monastic air. It was the first and last time I ever saw her with another person. They sat down at the same table as always and I wondered if the man knew that there, hours later, a memorable scene would take place. She looked a little different, with her red curls falling perfectly and a long, red dress decorated with blue flowers. Her face no longer held tiredness, but seemed to take on the authority of age. The spring suited her so well that for a moment I thought I could love her. It was then that I thought she noticed me. After long months of spying, I'd finally committed the capital mistake: I arrived too early. As if in that bar one had to respect a secret schedule that regulated visibility and invisibility. I felt terribly present, and I tried to hide behind my newspaper. People were dining and chatting all around us, while I drank one glass of wine after another. I had committed the sin of arriving too early, and the only way out I could discern was to get drunk to the point of invisibility. I remember that from behind the newspaper I could watch her talking with that man, who seemed plucked from a Hare Krishna sect. Somehow I felt betrayed, as if, behind the many nights I spent in that place, there was a pact of shared but unaccepted solitude. Perhaps, I thought, my early arrival had broken that imagined contract between insomniacs. I had arrived early to the bar, but late to Giovanna's story. The impossibility of arriving on time, I told myself, is another name for insomnia. At the other end of the bar, a blond girl was smiling mischievously at me.

On the right corner of the newspaper was printed "April 23, 1999." The new millennium was coming and everyone was talking about total collapse, an informational error in the way programmers had stored dates. I thought about the strange English name for that software error: a *bug*. I thought again about the insect that had bitten Giovanna, the way our conversations always ended up centering on some bug. And for a moment I saw myself again as a child, swatting at mosquitoes and tripping over my feet until I finally surrendered in frustration to the bites. Insects, there's nothing so annoying. With insects, the problem was that the slap always came too late or too early. I ordered another glass of wine and then, when the man left and the woman took out her newspapers, I ordered another. I was afraid my strategy would backfire, and it would be my drunkenness that gave me away. I laughed a little, thinking that something or other had bitten us all.

8

During Tancredo's younger years as an activist, he'd harbored his own obsession: he came up with a way to critique the system using what he called "practical reason." He lived in New Brunswick but worked in New York, so he took the train every day. It occurred to him to record all the train's arrivals, the discrepancies in its schedules, to highlight the delays. For him, every delay was proof that something in that supposedly perfect system didn't work. It all ended up in a little notebook with a red leather cover that was similar to the one where Giovanna would later sketch out her theories. I looked at Tancredo as he told me this, at his mustache with its pointed ends and his red-brimmed hat; I laughed a little and accused him of trying to hide his obsessive nature. You have to learn the art of patience, I told him, citing my grandfather. Maybe seven years have passed since he told me that story, but I feel like something in that whole question of schedules is starting to take on relevance, as my insomnia stretches out past two o'clock and the temptation to open the envelopes is gaining ground. Drink enough coffee, and the timing is always right.

I watch as a car pulls up and parks outside. Two people get out, a woman and a man. She is carrying a bouquet of flowers and he is dressed in an impeccable suit. Suddenly the woman turns and seems to rebuke the man. Impatient, he starts to yell at her. I don't know what the argument is about, but its intensity is growing. The window creates a frame, and the sound of the fan re-creates rhythms. I start to think that these kinds of scenes always happen while people are asleep, that certainly my neighbor is sleeping peacefully while, in his front yard, a couple holding flowers is fighting. I can't distinguish what they say, only the intensity of their gestures and the violence in his voice: the contours of an empty scene. Then I remember that during those months, I started to keep a notebook of possibilities, where I outlined different explanations for the scene I witnessed in the bar. It was a red leather notebook, like Tancredo's and Giovanna's, where I gave free rein to my imagination and placed the newspaper reader into broader stories. I had baptized the notebook on the first page with a playful title: *Reading Hypotheses*. Something in that title sounded like high school to me, like a science fair, a schoolboy's silliness. Maybe that's why I liked it.

So the thing is that I used the notebook to sketch out possibilities, from the simplest, which was madness, to the most complex, which was that it was all terribly normal and I was the one who hallucinated its strangeness. It was something like a notebook of stories for insomniacs, narrations skating over the void, like those stories Giovanna had to listen to during her months of convalescence. In some cases I wrote in the first person, but in others the protagonist was that New York ancestor I had created. I would reach the bar after one of my long conversations with Giovanna, open the notebook cautiously, and as I drank, I'd outline a hypothesis: my ancestor would appear suddenly—hat in hand, the face of a man with few friends— and he'd sit down beside the woman and they would start to talk. It was all in the dialogue: that's where the real hypotheses came into play, from madness to a search for a missing daughter.

I look out the window again: the couple is still there, but now they're quieter, embracing in the middle of the street, unabashed. We always ignore the fact that someone could be watching from a window. That's where the origin of fiction hides. The appropriate thing, then, I tell myself, would be to create empty images: images like little black holes, as Tancredo would say. The image of a pale young Giovanna in a hospital bed returns to my mind, a voice beside her reading fairy tales in Spanish, and around that voice the knot of an absence: her parents aren't there. From the day she told me that story, I knew, immediately, that nothing would be the same. Nothing can be once one of the players of the game believes he has the crux of the story, the key to filling the void. So after that day on the beach everything changed a little, enough to make me think I was falling into another trap, a more dangerous one, since it made me think that I finally understood something. The prankster's trick, Tancredo told me once, is making the victim believe he has control over the situation. Only then will he fall hard and unexpectedly. Perhaps I sensed this and it was what made me get blind drunk that night, until I almost went over to the newspaper reader and admitted the secret of my spying. I got lucky, and just when I wanted to approach her, my pen started to leak over the notebook, spilling out a new hypothetical story. Like now, as I look out the window and see that the couple has disappeared, and I start to imagine possible endings.

9

That night I dreamed. Afraid my bender would break my will for silence, I left the bar earlier than usual and managed to catch the last train of the night. A no-man's-land of two hours stretches out between the last train of one day and the first train of the next. By then I had become an expert in those indistinct hours. I knew to perfection that it's during those hours when Penn Station takes on its true density, when the drunks and bums commingle with dreadfully tired upright citizens. Then there are the accidentals: tourists in transit who would rather sleep in the station for a few hours than pay for a night in a Manhattan hotel. But that night I got there early enough to catch the last train. I slipped in among the drunk young people and finally found a seat across from an older woman who gave me the side-eye. Rarely have I felt tireder. The drunken shouting did not matter, nor did the swaying of the train. I fell asleep in a few minutes. That's when I dreamed I was little—not just young but truly small. I dreamed myself diminutive among a throng of soft-timbered voices, all nearly identical but slightly different, all demanding something from me. I stuffed my hands in my pockets as if desperately searching for something, but there was nothing there. In the background I heard Tancredo's laughter grow louder, until suddenly there were no more voices or laughter, just some kind of Caribbean music, salsa or *son*, and a man appeared and introduced himself as William Howard. His beard was overgrown and he reeked of beer, but I still tried to hug him. Impossible, however, to hug a drunk in a dream. The bearded man pushed me away and showed me a newspaper with a date long past. He was laughing as he showed it to me, and then he set it on fire. Then there was nothing left, no drunk or island or music, just a bunch of ants crawling around, impatient and teeming, on a sidewalk dotted with gum.

I was woken by a train whistle just as we were approaching New Brunswick. I looked around and saw some young people who were still keeping the party going, and then there was the ticket collector stamping tickets. The scene was full of anachronistic shadings: the ticket collector's clothes, the mechanical sound of the stamp, the swaying of the cars. An old loudspeaker blared the names of the next stations in a voice so fuzzy it was no help at all. I adored the train with all the intensity of a love for final things. I realized it was stopping, and caught a glimpse of my station in the distance. From so many early-morning trips my body had learned, even tipsy as it was, to track the distances. The station at that hour was almost empty, except for the usual drunks and a few dealers on the prowl. One of them approached me and I tried unsuccessfully to dodge him. He said a bunch of words to me that I didn't understand, and then he cursed me in a deep and serious voice. The truth is that I was still a little under the influence of all the alcohol, and when I saw him, the only thing I felt was the unexpected return of the dream I'd had. I hardly ever remembered dreams, and when I did they were always like a strange fog from which sudden, solitary images would emerge. But this time was different. Maybe it was the drunkenness, but I felt the whole dream in living flesh. I saw myself there, in that same station, tiny like an insect in the Amazon, listening to a bum who was none other than Tancredo's William Howard. In the dream I'd been surprised to see that the man whose story I'd heard so many times wasn't white, as I'd always imagined him, but a black man with imposing muscles. I saw myself there, in the middle of the station, listening to stories of islands while the ants crawled around us, invisible but real. Only then, when the fear reached its highest point, like a helium balloon about to burst, did the ticket collector wake me up to ask for my ticket, and I was able to breathe as I realized New Brunswick was still a ways off, more than four stations away. I can't remember any other time when my dreams ensnared me like that. I thought the insomnia was starting to take a toll and I should try to get more sleep. Outside, framed by the train car's window, the night ran by fast and dark, to the beat of that train rushing and shaking southward. Drunk, I felt a loss.

Giovanna called me again the next week. She had an odd request: she wanted to see me on my home court, at the museum. I didn't know how to say no to her, so two days later, in the afternoon, all my coworkers watched that strange parade of assistants followed by a woman dressed in black. It all had something circus-like about it, something of a children's pageant gone astray. I sighed at the thought that at least to a certain extent this would legitimate the strange attitude I'd had toward my work over the past year, my cold and distant mien as I'd set the catalogs aside to devote myself to perpetual insomnia. My appearance had changed. I had terrible circles under my eyes and at times I practically fell asleep in the middle of the exhibition hall, right onto an informational plaque. So that afternoon, when I saw the first assistants enter, I felt a little relieved, a little proud. That circus parade confirmed the few stories I'd told my coworkers, just when they were all starting to look at me with worried faces. I watched the helpers pass one by one, their faces young and ambitious, and something in me felt like I belonged to that race of impatient beings. Someday, we seemed to all be saying, our turn would come. She crossed the main hall of the museum, hugged me, and asked to see the gallery of tropical butterflies. Our museum was humble but extensive and twisted. I guided Giovanna through that odd maze until we reached the butterfly hall. Beyond the glass dome was a sunny day that shone in brightly. In the full light, her face, as she leaned over the multitude of butterflies on display, looked soft and delicate. Her false blue eyes reflected the butterflies' shades in an interplay of doubles where I briefly thought I saw something illuminated. She looked at me happily and said that she rarely went to museums—the crowds—but that she was grateful to me because my museum was a very hygienic place. I'll never forget that word, "hygienic," placed there like bait. Then, offhandedly, she mentioned a story that I didn't fully grasp. It was the story of a French poet who had edited a fashion magazine in the nineteenth century. Though I forget his name, I remember a quote that Giovanna assured me the poet had applied to the greatest fashion designer of the age: "He knows how to create dresses as fugitive as our thoughts." Though I didn't understand it, it struck me as a beautiful quote, befitting that gallery, which after so many years I finally saw in its true splendor. Giovanna went on with her anecdote. There, in that magazine whose name, *La dernière mode*, contained the key to the profession, the poet devoted himself to outlining, under crackpot and aristocratic pseudonyms, a theory of the fleeting: he tried to describe the relationship between thought and analogy, image and metamorphosis, clouds, seasons, and the reflection of the perfumes of thought. It all sounded a little cheesy to me, interesting but unsuccessful. I remember, however, that Giovanna closed with a withering, fatal phrase: "In sum, fashion is the art of prophesy, and thus of meteorology." She had that allegorical and epigrammatic way of speaking, as if she were leaving clues that one would have to think about later, once night had fallen, in a Bowery bar while watching a woman read. I felt it was all coming from somewhere else, from a place that was just starting to show itself from behind a series of stories that could well be false. That was the interesting thing with her, that feeling that everything could very well be fake, a kind of world in scare quotes, an immense joke that would end up falling on my head just when I least expected it. During that time she started to use a phrase that today has become terribly relevant. She'd come out with one of her epigrammatic phrases or stories, look at me tenderly, and then say: "One of these days I'll show you the papers." She'd say that and then go quiet, with the ability all great seducers have of proposing something and then showing you their empty palm. I'd be left there, a little tired and puffy-eyed, thinking of the mysterious cloud of papers that hid all of that woman's thoughts. Just like that, sentence by sentence, she was winning the game as if it were a chess match. Maybe that's why today, when the driver arrived with a package in hand, I thought about her strange way of speaking, as if it were all going to take on meaning in retrospect.

10

"One of these days I'll show you the papers": seven years later, the cipher is finally starting to unravel and show its seams. With the envelopes in front of me, scattered in childish disorder, I start to think about how easy it would be to burn it all in an absolute gesture. Get rid of the problem. Brush off this legacy that doesn't belong to me. A series of images from epic scenes of destruction come to my mind. The most famous and most often cited, the destruction of the Library of Alexandria; then I thought about the 1501 burning of the Arabic manuscripts under orders of Cardinal Cisneros, until I turned to less historic but equally disastrous burnings, like the ones perpetrated during the Chilean coup in 1973, when it's said that more than fifteen thousand copies of a novel by García Márquez were burned. Then my mind turned to Ray Bradbury's *Fahrenheit 451*, in which a fireman's job is to find and burn books. Another image, however, brought the epic list to a halt. I've been assaulted by the idea that, even if I burned it all, everything would stay the same. Surely she anticipated such a gesture and asked someone to photocopy all the documents before giving them to me. I've pictured myself receiving a slew of emails with copies of those documents after I thought I'd destroyed them, and the idea, though comic in a way, has struck me as dreadful.

Once, Tancredo and I tried to come up with a total and irreversible gesture. I suggested setting fires. I liked those final scenes in novels or movies when one of the protagonists, fearful that a secret will be discovered, burns the house with the enigma inside. Tancredo's reply was short and dismissive: fire is only good for lighting cigarettes and cooking stews. Now that I think about it, he was right: the copies of copies would win any race against the fastest of fires. Then I remembered another story of fire and manuscripts. An American friend told it to me during my first days as a student: the story of a literary critic who, during the war, literally smoked an entire manuscript. He didn't have papers, so he found himself forced to roll cigarettes with the pages of his manuscript. Supposedly it was a fat book, around five hundred pages of a bildungsroman. Poor guy, I say to myself now. A few years later and he could have photocopied that book all he liked, and smoked double. Then I see her, Giovanna, just as I saw her smoking in our meetings. She had a very strange way of doing it, without style, or with a very clumsy style, almost as if it were her first time holding a cigarette. Far removed from the chic gestures that distinguished the divas of French cinema. It was all more awkward with her, as if she wished she were smoking in secret. She'd stop in the middle of the conversation, take out the pack of cigarettes, and suddenly dart toward the door. You'd follow her without really knowing where she was going, and suddenly find her at the bottom of the steps with a cigarette in hand, shivering a little from the cold or sweating in the heat, her gestures evasive, as if her life depended on smoking that cigarette. She never finished one. She always stopped halfway through, when you least expected it, and stubbed it out. Then she'd halt the conversation and hurry back up the stairs like her lungs hadn't suffered at all. Once inside, we'd start talking again as if there'd been no pause at all.

And after I imagine her smoking, I also have to wonder whether she knew even then that her time was running out and that she needed to organize the matter of her legacy. "One of these days I'll show you the papers," she'd say things like that and then leave you hanging. No, I say to myself, fire won't be enough. I look at the envelopes. Even from the worst fires, some butterfly makes it out alive.

Thirty-three, the age of Christ, said Tancredo between chuckles. And then I added, bored: Christ died to leave a testament, twelve apostles, and a church. Tragedy or farce? It all depends on whom you ask. It's all about belief. He who believes sees tragedy, and he who doesn't sees a farce; the tale is the same, though it's told in a different voice. The protagonist bets it all on whether his story will provoke laughter or tears. I remember that while she smoked, she liked to speculate about the weather: looks like it's going to rain tomorrow, she'd say, while we looked up at an absolutely clear sky. And I'd sit there, a few inches from her, wondering if she was joking, whether I should laugh or not. Few things are as difficult as humor.

11

The image of young Giovanna, sick in some tropical hospital, increased its hold over me until it became an obsession. It was a strange thing, a minor irritation like the one the quincunx caused me as a student, only this time the story seized me emotionally. I could spend whole afternoons re-creating that scene, when I'd heard only a few circumstantial details. The pieces of an invisible chess game moved in my mind, placed the father to the left and the mother a little behind, in a wooden chair. In front I placed the nurse with her book of fairy tales. Something, though, didn't work. If the parents were there, then why was it the nurse who held the book? Why read in that foreign language if the parents were there to tell it all in English? Then the pieces of my chess game moved again and the scene emptied out to the minimum: the nurse and Giovanna in a shared solitude. But if the parents were dead, how had Giovanna reached the hospital? Something didn't fit. Deep though I was in a world of butterflies and fossils, I recalled my childhood years, when I could spend hours before a puzzle, turning the pieces until suddenly I saw something that had been hidden, the game's internal sequence, and hours later I'd start to recognize the image: a historical map, a watercolor of a flowery landscape, a little boat on a sunny day. One of my coworkers would wake me from those reveries. They'd notify me that a new collection of fossils had been delivered to the museum, that a group of elementary school students was just arriving, that someone was asking for me on the phone. Then I'd stop the puzzle for a while, knowing I'd return to it later on.

Those were the months when I obsessively searched online for biographical information about Giovanna. The dates progressed and all the newspapers talked about was the end of the millennium and the possible cybernetic catastrophe. There were retrospectives of the century: Einstein was everywhere, and then Hitler, Michael Jordan, and the fall of the Berlin Wall. I thought about the cybernetic bugs and laughed a little. Then I'd throw myself into a search for something that would give me an explanation for my own private bug: some allusion to an inheritance that would explain the parents' absence, some mention of her trajectory that would explain the unusual success she'd had at such a young age, something that would clarify the enigma of that scene that was expanding for me with the momentum of the jungles that grew in other latitudes. Giovanna had come, Tancredo said, to supplant my obsessions. She'd seen that I was obsessive, and she'd set out to change my fixation for me. To give me clues so I would create a false world on my own. I think Tancredo even started to worry about me. At first he thought maybe I was hallucinating, that there was no designer or project; after Giovanna's visit to the museum, he calmed down a bit. But even so, he worried about something else. He thought I was in love and maybe it would be best to put a stop to it right away. I remember he even came to suggest that we hire a detective who could clear the whole thing up. I laughed a little and went on with my search. In a way I had turned myself into a sort of private detective, with my visits to the Bowery, the feeling I was following in the footsteps of an imaginary ancestor, my little notebook where I dreamed up the possible lives of that red-haired woman who spent her time reading newspapers in a Lebanese bar. I searched and searched online, but the internet wasn't what it is today, and I found very little: details about Giovanna's most recent collections, some information about her early years, but nothing truly revealing. There was no mention of her family, not even of where she was from.

Sometimes the call came and sometimes it didn't. I still worked on my collection of notes, the *Reading Hypotheses* where I sketched out possible scenarios; I took the train to New York and wandered until I reached the Bowery. I'd see a girlfriend of the moment, or some school friend or another who'd moved to the city, and then, when the right moment came, I'd head to the Lebanese bar. I'd sit down, order a glass of wine, and feel enormous relief when I saw, reliable as ever, the same woman reading her newspapers. The scene, however, would start to mutate, and after a few hours the reader and the newspapers would be gone, replaced by the voice of that nurse who made the animals speak so tenderly. Beside her, a young Giovanna would be starting to understand those words that her mind turned over with the agility of a master chess player. Learning a language was like deciphering a riddle. I thought of Giovanna in the Hamptons, her neutral Spanish that betrayed no accent, and something told me the moment of illumination was near. Patience was the trick.

Two weeks after her visit to the museum, her voice surprised me on the phone. A blond coworker who'd been at the museum for only three weeks had interrupted me in the middle of a tour, and I'd slipped away from that troop of noisy kids thinking it would be the same as always: the soft voice of one of the helpers, whom I was now starting to recognize. Instead I was startled by Giovanna's voice, this time speaking in English. She spoke her mother tongue so rarely with me, usually only in search of some word whose Spanish equivalent she'd forgotten. That's why I knew from the start that it was urgent. I was right. She wanted to see me a little earlier this time, and not in the usual place. Without thinking much about it, I agreed and wrote down the address she gave me. It was in the Bronx. It had been a long time since I'd been there, maybe years, ever since I broke up with a woman who had a job writing obituaries, who lived there. I was pleased at the thought of returning, and I ended up telling her sure, I'd be there as soon as I finished work. So when I got rid of that quarreling crowd, I put on my sunglasses and went out to look for the driver. He and I had built a sort of friendship on a foundation of short conversations, so I didn't think it was out of place to ask him something about Giovanna's personal life. It seemed to make him angry, as if my question had crossed some unspoken boundary. He frowned in silence. Ms. Luxembourg, as he called her now with false decorum, greatly valued her privacy, and she never confided in him about her personal history. I felt bad at the thought that I'd committed some invisible transgression, so I decided to keep quiet for the rest of the drive. I worked a little on the classification of a series of Patagonian animal fossils that the museum had acquired recently, part of a large, anonymous donation that would allow us to add three more halls and even put a dinosaur in our main gallery. I sensed Giovanna hiding behind it all, but I chose to say nothing.

Two hours later, I felt the car come to a stop, and through the window I could see a kind of old warehouse hidden among ancient garages that were something like a used-car slaughterhouse. What was Giovanna doing there? Wasn't she afraid of dirty places? When I got out, I was met by a peculiar scene: there was a pile of dismembered mannequins in the mid-dle of the street, tossed out like garbage. As I was taking in the spectacle's apocalyptic mood, I felt a pedestrian collide with me, and when I turned around I saw a man in a black collarless shirt, whom I briefly thought I recognized as the man I'd seen dining with the newspaper reader weeks earlier in the Bowery bar. Only when I saw Giovanna's radiant face was I able to brush off the shock of recognition. She called to me from a glass door that opened into the warehouse, again with the warm texture her voice took on when she spoke in Spanish. I left the mannequins behind and went into that old storage space whose door opened onto a view that even today strikes me as beautiful: an enormous space where dozens of bent figures were cutting, sewing, and measuring cloths that would later adorn another dozen mannequins. Giovanna took my hand and led me farther into that deliciously artificial world. As we crossed the space, I felt amazement that she would take my hand that way, as if we were children playing, and she went along talking about things I didn't quite understand, until we came up to a cork wall where I thought I recognized some of Giovanna's sketches. I quickly realized I was wrong. They weren't sketches of dresses, but something stranger: photographs, clipped from newsprint, in which a masked face appeared over and over. With a happiness that had little to do with our surroundings, with an eagerness that bordered on insipid, Giovanna asked me if I recognized him. Furious, feeling the joke was growing more absurd, I dropped her hand.

Obviously I recognized him. The news had exploded five years earlier, accompanying the New Year like fireworks. A group of indigenous guerrillas had leapt from the jungle to declare war on the Mexican government. In the first hours of the New Year they'd taken control of the main municipal seats. From there they had read a manifesto in which they asked for equality, declared war on the state, and swore to march as far as Mexico City. I remember how when I read the manifesto for the first time, I said to Tancredo that the whole thing seemed orchestrated by a raving poet. What fascinated everyone, however, were the masks: ski masks, like the ones that Mexican aristocrats themselves used on their weekend ski trips to Colorado. Those masks seemed to re-cloak the jungle in its own anonymity. Still, looking past it all, past the masks and manifestos, past the high-level resignations and the newspaper headlines, the public had started to recognize the eyes of this man I now saw before me in a kind of photo collage, over which my friend had drawn red marker lines of possible connection.

Obviously I recognized the figure of Subcomandante Marcos, that *bandolero* of the last stages of the twentieth century, that Latin American cowboy, that Marxist John Wayne. I recognized, in fact, the central photo: the subcomandante on a horse, jungle behind him and the horse's imposing head in front, his eyes a little tired as he smokes his famous pipe. I had always been curious about it, about that photo, the fact that some kind of necklace seemed to be tied around the subcomandante's neck, a kind of amulet whose origin I never managed to decipher. I glanced at that enigmatic amulet and then got lost in that crazy collage. Finally, when my eyes were exhausted and the sound of the tailors' incessant labor behind me seemed to grow louder, I turned toward Giovanna and admitted that I knew his story. Giovanna looked at me eagerly, as if we were on the verge of a breakthrough, and she told me that just a week before, on a trip to Milan, she'd met a very interesting woman. A woman who had come to New York very young, wanting to start a career as a dancer, and after a few years, she'd done just that: she had performed with the most prestigious companies, until her body had failed her a decade later, and an injury forced her to reconsider her career. Then she decided to take up writing and journalism. Giovanna had talked to this woman about the history of masks. She then pointed to a couple of photos, one of a masked man who could well be the subcomandante and, next to it, close enough to force a comparison, a photo of a man with light skin and a well-trimmed beard. She said this journalist had been at the press conference when the Mexican government had tried to unmask the subcomandante. A very serious man had stood before a group of journalists with two enlarged photographs, one of a ski mask and the other an enlarged copy of this photo I had before me now. With a mechanical movement he'd superimposed the enormous cutout of the mask over the photo of the face, until everyone had seen appear, as if by magic, the initial image of that masked man who could well be the subcomandante. If she'd learned anything from that, the woman said, it was the strange power of masks. The government believed it was taking away the subcomandante's power by unmasking him. The result was the opposite. A week later, thousands of masked citizens protested in Mexico City under the cry of *"Todos somos Marcos"* (We are all Marcos). Giovanna's eyes lit up when she told me all this, as if she were finally understanding something. Then she went on with the story: her friend the journalist had convinced the newspaper to let her go to Mexico to see the subcomandante. And just like that, apparently convinced she could just dance her way through the jungle, she'd hacked through the underbrush to reach the camp where Marcos was said to be staying. She waited nearly twelve hours for him, until at dawn a masked man appeared. His eyes revealed no indigenous heritage. No, the journalist said, his eyes were marked by the perpetual energy of the insomniac. That mention of insomnia made me think of the woman in the bar, and I couldn't help looking at Giovanna with a certain distaste. Excited as she was over what seemed to be her great discovery, she apparently didn't notice my irritation. She had decided, she went on to say, that the new show would be a re-elaboration of the subject of masks. Tired, a little annoyed by the false theatricality, I moved my head in a vague sign of approval, while inside me I felt a confused indignation grow. Behind us, the tailor shop hummed.

I must admit that if I didn't leave the project then, if the cliché of a fashion designer's sudden obsession with Latin American politics didn't send me running for the door, it was because of my own strange fixation on Giovanna and her past. That was what kept me from turning away from the beginning of a story that, twenty years later, brought me exhausted to that wall full of photographs. I kept looking at the portraits of a masked man I knew of and perhaps admired, as one always admires people shrouded in mystery, but who, perhaps because of my own cowardice, I regarded as other. I looked at Giovanna with a coward's contempt, but in her I saw only the face of a ten-year-old girl, the marks of a deep-rooted passion that now had the soundtrack of a minimalist sonata of sewing machines. I looked at her resentfully, the way a soldier would look at the general who has led him into war under some false pretense, but I suddenly understood that everything about her was real, even her innocence, and that I would follow her even into the jungle. I thought of the story she'd just told me: the dancer-cum-journalist hacking her way through the jungle, afraid of the death she felt all around her, making her way through a forest that surely smelled of fear, only to find, at the end of a long wait, the eyes of an insomniac. Thinking of Tancredo, I told myself that the joke was flourishing like the jungle itself, and the saddest part was that I would never learn to dance. At the end of it all I'd find myself looking into the insomniac eyes of a William Howard, who would tell me the story of an island where a group of insomniacs risk their lives to become other people.

I thought about saying all this to Giovanna. I thought about telling her of the fear hidden behind Tancredo's jokes, behind my conjectures about her past, and the strange way that something in me was starting to love her, little by little and without passion, as the timid do. Still, something held me back. Perhaps, now that I think about it, it was the monotony of the machines. Terribly tired, finally ready to sleep, I kissed Giovanna's cheek, congratulated her on her evident achievement, and excused myself by saying I was needed at the museum. I practically stumbled past the machines to reach the door. As I left, I thought I saw the strange man again, but I assured myself it was a simple coincidence, just as it was, perhaps, a sad coincidence that I'd answered a certain phone call just past five in the morning.

I never slept better than I did that night. For the first time in a long time I let the driver take me straight to my apartment in New Brunswick, and when I got there, I felt something I had sensed for years but hadn't had the strength to articulate: that time passes stubbornly, even when there is a Manhattan bar where an old insomniac reads newspapers as if eternity were in play. The realization didn't last very long, however. After a few minutes I was sound asleep. They say that it's in that kind of deep sleep when the brain lets loose the most. Maybe that's why I had a kind of multiple dream. There was a mirror, and over the reflected image was a newspaper. I tried to read it, but suddenly the newspaper was covered with ants and I had to drop it. Then the man with the collarless shirt appeared and picked it up. He read something aloud, a few lines of something like a furniture assembly manual or a legal text, and I stood there without understanding, waiting for the man to reveal his identity. Nothing happened. And then, just when he stopped reading, a brief, precise sound started to repeat in the background, a bit slow and very quiet, but growing until it drowned out everything else. I stood there, waiting to finally understand the meaning of this dream image that was becoming long and evasive like a fish in the ocean. Some part of me accepted that that was the point, and sleep had to be a bit like an extended joke to which one could only surrender, accepting that understanding would come only at the very end. Something tells me that even today, seven years later, something in me is asleep, and something, finally, is waking up.

12

A week ago, when I found Giovanna's obituary in the paper, I felt tempted to write another one for her—anonymously, in the name of the museum—and then send it to the national paper of a country where no one knew her: a Puerto Rican or Dominican or maybe even Cuban newspaper, an island paper, in memory of all those islands she always talked about. To leave it there, a little lost amid all the other deaths, adrift as she said she'd been in the tropics. To leave it there like a message I knew no one would read. Then I remembered that old girlfriend of mine, a woman with dyed red curls and a mischievous expression who lived in the Bronx, heir to an intimate tropical battle—she was half Dominican and half Puerto Rican. Her job had been precisely that: to write other people's obituaries. It seemed that sometimes families, defeated by grief, couldn't gather the strength to write obituaries for their family members. So they tasked strangers with the terrible job of telling the world their loved one was no longer with them, but how very loved they'd been. One only had to call a number that appeared in the paper, and give the name of the deceased. A serene voice would offer condolences and assure them that everything would be taken care of. I always found it odd to imagine my girlfriend, who was so playful and saucy, modulating her voice to achieve an absolute serenity, assuring the stranger who could only sob on the other end that everything would be okay and that the world would know of their sorrow.

Several times, when I'd arrived after the long trip from New Bruns-wick to the Bronx—a trip that involved an infinite series of trains—I'd find her sitting at her desk, writing obituaries, while at her back rose the sound of a salsa whose rhythm she followed with slight head movements, making those curls that so enchanted me dance tenderly. And I'd wrap her in a spontaneous hug, and suddenly we were an enormous two-headed monster bent over a paper reading an obituary that to me seemed awfully sincere. She wrote with an intimate style it had taken her only a week to learn. I asked her if she wasn't caught off guard sometimes by the emotion of her work, the pathos in her labor, but she answered with the briefest of smiles that there was no better job in the world. And in her laugh there was a spark of morbid fascination that grew and melded with the salsa and became joy. Thinking of her, perhaps infected by a morbid happiness that itself was a strange form of mourning, I decided not to write the obituary and resigned myself to a humbler task: gathering the ones others had written for Giovanna—all I could find, print and digital—into a posthumous collection born of desperate mimicry.

Like those animals, Giovanna would have wanted to add, who see a predator coming and bury themselves in fallen leaves in a last-ditch attempt to escape. I compiled all the obituaries, one by one, until I was buried in a mess of papers that only pointed to her fatal absence. Among the dozens of obituaries I found, not one mentioned her parents. There were museums and institutions, private collectors and celebrities—one article was even written by Tancredo—but that was it. Then I remembered the boards where Giovanna used to unfurl the strategy of her madness, those boards where the photos built up, the sketches and press clippings, in a kind of megalomania that wasn't unlike the quiet frenzy—in a totally different kind of room, stripped of all luxury—of my old girlfriend as she went about her job writing death notices. Then I took Giovanna's obituaries and hung them up, one by one, on the corkboard I'd bought that summer. And then, briefly, I thought I loved her a little.

I look at the clock: three in the morning. I think how it could all be so easy, even easier than fire. As easy as finally setting my cowardice aside and opening the envelopes, looking at what I think I already know is there, the sketches and annotations, the papers that remained after those long conversations between two obsessives in the middle of the night. Even easier than writing an obituary. Open the envelopes and find everything that she, very much in code, had warned that she would leave to me. Arrive a little late and find it all laid out already, like the time I went to her house and there was no Giovanna, just a book open in the middle of the room. On closer inspection I found images and sketches of masks, with a word—*nahual*—underlined in red, followed by a very strange quote from a certain Díaz de Arce, a summons to listen to the voices of the children and women, because that's where true prophesies were found. I would only have to sit down the way I did that night, read the notes, and lie down to sleep. Swallow whatever dreams came and wake up again, ready for a new life.

———

But, as Tancredo says, distraction is our modern art. Something always opposes us, diverts us from our course. With that thought, a little tired but still charged with the strength of my last cup of coffee, I've returned to looking out the window, and I've noticed a young woman, maybe around thirty, walking her dog through the neighborhood in the wee morning hours. It's three o'clock, I say to myself. To say the "wee hours" is perhaps not to understand that in two and a half hours, at exactly five-thirty, the sun will rise and workers will spring into action, while the rest of us let ourselves sleep in two more hours. It's already Friday, I say to myself. Today I have to be at the museum by nine at the latest. But there is the woman, brown hair, tall, and thin, walking a dog that at times seems to emphasize her airiness. Then I repeat the phrase that always ambushed me on the trip from New Brunswick to New York: In this city there are no stray dogs. I repeat it, and nothing changes. Everything stays the same, hard as a rock in the middle of the night. And I say to myself, it may be three o'clock, but someone has to be awake to take in a scene that would otherwise be lost.

The early-morning hours, I think, set images to trembling. Everything takes on ambivalence and an oneiric shading: as if the false light from the streetlamps suspended time and lent reality an aura of possibility. I think of Giovanna, the enthusiastic tone of voice she reserved for conversations about fireflies and their playful relationship with light. I always wondered in what colors the ten-year-old girl saw the world as she lay convalescing, while beside her a foreign voice read her fables of the ends of the earth. I wondered what the ten-year-old girl would do when, as night fell, the lights went out and all that remained was her parents' absence, the silence without fables or fireflies marking the rhythm of the scene. I never found any answers, other than Giovanna's insolent enthusiasm as she threw herself into a political reality that was terribly foreign to her.

The early morning is the time of windows. Outside, the young woman continues her unhurried walk with utter naturalness, and what I see is a composition in which the solitary world of others steals our eyes to look at itself.

13

After our meeting in that immense tailor shop in the Bronx, the dynamic of our collaboration seemed to change. Something in me resisted participating in what I now thought of as a mere charade, the game of a spoiled little girl. Giovanna, however, had never seemed more enthusiastic. She had a newfound zeal for our conversations, though their subject was unchanging: masks, in all their forms. We could spend hours talking about camouflage, the mimeticism of certain jungle animals, but it always led to a midnight monologue by Giovanna. I let her talk, even came to have a little admiration for the frenzy of enthusiasm in her attempt to take the world by storm, as if every gesture were a battle. I let her talk, let her long, pale fingers play at sketching arabesques into the early-morning hours, but deep down I knew that no matter how much she talked, the war was lost and I was there only as a witness to the ravings of someone else's obsession: the obsession that drove her to fill enormous boards, to trace constellations in which I thought I could intuit an order, but whose cosmic patterns always wound up seeming a little vulgar. I sat there until suddenly I was there no longer, it was only her, in an accompanied solitude not so different from that of a ten-year-old girl in a Caribbean hospital. I stayed there until I became light and invisible, like the creatures she talked on and on about. Then I left her to her task and went out to walk the routes I knew well by then, the streets I walked along almost like a zombie, until I reached the same bar as always and made sure, glass in hand, that the same woman was still there, her newspapers spread out under her attentive gaze. Something in the world didn't change, I repeated to myself complacently, and later I'd head back on the two o'clock train to New Brunswick, which, strangely, I had learned to love again. A girl would be waiting for me there, and the museum and the daily beers with Tancredo, who'd interject the most obvious question: So why keep going? Why don't you tell her enough already, the project is all well and good but you're just too exhausted? He asked such questions, and I'd be left without much of an answer, except that some part of me wanted to keep her company, help her to better hide herself in that maze she was building so feverishly. That's what I told Tancredo, who smiled understandingly, thinking that deep down I loved her. But no, it wasn't that, it was something else, something known only to those who join in the great march of insomniacs: to an obsessive person, there is nothing more soothing than a shared mania. Tancredo couldn't understand, so I didn't talk about it. Tancredo's métier was something else: wild conjectures, the world made metaphor, the twisted reality of mirrors. And just like that, with the same punctuality as always, she would call again and I'd make the trip to New York, with no reason beyond keeping her company on that long foray toward dawn.

It must have been during those months when an accident slightly threw off my routine. And maybe it was in those months when I finally found— though I wasn't looking for it—a brief respite. One day I was at Giovanna's and she read me a few lines of the subcomandante's, poetic lines that told the story of a viceroy who dreams that his kingdom is destroyed. Terrified by cyclonic winds he believes he has foreseen, the viceroy sets about proving the dream wrong. So he travels throughout his land, asking his subjects about the event: he goes to his guards, who tell him they've had the same dream; then the feudal lords, who confirm the dream; and finally to the doctors, who try to convince him the dreams are the product of "Indian witchcraft." Fearful, psychotic, the viceroy orders all his people to be tortured and jailed. Giovanna read the subcomandante's words with the fury of fists, prophesies of a history to come that nevertheless occurred in the distant past. I remember the last sentence said, "He dreams and does not sleep. And the dream still keeps him awake." Without wanting it, without expecting it, the words touched something in me and made me think of that immense mural by Diego Rivera I'd seen in the National Palace as a child: that abbreviated history of Mexico where the shapes seemed to mix together as if they'd been drawn by the same insomniac cyclone. Two hours later, when I left Giovanna, I still had the image of the mural in mind, and maybe because of that, or maybe because of the cloudy sky that was already announcing a storm, I decided that that day, before I went to the Bowery bar, I would take the chance to visit one of the city's museums. And that was how I arrived at the Metropolitan Museum bearing the fears of a viceroy of a long-past empire who dreamed himself insomniac.

The accident, then, was a painting, or the conjunction of a painting and a phrase, or just the downpour that burst over the city as soon as I set foot on the museum steps—a complex weather front that forced me to wander longer than I'd planned through the wet halls of that many-faced monster, where I got lost and finally arrived, by no logic at all, at a small room of somewhat insipid paintings. Then I saw it: one more insipid painting among other bland portraits, as geometric and simple as could be, that nevertheless grew complex if you looked closely. It's not that the picture was an optical illusion. Nothing of the sort. Quite the opposite, everything in that painting seemed to be exactly what it was: a pale man sitting at his work desk and looking out a window. And even so, looked at more carefully, the painting began to take on a certain density: you started to see the man's terrible solitude in the fictitious city that was barely hinted at in the brief fragment of urban building that marked the lower corner of the image. Otherwise, that was the painting: a pale man sitting between windows, looking out at the clear sky of what could be any city. Something, then, started to mutate: there was that second window, our window, the one through which the observer looked at the man who was looking. I checked for the title and found in it the same flat literality of the image: *Office in a Small City*, 1953. The painter's name, Edward Hopper, sounded familiar, but I couldn't call up an exact idea of his work. I thought about continuing my walk, but for some reason I chose to stay there, take out my little notebook, look at the painting, and take a few short notes. The phrase I'd just heard from Giovanna came into my mind: "He dreams and does not sleep. And the dream still keeps him awake." And suddenly I saw it clearly: that image was the very embodiment of insomnia. It didn't matter that in that fictional city, so fragile and slight, the sky was clear and the man was lit by daylight. It was the image of a man who in daytime dreamed he was sleepless, doubled by windows, oblivious to real time. I thought of the viceroy, his fears and his eternal fury, and suddenly I felt terribly powerful, capable of moving mountains from a simple desk in a marginal city. For the first time in years I felt fury in my veins, the drive I'd had as a teenager, the caffeinated feeling of being capable of anything and wanting it all. And all right there in the gallery, museumgoers moved around me as I sank into my hushed megalomania, happy to have found the way back even if it was only a hall in a wet museum. A terribly geometrical hall where suddenly the pieces of the world were starting to fit together with the precision of a chess game. I sat there and started to think about the shape certain animals have when they stay silent, shrinking a little until they become light and anonymous, dangerously close to nothing. I felt a kinship with them and intuited their quiet power. Then I thought how the vitality of plants was even more complex, the secret strength of bonsais and algae, that way they had of huddling into themselves as if in a subtle display of omnipotence. And I saw all of us—Giovanna, the woman with the newspapers, me and Tancredo, the assistants and the man with the collarless shirt—I saw us all behind our desks looking at that same clear sky, which seemed now to emerge from the painting, flood the hall, and return to its fictional place as though nothing had happened. I jotted down the painter's froggy last name, tore out the paper, and stuffed it in my pocket, then left the museum ready to change my life. Outside, a handful of clouds seemed determined to contradict me.

I didn't tell anyone about what had happened. Not Tancredo or the Spanish girl I'd gotten entangled with in those days and who, as usual, had more or less ended up turning into my personal psychoanalyst. I went on with my routine, knowing that resolve was growing inside me, something like a plant or algae. Tancredo peered at me over his beer and thought he perceived something. "You're somewhere else," he said. But then he just repeated what he thought he knew: that Giovanna was slowly captivating me, beguiling me with her mystery, and that one day I would find out just how long a joke can drag on. I kept quiet, feeling the return inside me—so long delayed—of the same juvenile will that, in a distant past, had driven me to chase the silhouettes of the quincunx across a wide map of tropical butterflies. I kept quiet and gave a hint of a smile, as if I were the one proposing a final joke to the world.

The first thing that hit me about the Edward Hopper paintings was their crushing simplicity, their total literality behind which, little by little, something nevertheless seemed to withdraw. Something seemed to bristle inside an image that, otherwise, would have looked like a simple postcard.

Maybe that's why it took me two days to look for the paper where I'd written his name beside the painting's title. Finally I found it, hidden in the pockets of some pants I had sent to the cleaners. Though the letters were blurry I could make out the name, the title, and the date: Edward Hopper, *Office in a Small City*, 1953. Then I headed to the university bookstore and bought a small illustrated volume on his work. Two hours later, when Giovanna called and the driver came to pick me up, I didn't hesitate to bring along my new book. On the ride there I paged through the pictures: women naked in full daylight staring outside, office workers depicted from windows, men and women who drink coffee and smoke at leisure. Hopper is the great landscape artist of American insomnia, I said to myself, but the accidental echo of "American dream" struck me as vulgar. Instead I went with a quote that appeared on the book's cover: "Hopper is simply a bad painter, but if he were a better one, he would probably not be such a great artist." I liked the idea that he was essentially inept, an anachronistic painter, who, while his modern contemporaries spent their time throwing paint at the canvas, had dedicated himself to landscapes. That was Hopper's great skill: to depict the inner life of a landscape that was itself barely hinted at. As I flipped through the pages, I arrived at another painting. It was called *Morning Sun* and was dated 1952. In it, a woman in a slip sits on a bed, in profile and with her legs curled up. The picture is marked by the light that pierces the room and falls onto the woman's face, as she in turn seems to observe with utter patience the world just glimpsed through the window. Little is shown of what's beyond the window frame: just the top of an urban, red-brick building. Looking at that painting, I thought how that was what made Hopper the great American landscape artist: the way he inverted the logic of the genre. To show us the insomniac who looks and not the landscape. I glanced at the picture again and thought I saw Giovanna and the woman in the bar, I thought about the subcomandante and the insomniac viceroy. The bumping of the car as we hit the cobblestones told me we were arriving. She could be there behind any of the windows, in a room stripped of luxury—a Hopper-style room.

That night I didn't mention my newfound inspiration to Giovanna. I found her tense, more anxious than usual, moving with the bristly energy of someone suffering from a hangover. She seemed indecisive and impatient, her jitters concentrated in the muscles of her right hand, whose restless fingers held a little figure that after a while I distinguished as a small jade elephant. I merely observed her movements, mentally following the little elephant's adventures, until the memory of the painting I'd seen a few hours before made me see it all with different eyes. For the first time I imagined her naked in the middle of a room, her hands resting on her knees and her eyes a little lost, as if in a Hopper painting. I imagined her naked in her sleeplessness, terribly pale and anxious, like those fingers of hers that now seemed to clutch the jade figure with the nervous fury of a person risking her life. I looked at her fake blond hair, the black roots that now seemed to hide much more, and something told me the moment to act had come: to take a step forward and use sex to put an end to the joke that was threatening to bury us all. Maybe the code lay there: in the passion of one night that would reveal a sunny day. For a brief second I felt that Giovanna was thinking the same thing, that her fingers had stopped their restless probing and that she was looking at me deeply.

The ring of the phone put an end to that.

I saw her set the elephant on the table, cross the labyrinth of furniture that I now found unbearable, pick up the phone, and answer in a voice that somehow reminded me of the one from almost two years earlier, recorded on my machine. Anxious, still overwhelmed by the scene I'd just imagined, I leaned over the table in search of something to hold in my hand. Then I saw it: an open envelope with the stamp of a medical clinic on the back. I sat there, remembering the early call, the echoes of that recorded voice that now seemed to be sobbing into the phone even while she merely said yes and no, with the fragile strength found only in the ill. I picked up the little jade figure, put it in my pocket as a talisman. When she came back, I recognized on Giovanna's face the stubborn conviction of someone who intends to lie until the end.

Somewhere I read that what is forgotten is not a lie. In the months that followed that strange meeting, I remained faithful to that perverse intuition. I tried to forget, as I laboriously built my new project, the painful truth I believed I'd glimpsed. Later that night, I arrived at the Bowery bar feeling like my newly acquired powers were in danger. If I didn't make a decision now, I ran the risk of remaining beneath that strange shadow that is the lives of others. The lives of others: like that woman who spent her time in the same bar, compulsively reading the news. Then I took out my little notebook and there, where I had written *Reading Hypotheses*, I wrote another title that struck me as more apt: *The Invisible Border*. I looked around me, more out of modesty than anything else, and below the title I sketched those fake, light-blue eyes that just a few hours earlier had looked out at me from the empire of the sick. Only then did I feel the imaginary figure of my ancestor dissolve, as I finally became the story's protagonist. And I was the one now deciding to break down invisible borders, I was the one deciding to get up from the table where I'd kept quiet until then, and I was the one who, breaking all the unspoken rules, went over to that table where the newspapers lay exposed, and now, without an ounce of modesty, I pulled out a chair and sat down. I was the one who ignored the waiters who tried to dissuade me, and it was I who, finally sitting across from the woman whom I felt I'd been observing for ages, uttered the obvious question:

"What's with the newspapers?"

What comes next is almost an artificial memory, like the memory of a movie, pure image. The measured and deliberate way her face seemed to lift very slowly—refusing the violence I'd expected—from the paper. Her eyes had the glassy tinge that you sometimes see in digital photographs. A terribly empty gaze but not, for that, profound, a pair of eyes that simply refused to be more than eyes, mere surface without depth, much less abyss. From that abyss-less void I heard the reply that today, with Giovanna's notebooks strewn across the table, strikes me as terribly pertinent:

"What's it to you?"

Even today, past four in the morning, that would seem to be the question: What's it to me? That was always the question: Why do we decide to get involved in certain lives and not in others? Why, in the middle of the night, does someone decide to remember one story and not others? That night in the Bowery bar I learned that patience isn't always rewarded with stories, or, even more terrible, that sometimes curiosity is left there, at mere curiosity, without even rising to the level of anecdote. That sometimes surface is all there is, gaze without depth, glassy eyes dedicated to filling the hours with letters. Finally I thought I understood something: that woman wasn't reading anything, wasn't looking for any stories beyond those offered by the surface of the paper. Like ancient copyists, like current computers, her labor was limited to a register of the vocabulary that precedes anecdote. Or maybe not, maybe she was reading from the secret center of her particular obsession, but even if that were true, everything still ended there: at the armor of the private passion I'd intuited in her eyes. I didn't reply, didn't think it necessary to come up with an answer. I simply apologized, as if I'd done something rude, and put away my notebook. And as I left I felt I was reliving a scene: outside a nearby bar, two boys were in a fistfight. Only now I felt I was living it in my own skin, in the present and not the past, immersed in all the details: the boys' sweat, the stench of stale beer, the blood that traced one eyebrow on the face of a very tall boy who was now being held back by his friends, their fury a match for his as he struggled to escape. At the start of the twenty-first century, two boys were repeating a scene that had surely been lived by two gangsters of the nineteenth, with the difference that I was forced to watch the scene live and in color, in its absolute presence, with all the modern resolution of television. I crossed the street convinced that I was gradually starting to shed my old costume. After a few blocks I stopped at another bar, took out the notebook, and read that phrase I had written earlier: *The Invisible Border*. There was a project peering out from behind those words. The sketch of Giovanna's eyes, below, seemed to remind me that it wouldn't be an easy one; forgetting never has been easy.

You can read a cat's insomnia in his eyes, Tancredo says. He says it as if he knew them, as if he secretly frequented their meetings, as if he belonged to the animal world. He says it and then he corrects himself. Cats, he repeats, inhabit an in-between world. Scientists have demonstrated it, he repeats, as if it mattered to me, and then he goes on to explain what he calls science: the fact that it's been proven that feline brain waves are similar to those of human beings when they sleep.

Maybe that's why, the day I decided to shave, I thought of Tancredo. Shaving, now that I think about it, was my way of marking a change: a before and after that simulated metamorphosis. I saw myself in the mirror: tired and old, fatter than I used to be, but still willing to fight the last battle. And there was the beard, the beard I'd had since I was twenty, full at times and at others timid, but always there, hiding much of my face. I thought about how, though it seems strange in retrospect, Giovanna and I had never talked about the beard, hair as a mask. That was ultimately what my beard had been: at first a way to hide my youth, then a way to hide behind the anonymity of the ordinary, until it became the mask that hid a premature old age. But something in me now was starting to resist: part of me wanted to be a child again. I ran my fingers over my beard, and, to the rhythm of a Dominican bachata, I saw the fuzz fall until there was no more hair on my face but a lively mustache. I laughed at the thought that I had become, at the end of the day, one of those cats Tancredo talked about, a kind of eternal watcher of the sleeping world. I laughed at the thought that a man could come to look like a cat. It was then that I understood the meaning the words I'd written would have: *The Invisible Border* was another name for the gaze. I thought about Hopper and the characters of his paintings, those men and women in broad daylight who seemed to look toward an outside that was forbidden to the viewer. I looked at myself in the mirror, with the peppy mustache in the middle of my face, and I played for a few seconds at becoming unrecognizable. I played at losing myself in grimaces, with the plastic joy of a person repeating a word until it's deformed. Everything changed except my eyes. I felt a childish joy as I told myself that that was what *The Invisible Border* would be: an enormous exhibit on the animal gaze, a giant parade of eyes. I told myself this, and for an instant, while the razor removed the mustache, I forgot Giovanna's eyes, the medical envelope, the anxious fingers. I forgot that I'd imagined her naked in the middle of the room, that I'd desired her, even if for a brief instant. With the last swipe of the razor, I stared at myself again in the mirror: I looked young and strange, a cat without whiskers, anxious and ready to wake up.

14

When I was little I was always fascinated by that instant in cartoons when a character runs off a cliff and hangs there, his legs moving over the abyss, until he decides to look down and becomes aware of his folly. It didn't matter how many times I saw that scene, I was always hit by the same disappointment at witnessing the cartoon character's foolishness, his always inopportune decision to give in to the world of gravity and thus of logic. Cunning, as I think about it now, was in suspending the time of reason, in becoming weightless: in seeing how long one could run across the void, refusing to look down. Like now, as I realize that I'm the one who refuses to look down, to break the spell of the joke that's still growing now, past four in the morning. Outside, the night simply continues, while inside, I look at the envelopes again, the five points of the quincunx that now seem to want to take flight. "Tragedy or farce?" I remember then a question that Tancredo often asks: How long can a joke go on? Like in the cartoons, the jokester's trick consists of not looking down: to look down is to finally give in to the inevitable tragedy, while to go on running in the void is to choose the foolishness of laughter and of farce. The jokester's trick, says Tancredo, consists of keeping the audience on the edges of their seats, removing certainty, suspending them in a cloud of expectations, until he sees them emerge suddenly from behind a shared laugh. The jokester who doubts falls into the silent abyss. Now, after four in the morning, I start to feel like my time is coming, that the joke is reaching its end and the room for laughter is opening up.

Outside, in the house across the street, a light has come on, and I recognize, through the window, the silhouette of a woman making coffee. The day is here, I say to myself. The hour has arrived when people allow themselves to turn on the lights, make coffee, show themselves. Emerge from the anonymity of insomnia. I think of Hopper, of the strange light in his paintings, a shadow light, a silhouette light, and suddenly the image of an enormous fishbowl comes to me. I wonder whether there were fish in the fables Giovanna heard in that tropical hospital, and, if there were, what language they spoke. Through the now-illuminated window, the woman starts to read something that could well be a newspaper, but then I think it's too early for the paper, the delivery boy comes by at five. I look at her again, the honed feminine shape behind the window. I wonder if I could come to love her. That's how we private men are: we love what is behind windows. Closeness becomes unbearable for us.

Giovanna had an aquarium in her house, with many fish that she fed regularly. Fish of all colors. Orange ones with black-and-white stripes, blue ones and yellow ones, and my favorites: the catfish. Those creatures of the deep with the faces of grumpy little men, scavengers who spend nights cleaning the underwater subsoil, suctioning up the remains of their colorful compatriots' diurnal lives. Giovanna would stop the conversation, open a drawer, and take out a little box; then, with her walk that was itself a little like a fish or a manta ray, she'd go over to the tank and feed her pets. I felt a strange alliance with those scavenger fish. The last crumbs of the night belonged to me, too, while the day was for others. I never knew if Giovanna had lovers, although if she did, I told myself, they must be daytime lovers. Maybe on one of those sudden trips that took her to Milan, Prague, Barcelona, she read verses to a man who had learned to desire her better than I did.

Again, I observe the scene across the street: the woman has stood up and slowly, as if she were still asleep, walked to the coffeepot. She's poured a little more coffee and turned back to her reading. In one corner of the envelope I've written a phrase, almost a title: *Scenes from a private life*. And I've started to think about how Americans are really marvelous in those minor genres of private life. Suburban dramas, movies about hysterical men and women, tragicomedies about the malaise of the petite bourgeoisie. "What's it to you?" The words of the woman in the Bowery have leapt up unexpectedly, and a little voice tells me that we're all fish in small adjacent tanks trying to look at each other in the night, knowing there's an invisible barrier between us. Giovanna desperately wanted to leave all this ordinary life behind, I think to myself. She wanted to become invisible and anonymous, to then leap out and encompass everything. Through the window, two houses down, I see another light go on.

Private catastrophes, Tancredo sometimes calls them, as he scarfs down a hamburger. Private catastrophes, he says, and in his voice I note that acidic irony that annoys and entertains me: it's a way of suspending the truth, of offering words the way one hands over pieces of a puzzle, with the grace of the tightrope walker who bet everything on a simple metaphor. I sometimes feel, looking at Tancredo in his red-brimmed hat, the brushstroke of the solitary mustache across his pale face, that his strategy is to build a metaphorical world, a theory world: a strategy based on the future. Sometimes, though, his cynicism exasperates me, and I feel like his profile gives him away: a man at the end of times, a decadent man without a future who in a New Brunswick diner tries to dissolve the real in a giant net of kooky allusions. Private catastrophes, says Tancredo, and with that expression he tries to mock my theory of beginnings. According to him, there is no repetition or copy in the beginning, but rather a simple, small explosion that suddenly awakens something within a man. All this to say: the world is kept moving by the common man's hysteria.

And it's been precisely with the bravery of a common man, with the patience of an algae or a fish, that I have approached the envelopes and placed them all on the table. Three manila envelopes adorned with a red cord. I've placed the envelopes on the table, starting with that first one where I recognize Giovanna's fragile handwriting: *Notes (1999)*. I remember the parties on New Year's Eve that year, the call from Giovanna after ten o'clock: she was in Rome and she already belonged to the next century. Drunk, she'd said things that I didn't want to hear and that later I forgot or believed I'd forgotten, just like I forgot or pretended to forget about that doctor's envelope. *Notes (1999)*: the fears that were left behind, reduced to the ravings of the past century, and the fears that were only just starting to grow. Outside, a light in another house punctuates the still-dark scene, and I see a man in pajamas holding a small boy in his arms. I think of Giovanna, the medical envelope, and the ten-year-old girl. Moving closer to the fragile threshold that now separates night from day, I start to untangle the first knot of the cord.

15

After was after: days, weeks, months, years that started to pile up as Giovanna endeavored to disappear. Or maybe I was the one who, driven by a zeal for forgetting, finally started to emerge, thinner and beardless, from an even deeper neglect. Something in me seemed determined to do battle against that great farce of anonymity with a showy dramaticism. The museum had accepted my proposal, and the exhibition *The Invisible Border* was scheduled for the following year. Giovanna still called, but now nothing was the same: more than collaborators, we were like old lovers doomed to invoke the past and its now inaccessible nights of passion. Months would pass without a word from her, and part of me was relieved. Months during which I toyed with the little jade elephant I'd stolen from her. I fiddled with it just as she had, with unconscious worry, while I set to organizing the exhibition that was slowly starting to take on the shape of my ambition: I played with the order of photographs, switched out texts, I amused myself by sprinkling human gazes among that great parade of animal eyes. She disappeared for months and I swore she was headed for the jungle, that she was hacking through the weeds at night to reach the camp where an insomniac subcomandante's eyes would receive her. I merely followed her travels from afar, tracked the path of the subcomandante's poetic pronouncements, waiting for the day when the newspapers would announce the surprising meeting between a fashion designer and a leftist leader. I laughed at the thought of the barbarities the right-wing press would suggest: the love affairs they'd imagine, the perverse stories of corruption they'd weave around a simple and innocent image. Still, the months passed and nothing happened. She'd come back from her long trips thinner and more evasive, as if the project were now growing behind my back and the secret turning deep and unpronounceable. The idea, always present but ignored, that her destination in those months of silence could be another hospital ate away at me from inside. Our conversation continued naturally, but I felt that everything had ended some months ago, with Giovanna on the phone nodding yes. I felt that we were only there as part of a ghost story just reaching its denouement. What I liked most of all was to go out walking to the bar in the Bowery. I liked to sit there, and, freed now from curiosity but still accompanied by the newspaper reader, I worked on the exhibit with an absolute voracity, the same voracity with which, a few tables over, the woman devoured the news with a gaze I now knew was empty. I knuckled down over my red leather notebook and sketched out crazy ideas: bringing a live animal to the museum, creating an anatomy of the gaze, filling the hall with portraits of eyes until the gazes got confused and no one could tell which ones were animal and which human. I worked intensely until exhaustion or the image of a sick Giovanna came to me and stopped me in my tracks, and the idea of continuing became unbearable. Then I'd take the train, and when I got home, I'd fall deeply asleep as I hadn't in a long time, placidly surrounded by thousands of eyes, faint and indistinct, that seemed to keep watch over my dreams.

We expected the end times and what we got was a pointless hangover, said Tancredo. I nodded, not wanting to contradict him, but inside I was thinking that finally my time was coming. Something had changed irrevocably, though it had nothing to do with the end of days. Something had mutated and the shell had broken. Spring could already be glimpsed, and while the bars were full of people drinking, I told myself that now was the time for sobriety, the moment to grasp the reins and finally take a risk. I felt at ease, at peace within that strange habitat I had managed to build for myself. I had turned into a rare bird, an insect that buzzed its wings incessantly to keep from falling, but that, little by little, had learned such speed wasn't necessary; it was enough to keep up a moderate but practiced pace. Patience, I'd say to Tancredo, as I thought about how the metaphor was wrong, how it wasn't that I had spent years unnecessarily flapping my wings, but quite the opposite. I'd spent my time in stillness, to the point of disappearing entirely from the landscape. Only now, slowly, with reptilian stealth, was I starting to emerge from that lair I'd constructed so carefully. Haven't you heard of Gestalt psychology? asked Tancredo. Whenever one figure appears it's because something else has disappeared into the background. Something in me fearfully intuited the consequences of my awakening.

———

Whenever one thing appears it's because something else has disappeared, background and figure, repeated Tancredo, while in my mind the image of Giovanna returned me to a childhood memory. I thought back to the afternoons when my father took me to the zoo. I wasn't interested in the marquee animals—I was bored by the elephants and lions, the zebras and monkeys. I was saddened at the sight of their supreme boredom, where, now that I think of it, I saw glinting a kind of vulgar portrait of the adult world. I loved, on the other hand, the vivarium: those visual Pandora's boxes of hidden, living enigmas. I would stand fascinated before the boxes, and without looking at the name of the animal, try to decipher what it was all about. Life as a puzzle or a stereogram. In some cases, the answer was obvious: you could see the sinuous, damp shape of the snake on the dry trunk, the fluttering presence of the butterfly, the sinister tedium of the solitary iguana on the rock. But in other cases, you saw only absolute emptiness on the other side of the glass. As if the original animal had died and the zoo employees had forgotten to replace it with a new one. And I would hover in front of those apparently empty boxes, waiting for the figure that had been hidden to suddenly emerge: the singular butterfly that blends with the branches, the laborious ants in their heretofore unseen labor, the same iguana in whose stillness I now saw impudence instead of boredom. I loved those little captive tropics where nothingness at last became visible. And so I detested the impatient children who, seeing nothing behind the glass, dared to tap on it in a desperate attempt to make something show itself. I remember being in front of one of those tropical theaters where nothing seemed to be happening in spite of the other children's impatient tapping. Positive that nothing was there, they soon went on to other boxes. But I stayed where I was, in spite of my father's insistence; like the others, he thought nothing was there. Then I'd seen it slowly emerge: not merely the animal within the landscape, but the animal-landscape, the animal that was itself the landscape in which we'd looked for it. I turned to find out the precise name inscribed on the plaque: "Mula del Diablo (walking stick), Costa Rica." Below that, a subheading that stayed with me long after, read: "Phasmid." I had seen that small phasmid emerge with the impression that this was no typical camouflage, but rather something more sinister: an animal that, little by little, was devouring the landscape with the secret ambition of *becoming* the scene. Years later, in a book by a

French philosopher, I would discover the concepts necessary to grasp what simply unfolded that day: the copy was devouring the model. But that would come later. The twelve-year-old boy who stood before the empty cage that afternoon had a different impression: that he was facing an extraordinary animal, one more frightening than any other precisely because its ambition was not necessarily to survive, but to transcend life. A second discovery overwhelmed me as I got closer to the glass: this wasn't just one creature, but rather dozens of tiny insects that melded together until they created a kind of collective body seemingly set on emulating an absent landscape. A horrible confusion kept me awake that night as I tried to understand exactly what it was I'd seen. What had become visible, and what had remained unseen? During that now distant spring, the image of a swarm of insects stayed with me as a kind of warning: what appears out of nowhere is always something close to nothingness itself. A terrible nothingness that still aspires to encompass everything.

As I thought back to that day I was certain that Giovanna and I were something like those phasmids, a paired background and figure, our secret ambition to meld with absolute nothingness. And thus the spring lengthened out like a tightrope between all and nothing, while I tried to convince myself that the only way to truly keep Giovanna company was to learn to lose her. I saw her return from one of her enigmatic trips, thinner and paler, but I soothed myself by saying it was all pure illusion. Soon we would change perspective and the real image would emerge, masterful and precise: we would realize that her thinness was nothing but one side of another, more ferocious reality, one that impelled her to meld into the landscape with the strength of that elusive insect from my childhood. Whenever one thing appears it's because something else has disappeared, background and figure, asserted Tancredo, while in my mind it wasn't the real Giovanna who was disappearing, but the ten-year-old girl she'd been.

One might say, then, that the project dissolved as spontaneously as it was conceived. It could also be said that, to this day, I don't know what the project really was. My life was interrupted by an early-morning phone call, and after two years I still wasn't clear on where the thing was going. I liked to think that one day we'd see the subcomandante in some more fashion-able ski mask, something colorful and flashy. And beside him, Giovanna would laugh into the camera as if she were looking at me. I smiled at the thought of how it would irrevocably interrupt the war, just as a simple call at five in the morning had disturbed my life. But my hallucinatory come-dies were never acted out. The war went on being a war, in a far-off country and a new century. And, just like that, the project vanished like a dream.

The last time I saw her she wasn't wearing any makeup. Or she was, but only half-done, as if she'd tried to remove it quickly but had stopped halfway through, maybe when she heard me knock at the door. She was dressed in black as always, but it was a tired black that now extended to the roots of her hair, which, neglected, seemed determined to return to its true color. I felt that her disguises were fading away, and perhaps very soon I'd have the real Giovanna in front of me. She, however, seemed resolved to remain unchanged. She told me something about her travels, and went to sit down in one of the many chairs. On the table there was a pile of puzzle pieces whose box was propped beside the fish tank. The fish floated above the box as if they belonged to its world. The puzzle depicted one of Monet's luminous scenes: a garden of little flowers with petals where the purple seemed to flirt with turning white. Breaking the painting into a thousand pieces made it clear: most of them just suggested a touch of purple. That was when she made her move: in a very light voice, she suggested that the project was coming to an end, and said she wouldn't need my help in the coming months, as she planned to spend some time abroad. She used that word, *abroad*, and it struck me as a strange expression, an old-fashioned word. Then, smiling, she picked up a greenish piece—a leaf, I thought distractedly—and fit it into a small fragment that was starting to take shape. I imitated her, not thinking it necessary to even reply, under-standing that she was not asking a question but only offering information, a sentence she tossed into the air for it to hang just so. That's how we spent the rest of that night, reconstructing a painting of weightless flowers, wrapped in a tense silence that insinuated a slight dispute. It would have been more appropriate, I thought, for us to play a game of chess that night, or, better yet, one of those board games I'd liked so much as a boy: a game of war, with the world map drawn in colors and little soldiers jumping borders. Something, I repeated to myself, that would have made it clear that what we were playing was a final game. But that wasn't Giovanna's style. Hers was a lighter and more subtle approach, like that of the Monet painting we were reassembling, which seemed to be drawn by the delicate hand of a terribly bored god: here a stroke of purple, there a touch of white. One of those terrible exercises in patience that she liked so much. We kept it up until the early morning, when Giovanna fell asleep. I stayed half an hour longer, trying to finish the puzzle, but then I thought the appropriate thing was to leave it just like that, half-finished. I looked at her sleeping like a little girl while I tried to convince myself that endings never happen just like that. Something is always left behind. On my way out I noticed it was already dawn.

16

Five years later, a mess of pages lies on my bed like a jigsaw puzzle. Outside, a man closes a door and starts a car engine. I become aware that seven hours have passed since a different man handed me this package that now lies scattered in pieces. I look at the clock as though seeking confirmation. It's five in the morning, and again I think of the original call that came right at five. I'm pleased at the thought that my theory remains intact: every beginning is only a copy. Then I start to sort the documents, in an attempt to understand the story Giovanna wants to tell me.

The first envelope is filled entirely with photographs. There are maybe fifty undated photos that, after a while, I manage to organize into three basic categories. In the first group, perhaps the most noteworthy, I place the fashion photos: women wearing bathing suits from the fifties, voluptuous young women made up à la Marilyn Monroe, à la Jayne Mansfield, à la Grace Kelly. Young women with false, nearly white dyed hair, perfect curls, and accentuated cleavage. Photographs of models who slowly become less imposing and more delicate, less like Marilyn Monroe and more like a tender Audrey Hepburn. Until I reach a series of photographs taken not on set, but in the middle of what seems to be the nocturnal frenzy of the Caribbean, with its palm trees and the baroque Tropicana-style suits. Then, in a second group of photos that seem to have been taken later, natural, full-color landscapes start to emerge: photographs of rocky mountains in the style of Ansel Adams, photos of a lusher, more tropical jungle where, when I look again, the face of one of the models from the previous images appears. A blond girl, very young, who playfully covers her face with a broad green leaf. Her eyes, though, give her away: she is recognizable in her hidden laugh, in her expression as she lightheartedly refuses the camera. Then there are more landscapes: the jungle seen from the air as though taken from a helium balloon, some photos of a swollen river, and, to finish off, a series of birds in flight. The third group of photographs is the most disconcerting. It's composed of a series of images of what seems to be a mining town: the blackened men, the carts, the underground tunnels. These photographs are black-and-white again, but they do not seek to move the viewer. They seem to be after another effect: a kind of absolute objectivity. Here there are no faces, and the images are merely outlines of laborers in poses of work. Among them, a bit out of place, I find an image of a little blackened canary. A canary in the coal mine, I say to myself, as I remember the story my father told me about a bird that changed world history: one humble bird's suffocated silence saved Churchill's grandfather, and thus Churchill. My father laughed and then took the inevitable leap: that canary had saved us all. I separate the image of the canary and start to look over the photos again. I search for some letter from Giovanna explaining all this, but there's nothing.

I think for a second that it's all a mistake. Giovanna must have gotten something wrong when she stipulated that I be sent these files after her death. She must have drawn the quincunx and then gotten mixed up as to the recipient. I go back through the photographs until I return to the one showing the blond girl playfully covering her face with a tropical leaf. Something in her eyes reminds me of Giovanna's habit of turning away when she laughed, a certain pendular movement in which I thought I intuited a game of absences. The similarity, however, soon vanishes. I go over the other photos of the model, those where she appears a little younger and more voluptuous, a little more Marilyn and less Audrey, in what must have been the fifties. I again find a similarity, the same gaze of wide, round eyes playing hide-and-seek. Then I tell myself: here's the trick, Tancredo, just as we expected it. The puzzle pieces vaguely set out for the obsessive to start tracing. As though refusing my intuition, I try to distract my gaze. I put the photos of the woman aside and focus on those of the mining town. The real discovery, I think, is there, in those images that refuse to fit into the overall pattern. I look at the canary and tell myself that if there's a story here, it would have to start with the canary's song in a distant town. Outside, the day starts to show itself.

The second envelope is made up of five essays. They all focus on photography. The first, dated 1966, is a kind of reconciliation with the artistic nature of fashion photography. The second, dated eight years later in 1974, is an investigation into the relationship between photography and history. So far, so normal. The essays are written in elegant but severe prose, as if the author sincerely believed in the parameters imposed by the academic world to which they're apparently addressed. It's in the third article that things change. "The Silhouettes of Clouds," published in 1975, has eleven epigraphs and a hallucinatory prose behind which you can sense a certain poetic vocation. Its subject: photography as meteorology, or photography and the future. The fourth article, titled "From a Bird's-Eye View," is made up of seven aerial photographs of a mining town around which winds a small epic on distance. The text is dated at the end, location included: "San José, Costa Rica, 1977." Finally, there's an article from 1983 about photography and reproduction, about photography and having children. I think about Giovanna, the ten-year-old girl sick in a Caribbean hospital. I think of the parents' absence and I find myself touched by an unexpected sentimentalism. I stop. I page through the texts and notice that they are all signed with the same name: Yoav Toledano. I repeat the name three times, but nothing happens. Then I stop at a small poem that appears in the last article, set in the form of a kind of cosmic spiral that makes me a little dizzy. I think that the figure isn't so much like a galaxy as a small tropical hurricane. I think of the black holes Tancredo likes so much, and I remember that Bowery bar where I dug in for two years. I think that some secrets are barely visible, and behind them lies nothing but a great void. I start to read the verses in search of some pattern, but after a while I get bored. Something in me says that perhaps that's the story: a great epic of boredom that Giovanna wove to fill the empty hours, a kind of vain voyage after an invented white whale that will vanish as soon as I start to chase it. I return to the article called "The Silhouettes of Clouds" and underline some phrases with a red marker: "A photograph, like a cloud, is never a thing in itself, but rather the sign that something will happen." I think the sentence is wrong: the photograph doesn't point toward the future, but the past. Still, I like the idea: to take a photo of the future. I look back at the texts and tell myself it's too much reading. Careful to maintain the initial order, I put the articles back into their envelope.

The third envelope contains a series of newspaper articles. They report on a growing underground fire in a small mining town. The first one, from 1962, relates the initial event without yet grasping its repercussions:

according to official information, as stated in the police reports, the fire was ignited by an error in the process of burning garbage in the municipal dump. Some part of the initial fire was left burning, and as it grew it moved into the labyrinth of abandoned coal mines in the vicinity. That's as far as the article goes. It mentions that the town is being monitored, and that the authorities will soon be able to put the fire out entirely. The second article, dated seventeen years later, in 1979, traces the outcome of that first event. Apparently, the owner of a local gas station had been trying to measure gasoline levels when he noticed that his measuring needle emerged unexpectedly hot. He decided to check the temperature of the gasoline and was surprised to find it was 172 degrees Fahrenheit. Only then did he realize the fire was all around him. The third article dates from 1981 and relates a frightening event that happened in a nearby town: a twelve-year-old boy was plunged 150 feet deep into a sinkhole that opened suddenly in his front yard. The article tells of his heroic fourteen-year-old cousin, who was able to pull him out of the hole and save his life. The column of smoke exhaled by the sinkhole was analyzed and found to contain lethal amounts of carbon monoxide. The fire was silent, frenzied, as it ran through a town where children still played. I stop reading the article and think that Giovanna would have been around fourteen, too, at the time. I think of the story of Giovanna in the tropical hospital, and something returns me to her strange way of smoking. I think of the photos of the model whose eyes recalled Giovanna's evasive gaze. The fourth article is from 1987 and tells of a reporter's trip to the town after it has already begun to empty. What starts to emerge is the reporter's fascination with those who decide to stay, though the article is mostly dedicated to describing the incentives the government offered citizens to encourage them to abandon the town. Ten years later, in 1997, the same journalist pens an article in which his curiosity is made manifest: he returns to the town to interview the few people who've decided to stay on. He manages to talk to almost all of them—only three refuse to participate. The article, however, mentions the names of these three: a married couple, Richard and Roselyn Cena, absent from the town at the time of the interview because of a sick daughter, and a foreign photographer who gives his name as Yoav Toledano, in spite of the fact that everyone else in town knows him as Roberto Rotelli. I recognize the name with tired happiness, like someone spotting a church after driving around lost for hours in search of it. I close the envelope knowing that there is still a long way to go. Outside, two men shout as daylight grows.

So, at the end of this story there is only a name: Yoav Toledano. I repeat it to myself until it loses all meaning, and only then, when the syllables separate and become anonymous, do I turn on the computer and enter the name in a search engine. There are photographs of a handsome man, sometimes impeccably neat—clean-shaven with his hair slicked back fifties-style—and others where he appears bearded and more playful, photographed alongside figures from the bohemian sixties and seventies. Farther down I find other photographs whose style I recognize immediately: fashion photos like the ones in the first envelope. I stop on a fascinating image in which the photographer appears, bearded and with one leg in a cast, alongside a model who is lying on her back, with the look of a dancer, her back arched. Toledano is wearing swim trunks, and he's roguishly brandishing a shotgun that seems to have been turned into a fishing pole. Behind him is a map of the world. I recognize the woman's eyes, the same gaze in which, half an hour before, I thought I found Giovanna. It's the same model, but now she looks darker and more tropical. I close the image search and look for any information about this character named Yoav Toledano whose importance now grows by leaps and bounds. After a few minutes I find a detail that links the threads discovered so far: "In 1976, the Israeli photographer Yoav Toledano, famous for having captured many of the most notable faces of New York counterculture, vanished without a trace." Every story, I tell myself, begins far from home.

17

After that last meeting, I went on taking the train to Manhattan as if Giovanna still summoned me. I'd arrive in the city and head southward, happy to be able to walk, notebook in hand, through those same streets I'd spent two years wandering. I walked the way tired birds walk, with a certain happy sorrow, until I reached the Bowery bar. I recognized the woman with the newspapers and the waiters. Then I'd open the little notebook with the red leather cover and start to work on the exhibition. I toiled under the shelter of the lamps of routine. Night after night I went back to that place that I believed was the origin of fiction, the origin of delirium, until one night she didn't come. I spent hours staring at the empty table where there had always been newspapers, and after two glasses of wine I told myself it was time to leave. I remember that when I left, I felt the night was opening up. I walked without pause or direction, randomly yet searching for something, though not a location or even a surprise. I walked in search of a feeling only to realize I already had it, and that it was enough to keep walking until it was all spent, until I reached the end of the night and realized there was nothing to do but use up my happiness.

Three Questions for Giovanna Luxembourg

(Unpublished Interview, December 2005)

How and when did you decide to work in fashion design?

I was sixteen years old, and I felt an intense desire to escape from my-self—my voice, my body, the fixity of those mirrors that seemed to chase me everywhere. That was when I started sneaking out at night. I ran away from the house where I was living then with an old retired couple who'd adopted me. It was then, as well, that I decided to dye my hair black for the first time. But it wasn't just the hair. Some part of me wanted to become the color black: a void that would escape all mirrors. I dressed in black, I wore black lipstick and nail polish, I looked for a vacuum in the color black. My adopted family got worried, and they decided to send me off to Europe with a distant aunt. To this day I don't know why I agreed to go, but I did, and a month later I was across the pond. It was while I was there, in one of those little white villages that overlook the Mediterranean and always seem to want to empty of themselves, that I decided to run away. I took my chance when my aunt had gone to the bathroom and I ran, not knowing that the village was so small they'd find me without even look-ing. I ran like never before, until after a few minutes I saw a small chapel at the end of a narrow street. I went in and hid. My plan was to stay there until night fell, and then disappear into the town. Flee on foot to another village, cross even more daring borders. But I was afraid, and in my fear I screamed. I let out a prodigious, thundering scream, my fear now imbued with fury. I screamed loud, and to my surprise my voice disappeared in the nooks and crannies of that chapel, to the point where I thought I'd lost it. I almost thought I was dreaming when finally I heard the scream come back to me, now converted into something else: it was my voice, but different. It was an echo in which my voice played at camouflaging itself among other voices, past and future. Something told me this was what I'd been looking for: a hiding place within my own voice. And then a forgot-ten childhood memory came back to me: I recalled a lush jungle, and in it the figure of an insect disguising itself in the branches. I remembered that playful animal, dressing and cross-dressing in the middle of the rain forest, and somehow I understood that the only escape from the fear and fury I felt was there: in the tricks of that little creature and the echo of my voice that was now coming back to me, the same and yet transformed. Hidden within itself. When the sun came up the next morning, I finally came out of hiding and told my aunt I would never run away again under two conditions: I wanted to change my name, and I wanted to study fashion design. A week later I told all my friends that my new name was Giovanna Luxembourg. They all laughed, but I just heard the echo of that fantastical chapel.

What is your real name?

Carolyn Toledano. But to say "real" is to not understand anything I've just told you.

And what kind of relationship do you have with your parents?

None. Let's just say they're dead. Or let's say, more like it, that I feel like I talk to my mother sometimes: in the middle of the night, her voice tells me what path to follow. And let's say that my father is a man who sits in a small mining town and tries to forget the end of the world. Changing your name is a little like changing family.

The road would be long. All roads are long that
lead toward one's heart's desire.

—Joseph Conrad, *The Shadow Line*

1

Every afternoon the order repeats like an empty ritual: five o'clock arrives and the old man stops bustling around the garage, pours himself a blond beer, sits down at the table in the yard, and, one by one, sets up the chess pieces. With a cat's ever-attentive calm, he takes off his boots, rolls up his sleeves, puts a hand to his beard, and then, sitting and facing the afternoon that now begins to sprawl out, he gives the deep-throated shout that tells me he's ready. I toss my novel onto the cot and cross the living room, where I hear the sound of the canaries' frenetic fluttering in their cages, then I open the door and, as I go outside, see that the ritual is now complete. I see him in his chair looking toward the old school that's now become a vacant lot, his face cured by the sun and the years, his eyes fixed on the chessboard as if he were plotting his moves, his prominent bald spot surrounded by his elegant white curls. Three dogs ramble around him, trying to escape the afternoon heat. He gestures with his right hand while the left gives a little pat to the other chair. The signal for me to sit. Like that, without many words, the day ends and the game begins.

Every afternoon since I arrived has been the same. Sometimes we play several games and other times only one, eternal and multiple, which makes me think the old man is inventing games within the larger match, private rules within a universe in miniature that he himself built. We play to the afternoon heat, from one beer to the next, with the dogs wandering around us and the constant murmur of the canaries as background music. He always faces westward, I always look to the east, toward the house old Marlowe abandoned, where dozens of chickens now scrabble aimlessly. "He trained them to compete," *the old man told me at the end of the second day.* "He'd take the chickens a mile away and then let them go, and he and his friends bet on which bird would make it home first." *Then he spat on the floor, as if putting an end to the conversation.*

And like that, watching the restless chickens that in the end returned to a house that could give them nothing more, we play for hours in a companionable silence, until I feel the boredom start to get to him. I see him sit up straighter in the chair and he seems much taller and younger, with his eyes wide open and his face more expressive. That's when I recognize him just as I've seen him in the photos in Giovanna's file: the mischievous gaze, the half-smile, the well-defined eyebrows, now white. I recognize the man who, forty or fifty years younger, appears in the photos accompanied by tropical dancers, but I still try to hide the discovery. If he finds out I know, I tell myself, he'll refuse to help me. Without stopping the game, between sips of beer, the old photographer starts to tell me a story that grows windingly: a long, thin story of detours and journeys that ends by depositing him here in this town that stretches out behind him, a town whose tired spirit as it empties is the same spirit with which he decided to adopt it as his own. He tells me the story in fragments, as if we were looking at photographs, until suddenly, weary, he cries out the inevitable checkmate. Inside, the silence of the house signals that the canaries have accepted the end of the day.

Still, I know his day doesn't end there. I know that past nine o'clock the old man will return to the garage to contemplate the progress of those enigmatic models he spent the day creating. I know because I've seen it, that when he finishes dinner he opens the door of the house again, crosses the little patio, goes into the garage, and sits down to gaze, with the eyes of an age-old elephant, at those models that bear the outlines of half-drawn maps. Maps to different scales, full of eraser marks; maps that seem to dissolve the way a memory or a scent fades away. They apparently show the same city. They differ, though, in scale, and in the singular ways they've been distorted. Amid the mess of old magazines, newspapers, and beer cans that clutter the garage, there is a wicker rocking chair. He sits there, and with his elephant eyes he contemplates those ephemeral monuments, his movements as slow as when he moved the chess pieces hours earlier. I secretly watch him in that strange ritual until the question becomes obsessive: Why didn't he leave when everyone decided to go? Why did he stay in this town that wasn't even his? One of the dogs comes over to me and licks my hand, like an offering of friendship in the middle of the desert.

2

Yoav Toledano is twenty-three years old the first time he thinks about Latin America as a real possibility that exists beyond all the dismal maps. A growing allergy to war, product of his participation in Sinai in 1957, has ultimately instilled in him the secret vocation of a globe-trotter. He thinks, at first, of visiting some Asian country, green palm trees and clear coasts, but the poetic resonance of Tierra del Fuego manages to dissuade him. The terribly romantic idea of the solitude at the end of the world makes him feel he is fleeing a history that encloses him on all sides. A photograph he finds in an old fashion magazine of Bariloche, with its snowy mountains and beautiful lake, confirms his intuition. He imagines himself at the end of the world, in the company of penguins and polar bears, surrounded by the taciturn solidarity of the color white. He tells himself that on arriving in America he will need three things: a camera, a map, and the voracity that has guided his family throughout a seemingly endless pilgrimage of four centuries. Though he's never seen the snow, he imagines himself photographing enormous ice floes aboard little boats struggling to go ever deeper south. He conceives of his mission in epic terms: he will travel west like the sun and south like the stars. To his family, however, he explains the trip as a youthful sowing of oats. He'll return after a few months, as soon as he's learned to recite, in perfect Spanish, the poems of his father's favorite: the Nicaraguan poet Rubén Darío.

Once his parents are convinced, he turns to the selection of a camera. In a little book on the history of photography he finds the necessary inspiration: he reads about Niépce's camera obscura and Daguerre's device, about Talbot's experiments, the emergence of Kodak's first cameras, and the invention of the instant photograph. This last event fascinates him: he cannot imagine photography without that instantaneous lightness. It's only natural, then, that when it's time to buy, he decides on a Polaroid Pathfinder he comes across in a small electronics store in Tel Aviv. The choice of the map is simpler, but no less suggestive. In a history book, he finds a map showing the routes of Alexander von Humboldt's American travels. He tears it out and draws over its wrinkled surface the trip he has imagined. It has four points. The first, a star drawn in red marker, is logical: the Haifa port. The second point, marked with a postage stamp, is on the southern tip of Spain, as if any transatlantic trip called for a repetition of Columbus's voyage. The third, modern and dreamy, is New York. From there he draws a zigzagging line that again crosses the Atlantic, this time with an enormous arc that finally alights on the southern tip of South America. Marking this last point, Toledano decides to draw a little penguin, below which can be read, in Hebrew letters, the name that so fascinates him: "Tierra del Fuego." And like that, inevitably romantic and with an imperious youthful will, he prepares himself during the winter while he waits for a trip he can only imagine under the rubric of other classic voyages: the one that deposited Charles Darwin on the southern tip of the same continent he's headed toward; the famous circumnavigation of the globe when Magellan discovered the beauty of spheres; the sad flight that ended when Amelia Earhart disappeared, her aerial dream along with her. He traces routes, imagines sojourns, sketches projects. But mostly, he takes photos.

In the absence of a gun, the portable camera quickly becomes his greatest ally and defense, not to say his obsession. He travels the country north to south taking photos, from the Sea of Galilee to the Negev Desert, from the Roman ruins in Caesarea to the dimly lit alleys of Jaffa. After a few weeks he is an expert. His friends ask for portraits, his relatives, postcards. A family acquaintance who is an art collector even offers a commission in exchange for photographs of the five new pieces he's just brought back from New York. Toledano doesn't hesitate. He feverishly shoots those paintings by a young artist whose name he doesn't know and whose style confuses him: he can't know that behind the violent brushstrokes of a certain Willem de Kooning is a painter with whom he will soon rub elbows in the Big Apple. He can't know and doesn't want to. More than the art, more than painting, he is interested in the essential nature of color. And well does he know that there are two colors absent in his collection: the white of the southern snow and the green of the Amazonian jungle. So, on the sunny spring afternoon when he learns that his travel papers are ready, Toledano can only imagine himself surrounded by that Latin American world he pictures as a terribly natural monster. Anxious, he realizes that he has reached his twenty-third year without ever leaving the little clod of dirt that saw his birth. He calms himself by repeating a schmaltzy phrase that at his young age still sounds daring and poetic: "Soon I'll photograph the end of the world." He ignores, without the slightest qualm, the fact that the beginning of any trip is a detour.

The day of his departure, his father gives him two books. More than books, they are amulets, objects that will be with him throughout the trip as reminders of a promise of return. At least, that's how the father imagines it; as his family looks on, he opens the first book and reads, in a very Ladino Spanish, some verses that no one but him understands:

> *Y llegué y vi en las nubes la prestigiosa testa*
> *de aquel cono de siglos, de aquel volcán de gesta,*
> *que era ante mí de revelación.*
> *Señor de las alturas, emperador del agua,*
> *a sus pies el divino lago de Managua,*
> *con islas todas luz y canción.*

In the father's voice the syllables are rough, the *r*'s scratchy, the pauses uncomfortable. No one knows why he adopted as his preferred poet that Nicaraguan writer of somewhat grandiloquent phrasing, but that day, gathered around the departing son, they all take it as a kind of bad joke. All except Yoav, for whom this secret language represents a world. Still, curiosity wins out, and he puts aside the book of Darío's poems and opens the second volume. A biography of Nadar, a photographer he's read something of in his little history of photography, but about whom he knows only the basics: he was born and he took portraits. Soon he'll know more: he will know, for example, that the same man who photographed the distinguished Baudelaire also depicted the Parisian catacombs. Years later he will wonder what would have happened if, instead of a book by Rubén Darío, his father had given him one by Baudelaire. But that will come later. On the day of his departure the book on Nadar is nothing more than a book. With eager curiosity, Yoav reads a few pages and stashes it in his backpack, between the book of poems and the history of photography that has kept him company during recent months. He kisses his father, kisses his mother, kisses his little brother, and leaves.

———

First stop: Spain. His parents have asked him to visit the place of origin that is tattooed on his name—Toledo. So when he disembarks in Madrid, the first thing Yoav does is determine the cardinal points. He will travel south in what he considers a practice exercise for the final trip that, according to his plan, will leave him at the southern tip of the American continent. His parents have asked him to try to take photos of the famous Toledo Synagogue, where the family history began. Yoav, however, is more interested in the beautiful name the Christians use: Santa María la Blanca. More than history, he is chasing the twists and turns of his name. Two days later, after a pilgrimage that involved a train and two buses, Toledo welcomes him with the uncertain melancholy of a parent receiving a prodigal son. As afternoon falls, Yoav recognizes the old synagogue and repeats to himself that this is where the whole story begins. It's six in the afternoon on a Friday. This Sabbath will find him far from home, alone in a postcard landscape.

His grandfather has told him the story over the course of many evenings, in fragments scattered over countless Sabbaths. The story, as he's heard it told, begins precisely there, in Toledo, when Yusef Abenxuxen, son of the most skilled finance minister of Alfonso VIII of Castile, decides he will be the one to convince the king that his people's prayers also deserve a home. He will convince the crown that Toledo needs a synagogue. The twelfth century is approaching and a new wave of anti-Semitism has awakened anxiety in Toledo's Jews. Using his influence and going against his father's wishes, Abenxuxen secures a meeting with the king's adviser. On a rainy afternoon, sitting across from a man who doesn't seem to be listening, he tries to explain the need for this temple that he imagines, per the concepts of sacred scriptures, as a space for silence, prayer, and law. After an hour, tired of struggling with this enthusiastic young man's rhetoric, the consul sends him away with the assurance that he will bring his complaints to the king, though he doubts the reaction will be positive. So, two days later, when the reply reaches Abenxuxen mid-supper, his surprise is considerable: the king has accepted. The problem is that Jewish architects aren't exactly in abundance. The building, emphasizes the messenger, will have to be designed by Moorish architects. Yusef does not despair. Young and pragmatic, he knows that the important thing is to get the building up.

But then comes the problem of convincing the old rabbis. Before long, he sees another way out. He remembers a friend of his who could always be found drawing architectural designs that never materialized. It occurs to him that if he can convince this architecture aficionado to join the team of Moorish architects, the rabbis will agree. That original architect, Yoav's grandfather told him, was the first of their family line.

His name was Yosef Ben Shotan, but after two weeks go by, the Moorish architects with whom he now shares the joy of a profession baptized him with a more neutral name: Toledano. The shyness of genius lent him a chameleonic aspect. He could go an entire afternoon without uttering a word, but when he did say something, it seemed as though he'd been there speaking from the start. He had the ability to fit in anywhere, to harmonize in any group. "He was the first Marrano," his grandfather said, while little Yoav looked at him and nodded, not knowing what that word meant. He was only eleven years old, and history was already starting to intrigue him, even when it seemed incomprehensibly distant. "He was a few centuries early," the old man went on, "but his expression already held the bravery of the Marranos." Hours later, hidden among old volumes of Shakespeare in his father's enormous library, captive to the bewilderment those family anecdotes made him feel, Yoav would find in an old encyclopedia a brief article on the secret systems of the Jewish conversos and the clandestine practice of religious traditions. He would find, scattered throughout the article, words that would confuse him even more—shining, winding words, like *crypto-Judaism*. Farther down, as one final aid, he would find a pictorial rendering that showed a group of Jews gathered in the dark, praying among candles, clearly in an age long past. Yoav forgot the rest and retained only that image. Every time his father repeated that Yosef Toledano was the first Marrano, he imagined a shadowy scene with ancient people chanting over candles. The secret of that word, for him, had much to do with twilight. So, eight years later, when he reaches the old synagogue of Santa María la Blanca past six in the evening, Yoav thinks to himself that his arrival could only be thus: late, Marrano.

The photograph of Toledo that he sent his family shows Yoav between two of the synagogue's famous white arches, smiling in the sunset. He looks tall, handsome, his hair short and neat, just as he was when his parents said goodbye to him. There is a hint, however, of a certain nomadic inclination. Turning the photograph over we find a short note, written in Hebrew: "Here at the first temple, during a Marrano sunset. Hugs." Farther down, in a nod to the books his father had given him, there's a quote from Nadar: "There is much photography in the sunset." He has barely left his house behind, and already he seems to have found a second home. He's imagined the trip as an odyssey to the end of the world, but this first stop already strikes him as conclusive and comfortable.

He spends two weeks in Spain. He wants to finish his tour of the family history hidden behind that first name, Yosef Toledano. He has only the information his grandfather gave him: dates, a few names, general outlines of the story of the Marranos in old Spain. Still, he doesn't give up. Nor does he care that he doesn't speak the language. He has picked up several key words, which, combined with a few gestures and a dictionary, are enough to survive on. In the mornings he explores the streets of the old Jewish quarter, those aged sectors that stretch through the city with the force of a secret. He walks the streets of the walled city, crosses St. Martin's Bridge to the Puerta del Cambrón, from the old Assuica district to Santo Tomé. He sits down to drink a beer in Montichel, enjoys a sunny afternoon on the outskirts of the Bab Alfarach neighborhood. In an alleyway in Hamanzeite, a couple of Gypsies try to steal his camera, but he fights them off. He knows the camera is his true language. Everywhere he goes he takes a lot of Polaroids; after lunch, he arranges them in a travel album, and at the end of the day, he sits down to write a diary that snakes among the photos as it grows. A luminous intuition tells him that the novels of the future will be something like this: illustrated almanacs, enormous catalogs, curiosity cabinets on which the authors, mere copyists, write commentaries.

One afternoon, looking for a map, he enters a small store in the old Arriaza neighborhood. He's greeted by an enormous man, fat and stinking. The whole place smells of old alcohol and fermented food. The scene is completed by a half-dozen cats that wander around the truly tiny space, whose walls are adorned with dozens of useless artifacts: broken record players, rusted rifles, a decrepit phonograph. Yoav considers leaving, but his politeness makes him stay. Winding his way through the cats, he picks up a map and tries to locate the Samuel Ha-Levi synagogue. The man asks what he is looking for. Yoav, shy and unable to express himself in that still-foreign language, shows him a photograph of the synagogue and merely pronounces the key word: *Marrano*. The man doesn't understand. Then he switches languages. It's the first and last time, in his entire trip through Spain, that someone will speak to him in English. And in perfect English, no less, in spite of the booze on his breath. The fat man tells him that years ago he'd studied architecture in England—Cambridge, specifically—among British aristocrats and buttoned-down ladies, until one day, sick of libraries, he opted instead for cats and alcohol. He talks to Yoav about the London afternoons that tended to encompass all four seasons, about the ever-lukewarm English beers, about the Natural History Museum, about girls he kissed in the rain. Then, between sips of liquor, prisoner of the nostalgia brought on by the English language, he shows Yoav an old folder. And there, among papers dotted with coffee stains, Yoav glimpses what seems to be a map of the entire city. Between grotesque peals of laughter, the fat man swears this map depicts the Toledan underground. It looks, rather, like two maps superimposed, one over the other, doing battle. He said the map had once been part of his doctoral thesis, which had promised to discover, through an archaeological study of the Toledo subsoil, the ruins of ancient cemeteries. According to him, right there beneath the living city, there was a subterranean history that included remains left by Romans, Visigoths, Jews, Muslims, and Arabs.

"Our own private Hades," he repeats.

Yoav finds the story fascinating, loves to imagine that he's walking on a secret world, the underground history that, according to this drunk archaeologist, at times emerges into the city's surface. The fat man tells him there are some corners of the city where intact traces of the cemeteries remain: a half-erased gravestone can be found in Calle de la Plata, another one persists near the Santo Tomé bridge.

Toledano spends the following days sunk in his diary, sketching out diagrams, drawings, commentaries, aphorisms. In school he was precocious in math, and that skill is evident in his notebooks, which seem to adhere to a precarious order. An ordered chaos, that's what stands out in the pages he devotes to the most insignificant occurrences: notes about the southern sunset, comments on photographic texture, sketches of cats and even a train ticket. More than a diary, it's an almanac, a conceptual collage, a little like those magazines from the turn of the century that diffidently featured, side by side, short stories by Poe and the most frivolous fashion ads. In the afternoons, when the heat becomes unbearable, he takes shelter in some small, fanned café and reads, with a joy not free of restlessness, his little book on the history of photography. He returns over and over to the same stories: the camera obscura by Giovanni Battista della Porta, William Hyde Wollaston's magic lantern, the complicated and treacherous story of Daguerre and Talbot. He likes the way the characters of this story bet everything on ideas that seemed crazy at first. He is fascinated by how, in the name of the purest science, they pursued projects that must have seemed like hallucinations. In that same book, between liters of beer that he's slowly learned to drink without disgust, he reads of Niépce's heliographic project. *Heliography*: he likes the word, distant and light, but he likes even more what it means. "Sun writing"—he repeats the definition in the middle of the tavern and the idea lights up the afternoon.

In the midst of the Enlightenment, two brothers, tired of listening to old Kant go on about the light of reason, say to each other that it would be better to invent an apparatus that could write with the light of the sun itself. Shrouded as it is in romantic frenzy, the project strikes Yoav as intensely poetic—to defy reason, in the full swing of the Enlightenment, by imagining an impossible artifact that could illuminate everything the old philosophers talk about. To add a pinch of luminous darkness to so much conceptual blather. Yoav soon discovers that there is indeed a lot of darkness in early photography. Paging through the book's illustrations, he finds a blurry photo that looks more like an inky blotch than anything else. Below it is an explanation that declares this image the very first photograph, a reproduction of the landscape just as it looked from the window of Niépce's studio one morning in 1826. Overcome, he thinks how photography is an art of pause and suspension, an art of static light that nevertheless contains a great deal of darkness. Surrounded as he is by drunk men, he says, "It's something like that, slow and light like alcohol."

Of all the information in his book, one story quickly becomes his favorite: the invention of the photographic negative by the Englishman William Henry Fox Talbot. He is so interested in the anecdote that, so as not to forget it, he copies it out word for word like a primary school child. It's the story of an invention that, like all inventions, is more of a stroke of luck. One afternoon when he's vacationing near Lake Como, Talbot decides to put a few leaves out in the sun on paper that has been immersed in silver nitrate. After a few hours he finds that the light has traced an inverse image of the outline of the leaves. All that's needed is a little salt, and those inverse shadows are fixed to the paper. Years later, the Englishman would be able to transfer his technique to the camera obscura. It's the true birth of modern photography, of mechanical reproduction, the visual universe that sometime later Toledano himself will try to escape. Young Yoav, however, is interested not so much in the invention itself but in its conceptual implications, the metaphorical flight of the anecdote. He likes the idea of photography as an art of inversion, like a mirror in which reality finds its subterranean opposite. The anecdote brings him immediately back to the fat man's story, the image of that sepulchral city that exists below Toledo's surface. He pastes Talbot's first photograph in his notebook beside the anecdote he's just copied, and then he writes a reflection that he titles, not without irony, "Toledan Sunset." It's a small reflection on inversions, shadows, and invisibilities. Here he notes that he has read little in his life, really very little. He spent his school years on equations and soccer games. Now, when he sits down for the first time to write something he considers legitimately literary, the words arise freely, if orphaned. They have no tradition, no base, no territory. Yoav, however, likes that state of absolute contingency, the innocent power of one's first writing, the tabula rasa that belies an errant reflection on his own lineage. "Toledan Sunset" is a text of conceptual contretemps that hides something more: for the first time, the young photographer is imagining photography as the possibility of escape. More than the visible, he tells himself, photography pursues the invisible. More than light, darkness. More than the ground, the underground. He writes everything like that, couched in somewhat pathetic reflections. He is ignorant of tradition and a long way from satire, and pathos doesn't strike him as a problem. He reads over what he's written and his prose convinces him. He feels for the first time the pleasure of a voice of his own, even when it's precisely that voice he wants to escape. *Toledan* is, at the end of the day, not just an adjective but also pretty much his own last name; his writing is ultimately a veiled reflection on the secrets of his name. Among the terms he writes down, there is one he finds particularly suggestive, one he will return to many times: *negative history.* Behind every event, behind every story, Yoav says to himself, there is something more, a kind of photographic negative of meaning, a historical shadow of what has been.

That night he dreams. He dreams he is back in the archaeologist's shop, searching through papers in a file that grows along with his confusion. He doesn't know what he's looking for, but he keeps looking, as if the meaning of the task lay in absurd repetition. In his dream he hears something. An echoing laugh that he quickly recognizes as the fat man's. Then he notices that at the back of the store there's a small staircase that leads to a basement. When he goes down, he finds himself in a much larger underground space. It seems to be an art studio. And it is: there, among dozens of identical paintings, the fat man is ambling around and applying the final touches to one of the mountainous landscapes. To one side, an old man completes crossword puzzles while the room starts to fill with cats. Then Yoav wakes up, terrified, swearing it's time for him to depart.

3

He tells me everything—his story, the trip, that youthful picaresque—with a devilish neutrality, as if he were talking about someone else. I let him talk, while the dogs wander around us like leisurely witnesses. From time to time one of them approaches in search of a caress, but the old man smacks it away. Then he continues the story, seeming to punctuate it with chess movements: he tells an anecdote and then moves a rook, tells another and moves a queen, remembers an afternoon in Montichel and moves a pawn. This, I tell myself, is more than a simple game. I let him talk, let him go on with this long, thin story, while my mind starts to associate images of that remote past with others of this smoke-filled town. I think of his reflections on the Marrano sunsets, I think of the story I've just heard about the sepulchral underground of Toledo, I think of his theory on negative history, and I think about how it all leads to this town. I think of his desire to reach the end of the world and I say to myself that perhaps, after decades, Yoav Toledano understood that the true end was not at the world's southern tip but rather in a small mining town two hours from home. I look back at old Marlowe's empty house, where the chickens flap incessantly, and I say to myself, every dog will have his day.

John, the youngest of the remaining nine, the one who was barely four years old when the fires became inevitable, has shown me around with the pained elegance of a man tracing an invisible history. He pointed to a barren lot and said, "That's where the church was." He pointed to some trees and said, "That's where the school was." We walked on a muddy plot and at the midpoint he murmured, "My uncle's house was here."

He shows me things in the mornings, taking advantage of the fact that during the early hours the old man is caught up with his models, the purpose of which John doesn't know either, though he's heard theories. "My uncle said that the models depict the town as it would look from the sky," he told me. But then he added, "That old guy is crazy. I don't know why you're interested in him." And I thought how that's precisely why I'm interested, because he's the one who stayed, though neither family nor history tied him to the town. He arrived a year before the fires took control—he says he came to photograph the mines—and two years later he was still there, even after the news spread through the town and the main highway filled up with fleeing cars. He had no wife or family, or at least he made no reference to any. He spent his days with the camera slung over his shoulder, making notes in a little notebook with a red leather cover. It was clear he had been someone more, a city slicker, elegant and sophisticated, but now he seemed to have closed himself off behind a hermetic seal. Still, there was no tragedy about him, no alcoholism. He just took his pictures and then went home. And no one knew what he did there. He locked himself in the house he'd bought with who knows what money, and he wasn't seen coming back out until the next morning, again hoisting his camera with the conviction that nothing had changed. And that's how it was, day after day, while around him the town slowly emptied. Until one day he emerged without the camera, and those who saw him thought he would finally leave, that he'd finally realized there wasn't much for him to do there. They were wrong: he'd never been more resolved to stay. As if he had come here specifically to watch the town burn.

John tells the old man's story just as he heard it. Then he gets tired and returns to what must be to him the only story, the story of the mining town that woke up one day to learn that its underground is an inferno. Together we walk around the town that now, twenty-five years later, seems more like a scattered village: a house here, another there, but everywhere a feeling of imminent vertigo, an intuition that there was once something more. We cross the emptiness of what used to be—the church, the school, the bookstore, the old mining company headquarters—until beyond all the grassy fields I see an enormous mountain rise up. Here, says my new friend, is where it all started. Here, at the dump, a fire that was meant to burn garbage came into contact with the coal of the underground mines. He makes the sound of an explosion, and his hands imitate the force of an expansive wave. At the edge of the dump I catch sight of some plumes of smoke that sigh slowly, as if responding to an ancestral voice, ancient and slow. John repeats the town's story, but I get distracted. Two sparrows swoop down above us, while in the distance I can make out the main highway. I imagine that initial spark, like a camera flash.

In the afternoons, when John heads off to work, I go back to the house with-out making much noise. I see the old man in his hallucinatory task, deep in the creation of those strange models, and something makes me remember the old reader at the Bowery: the same blind and stubborn obsession, the same empty gaze. Facing the dogs as they sleep away the afternoon heat, with the canaries providing background music, I stretch out on the cot and finally pause to observe the old man's house. It gradually dawns on me that the space is punctuated, very subtly, with Latin American elements: in one corner, on two old shelves, I see some novels by Latin American au-thors among the books. The big names: García Márquez, Cortázar, Cabrera Infante, a weathered copy of Rubén Darío's complete works. Farther down, lost among anthropological treatises, I find a copy in Spanish of Los ser-tones, by Euclides da Cunha. Then, two names I don't recognize but whose books bear titles in Spanish: Salvador Elizondo and José Revueltas. And it doesn't stop there. On the same wall, a sign in primary colors commemo-rates the first years of the Sandinista struggle. Even more hidden, in a cor-ner that I hadn't noticed until then, I see a small shrine, the colored candles half burned down, some with images of saints, others of virgins. Beside an old radio, a plastic bust of Simón Bolívar, the Liberator, completes the unexpected scene. Never, I think to myself, could old Simón have imagined he'd end up in plastic. The canaries flutter around the little Bolívar without the slightest respect. I turn back to the saint candles, and my mind flashes onto the long afternoons of darkness and heat that followed the hurricanes of my childhood. Then I think of Giovanna, the way Latin America had slowly begun to arise from her story, too, subtle as the reptiles that so fas-cinated her. I picture Giovanna sick in the tropics, and my mind turns to the photo of Yoav Toledano that has him in shorts with his leg in a cast, beside that woman whose gaze so reminds me of Giovanna's, but who still refuses to appear in this story. I think of the world map behind him, and I wonder again what this old Israeli has to do with a plastic Bolívar. After a while the whole thing starts to take on elements of kitsch. Then, to battle the distaste and boredom, I lie down on the cot again and start to read the book I brought with me: a novel by Malcolm Lowry about an alcoholic consul who tries to get back together with his wife. I read sporadically, in fragments, until boredom wins out. Then, thinking of the story I've just heard from John, I take out my backpack and go through the papers from

Giovanna's file. Carefully, afraid the old man will catch me, I take out the newspaper clippings. There is the story in pieces, fragmented: from that first clipping dated 1962, which relates the origin of a disaster that doesn't yet seem fatal, to the last article, from 1997, with interviews of all the people who decided to stay.

4

Crossing the Atlantic turns out to be more pleasant than he'd imagined. A far cry from the epic, torturous crossings of Magellan and Columbus, Earhart and Darwin. His is something else, a simple postwar voyage, a mere tourist trip that he, nevertheless, views with Homeric eyes. Yoav Toledano demands disruptions in a time of peace. Years later, wrapped in a messianic whirlwind that again he won't know how to relate, he will understand the resonance of unresolved desire.

Still, that will come later. On May 6, 1957, on boarding the immense *Almanzora*, Toledano meets a muffled reality. Not that his trip is to be short or even comfortable. On the contrary: he is separated from New York by three weeks and a third-class bunk where every breath taken seems like a miracle. The true enemy of his heroic epic, however, turns out to be something simpler and unexpected—as soon as he boards, his youth and vigor win the attention of two moneyed girls. The trip hasn't even started, but Toledano instinctively understands something that many people take lifetimes to comprehend: there's nothing keeping us in the place we're born into, especially if genetics have granted us an agile body and a pair of striking eyes. Two Italian cousins, heiresses of a textile empire, take the youth by the hand and introduce him to the first-class bunks and luxurious parlors. He drinks champagne in salons denied to his third-class companions and surprises himself trying exotic foods: lobster, shrimp, octopus, caviar. Long gone is the kosher regimen of his childhood. He discovers, along with the cousins' nocturnal company, that while all bunks may seem the same in the dark, some lend themselves better to six-handed games. His inhibitions loosened by alcohol, he realizes that being handsome is another way of being rich. It's not long before he glimpses the unhappy corollary of this pleasing intuition—that wealth can bring the worst deprivation. One day, in the middle of a luxurious dinner, he realizes his betrayal: he's gone a full week without taking a photograph, a full week without reading from his father's book of poems, a full week lost amid the tantalizing laughter of two insatiable cousins. Years later, deep in a game of chess, he will remember that mistake with the following words: "That's how life passes, in those detours that rob you of a decade." His story, it could be said, is not only the story of his obsession, but also of its detours.

Saddened by this brief distraction, he returns to his reading. In the shelter of the colored map of Latin America he's hung on the wall beside his bunk, he rereads, in a bilingual translation, his father's poet, Rubén Darío, until he tires of so much grandiloquence. He tosses the book aside, and from that day on he spends the mornings reading exclusively about photography. As he returns to his passion for reading, his practicality also comes back. Now he is seen in the luxurious salons hoisting his camera, his attentive eye always looking for just the right moment. Thus Toledano believes his dilemma resolved: photographing leisure is still a photographic act. To depict life as it's lived is another way of living it. He hopes that this way he can escape distraction without denying himself the minimal pleasures that are slowly starting to tempt him. Perhaps unfortunately for him, the camera only serves to accentuate his allure. In his case, he quickly understands, being a photographer is a most potent aphrodisiac. Before the jealous eyes of the two aristocratic Italians, Toledano watches other girls approach him, curious about the camera's workings. To them, weighed down by their parents' conservative and aristocratic tradition, this ungainly but athletic boy, the camera over his shoulder and a devilish smile on his face, soon becomes a symbol of all things modern. And the modern, in those years leading up to the sixties, is synonymous with the sensual. Without expecting it, without seeking it out, the young man finds he is contemporary, sexual, attractive. Women fight over him, over a lens that is suddenly capable of touch, impulse, caress. Even more importantly, Toledano catches on, for better or worse, to a fact that will stay with him throughout a trip that's only getting started: just like the very first Toledano, everywhere he goes, people seem to accept him as though he belongs. Wherever he is, his presence seems not just acceptable but necessary. Far from making him invisible, this chameleonic effect grants him a certain omnipresence. That's the only way to account for the string of girls he shares his nights with during that voyage of only three weeks.

And that's how we could summarize the trip that ends by dropping him off in fearsome New York: Yoav Toledano's second life began on an enormous cruise ship the moment he realized that fiction truly begins with the one who holds the camera. Years later, burdened by the consequences of this terrible intuition, he will seek total invisibility in a mining town—the dark underside of this story of lights.

There's one girl, however, with whom he falls in love. Her name is Lucía Ferrer, she is Catalan, and she comes from an affluent family of bankers. Among all the women who try to get close to him during those three weeks of nautical travel, she, haughty and fierce, will be the one to make him feel something different. Lucía Ferrer is the bad girl, the faded aristocrat, the rebellious alcoholic, the ironist. And it's precisely that aura of punk *avant la lettre* that attracts Yoav. He's captivated by her way of dismissing everything with short phrases that pound like fists, by the graceful way she turns her back on that whole world of champagne and caviar. She is, as well, the only one who refuses to utter a single word in English. All the other girls have given in to the traps of understanding, they've searched through memories of school days until they found the English words by which to communicate with this young Israeli who can barely stammer out a few syllables of rough Spanish. She, however, refuses. Though she speaks English to perfection, she refuses to pronounce a word of it during that final week they spend together. In a gesture of combined hubris and defiance, she forces Toledano to move closer to a language he still doesn't understand exactly but in which he's starting to feel more agile. In a curt but perfect Spanish well suited to her personality, the girl tells lies that Yoav, still innocent, believes are the feats of a precocious adventurer. She tells him political stories, personal stories, school stories. Multiple stories that depict her most rebellious sides, stories that liken her to a contemporary Marie Antoinette. Suffice it to say, Lucía Ferrer is a modern diva. Anachronistically aristocratic, cavalierly modern, she's the living body of a contradiction. It's no wonder, then, that young Toledano listens to her with the attention of one unraveling a paradox. And then, among the many names that appear in those transversal stories, Yoav thinks he recognizes one: Josep Lluís Facerías. It takes him a bit to remember where he's heard that name, but when he finally does, it dawns on him clearly, precise as the image that accompanies it: he remembers the very day of his departure, in a Toledo eatery, hearing some old men shout the name of that man who, Lucía says, has been her mentor. And his girl goes on to claim she has participated in anarchist coups, leftist conspiracies, in urban guerrilla forces. Indecisive, unable to figure out whether this strange aristocrat is pulling his leg or not, Toledano opts to move the question into the only possible tribunal: bed. There, after two hours of struggle and strain, the evidence is clear: only an anarchist, he thinks, could move like that, kiss that way, bite like her. Only a clandestine guerrilla would dare kiss him like that, crying out with such passion. Sore and exhausted, Toledano accepts the incontrovertible evidence of her singular sexual fury, only to find that, once the act is over, Lucía Ferrer bursts out laughing. She is laughing at him, though not, as Toledano thinks, at his abilities as a lover. She laughs, rather, at the ingenuity that lets him believe she could be part of the anarchist guerrilla groups of Josep Lluís Facerías and Quico Sabaté. Only an unfledged child, she says, would believe she would waste time on political games. Sitting at the table and sunk in shame, Yoav watches her laugh, naked and happy, until suddenly the ideal revenge dawns on him. He gets his camera, raises it, and without a care for her nudity, he takes her picture. The expected accusatory cry never comes. To the contrary, Lucía Ferrer laughs harder, breezily ironic, without losing an ounce of grace. In other words, no sooner does she feel the camera's eye upon her than the girl decides to pose. Without realizing it, Yoav Toledano has taken a first step toward the fashion photography that soon will earn him his living. He has crossed a border that will mark an era. Years later, a British journalist will ask him at what point he decided on fashion photography as his genre. His reply will be brief and enigmatic: "The day I discovered that the camera could make an anarchist smile." The nudes of Lucía Ferrer in the fullness of youth are the first sign of a curiosity that suddenly shifts away from the natural world and comes to rest on that convulsive and instinctive animal that is the human being. From that moment on, the agreement is mutual. They are only seen together, laughing, always with the camera close by. He has imagined his voyage as a long crossing to the end of the world, but only a month and a half later he seems to have found an ending in the laughter of a vivacious young woman. Lucía Ferrer, then, marks the complicated beginning, learning as laughter and detour, the brief intuition of a different horizon, full of biting and champagne. Lucía Ferrer is the harbinger of a truth that will become visible only years later, under the heat of a long tropical summer: Yoav Toledano's political commitment began as the joke of a spoiled girl posing as an anarchist.

Every voyage, however, ends with a port. And this one is no exception: on May 27, 1957, the *Almanzora* sees the silhouette of the city of New York rise up in the distance. It's time to go ashore.

What does he know about New York? Nothing, or very little. The image movies have given him of a greedy and gluttonous city, the winding image of a city where reason is pushed to its limits. He'd seen *All About Eve* at the Armón theater in Haifa. New York, then, is tied to a story of betrayal, the decadent image of the always beautiful Bette Davis, the triumph of the bad girl. What he knows of New York, or thinks he knows, is the strident image of a skyscraper in mid-construction, the lists of Broadway shows, news about the stock market, the New York Yankees' uniforms. Of the city he knows this: its iconic face, its kitsch facade, its most hackneyed side. He's heard of Babe Ruth, of Mickey Mantle, the slums of the Bowery, the lights of Madison Avenue, and the famous hot dogs. As soon as he moves farther into the city, he understands that none of that will help him. The city is something else: a constant background noise that forces the masses to move, a great dumping ground of sound with no possible escape, a great upswelling without sky. Alone and adrift, he lets himself be carried along on that vital impulse that pushes and displaces, until he understands that this city is unlike any other. He's left behind the amiable strolls of his native Haifa, the pleasant bike rides through Tel Aviv. New York is something else: an anxious body that shakes and contorts and never asks permission. On edge, with no shelter, and faced with the portents of nightfall, he realizes he'll have to seek help. He remembers having stashed in his backpack the number, name, and address of the gallery that belongs to his parents' friend, the one who'd hired him to photograph some paintings months before. He thinks about calling, but he's ashamed. He can't give in to cowardice. He has to taste New York, he tells himself, at least for one night, with the brave and sudden patience of a person trying an unknown liquor. Lucía Ferrer's anarchic smile is already far behind.

———————

That day he doesn't go far from the port. He'll have plenty of time, he knows, to explore the north. He'll have time to attend the great theaters of Broadway and visit the glorious and decadent New York of Bette Davis. Today, though, he is interested in another kind of decadence, the kind that's found in the dark alleyways of the Bowery, that zone of prostitution and parties he's seen depicted in the social photographs of Arthur Fellig, better known as Weegee. Nadar, he tells himself, depicted the Parisian catacombs. He will depict the New York underground. He's seduced by the idea of photography as an art of the flip side, an art of opposites and negatives. He is seduced, from that first day, by the thought that photographing the bums of the Bowery is another way of depicting the paradoxical megalomania of the metropolis. That day, though, he doesn't take pictures. He merely walks the streets of Lower Manhattan: from the Greenwich Village of Allen Ginsberg, a poet he has barely read in English, passing through a deserted SoHo, until he reaches the infamous Bowery he's heard so much about. In each place he sits, drinks a beer, and goes on, until the night finds him seated in a small tavern on the Lower East Side, with no hotel or place to stay. When he hears the echo of some congas across from the tavern, he understands that, without realizing, he's arrived right where he wanted to be. The murmur of that Spanish he still doesn't know how to distinguish as Caribbean lifts his spirits. It's not long before he joins in song with the group of Puerto Ricans who adorn the sidewalk. Three hours later, with the last sip of rum, he realizes it's time to look for a roof, and he asks one of his new Latino friends if they know of a place where he can sleep. Fifteen minutes later, a woman opens the door of what will be his first lodging in the new world: a small room without a bathroom that he will share for three months with three Puerto Ricans newly arrived at what they, with their usual impudence, refer to as "Loisaida."

Wherever he goes, Toledano *fits in*. Chameleonic, cheerful, easy, Toledano lands on his feet anywhere, among Puerto Ricans, among Italians, Irish, Jews. The next day, he visits his parents' friend's small art gallery, and a week later he meets a Romanian Jew who will give him his first job, at a small Brooklyn newspaper. Every morning from then on, he will write small, lurid stories to accompany news images. Every morning, he'll concentrate all the English he knows in order to synthesize, in ten words, the meaning of an image. Unworried about sounding pretentious, he'll describe his work with its elegant French name: "I write *faits divers*," he'll tell anyone who asks. The afternoons, on the other hand, will be spent wandering, south or north, always carrying his camera, convinced that at any moment the perfect photographic framing could arise, the decisive photo that will make all others pale in comparison. Nights he will spend in groups. With the Puerto Rican friends he's made at his lodgings, or in the various bars where they take him once evening falls. Chameleonic, cheerful, easy, Toledano gets to know the big city at the same runaway speed with which he consumes alcohol and women, with the happy lightness of a man who knows how to capture an entire story in three phrases. He has learned that in Bette Davis's New York, the only important thing is to adapt.

They are days of readings and obsessions. In the afternoons, when he goes out to walk, he always brings a book, and he devours one after another: from the books of the beat generation so prevalent in those days, Kerouac's famous *On the Road* and Ginsberg's *Howl*, to modern American classics, *Manhattan Transfer* by Dos Passos, the poetry of Hart Crane, the great Southern tragedies of William Faulkner. He likes the beatniks' experimental aspect, their eagerness to see it all, the hallucinatory trips to a Mexico that he still conceives of in epic terms. He swears to himself that, very soon, he will travel south. In Faulkner, he likes the strength of the writing, the bravery of setting everything else aside to delve into the ruins of the South. One subject, though, continues to fascinate him: the history of photography. Once he finishes the book he's brought with him from Israel, he wastes no time buying others. Multiple histories of photography that end up nurturing the projects he patiently sketches out in the little red leather notebook that he buys with his first paycheck to replace the travel diary, and that from then on goes with him everywhere. Of all the anecdotes of photography's history, two continue to pursue him: the idea of photography as an art of negatives coexists in his mind with the image of Gaspard-Félix Tournachon—also known as Nadar—moving deeper into the Parisian catacombs, ready to shoot the Parisian underground from inside. Nights, over drinks, his Puerto Rican friends talk to him of beaches and islands; meanwhile, Yoav Toledano dreams up projects as grandiose as Nadar's: he imagines an enormous photographic atlas of the New York underground, a catalog where New York's misery coincides with its greatness. He even imagines himself finding a perspective from which the city would appear identical to itself, reduced to the scale of ambition and bewilderment.

Those are years of unexpected, at times silent, coincidences. Often without knowing it, Toledano coincides, in bars and parties of south-side bohemia, with many artists and writers who would set the standard for the rest of the century. He will drink, unbeknownst to him, two tables away from Jackson Pollock and Willem de Kooning, whom he will not recognize even though he began his photography career only months earlier by shooting de Kooning's paintings. He will sing a bolero by Daniel Santos six elbows away from a very drunk Ken Kesey. He will charm women in the same SoHo bars through which a still-unknown Andy Warhol moves. But he will know little about those people. Always accompanied by his Caribbean friends, he will feel that his heritage lies elsewhere. He'll imagine, like the beatniks, that his tradition is a line fleeing southward, the epic voyage that he is sure will end in Tierra del Fuego. New York, he tells himself, is just a detour. And though he doesn't know it, New York is indeed just a stop on an odyssey that will ultimately lead him to a ghost town occupied by dogs and canaries, where he'll play chess as evening falls. But he can't know that yet. Yoav Toledano cannot yet know that he will never reach the absolute south, just as he cannot know—as he drinks rum among his island friends—that 1,001 detours from his southward voyage still await him. Ignorant of his destiny, he merely drinks, aware that there are two things in this life that do him good: women and alcohol. He doesn't understand yet, young as he is, that the two of them conspire to avoid straight lines.

———

And so, it's no surprise that a second detour interrupts young Toledano's southern pilgrimage. On May 16, 1959, while he is packing his suitcases to finally set off for Tierra del Fuego, he is invited to a party in the house of his father's well-to-do friend. That night, lost amid champagne and canapés, he meets a girl as young as she is beautiful, in whose name he thinks he can already recognize her future triumphs: her name is Virginia McCallister, she is seventeen years old, and, word has it, she is the most sought-after model on the entire East Coast. He has only to see her to know that she is his great detour.

5

Chess is a futures game, says the old man, while around him the dogs doze as if resting atop the tedium. Doesn't matter. With the aura of a tired elephant, patient and immemorial, he moves a piece, then another, and the sound of the canaries abruptly falls silent. Then I start to think about the numbers I've read: the four thousand people who lived in the town in 1962, the thousand people who remained in 1979, the two hundred left in 1985, the nine in 1997. I think about those figures, and the resulting image is of a city that slowly emptied of people so it could be filled by canaries.

    My friend John told me the story. He's told me how, when the town's inhabitants found out about the fires, they decided to turn to the old trick of the canary in the mine. Over half the town went out and bought a canary. They brought them home and set them to singing, he explained, afraid that one day a canary's silence would indicate the end was nigh: methane, carbon monoxide, any of those gases whose presence foretold death, one way or another. As John told me on one of those long walks we took through the ghosts of the absent town, the canaries lasted longer than the townspeople. Month by month, week by week, day by day, you heard of another family who'd decided to leave town. And they left behind, as a legacy of catastrophe, their little mine canary. They'd leave it with a mother, a brother, a friend: someone in whose character they detected fidelity and permanence. And that's how the canaries began to pass from hand to hand, until one day the townspeople all understood, not without surprise, that the only one who would stay to the end would be the foreign photographer. They started to come to his house, canaries in hand. People who had never even said a word to him. People who had maybe heard of him once or twice. People who one day found work in a nearby city, and, in the bustle of the move, decided to resolve the matter of the canary with an expression equal parts unexpected and conclusive: "No problem, we'll leave it with the photographer." The town was emptying out, but his house filled up with feathers and song. The canaries would be, so to speak, his inheritance, just as mine would be that series of envelopes full of photos and articles, newspaper clippings, and half-drawn clues that would end up returning me, unwittingly, to the imagined scene of a young Giovanna lost amid the empty alleys of a remote mining town.

———

And so, in the evenings, while the old man works on his models and I hear the creak of wood coming from the garage, I open the envelopes and find Toledano's writings among the legacy of orphaned papers. Then I sit down, putting the novel aside, and read. I read the occasional phrase out loud. For example, this sentence of his that I like so much: "A photograph, like a cloud, is never a thing in itself, but rather the sign that something will happen." I repeat the words until they no longer mean anything, and then I sit and watch the clouds go by, the passing tedium, and hear the strange way the canaries have of spacing out silences between their songs. I repeat the words until suddenly I understand that this man bet it all on an empty future. His wager is on leaving no legacy. Farther on in the same article I find an encyclopedia definition of the phenomenon of combustion. A terribly boring definition that I think Toledano must have copied out feeling that the future was a thing that could be consumed bit by bit, a substance as flammable as the lands that surrounded him. A canary sings again and I read:

> Combustion (from the Latin combustio) is a chemical reaction of oxidation, in which a large quantity of energy is obtained in the form of heat and light, manifesting visually as fire and other phenomena. In all combustion there is an element that burns (fuel) and another that produces the combustion (oxidant), generally oxygen in the form of gaseous O_2.

Farther down is the chemical equation of combustion. I sit thinking about it all, that strange intersection of poetic and scientific language. In this story, I think, it's not clear what was fuel and what was oxidant, what set fire and what burned. Then I stop reading. I approach the garage slowly and stop to look at the old man as he builds his models, until he realizes I'm there and stops working. I don't say anything. Nor do I look more closely. It scares me to think that in those models lies the key to the story. I'm afraid to see what I already know. I'd rather listen to him talk. That's why, as soon as I realize the old man has noticed I'm there, I go back to bed and stretch out to go on reading my novel, knowing that in a few hours I'll hear another whistle, and when I go outside I'll see the chess pieces arranged over the exact shades of this provincial dusk. Chess is a game of futures, I'll think then, just as the old man said.

6

They grow together. She as a model, he as a photographer. That same night, after they flee the party, she makes him repeat three times that he'll delay his departure. Not only that: she convinces him that he deserves a more respectable job. That's the end of the *faits divers*, the three-line stories, the journalistic epigrams beneath photos. From now on he will dedicate himself only to his two great passions: her and photography. Virginia McCallister says it like that, decisively, with character, and young Yoav Toledano can only accept the all-consuming strength of this girl who hasn't even come of age. That night they escape together. Sick of champagne toasts, tired of the anemic conversations of the rich, they take a taxi and head south. Half an hour later the night finds them sitting outside a small bodega on the Lower East Side, listening to the drums of a couple of Caribbean musicians. They're enjoying a little taste of what in less than ten years will become salsa music. For them, however, the future holds little interest. That night, they're interested in the intensity of the present, the precision of voices and kisses. They're interested in being complements to each other. From then on, that's what they'll be: two opposing worlds in conversation, the photographic negative that Toledano had sought. Northern, rich, and sedentary versus southern, poor, and nomadic. In the years to come, growing together will mean, more than anything, sharing a two-way highway: one that will lead them, always, from the Upper East Side mansions to the bohemian underworlds of the Bowery, and from Warhol's SoHo to the Upper West Side of Virginia's parents. Growing together will mean, above all, repeating every once in a while the initial act of rebellion.

One week later, Toledano quits his job at the newspaper and starts to work as a photographer for an art gallery owned by a friend of Virginia's parents. Two months later, Virginia herself, tired of not having him nearby, convinces the editors of a prestigious fashion magazine to hire the young Israeli. From then on, they are only seen together: in the studio and out, at rich people's parties, and in downtown taverns. They share everything: reading, a bed, obsessions, and even the drugs that are starting to be consumed in those days at the parties of New York bohemia. Their ascent is meteoric. After two years, they are both fashion-world darlings. New contracts come in. Virginia films her first movies, while Toledano makes a name for himself in fashion photography. Never, though, do they forget the first night. In the glamorous world where they live, it's well known that they take excursions to southern Bohemia, that they're aficionados of Caribbean rhythms, and it's even rumored that they share a house in the Bowery with dozens of Puerto Ricans. The rumors are part of their glamour and charm: a couple living outside the rules of society. A magical couple, able to combine luxury with an incendiary private life, from whose secrets the press is necessarily excluded. Perhaps that's why no one, not even their parents, is surprised to hear, from third parties, that the couple has begun to travel—to Atlanta, Florida, Tennessee, to Haiti and Cuba—to the south they find so seductive in its intensity.

Then other rumors start. Word begins to spread that they're caught up in red networks—Communist groups. Those are the years of the Cuban revolution, they're McCarthy years, and although their southern trips happen just before the embargo is declared against the Cubans, the coincidence only increases the story's morbid appeal. Nor does it help that, after meeting some Cuban leaders on a brief visit to New York, Toledano has stayed in touch with them. Even less that he's taken a photograph or two of Cuban leaders, a certain portrait that as the years pass will take on iconic weight. People start to label them Communists, they're branded as witch doctors, people associate them with esoteric beliefs. The strange thing is that for once the tabloids are not wrong. They may have unsound sources, they may exaggerate when they say the couple was spotted drinking crocodile blood, but the truth is that those who know them also know that they've traded in their old friends for new ones. They seem to be called, so to speak, to act in the service of some strange illumination. They turn up to fewer showbiz parties, they're seen with different groups of friends, and those who do see them notice a peculiar spark in their eyes. And what they see, more than anything, is a quest: Yoav Toledano and Virginia McCallister seek, with the fury of the worst kind of fire, a way out of the whirlwind growing around them. First they escape into fame, then into religion, then down the path of politics, only to end up mixing all those routes together in a hallucinogenic cocktail that, toward the middle of the decade, begins to soak their days.

Now that he's telling his story of the pilgrimage that ended when he came to this empty town, he doesn't remember the moment perfectly, but he conjectures that it was in those drugged-out days when a crazy idea started to rattle around in his mind. He doesn't know if it was the drugs, but it was during that time when he started to glimpse the idea that would eventually bring them to the middle of the jungle, in search of a lost city that few had ever seen. The idea, fixed and absurd like all obsessions, was this: Just as at the end of history the beginning was to be found—divine justice, angels, and God—likewise, the end of the left's political journey would be the right: the divine point where violence would coincide with itself and opposing political forces would stare each other in the face. A sort of angelic epic poem. He spent his days thinking about his theory, searching for books that would confirm it; he even remembers having outlined his ideas in a new little red leather notebook on whose first page he had scrawled a memorable title: *Notes on Beauty and Destruction*. A perfect title for the couple and for that pack of beautiful beings with whom they spent their mornings, among cameras of all kinds. A title under which Toledano composes, over the course of two years, an impressive theory around what he calls the end of history. A compendium of examples that include reflections on the atomic bomb, the burning of the Library of Alexandria, the years of Jacobin terror, his own family history. He makes his notes in secret, convinced that someday they will explain the political turn he is taking during that time. One day, in 1966, Toledano stands up and proclaims there is nothing more beautiful than destruction. Two days later, his wife wakes him with unexpected news: she is pregnant. That day, Toledano anxiously looks through his notebooks in search of a reply. He can't find any answer other than the face of horror.

After a long conversation that stretches into dawn, they decide to have the child on the condition that Virginia cuts down her drug use. From that moment on, Toledano seems like another person. He sets aside the drugs, submerges himself in the world of Santeria, tries to distance himself from the theories that have brought him to the edge of Nazism. It's Virginia McCallister, on the other hand, who seems to take up her husband's conceptual delirium. One day she finds his notebook tossed onto the bed, and what she reads there enchants her. It occurs to her that this is the only way to explain her lifelong fascination with a certain family anecdote: During the civil war, her great-grandfather had marched his men southward, and they burned everything in their path. This is the only way, the model says to herself as she reads her husband's notes, to explain her strange fascination with her great-grandfather William Sherman and his infamous March to the Sea. Starting that day she makes notes of her own, and she decides to take up old Sherman's lost tradition—finding there, perhaps, the euphoria she needs to replace the energy of the drugged nights. Perhaps. What is certain is that from that moment on, the red leather notebook is hers. It's where she jots down her ideas, where she imagines, during the long and tedious nine months of her pregnancy, another possible story. There, in the margins, she starts to draw little maps, trajectories outlining alternative histories, pilgrimages to the south, just what her husband is trying to forget by throwing himself into work. But she doesn't want to forget: quite the opposite, she wants to remember, just in a different way. She writes frenetically, without pause, even when they tell her she's carrying a girl, even when, months later, they tell her the girl could be born deaf, even when she knows she'll give birth any day. The first contractions, in fact, catch her with pen in hand, sketching the routes of destruction that her forebear took, trying to forget that in a few hours she will bring her first child into the world. Even twenty hours later, when she's presented with a tender little pink-and-white blob named Carolyn, Virginia smiles briefly, caresses and kisses her, but minutes later she returns to her writing and reading, as if her life depended on it.

These are misleading years. On the surface, nothing seems to change their careers' upward momentum. The projects multiply, the movies, the photo shoots. They're seen along with the little girl in recording studios, at this or that movie premiere, in fashion magazines. A model family, that's what anyone would see in those ubiquitous photos—and yet it's precisely during that time when Virginia McCallister's esoteric theories turn their most hallucinatory. It's during those days that she returns to Toledano's premise about the end of history, and she combines it with her own theories of destruction. Starting then, behind a facade of normalcy, she becomes obsessed with an idea: of finding the way out before it's too late. Those years pass quickly, in a whirlwind of ideas and conjectures that end up returning her to the world of hallucinogenics she thought she'd left behind. Breakneck years that lead up to the night when, for the first time, she hears about the commune.

Now that he's telling the story, Toledano doesn't remember exactly who first mentioned its existence, but he does remember that they first heard about the commune at an entertainment-industry party. There, amid acid and mushrooms, someone first made mention of an anarchist commune deep in the jungle, where a young seer said he'd had a vision, in a divine revelation, of a vast fire devouring the tangle of trees. And that same boy, an indigenous child just seven years old, had predicted the end of times and the dawn of a new era. From then on he was surrounded by a large community of enlightened hippies, art house celebrities, people seeking to build a new society around the child, awaiting the foretold end of times.

Now that he's telling the story, Toledano seems to notice how ridiculous the thing sounds, how ridiculous it all must sound to a forty-something like me, who never lived through anything like that historical euphoria. Still, he doesn't hold back. He tells the story the same way he tells everything else, with a cold and objective tone, as if he were talking about chess moves. He tells me that, starting that night, Virginia McCallister never stopped talking about that commune, or researching the child seer. For her, commune and seer came to symbolize a divine omen, one that fit perfectly with the theories she had been elaborating, and with the mythical figure of her incendiary ancestor, William Sherman. After that, she started to frequent secret meetings, meetings that Toledano never seemed to be invited to or that he preferred not to attend, dedicated as he was to raising the little girl who was growing in leaps and bounds, still unaware of her mother's delusions of grandeur. That little girl who grew, pale, fragile, and fearful, in the arms of a mother who told her bedtime stories of a faraway land where a boy, young like her, had seen the end of the world.

Now that he's telling the story, the sound of the canaries in the background, Toledano can't help feeling the pathos of his confession. And without knowing why he tells it, or what he gains in the telling, he relates how one afternoon his wife came home with a ticket in hand, a ticket that would carry them, finally, to that commune and that jungle, to come face-to-face with the seer. That afternoon, with the cold of the New York winter just around the corner, Yoav Toledano told himself that perhaps this was the only way to shake off her obsession: give her a trip and dismantle her fantasy. Looking at the tickets, he remembered his youthful obsession with reaching the infamous Tierra del Fuego. He knew he wouldn't be heading for the south he so longed for, but he told himself that if he agreed to go, it was precisely in order to remain faithful in some way to the stubborn boy he'd once been. Beside him, little Carolyn wants to know, where is that jungle they talk so much about?

7

I listen to the old man's anecdotes and I say to myself that telling stories, much like playing chess, is the act of proposing false futures. Like the chess player, the narrator produces false expectations. Then I think again of Giovanna, her strange way of punctuating time with silences, of leaving the conversation always on the verge of an inconclusive revelation. Revelations are always a bit vulgar, says Tancredo, and maybe he's right. Art is just the opposite, producing half-seen subtleties: imagined dioramas in the middle of the desert. As the old man starts talking again, I can only think of the sequence of events that have led me to this empty town: Giovanna's first call, her always opaque proposal of collaboration, my walks through the New York metropolis, the hours I spent imagining stories that would end with the image of an insomniac woman, reading. I've remembered the happy period of silence and peace that came after that strange project, Giovanna's partial disappearance, and then the arrival of that dreadful archive that has brought me here. The trick, I tell myself as I go back to listening to the old man, is to propose images and futures as though proposing a life.

Today, sitting across from the town mayor, I felt a sudden consternation, and I understood that I was annoyed by the same question as always. The question that has led me here and toward whose reply old Toledano's story seems to be heading, but of which only today I realized also implicates me: How does one end up in an empty town? The question hit me suddenly, while the old mayor, an ex-miner almost ninety years old, was trying to tell me the town's story year by year. For this old man, I thought as I watched him struggle with his memory, there's nothing left: his life was written here. His life would end here because that's how men live and die. Then I asked him about Toledano, and I noticed his hesitation. I thought his memory was failing him again, but after a few seconds John interrupted to ask who I was talking about. The photographer, I replied, and the mayor corrected me, insisting: "Ah, crazy old Roberto Rotelli." Only then did I understand the obvious: the old man was never Yoav Toledano to them. Then I remembered that in one of his last articles, Toledano started with a citation I'd always liked, attributed to a certain R.R., that said: "In 1912 I decided to be alone and to move forward without destination. The artist must be alone with himself, as in a shipwreck." Perhaps, I said to myself, it was this R.R. who inspired the old man's decision to become Roberto Rotelli. But I didn't say anything out loud. As always, I simply listened as the mayor told the story I'd already heard, but that he tells better than anyone: the story that for him ends the day the highway that led to the town split in two. That day, he repeats patiently, he realized he would die in a ghost town, unable to betray the memory of five generations. He tells it to me straightforwardly, and I start to think of old Toledano's many masks. In learning to tell a story one must self-impose a shipwreck, I tell myself, thinking again of the epigraph. We stay for coffee and then, when we see that the mayor is falling asleep after half a cup, we take our leave. Outside, I start to tell my friend about the game of names, but I immediately realize I would be betraying a man who has wagered everything on becoming anonymous.

8

The rest belongs to fantasy. On November 23, 1976, with nothing but a couple of suitcases, the family takes a plane toward the south that they've never seen but on which they've placed all their hopes. Two days later, with little Carolyn showing the first symptoms of the illness that will accompany her throughout the journey, the old bus they're riding in arrives at a jungle, imposing and lush. Then comes a Latin American journey that is a kind of photographic negative of the great adventurers' classic voyages. Where Humboldt found a wild and sublime America, they meet a ruinous nature brimming with garbage. Where William Walker found the total absence of the state, they encounter the signs of state power all around. Where Franz Boas found the nature of the unknown, they encounter what seems to be a sinister mirror of their own selves.

Everywhere he goes, Toledano feels that his voyage is, more than anything, a repetition tinged with farce. Perhaps that's why after the first night, while his wife and daughter are sleeping, he takes his wife's notebook and copies in two fragments from the diary of one of his favorite philosophers. Two dreams that, according to Toledano, suggested that at the end of any voyage there is nothing but a laugh of disillusionment. The first, which Toledano underlines with red ink, is called "Mexican Embassy," and it goes like this:

> I dreamed I was a member of an exploring party in Mexico. After crossing a high, primeval jungle, we came upon a system of aboveground caves where an order has survived from the time of the first missionaries till now, its monks continuing the work of conversion among the natives. In an immense central grotto with a gothically pointed roof, Mass was celebrated according to the most ancient rites. We joined the ceremony and witnessed its climax: toward a wooden bust of God the Father fixed high on the wall of the cave, a priest raised a Mexican fetish. At this the divine head turned thrice in denial from right to left.

He feels morbid fascination with the idea that, at the end of the jungle, he will find a mirror image of western misery. He feels morbid fascination with the thought that this trip to the end of the jungle is nothing but a voyage toward the malaise of his own culture. It pains him, however, to think of how, in search of that farce, his wife has impelled a sick child to cross a jungle, one with very little of the natural about it. In those first days, when he finds himself facing these doubts, he returns to the fragment he wrote and tells himself they must go on: they must reach the end of the dream and learn how to laugh on waking. Beside him, the little girl coughs again in her sleep.

They are long days. Led by a tattooed man who calls himself the apostle, a group of pilgrims crosses a jungle full of strange noises, animals, and smugglers. Long days in which Toledano comes to comprehend that his wife's madness knows no bounds. Days when Toledano intuits that only by maintaining his sanity will he manage to return home with the girl alive. One idea keeps him sane and soothes him: the thought that on reaching the end of the road, his wife will understand the futility of her project, the uselessness of her passion.

Because of his profession and prestige, he's been given the task of photographing the trip. Acting as witness. Still, as he tells me about that trip now, he doesn't remember taking all that many photos. He remembers, instead, the insect buzz, the croaking of the frogs, the ever-present sound of the rivers, the little girl's cough that grew with astonishing alacrity as their trek advanced. As he recalls walking with slow steps toward the decisive moment that will mark his life, he remembers the tedium of the nights they spent under mosquito nets, nights when the little girl asked him when they could go home. He remembers the apostle's proclamations, his wife's passion, the disconcerting feeling of having wandered into a maze with no way out. He remembers a town full of smugglers; a crude, fat man; a German hippie who acted out eighteenth-century plays for the natives; and a young Polish woman who spent her leisure time telling stories about the pampas. Then he stops, as if, finally glimpsing his destination, his memory has refused to bear witness.

———

Later on I came to understand that the true history of that unusual family lay in those silences. My grandfather used to say that a story's silences will show you the doubts and fears at play within it. Its meaning too. If Toledano paused then before going on with his story, it was precisely because there, in his silence, lay its direction and its meaning. But that realization would come later. That afternoon, sensing the end was close, I merely listened to the story stretching out before me, untamable and strange, with the disquieting feeling that I'd heard it before—in those silences I'd shared for two years with Giovanna.

In the story, there is a family and a journey. There is a sick child and a man who at night recites prophesies before a bonfire. There are pilgrims and smugglers, there's a little girl who learns to play hide-and-seek from the animals. There are long nights when the father consoles the girl by charting constellations and stories, while the mother sketches theoretical fancies. It's a story of expectation and disillusion that culminates the day when, after climbing an enormous mountain, the pilgrims see a startling city appear before them. And in that city there is a boy who says he has dreamed of the end of time, the arrival of the fires, and the inauguration of a new time. There is a long, prophetic wait, a kind of Advent anticipating a sacred event. There is a man who understands he is starring in a farce but who decides not to abandon his wife, believing that after disillusion will come reason. But to Toledano's disappointment, not even at the end of the journey does his wife recover her sanity. Rather, she asks him—a request he will remember for the rest of his life—to take a photo of the little girl beside the young seer. In the story there is a final photograph, and it's that absent image that depicts the journey's meaninglessness, the innocence of the age and the feeling of nakedness and exposure that was to come. After he takes the picture, Yoav Toledano decides to depart from the city. He leaves the girl in a small provincial hospital, kisses her, and promises he will see her again in no more than one month.

That day, looking at his sick daughter, Yoav Toledano tells himself that it's time to go, and that there is no place for a child where he's going.

Remembering the figure of Nadar that so tempted him in his first years, he says to himself that only one profession would be appropriate for a man who has seen what he has: photographer of mines. Remembering Nadar in the Parisian catacombs, he tells himself that only there, underground, will he find the right place to bury his secret. In the grade-school library of a small town on the jungle's edge, he finds an atlas; after a few hours of inspection, he locates a small mining town. Three days later, the town's post office clerk sees him enter carrying a couple of suitcases and a bag full of what seem to be old cameras. He is beautiful and tall, she thinks; he has the air of an English gentleman and the lost gaze of those foreigners who, having seen it all, are content to withdraw one day to their own little plot of land. That afternoon, after he asked about a nearby hotel, she sees him talking with Marlowe's widow. Two days later, when the mayor goes to see him and learn his intentions, all he finds in the house is a heap of old cameras on a wooden table. Yoav Toledano is already out, desperately seeking the oblivion he will find two years later, when he reads, in a local newspaper, about the initial sightings of smoke.

Between turns, without changing his pace or his tone, with the monotony of the resigned, he tells me everything: he tells me about the bus that dropped them off at the edge of the jungle, he tells me about the little girl's illness, he describes the mother's fearful fascination. He tells me everything as if I knew nothing: the interminable nights of insomnia, the days spent crossing the jungle on foot, the sounds and the dreams, until they reached that luminous moment when he was asked to take a photo, and, at the precise instant he presses the button, he realized he would never be the same again. He tells me everything and then cries checkmate, as if the game had to end when the story did. Then, without showing the slightest consternation after his apparent confession, he stands and says we're short on beer, and the store is closing soon. He says this, gets into his old, green jeep, and heads to town without even asking if I want to go with him.

Only then, once the story is finished, knowing that my time here is coming to an end, do I store the novel I'm reading in my backpack and finally dare to venture into the old man's private world. With slow steps, the dogs' eyes heavy on my back, I step into the garage with its smell of sawdust and beer, aware that I don't belong. Outdated newspapers, beer cans, old tools, and an empty birdcage or two. Then, as I leave the canaries' song behind, I see them. Over twenty models: all identical, all different. Models that seem to depict a small city in the shape of a quincunx. Identical models that the old man has tried to erase in different ways, perhaps trying to understand the nature of forgetting. One of the dogs licks my hand and I start in fright. Maybe that's why I don't linger. I continue to the back of the garage, driven mainly by fear, until I'm facing a door I open without hesitation. There, perfectly arranged on a shelf, are over a hundred old cameras, from the Polaroid Pathfinder that Toledano had when he left Haifa to the Nikon F that Larry Burrows used to depict Vietnam. A great parade of devices where photographic history accumulates like a junkyard of brands: the Canons alternate with Nikons, then Olympus, and then back to the Polaroid that started Toledano's career, which today seems to be ending in an emptied-out town. Along with the cameras, distributed in half-closed drawers, are thousands of photos. Pictures of all kinds. Fashion portraits the old man must have taken during his New York years, still lifes that maybe he took in his very first forays, photos of a lush jungle that is perhaps the one he's just been telling me about. The idea gives me a thrill. I'm intrigued to think that among those thousands of photos is the very one that depicts the end of the story as Toledano has just told it to me. I investigate. I search among those thousands of images to find the one that shows Giovanna's tiny face, her con-fusion and resentment. The one that shows Giovanna lost deep in the jungle, prisoner of her parents' hallucinatory passion. The one that shows her the way I knew her, timid, distant, and fragile. But I only find a jumble of im-passive faces, a snarl of cold and remote gazes that refuse to look back at me.

Posthumous Notes

(Letter from Giovanna Luxembourg, never sent)

I'm tired. Tired of wills, doctors, and so much funereal red tape that only returns me to the image of my own death. Maybe that's why, in my few free moments, I shut myself in my studio where no one dares to disturb me, and I prepare the papers I plan to send you one day. I don't say anything to anyone and I come here to feed the fish, to listen to a music that's pale as the night, and to prepare this file. There is our project just as we imagined it years ago, reflected in a future I will no longer be a part of. It will be your small inheritance. But tell me: What is an inheritance? I, who believed myself an orphan, who changed my name to lose a family whose history I didn't understand, today I inexorably return to that family. I never told you, but that night when you came to my house and saw the medical envelope on the table, a man had just told me that something inside me was preparing to betray me. That afternoon I chose not to tell you, even though I could see how you were looking at the envelope and your face gave away your discovery. I chose not to tell you what I'd heard that day: the story of the genetic mutation, the illness that was starting to eat away at me, the long road ahead. I, who believed myself an orphan, who changed my name to lose a family whose story I didn't understand, didn't want to tell you my inheritance was returning in the form of a mutating gene, a gene that was turning into something else, something lethal that now seemed determined to annihilate me. Ironies of life. Inheritance, I said to myself then, was an incurable illness that one day leaves us terribly tired, contemplating a pile of papers that describe an unfinished project. After you left that night, I thought about my parents again, and I started to organize that posthumous project of which you are now a part. No one chooses their inheritance. More than once I thought about telling you everything, leaving the pieces fitted together, the puzzle complete, the intrigue resolved. Then I understood that if I did, you would never come to understand me as I am. You would lose focus on my story if I didn't force you to relive it, just as I had lost focus on the inheritance whose echo was now invading me from inside, transforming my body into an enormous theater of death. Perhaps that's why, tired as I am, I'm sitting here to write this letter that I know full well I'll never send you, aware as I am that it's always best to leave the image half-assembled. Like that final night when you came over and I didn't want to talk. We just sat down to put together a boring puzzle, and halfway through, sorrowful at saying goodbye, I pretended to fall asleep. And I watched you struggle with the pieces, knowing you wouldn't find the image you wanted there, only the banality of a lake covered in flowers. That night I realized you would know how to navigate your inheritance, as I had struggled to navigate mine. My inheritance, which today is forcing me to sign estate papers with a name that isn't even my real one, aware that my body is mutating and betraying me. Aware also that this letter will not reach you, and that somehow you will have to intuit it for yourself. Inheritance is a bit like that: a letter written from the past that never reaches the present. And your task is to reconstruct that absent conversation.

If a rumor strikes a place at just the right
moment in history, if it manages to materialize
a fear or expectation, only then does it grow.
It starts to spread only if it touches a nerve.

—Francis Alÿs

1

It was Tancredo who gave me the newspaper clipping. We were in a New Brunswick bar one afternoon in the fall of 2008, just when the financial crisis was starting to become a topic of conversation. The central image was of two photos. The first was of an older woman around seventy years old, dressed entirely in black. Dark turtleneck sweater, solemn expression, few wrinkles. In spite of her age, her face projected a certain atemporal elegance, a beauty that seemed to be repeated in the next photograph, which showed a model in the kind of bikini that was in fashion in the United States in the sixties. I recognized that face immediately, but decided not to show any emotion. Instead, I traced the similarities between the two photos, the way a face changed over the years, crossed half a century and emerged again, now marked by the passage of time. Above, a headline, a brief sentence completed the news: "Missing Ex-Model Found Alive, Accused of Multiple Crimes."

The article took up barely half a page. It began by outlining the strange disappearance in 1976 of the famous model Virginia McCallister, then delivered the shocking news: after thirty years, the actress had been discovered by the authorities, who accused her of being responsible for more than five hundred cases of interference in the stock market, crimes they said she'd been perpetrating from the beginning of the eighties until she was discovered early this month. In those thirty years of supposed disappearance, while the authorities were trying to track down both McCallister and her equally disappeared husband, the photographer Yoav Toledano, she had been falsifying more than three thousand events whose movement through media outlets had cost the stock market millions of dollars. Three thousand events that never happened, but that the actress, shrouded by a series of pseudonyms, had managed to circulate in the media, in some cases shifting market trends.

The most interesting part, however, was what came next.

When asked if she pleaded guilty, the accused replied that she didn't feel the slightest bit guilty, precisely because she considered it all part of her artistic oeuvre, and art, as has been known since the Greeks, is a sovereign realm beyond good and evil, beyond moral and legal judgment. She emphasized that she had not received any monetary benefit from her little interventions. To support that preliminary defense, she decided to cite, as precedent, the piece *Happening para un jabalí difunto* (Happening for a Dead Boar), produced in 1966 by the Argentine artists Raúl Escari, Roberto Jacoby, and Eduardo Costa. The artists had managed to get the popular media to report on an event that never occurred, something that could have been but wasn't. If that was art, McCallister argued, then so was her project.

I spent that afternoon reading about the lunacies of Escari, Jacoby, and Costa. I tried to avoid, at all costs, thinking of Giovanna, of Virginia McCallister, of the story that an old man in a mining town had recently told me. I found a manifesto online in which the three artists issued an appeal to imagine a new form of art, one based on the way mass society produced meaning through the circulation of information. An event, they said, was no longer merely the event itself, but rather the images the media produced of the event. They wanted to show the world that a nonexistent occurrence could easily exist if the media wanted it to. I liked the idea. I remembered the old woman who used to sit in a Manhattan bar at nightfall to read obsolete newspapers, and it seemed beautiful: inundating reality with small fictions, interrupting the world with little lies that, days later, an insomniac would read about in a Lebanese bar. It occurred to me that maybe universal history was similar: a great lie in which historians had conspired against us. A great lie we would only wise up to once it was too late.

Two days later Tancredo called me. The initial article that he'd given me, which the journalist may have written in reckless enthusiasm, had left out a fundamental detail. The writer had forgotten to mention where the events had taken place, a piece of information that, though irrelevant for many, held special importance for me. Authorities had apprehended Virginia McCallister in an enormous abandoned high-rise on the outskirts of San Juan, Puerto Rico. She lived there alongside five hundred poor families who, after builders had abandoned the structure at the start of the decade, had decided to take it upon themselves to convert the tower into housing. According to Tancredo, the story of the tower was just as crazy as the artist's crimes. A Russian billionaire had ordered construction to start in the early 1990s, but it was halted when the billionaire's network of fraud was exposed, and the building had ended up in the hands of a series of foreign bankers and investors. By then the tower already had more than twenty-five floors. Unable to decide what to do with that immense, half-finished structure, the investors had decided to abandon the project until they came up with a plan. A year later, when they received the first letter complaining of the initial illegal invasions, there was little they could do: for months, more than a hundred poor families had occupied the place, building impressive apartments complete with bathrooms and dividing walls, kitchens and living rooms. Lacking elevators, they had even started a ramp system for motorcycles that carried them to different floors. The investors preferred, then, to let time pass. The right moment would come. Two years later, when the government tried to mediate in the matter, their agents couldn't even get in. By then, the place was a true city: shops, barbers, dentists, day care, general stores, drug corners, and even a brothel. A small city built into the ruins of that immense tower.

When they caught her, Virginia McCallister had been living in the building for almost a decade, among hundreds of families who surely looked at her with suspicion. According to the second article Tancredo showed me, published in a local paper three days after McCallister's arrest, it had been one of those neighbors who turned her in. She'd knocked on the door one day to discuss a community matter, and, finding her neighbor away, she'd gone in and found herself looking at a bulletin board covered with newspaper articles, which reminded her of the detective series she'd watched as a child. Her first thought was that her neighbor was a mole, an undercover agent sent by the government to gather information on the tower's inhabitants. Looking at the clippings, she realized this was something else: these weren't notes about the community, or even local articles. Dozens of heavily underlined columns about matters of global reach, which the woman had linked by arrows that seemed to trace a worldwide conspiracy. She grew convinced that this strange woman, with her black clothes and arrogant airs, couldn't be a spy. Too obvious, too glaring: spies weren't gringos and they didn't wear luxury clothes. So a week later she marched into the station and blew the whistle. When they asked her under what suspicion she was filing a complaint, the neighbor merely said she didn't know, but that the woman was up to something strange. When she heard the officer's laughter, she threw out a final warning: "You laugh, sir, but that gringa has bulletin boards covered with articles in her room, and hundreds of notebooks everywhere. You laugh, but something fishy's going on there." Then she left. Later, when boredom brought the scene back to his mind, the policeman decided it would be worthwhile to take the clue as an excuse to venture into the tower's labyrinthine world. Five hours later, when he and his partner entered the building, he found himself blown away by a macrocosm that seemed to obey its own rules: a world drawn to a scale, as if some painter—bohemian, drugged, and poor—had dreamed it up one magnificent afternoon. Like in a futuristic dream, everything fit there, even poverty itself, sketched on the face of a bum he met near the entrance. They were welcomed by a small guard, a man with a salt-and-pepper mustache. When he saw them, he turned off an old TV that was showing a horse race and asked them for the necessary documents. They mollified him by mentioning the suspicions they'd heard about one of the neighbors.

"Yeah, that old lady is something strange. She arrived one New Year's, settled in with dozens of computers, and since then barely any of us have talked to her. I think she's crazier than a loon." Ten minutes later, after a motorcycle ride that carried them through the strange tower's mazelike twists and turns, they came upon a door painted entirely black. At the third knock, Virginia McCallister opened it without betraying an ounce of fear.

They called her "la gringa." She'd arrived on January 15, 2001, when the tower's inhabitants consisted of a hundred vagrants, a few dozen heroin addicts, and fifteen families living in extreme poverty. She'd turned up one day along with two men, and after two weeks they had built a private home; then the two men left and she stayed put, living in the tower but enclosed in a carapace that no one had breached until the day those two policemen knocked at her door three times and she opened up, ready to tell them everything. All it took, once inside, was for one of them to ask about the articles adorning the wall, and she started to spill: she said she was an artist and that her works were about the media. When she realized the cops were looking at her like she was crazy, she elaborated. She told them, always with her eyes fixed on a little cup of tea she had poured but didn't drink, that her art was political and it followed the tradition of Escari, Jacoby, and Costa, three Argentine artists who had conjured up a happening where there'd been none. She told them she invented false news items and inserted them among the true ones. She mentioned three news stories that neither policeman had heard of, and when she saw from their lost looks that they still didn't understand, she repeated the Argentines' names, then mentioned, very much in passing, the only detail that managed to resonate: her interventions had cost the stock market over a hundred million dollars. She finished with an example: she told a strange story of a mountain in the middle of a jungle, and how on the mountain a boy said he had seen strange things, sacred images. She mentioned some names, including the boy's, and explained that on that mountain, hundreds of foreigners paid homage to that child. She told them how it was enough to say, for example, that among the pilgrims present on that mountain in the last month of 1976 was the current vice president of a powerful company, and the market's course changed. She told it all with utter elegance, with a grace that seemed innate, and the two cops could only think that this was a very sophisticated, yes, but crazy old lady, crazy as could be. She told her story quickly and without pause, as if each word relieved her of a very old weight, as if she'd been waiting a long time for someone to come and ask her what she was up to. And then, on finishing, she said goodbye to them with the excuse that she had to get back to work. It was around two in the afternoon when the policemen left the tower laughing about the absurdity of what they'd just heard.

Tancredo took care to fill in the details of her capture. He had called the journalist who'd written that second article and found out the rest of the story.

That same night, one of the cops, unable to sleep, had lain there thinking about the strange scene he'd witnessed that afternoon, and in particular about a book he'd seen as he was leaving: a voluminous tome whose cover showed an old photograph of a model with the same sharp, refined face as the woman who had just told them a bunch of nonsense. He remembered the title: *Virginia McCallister, 1955–1975*. Puzzled, he thought about the name she had given when she said goodbye: Viviana Luxembourg. Something didn't fit. More out of boredom and insomnia than real interest, he got out of bed, sat down at the computer, and searched for the name online: Virginia McCallister. And then he saw dozens of photographs that were unmistakably of the same person he and his partner had spoken to hours earlier, photographs in every pose, in bathing suits and ball gowns, beside celebrities and politicians. A beautiful woman, with long legs and a finely chiseled face—the same face, no doubt about it, that he'd seen that very day, giving a delirious speech.

Then he looked up Viviana Luxembourg. He found very little. He went back to his previous search, to the images of Virginia McCallister. Then he looked at the news. That was where he found the detail that would keep him awake until well into morning: a series of articles that documented the 1976 disappearance of Virginia McCallister.

From two until five in the morning, possessed by a curiosity that exacerbated his insomnia, Sergeant Alexis Burgos read everything he could find about the disappearance. On November 23 of that year, the family—Virginia McCallister; her husband, the Israeli photographer Yoav Toledano; and their young daughter, Carolyn—took a flight from John F. Kennedy Airport in New York to San José, Costa Rica. Their return was set for December 2. When Virginia's agent called ten days later, he was surprised when no one answered. He tried again the next day, and again no answer. He decided to visit. He found the door open, the house empty, the dog fierce and hungry. Then he figured the family had decided to extend their stay, but would surely return soon. He went back every day that week. Every day it was the same: he rang the bell, waited for the reply that never came, and then went in, and every day he saw that no one had returned. On the tenth day of his vigil, as had become routine, he fed the dog. Then, tired of waiting, he picked up the phone and called the police. Two days later, still without a word from family or the police, the papers published the first article: "Virginia McCallister and Family, Missing." It was accompanied by a family photo showing the three of them—mother, father, daughter—at some New York gala. Wrapped in the dense wee morning hours, the sergeant looked at that photo and thought that, without a doubt, this was a model family: beautiful, warm, successful. He, on the other hand, had no one. He deflected the thought by searching for more information.

What he found helped complete the story. After that first article, published in a New York paper, the following months saw dozens of follow-up articles in all the major media. They talked about the couple's ties to the Latin American left, about the esoteric tendencies that had started to mark the model's life in recent years; the photos of the couple alongside political figures resurfaced. The press invented horrible hypotheses: a suicide, Toledano's spiraling drug addiction, the possibility that the couple had been, all along, spies for the Castro regime. That last possibility struck the press as particularly attractive, given that Virginia McCallister, though descended on her father's side from the Scottish McCallisters, carried illustrious Yankee blood in her veins. Her mother, Catherine Sherman, was the granddaughter of the infamous general William Tecumseh Sherman, the Union general whose legendary and merciless March to the Sea had handed victory to Abraham Lincoln. The idea that a descendant of old Sherman's could be a Cuban spy sounded so exotic that one old Republican senator, still resentful about the Bay of Pigs, came to blame the Cuban government for the family's disappearance. A Cuban vice-minister dressed in an impeccable guayabera expressed his sympathies but said the allegation was totally false. Over time, the thing became diluted, like everything in the news: sporadic false sightings; people who claimed to have seen the family in Peru, Brazil, wherever. Alexis Burgos read all of this, and he was left with a frail image not of the woman he'd seen that afternoon, but of the little girl in the first photo: a fragile child, pale and timid, who seemed to hide behind her mother's long legs. A girl like any other, who on one winter afternoon had started off on a trip with no idea of what awaited her. He spent hours thinking about that girl, until the image of the mother emerged as he'd seen her that morning: haughty, decisive, beautiful in spite of the years. He felt a strange pride when he thought that of all the possible places, Virginia McCallister had decided to hide out on his little island. At six in the morning, he fell asleep.

The next day, wrapped in the confused whirlwind of emotions that so much information produced in him, he felt a strange immobility. He didn't know how to proceed. For the first time in years, he felt that the case he had before him was something different, not a police case, but something else. He thought about returning to the tower and confronting the old woman but ruled out the possibility. She might flee without saying a word. Defeated, unable to specify what it was that so confused him, he picked up the phone and called the only person who seemed appropriate: Danny Limes, a gringo working for the FBI, whom he'd met playing pool in a San Juan dive. Five days later, five agents went into the tower, ready to capture the woman who called herself Viviana Luxembourg. They found her sitting in front of the bulletin board, her face placid and congenial, as if she'd been waiting for them for years.

The first thing that surprised them was the total order that ruled the room. Everything in the place seemed designed to be recorded and archived; it all seemed arranged for the exacting eyes of the police. The corkboard where dozens of newspaper articles hung in perfect disorder; the bed, flawlessly made; and then, on a dozen perfectly tended shelves, the notebooks. Over 200 notebooks—247, to be exact, all identical, all numbered—full of notes that the agents looked through without understanding much, but that a specialist would identify, after two days of examination, as two different projects.

The first, composed of 174 notebooks, was called *Art on Trial*. In delicate but haughty handwriting, the project detailed more than five hundred cases in which artists had been brought to court, from the Renaissance judgment against Paolo Veronese to the case against Constantin Brancusi, from the trial of Benjamin Vandergucht to the famous Whistler vs. Ruskin trial. Still, it wasn't a book, per se—more like a great archive of cases where the author had written, in the margins, some theoretical notes. The second project, written in red ink in the remaining seventy-three notebooks, was called *The Great South*, and it laid out an eschatological theory around the history of millenarian anarchism. According to the specialist, this one also centered on a series of specific cases, around which the author built a fierce yet arbitrary conclusion: that the apocalypse would come from the south, and its sign would be a great wave of fires. Along with the notebooks, the police seized hundreds of press clippings, two empty diaries, and half a dozen computers. They found little there; apparently, someone had definitively erased the hard drives just hours before. Nor did they find the fashion book that Sergeant Burgos had mentioned, or any other reference to Virginia McCallister. Each of the 247 notebooks, Profile brand, was signed on the first page with the name Viviana Luxembourg.

2

That same day, the defendant, dressed in an impeccable black suit, was taken to a correctional facility on the outskirts of San Juan. There, a policeman handed her a cream-colored jumpsuit and asked her to change. When she came out of the bathroom, for the first time in years, her usual all black had given way to even simpler attire, closer still to that anonymity she seemed to have been seeking for ages. Against the background murmur from the receptionists and a few inmates, they took her information, her fingerprints, mug shots, her first statements. She replied with a minimum of words in the monotone of calculated indifference, alleging her innocence just as she had at first, with the argument that it was all part of a great artistic project whose logic she would explain if necessary.

Then she asked to speak to her lawyer in private. Little is known of that singular meeting. What is known is that they spoke for hours, at the end of which the lawyer, a young and nervous man in thick-rimmed glasses, asked for access to the 247 notebooks that the police had found in her apartment. He spent that afternoon there, immersed in the notebooks, looking for the secret key that the defendant claimed to have written, trying to understand why it was his bad luck to be assigned to a crazy gringa in his third case ever. In one notebook, he found a note in the margin that convinced him of her madness. The fragment, written in red ink and dated two weeks earlier, said:

> All art leads to trial. There is no art without judgment, just as there is no sport without an audience. The artist presents herself before the jury and tries to demonstrate that the logical categories under which the law functions are not sufficient. All art leads to judgment, all true art tries to demonstrate that the law is antiquated, insufficient, limited.

Without a doubt, thought the young lawyer, this woman seemed convinced that her only way out was to confront justice. Immersed in the notebooks' theoretical madness, among drawings of circular cities and mathematical equations, he grew convinced that this woman had arranged for her own capture, just as she now was laying out the conditions of her defense. He left at five, convinced that the most logical choice was to plead insanity.

When, three days later, Sergeant Alexis Burgos recognized the face of the accused woman in the newspaper, he thought it was strange to see her like that, dressed as a prisoner. He remembered the peculiar way, outrageous but elegant, that the defendant had explained her art just a week earlier, and he felt that perhaps he'd made a mistake. That woman didn't belong there. She wouldn't survive prison. Nor, he thought, puzzled, did she belong in a home for the elderly. That day, overcome by a strange feeling of guilt, dressed in civilian clothes, he returned to the tower and walked around its floors, trying to understand what had led this woman to choose such a strange place to live. Shrouded in an anonymity that brought on an unexpected joy, he saw whole families living there, he saw boys playing basketball, he saw TV sets, restaurants, and barbers, and at the edge of all that he saw two older women in rockers. Deciding that they would be the best witnesses of what went on there, he approached them, and, taking the opportunity of a stray comment, started a conversation. Minutes later, he decided to pose his question:

"So, how about that gringa they caught?"

The old women looked at him in distrust and asked if he was a journalist—ever since the incident, they said, journalists had all but taken over the tower. When he assured them he was not, they told him that everyone had left the gringa to her own devices, almost as if she didn't exist, or as if she were a ghost. She didn't talk to them, they didn't talk to her. Except for one person, Miguel Rivera, a withdrawn, possibly autistic boy who, they said, helped her with the shopping and sometimes spent hours in her apartment. Then they laughed that capricious laugh that lets you know there is gossip behind the story. The sergeant merely took note.

Miguel Rivera lived alone in an apartment on the twenty-seventh floor, the tower's top floor. They called him El Tarta because of his stutter. They said that he'd moved to the tower after his parents died and that, furious with the world, wanting to get away from everything, he'd decided to settle where no one could find him. He had almost managed it. The motorcycles that the inhabitants used as an elevator only went up to the fifteenth floor; from there, you had to walk. Few people took the trouble to climb to the twenty-seventh floor. As Sergeant Burgos learned that day, it was no easy task. When he reached the boy's floor after twenty-five minutes, he was sweating like a pig and felt he'd caught a glimpse of hell: dozens of heroin addicts occupied the upper floors, and among them scampered a crowd of children. He was surprised to find the walls covered with political posters and flyers, which on those floors hardly anyone would see, but he told himself that was island politics: a poster lost among rubble and syringes. He knocked five times, and when no one answered he felt like an idiot. To have climbed twelve floors on foot for nothing. He was starting to leave when he heard the door open behind him, and when he looked back he found the emaciated figure of a boy who greeted him with a tenuous, timid voice. A skinny and pale boy whose face didn't show, however, any trace of addiction or of dementia, just the marks of prolonged insomnia. His skin was tattooed everywhere, little symbols whose sinuous shapes Burgos couldn't decipher, but that grew over his small body like an enormous vine sprouting calligraphy, even invading his face. Seeing him up close, Burgos thought the boy couldn't be more than twenty years old, but he seemed to have already lived sixty years.

In his police work, the sergeant had seen how drugs and alcohol devoured young bodies. Often, at the scene of an atrocious homicide, it was the thin, broken, disjointed voice of an addict that confessed to the crime. That was not the case he now had in front of him. The boy's voice emerged fitfully, sporadic and tremulous, more violent than an alcoholic's mellow voice. In answer to a question from that voice, the sergeant merely stated, "I'm looking for Virginia McCallister." The result was that Rivera, clearly nervous, tried to shut the door on him. He stopped the boy with a spontaneous and terrible phrase: "I have news about her daughter." He said it just like that, without further ado, with a will of unknown origin. "I have news about her daughter," he repeated, when he saw the words had an effect. When the kid took a step out of the apartment and closed the door behind him, he understood he'd pressed the right button, and it was too late to turn back. With his memory on the pale, fragile girl he'd seen in photographs a few nights back, he imagined possible futures that could include her and he recounted them, one lie after another, until he thought the boy seemed to notice his deception. When Rivera opened the door and invited Burgos in, the sergeant felt the implacable shiver of one who believes he is committing a crime, though an accidental one. When he stepped inside, he felt that he was finally gaining access to the world of the tower. He thought about turning back, but it was too late.

What he saw then wrapped him up in a sheet of fear and cold. He saw a room that looked like a dark cave, with walls covered by an enormous mural whose shapes he couldn't decipher immediately but that somehow made him think of a long night deep in a dark forest. A huge mural that sheltered the place like the arms of an abusive mother, with simultaneous love and contempt, in which he thought he could make out, on second glance, a kind of animal epic, an underwater kingdom that seemed to start with small organisms and slowly evolve to become an anarchic and violent world where humans, reduced to small serpentine cells, seemed to be struggling in a sacred orgy. He took it all in at once, and he didn't know what to do. He thought he'd seen the image before, but he didn't know where. Still enveloped in that cold shroud, he spotted three computers, and on their screens were the images of half a dozen faces. He realized they were the faces of children, young people, teenagers, and they made him think of the words he had just pronounced and that were now forcing him to speak.

"So, as you were saying—the daughter?" he heard the boy stammer with difficulty, repeating his words while, one by one, he turned off the computers, and with them, the faces. Instinctively, Burgos felt for his gun, but he realized he hadn't brought it. It was his turn to speak. He looked at the boy and told a long, thin story, a lie that stretched out over decades and culminated at a Swedish beach resort where men spent hours waiting for the sun to come out. He told the story, swallowed hard, and waited for the boy to speak again.

Perhaps in an attempt to unmask the sergeant's lies, or perhaps just wanting to propose a final tale that would banish the visitor, the boy told an even stranger story. A sharp, precise account. It was the story of a circular kingdom where children were the sovereign rulers, a kingdom full of temples looking toward the sea. He told the story in a slow voice, as if narrating a documentary, and Burgos couldn't help thinking that this boy came from that kingdom of illuminated children, the magnificent land of a visionary boy. He told the story without pauses, in a perfect rhythm that accommodated interruptions from his stutter, and then, when fear started to show in Burgos's eyes, he finished the tale and burst out laughing. His laugh was long and intermittent like his voice, and it made the sergeant feel like an idiot, and he understood that his own lies were surely just as laughable and unrealistic. Without a second thought, Burgos stood up, confused and humiliated, and walked out of that delirious apartment that now seemed to him a den of frauds. He went down the tower's many floors, one by one, wrapped in an acute anxiety, convinced that the stuttering boy and the old woman had planned it all as a bad joke. When he finally reached the bottom floor, he felt a slight relief on finding the old man still there, stretched out on a leather sofa and watching horse races. Consistency, he reflected, overwrought, was a beautiful thing.

That night, again, he couldn't sleep. He spent it thinking about the story he'd heard, tormented by the stutterer's laughter, by the impossible image of a wild city full of children. In his career he'd seen atrocious crimes, drug murders and the like; he had participated in dozens of operations that had brought him close to a world of horror and violence. That night, however, he felt like the world that was now starting to surround him harbored a different horror, intangible and irrational, a horror that had to do with the tower that grew with the implacable will of the dispossessed. He took two pills and tried to sleep. The sedatives left him sunk in a strange half-sleep populated with brief, painful images: the half-dozen childish faces he'd seen on the screens that afternoon, the boy's tattooed face, the forced and precise voice he had used to narrate that joke as if it were a true story. From within his drugged fog, he thought that perhaps the story wasn't entirely false, that the boy had been trying to bury his own fears. He wished he hadn't taken the pills. He wished he'd never gone into the tower or met the old woman, but he told himself it would all pass, that soon it would be five in the morning and the heat of dawn would make him sweat out his dread. Exhausted, he convinced himself the best thing to do was turn on the TV. He found only religious programs. Evangelical pastors, Baptists, Pentecostals, all caught up in endless sermons, all doing battle against tedium and desperation. Dozens of parishioners looked on in rapture. Faces full of desire and hope, faces capable of reconciling empty gestures with late-coming epiphanies. He wondered why the dawn so suited pastors and their sermons. He found no answer beyond the bored face of a little boy in the pews, a round, dark face like a ripe fig that made him think again of the children he'd seen on the screens that afternoon. He remembered how, as Virginia McCallister was explaining her odd art two weeks before, she had brought up the sacred mountain where children congregated around a small seer. He wondered if it all led to a solution, or just to more dreadful laughter. Unable to find the answer to the riddle, he surrendered to compulsively flipping through channels, jumping from image to image, until, hours later, with the first rays of sun marking a small square on the wall, he understood that it was all a waste of time. He wouldn't sleep that night. Feeling the first tentacles of paralysis and immobility, he told himself it was time to act. He fixed the same black coffee that he'd drunk every morning for the past twenty years, took a shower as he always did, and went out for a walk. After an hour he returned home. He put on his police uniform and, without a word to anyone, without even checking in with the station, he headed for the tower.

That morning, the tower seemed like a dead world: calmer than usual, tireder, more ghost town than anything else. Seeing that the TV at the entrance was dark, he missed the horse races; consistency, he thought, was beginning to crumble. The sight of the two little old ladies in their rockers revived his hope. They greeted him with a kiss on the cheek, as if he were already part of their crepuscular world. When he didn't find any motorcyclists who would take him up, he had no choice but to make the climb on foot. In spite of his exhaustion, he wasn't willing to turn around. An hour later, after passing painful scenes of suffering that would stay with him, he reached the twenty-seventh floor. He reached the stutterer's blue door and was about to knock when he was suddenly invaded by a fear he hadn't felt since his first years as a cadet. He reached for his gun and was relieved to find that this time it was there. Then he knocked. He knocked once, twice, three times, then called out a few words. The silence only grew louder. Then he noticed the door was unlocked. He went in slowly, as if expecting an ambush. His fear grew when he saw the place was empty. In the past twelve hours, someone had removed everything: the bed, the shelves, the speakers, the clothing that he'd seen strewn about the room the previous day. He thought he must be going crazy. Too much work, too little sleep. Perhaps, he thought, he hadn't even been there before, perhaps he had been sleepwalking, like his father used to do. But there was the mural, terrible as eternal insomnia, and even more imposing in the absence of furniture. The room was, without a doubt, the very same.

Now that the stutterer had disappeared without a trace, Burgos took the chance to look carefully at the mural. Something in the way it swelled over the four walls made him think that it told a story—he didn't know what about, but its strength trapped him and forced him to look more closely. Thousands of little shapes populated the mural. Shapes that at first he'd thought were tadpoles, deformed marine cells that now, on a second, calmer look, became recognizable: hundreds of human figures were scattered over the first three walls, engaged in what seemed to be a divine orgy, a frenzied tumult that made the sergeant think of the hurricanes of his childhood. A termite's nest, he thought. He was struck by the level of detail, the way the bodies mixed together without losing shape, each one frozen in a different pose. Some images caught his attention: an enormous ear from which a dark devil seemed to be pulling a naked man out by his own ears, a shipwreck around which men seemed to be struggling to stay afloat, a giant broken egg in which a group of animals-turned-men played cards. In the upper part of that wall, Burgos discovered an apocalyptic sky benighted by catastrophe: volcanoes, fires, and wars that made him think of the stutterer's tattoos. He moved on to the second wall, adorned by a painting equally jumbled but lighter in color, a kind of lucid version of the previous wall, the same tiny human figures now strangely weightless. Somehow the discrepancy bothered him, something about how the darkness and utter pandemonium transformed into a lighter chimera. His eyes lingered on the only black man drawn among the multitude. A very tall man, elegant, surrounded by pale white women who looked at him as at a prodigy. He told himself that perhaps the painter had wanted to be that man, the only singular specimen in a motley and multiple landscape full of clones, like a terrible dream. Unable to bear it, he moved on to the third wall, where there were only two human figures, a man and a woman, beside a figure that seemed to represent the sacred. He thought then that the three-part story of divine ascension was being told, but he still didn't feel he fully understood. He thought of Miguel Rivera, his stammering voice and tattooed face, and he told himself that this was not a story but the ruins of one, the broken reflection of what could have been a world.

He was about to leave when he saw what at first glance seemed to be a letter. Someone, probably the boy as he was leaving, had left it on the only piece of furniture that remained in the room: a small wooden desk placed in the corner farthest from the mural. Something told him that this was what he was really hoping for: a letter that would make him feel that all was well, that the artist's arrest hadn't been his fault. He found neither letter nor explanation. Just ten loose pages on which someone had written a story by hand. A story that was strange as any obsession, a story that entered into a simple logic, until it was reduced to its purest unreason. Burgos, who never read, who had thought since childhood that books were for girls and fags, read then, without a pause or a yawn, this story that seemed like something more.

It was called "A Brief Tale of Blind Construction," and it told of a town whose architectural ambition led its inhabitants to the verge of madness. The construction of hell, he thought. Burgos kept reading until he came to a paragraph that struck him as beautiful, and he read it three times, trying to understand what the words were hiding:

> Although I left the village some time ago, the nightmares have come back to plague me. Simple and contradictory things, my nightmares. Sometimes I dream of a desert, a long and silent desert that reaches out its arms of sand and covers everything. Other times I dream of a green and undefined expanse, a nameless field where, before my eyes, the reddest rose I've ever seen is born.

Then, just as red and intense, another one appears, and another, until the whole meadow is full of roses that cover all the green, as if the field itself were turning into an immense crimson rose. When I wake up, barely containing a scream, I can't understand why a dream that could even be called beautiful would cause me such horror.

Burgos likewise couldn't explain his own fascination, but something told him that true beauty was like that, a flower that grew in an immense desert until it became a nightmare. He reread the text, and without knowing exactly what kind of story this was, he felt it was one of violence: alarming, impossible, like the stubborn strength of ants. A useless, dystopian story, he thought. On the lower corner of the page, in the same rounded handwriting, some bibliographic information was written: Bruno Soreno, *Breviary*, 2002. Soreno: the name wasn't common on the island. Bruno: it sounded like the name of a gringo's dog, or maybe an Austrian duke, but it wasn't Puerto Rican. Farther down, a little drawing seemed to depict a very long wall, like the Chinese wall that Burgos's father told him about when he was little. It occurred to him that life was a project that men took on in order to pass the time, to hide the fact that the works of men, however magnificent, are useless as a pheasant's beautiful feathers. Without thinking twice, he took out his lighter and set the pages on fire. A buoyant happiness overcame him when he saw that strange story reduced to ashes. Then, soundlessly, he closed the door behind him and walked down the twenty-seven floors, and when he finally emerged onto the street, he told himself that he would never go back to the tower again. It was a den of incomprehensible beasts. He intuited, however, that his fascination would betray him.

3

The media was all over the case. They were drawn to the allure of the defendant's glamorous career, and almost every media outlet sent a reporter to cover the story. Nearly all of them, too, worked in a mention or two of the defendant's illustrious lineage as a descendant of old General Sherman. When the authorities found out that many of the falsified articles were about U.S. politics, the story's morbid interest grew. *Treason* was the word that arose most often in the press during those days. It didn't help much that precisely in those months, after two weeks of free fall, the pundits had finally declared that the market was in crisis. That a famous actress and model, the heir of Sherman's madness, had been accused of distorting not only the markets but American history itself seemed outrageous. After a few weeks, Virginia McCallister became the obsession of a country that didn't know where to place her on a chessboard on the verge of collapse.

All the while, the defendant refused to acknowledge her identity: she claimed until the end to be Viviana Luxembourg, even when no records existed of such a person. There was no logic to her attitude: rather than denying the charges against her, she seemed determined to defend herself; rather than declaring her innocence, she seemed determined to demonstrate that there had been no crime at all.

The fact that the defendant was detained in Puerto Rico also increased media interest. It turned the story strange, exotic, Caribbean. The Americans asked that she be tried in Virginia, New York, New Jersey, any of the states where she had resided before her sudden disappearance. The island authorities, however, refused the transfer, arguing that the defendant had also committed a local infraction the moment she'd entered the tower. Like the other squatters, she was living in the tower illegally and had to be tried locally.

The decision took three weeks, but when it came down, the news was explosive: the trial would take place on the island, and it would be open to the public and the press. Two days later, after a long conversation between the prosecutor and the defense, a final clause was added to mollify the media: the trial would be televised. After forty years of anonymity and invisibility, Virginia McCallister was returning to the spotlight, dressed as a prisoner and speaking Spanish.

Some would say that Virginia McCallister had planned the perfect return: she'd disappeared at the height of her fame and was returning now in a cloud of exotic elusiveness, enhancing the allure of a misunderstood woman. She might have organized it all to give herself one last show before the final goodbye. She refused, however, to speak English. When she did speak, which was rare, it was in perfect Spanish, with a neutral accent that was impossible to place. Her final show, if that was what it was, would be in an assumed language.

She wrote a lot, letters to professors, artists, and writers, letters full of half-formed political theories, with analysis of cases she had been archiving for decades, letters that touched on a theory of the relationship between art and law, all written by hand on pages she tore from Profile brand notebooks that her lawyer ordered online. One might think that she had turned herself over to the law in search of the solitude necessary for thought and reflection. At least, that's what she seemed to indicate in the letters she was compulsively sending to the legion of collaborators who'd been caught up overnight in her methodical madness. Letter by letter, Virginia McCallister was preparing her true defense. She was organizing thoughts, outlining theories, searching for possible witnesses. She was preparing for her private war.

4

When Gregory Agins, a retired professor of aesthetics at the University of California, Santa Cruz, received the first letter, he thought it was a cruel joke from one of his former students. The letter began by citing an article about the case *Brancusi v. United States* that Agins himself had published decades earlier. The article began with an overview of the case: how, in 1926, the Romanian sculptor Constantin Brancusi had sent his piece *Bird in Space* from Paris to New York for an exhibition of his work that was to take place at the Brummer gallery. New York customs had detained the piece, arguing that, as it didn't resemble the bird its title suggested, it didn't qualify as art and fell under the category of useful objects, on which there was a 40 percent import tax. Brancusi, furious and unable to understand how his piece had ended up classified alongside kitchen utensils, decided to take up the matter in court. Agins proceeded to explore the figure of the art critic as defense witness, analyzing how critics of great renown were called to demonstrate that the thing was, without a doubt, art. Through Agins's argument and the New York courtroom passed Edward Steichen, who would later become director of the MoMA photography section; Jacob Epstein, a renowned British sculptor; and even William Henry Fox, director of the Brooklyn Museum. But for Agins, the central critic was Frank Crowninshield. When questioned about how exactly the thing the jury saw before them was similar to a bird, he dared to say: "It has the suggestion of flight, it suggests grace, aspiration, vigor, coupled with speed in the spirit of strength, potency, beauty, just as a bird does. But just the name, the title of this work, why, really, it does not mean much." According to Agins, with that relaxed declaration Crowninshield had shaken off thousands of years of art history and established a new relationship between art and law.

Gregory Agins never imagined that his arguments would lead him to the witness stand himself. Nor did he know what to make of the defendant's theories, which seemed to him ludicrous in a certain sense, but for which he felt a strange sense of responsibility: after decades of thinking that his work was mere mental masturbation, a probably crazy defendant was giving him the chance to put them into practice. He wasted no time replying, sealing his alliance with a brief "Confirmed."

The second person to receive a letter was the Venezuelan researcher Marcelo Collado. One day in his premature retirement, he read a letter that began: "I'm writing because no one knows more than you about Macedonio Fernández's legal function as a prosecutor in Posadas." Collado, a boy of only twenty-six, a great lover of cannabis, had just finished his doctoral thesis on the Argentine writer's judicial phase. It was called "Macedonio Fernández: The Legality of Art (1891–1920)," and it explored the various arguments and accusations that the writer had given during his period as justice of the peace in Misiones. A brave thesis that ended with an invented conversation between Fernández and Horacio Quiroga, another writer who had held the same legal position. The dissertation had earned Collado his doctorate, but not much more. Since then he'd jumped from job to job, teaching at multiple universities at once; he had—like many of his generation—the sense that he was living in a precarious world that seemed every day on the verge of collapse. Collado, unlike Agins, wasn't surprised to receive the letter. Still reckless, he thought that academic knowledge was unquestionably tied to the day-to-day, or that it should be, at least. He did find it odd, though, that the defendant should refer to his imagined dialogue between Quiroga and Fernández, still more that she would correct him: "About your final section, the conversation between the two writers, it should be noted that they did in fact meet, but on that occasion the dialogue was about José Enrique Rodó, a writer they tore apart in a matter of minutes." Overwhelmed, he left the letter aside and only picked it up again thirty-six hours and five joints later. Then the matter struck him as terrifying but grandiose, a kind of postmodern epic into which he'd been granted an unsolicited invitation. He sat down at his computer and typed out a long letter, almost twenty pages, in which the coincidences multiplied into a paranoid web, closing with a noble, innocent, and dazed, "Count me in."

The third letter caught the Costa Rican Guillermo Porras with a beer in hand, sitting in the stables at his grandfather's estate, where his family spent every Sunday afternoon. His mother brought the envelope to him with an air of confusion and dismay: "Look, what could this weird gringa want with you?" Porras, who had graduated with an art degree from the

Rhode Island School of Design, looked at the name at the bottom of the letter and was equally perplexed. He didn't remember ever meeting any Viviana Luxembourg. It had been a long time since he'd received any letters from abroad. It didn't matter. As the horses neighed in the background, it took him barely ten minutes to read the letter. When he finished, he read it over again, trying to understand how it had come to be. More than anything, he was surprised that someone had learned of his student work. Until that moment he would have sworn that not even his adviser had read his monograph on John Reid, a fictional Australian artist from a book by the anthropologist Michael Taussig. After selling the family farm for a fortune, John Reid had conceived of an enormous collage depicting the Latin American *desaparecidos*, made out of cut-up money. Months later, when the counterfeit squad of the Australian Federal Police showed up at his house, Reid argued that the enormous monetary mutilation was his masterpiece. Porras's monograph, imagined as an artwork in itself, consisted in building, around John Reid's collage, a great catalog of the history of currency manipulation as art form. His epigraph was from the Crimes (Currency) Act signed by the Australian court in 1981. Starting from there, he began a parade of a hundred alchemists and vagabonds, falsifiers and artists, and their various attacks on money. In the modern art world, argued the Costa Rican, the true artist constructs their own historical tradition, one that will allow a given madness to be read as art. That assertion was the end of the project, which would earn him a simple diploma. Three years later, it also gained him an appreciative letter from Viviana Luxembourg, who ventured to call his project "one of the most interesting commentaries on conceptual art in recent decades." The letter mentioned the work of a certain Sergio Rojas, a Chilean philosopher Porras had never heard of, and ended by elucidating a theory about what the defendant, following Rojas, called the depletion of art history.

Reading the letter, young Porras tried to ignore, with a shy man's modesty, the pride he felt at the praise. He couldn't. A happy energy invaded him and made him leap up, take the reins, and gallop across the estate. Hours later, after his happiness had run its course and he sat down to read the letter again, he found the project truly great: the accused was attempting to illuminate the mechanisms by which modern art did or did not enter the public sphere. The idea that his little college project would play a part made him think that his choice to abandon his scientific career to bet everything on art hadn't been in vain. Still, he didn't answer the letter right away.

That week he stuck to his plans. He traveled to the coast, to Puerto Viejo, where he worked as a tour guide; he slept with an Israeli with blond braids; fought off boredom by taking still-life photographs. He tried not to think about the letter that had so excited him, until Friday came and he was preparing to go back. He tried to be objective. When you came down to it, this was a criminal trial. He tried to convince himself that getting mixed up in it all was a bad idea, but his youthful enthusiasm at seeing his art career renewed won out. He spent that morning in the hostel, sweaty and tired, writing a letter that began like this: "Dear Viviana: You are completely right. Modern art is nothing more than art history. The modern work is only the construction of the frame from which an object becomes comprehensible to the public as art. I don't know Sergio Rojas, but I appreciate his work; it strikes me as outstanding." He continued the letter with a great intellectual exposition, immodest and ambitious, then closed with a more humble: "At your disposal for whatever you need." That afternoon, he tried to forget the card he'd played. He had sex with the Israeli girl again, walked along the beach again, and then, at noon, headed back to San José. Five hours later he confirmed that it was still raining in the capital.

The fourth letter was, in fact, perhaps the first one the defendant sent. When it finally reached Sofia Baggio, it had already made three complete trips around Mexico City. The Italian wasn't surprised by the delay: if she'd learned anything in the five months since she'd moved to the country, it was that postal delays were the only thing you could rely on in Mexico. Sending a letter meant daring to engage with the labyrinths of time. When she saw the postmark she thought it was from her friend Luisa Burgos, who had just returned to the island, but then she realized she was wrong. It was signed by a certain Viviana Luxembourg, whose name made her think for a second of a fashion designer who had died a few years back. But the letter went in an unexpected direction. After explaining her judicial situation and setting out the bases of her defense, Luxembourg congratulated

Baggio on the work she had done as a doctoral student at Birkbeck, University of London. Her monograph, called *Francis Alÿs: Toward a Poetic of Rumor*, was about the conceptual ramifications of the Belgian-Mexican artist's work, paying particular attention to the way he used fiction to intervene in reality. Baggio found the praise so excessive and strange that she came to wonder if it weren't Alÿs himself playing a mean joke. A simple Google search was enough to prove at least that the defendant existed. She was surprised at the image of the woman, elderly but elegant, in prisoner's clothes. It was hard for her to fit that image with the tone of the letter, a severe and scholastic voice that said things like, "Someone like you, able to see the conceptual resonances of Jacoby's, Escari's, and Costa's work with that of Francis Alÿs, will be able to understand the tradition within which my project is inscribed, a project that now has me in jail, awaiting trial." Then the letter went back to discussing some of the Belgian's main works, like *The Collector*, *The Rumor*, and *Doppelgänger*, which, according to Luxembourg, "circulated false fictions within the circuit of official fictions." Baggio finished the letter in one sitting and immediately, without thinking about it much, wrote a reply:

> *Dear Viviana:*
> *Thank you very much for your interest in my work and its*
> *ramifications, but, due to a small work accident that happened*
> *last year, I've decided to put a (premature) end to my academic*
> *career and to dedicate myself instead to a small hostel my*
> *husband and I built on the outskirts of Mexico City. I hope you*
> *understand. I wish you all the best in the trial.*
> *Affectionately,*
> *Sofia Baggio*

And she closed the letter, walked to the post office, and mailed it, sure that it would take ten turns around the city before making it to the Caribbean. She spent that afternoon stretched out on the mattress at home, watching cartoons, contemplating the tedium like a person watching a fly, trying to convince herself that things were better like that—best to stay away from her old vices. She thought of the career she'd left behind, the hours she'd dedicated to that academic project, hours that now felt distant and useless, without consequence or results. She told herself it was for the best not to think about the defendant or her crime. Not to stick her nose into other people's business, even when they asked her to. At three in the afternoon, tired of searching unsuccessfully for anything interesting on TV, she poured herself a glass of wine. An hour later, when her husband came home from work, he found her snoring with the television on.

The strange thing, thought Viviana Luxembourg's lawyer, was that the people the accused woman summoned for her defense didn't seem to be recognized critics, or even established professors, but rather a battalion of the exhausted, a vanguard of the irrelevant and invisible. The strange thing, he thought as he read the letters, was that his client had to have searched for those names ahead of time, in a premeditated way, expecting that ominous day when the police would come after her in the tower. Strange, he said to himself, to declare war when you lead an army of one-eyed soldiers. He was attracted by the idea of going to war with an army whose bravery is in doubt, a contingent that all other colonels would have ruled out. He was left with just one question: Did he, too, belong to this strange vanguard that, hidden in her tower, the artist had gathered for a future war?

The fifth person to receive a letter was the Guatemalan artist María José Pinillos, who had been brought to the brink of catastrophe by her life as a poète maudit. So drunk was she in those days that it took her almost two weeks to even realize she'd received a letter. Finally, she stumbled over a small mountain of mail as she entered her house, and when she picked up the first letter, she realized, even in her alcoholic stupor, that its subject was precisely the one she was beginning to tire of: art and destruction. In the early nineties, Pinillos had erupted in local art circles with a brief text titled *Thesis on Iconoclasm in Art*, a sort of manifesto that posited the iconoclastic, destructive, and violent nature of all art. The corollaries of that seemingly theoretical text were unexpected. Two weeks after launching the manifesto, when observers were starting to comment that it was all just theoretical posturing, the artist had burned a dozen Guatemalan flags in twelve different ways. That was followed by other radical acts: book burnings, exhumations of cadavers, the destruction of civil registries. However, infamy, or fame—depending on one's perspective—had only come a decade later, when, along with a group of collaborators, she had organized the simultaneous burning, in church, of a dozen statues of saints. The incident landed her in jail. She was saved by the international fame the performance had generated: hundreds of recognized artists interceded on her behalf, which was enough for the government to decide to free her after fifteen days. Spending even two weeks in a Guatemalan prison at the end of the nineties was not, however, an easy matter. When she got out, she wasn't the same. She'd moved far away from the intellectual passion that had distinguished her in the past, the analytical enthusiasm that, on more than one occasion, had carried her to the border between art and madness. Prison had done its job.

A decade later, the last icon the artist seemed intent on breaking was her own body. She'd given herself over to alcohol like it was a furiously poetic act. She was seen on the streets of her university town, dressed as a clown or a bride, bottle in hand, stammering verses that verged on nonsense, usually surrounded by stray dogs she found on the streets. Then, when night fell, once she'd collected enough money to feed her vice, she would disappear into the bars. To say that this woman had been one of the nation's great artists could seem, at times, like a joke in poor taste. A joke that Pinillos herself would have laughed at. A joke whose real punch line would come the day the poor woman opened an envelope at random and found herself involved in a trial whose components struck her as strangely beautiful. Minutes later, she looked around and said to herself, "Well, maybe this is how I finally get out of this pigsty." Then, for the first time in almost a decade, she took out all the old papers, the manifestos that this Viviana Luxembourg cited with such erudition, and her hungover fury couldn't obscure a certain pride. It took her three weeks to answer, because three weeks was how long it took to come out of the alcoholic maze she'd been wandering in for the past ten years, but when she did, the reply came with the intellectual precision that had always characterized her work. She cited Bataille and Nietzsche, she mentioned Cioran, she quoted all the furious philosophers she could remember, and then she closed the letter with a quote from Hegel that she'd always found memorable:

But the life of Spirit is not the life that shrinks from death and keeps itself untouched by devastation, but rather the life that endures it and maintains itself in it. It wins its truth only when, in utter dismemberment, it finds itself. [. . .] Spirit is this power only by looking the negative in the face, and tarrying with it.

A brief smile, impish and restless, appeared on her face as she finished writing the quote. A joyful and pleasant smile that made her remember the good times, when she could spend an entire day in the sun reading an incomprehensible book. Under her signature, she added a final note: "Be sure that the ticket is one way: Guatemala City–San Juan." As soon as she mailed the letter, she called her colleagues and told them what had happened. No one believed her, not that it mattered to her much. She put on her clown clothes, went out for a walk, and when she found herself facing a little girl who stared at her in surprise, she recited the most beautiful poem she knew: a poem that spoke of a frog who frequented a dark pond and who one day decided to stay and discover the pleasures of the night. When the little girl laughed, she knew she was on the right track.

For each letter she mailed, the defendant also prepared a file for the lawyer that included the possible collaborator's name, a copy of the letter they'd received, and an extensive theoretical discussion of their relevance to the case. Each week, when he was allowed to visit her, the lawyer picked up the file and, after discussing some details of the case, headed for the library at the university's law school, where he spent long hours trying to decipher his client's theoretical digressions. The first week he thought it was all simple madness; the second week he thought it was a great farce; by the third he thought it was an obsession. By the fourth week he understood that the project in his hands obeyed a strange logic, but one whose purpose still eluded him. It was during that fourth week, reviewing the file of the Guatemalan artist María José Pinillos, when he found, lost amid the thousands of words, a phrase that would help him understand the systems by which the defendant seemed to navigate. Written in the margins of the file, beside a paragraph on iconoclasm in medieval art, he found the solitary phrase: "This prison is my private Ustica." Ever since he was a child, he'd been unable to skip over unfamiliar words, and that night was no exception. A simple search was enough to find a Wikipedia article that explained, in English, that Ustica was a small Italian island in the Tyrrhenian Sea. Unsatisfied, he searched for more. Then he came across an interesting detail: a small subsection that described how the island had served as a prison during the years of Benito Mussolini's fascist government. Thousands of political prisoners had ended up there. Two of them deserved particular mention, in Wikipedia's opinion: Amadeo Bordiga and Antonio Gramsci. Thinking that he recognized the names, he decided to explore Bordiga first. When he didn't find much that would link him to Virginia McCallister, he turned to Gramsci.

With his round glasses and slightly disheveled hair, the man reminded him of one of his high school teachers. Farther down the page he found a section titled *"Prison Notebooks"* that explained how, while imprisoned, Gramsci had filled thirty-two notebooks, 2,848 pages outlining one of the most relevant political theories since Marx. Beset by health problems that had afflicted him since he was a child, he died on April 27, 1937, just six days after he was let out of prison. After his death, his brother-in-law managed to get the notebooks out of the hands of the police, and after assigning them random numbers, he gave them to the banker Raffaele Mattioli, Gramsci's secret patron. Mattioli then entrusted the writings to the leader of the Italian Communist Party, Palmiro Togliatti. Eleven years later, between 1949 and 1951, the notebooks appeared in print, published in six volumes by Einaudi, a small Turin-based press. The lawyer noted the titles of the publications:

- *Historical Materialism and the Philosophy of Benedetto Croce* (1949)
- *Intellectuals and the Organization of Culture* (1949)
- *Il Risorgimento* (1949)
- *Notes on Machiavelli, Politics, and the Modern State* (1949)
- *Literature and National Life* (1950)
- *Past and Present* (1951)

He felt a strange relief on realizing that he was finally starting to make his way into the maze that McCallister seemed determined to build. He also felt a kind of inverse vertigo as it dawned on him that the systems his client seemed to operate by were driven by glorious failure. That night, he didn't go back to reading about iconoclasm or the Guatemalan artist. He spent hours searching for information on that Italian intellectual, imagining him deep in the solitude of an island prison, sketching theories from his confinement that would come to describe the social mechanisms from which he'd been excluded. Strange, he thought, that a man in prison could imagine the laws of what's happening outside. When the librarian turned off the lights, she caught the lawyer midsentence, reading a letter Gramsci had sent to his son from jail. He wondered then what had become of his client's daughter, that little ten-year-old girl who had taken a plane to the tropics and never come back. The librarian interrupted his thoughts: "Esquilín, it's time." He nodded, worn out. It dawned on him that it was Friday.

His name was Luis Gerardo Esquilín, but from an early age his schoolmates had called him just Esquilín, and he liked it. When he was asked what had driven him to study law, he would answer, a little in jest, a little in earnest: I liked the sound of it, Esquilín, esquire. The answer hid, however, a void: Luis Gerardo Esquilín didn't know why he'd studied law, or, at least, he was afraid he didn't know. Like many people, he had entered law school a little reluctantly, driven by his parents' admonitions. He felt that at a certain age one had to come down from the idealist clouds and give in to the real world. Studying law was just a way of saying that he agreed to enter adulthood, that he intended to be a model citizen. His three years as a student were therefore directed toward forgetting his humanist past and what could have been, and becoming, through study, an exemplary adult. He'd done it. His long hair had been replaced by a precise cut; the hippie clothes had been supplanted by suits with British labels; his playful, Caribbean diction had given way to a slightly forced verbal correctness. In order to feel comfortable with himself, as if his change weren't a betrayal of his past, he bought some black-rimmed glasses that gave his look what he thought of as a postmodern twist. Law, for him, was the path to respectability and adulthood. He had imagined the law as black-and-white, but now a single case was demonstrating that the whisper of art was enough to destroy its respectable certainties.

After a month, his friends realized they were losing him. He stayed at the library late into the night, reading the cases his client suggested, searching for precedents, digging into monumental books of art history in search of the details that the defendant had forgotten to explain. More than once, during those first months, he feared that Luxembourg's fictions would start to infiltrate his life just as they had, for years, infiltrated the media. In those moments, he tried to get back to the basics, to tell himself that, at the end of the day, this woman was not Viviana Luxembourg but Virginia McCallister. In the middle of the night he sat down to look at old photos of the model from the fifties, or watch the movies she starred in alongside the heartthrobs of the day, or pore over the photos of her alongside her vanished family. One photo in particular caught his attention: an image the press had distributed after her supposed disappearance, showing the three of them in front of an enormous Christmas tree. The child must have been around ten years old, and the parents around forty, though they looked younger, more beautiful, more perfect. That photo, terribly familiar and quotidian, gave him a strange feeling. It forced him to think that there was another story hidden behind this whole project. He had tried during many meetings with his client to elicit that other story, not Viviana Luxembourg's but Virginia McCallister's, heir of old William Sherman, wife of the Israeli photographer Yoav Toledano, mother of little Carolyn Toledano. He had tried many times to learn the whereabouts of husband and daughter, the circumstances that had led to their disappearance. But the defendant kept quiet. Showing no emotion, she just said that it all belonged to Virginia McCallister's life, not hers. A person has the right to change her life, she said. Not wanting to contradict her, Esquilín still tried to convince her that the story would be crucial for the trial, that she could be accused of concealment, but he had no luck—the defendant went on with her monologue, and he was again caught up in its possibilities. However, the night he found the strange phrase—"This prison is my private Ustica."—he thought that this woman, like Gramsci before her, surely spent nights thinking about the child she'd left behind. That night, unable to sleep, he decided to go out walking through the streets of Santurce. He felt confused at the realization that his strange obsession had little to do with what was happening outside. Obsessions are always private, he thought, as he moved deeper into the night.

The sixth and final letter was addressed to a married pair of artists, the Chilean Constanza Saavedra and the Brit Arthur Chamberlain, residents of London, where decades earlier they had been the center of attention in one of the most talked about art trials ever. As Esquilín understood from the file, the couple had been accused of reproducing—with remarkable accuracy—pound sterling banknotes. One morning at the beginning of the decade, while he was having a donut with coffee at a New York diner, Chamberlain, distracted, had started to draw a dollar. When she saw how perfectly the Englishman was copying the bill, the waitress had started up a conversation and tried to persuade him to sell her the drawing. Chamberlain decided, then, that it would be fair to pay for his breakfast with that false currency. When he gave her the drawing, the waitress said that the breakfast cost only ninety cents—would he please take ten cents as change? Back in London, Arthur laughingly told the story to Constanza, who was fascinated: it presented a solution not only to the conceptual problems of realism that so interested her in those days, but also to the financial issues that plagued them. The transaction had established a new relationship between art and currency, art and the market. From then on she set the pace of their little performances, accompanied by her husband's prodigious hand: they'd go to a bar, talk for a bit, and then, pretending to be bored, Arthur would start drawing pound sterling notes on a napkin or whatever paper was handy. As soon as the waiter noticed his skill, the Chilean would interrupt and start the negotiation. From then on, life got easier. Art had become a mode of exchange that skipped over all the dreadful commercial logic.

However, it wasn't just the waiters who noticed and admired Chamberlain's skill. Rumors started to spread in the art world as well, and two years later the owner of a prestigious Parisian gallery contacted them to express interest in a solo show. The event was a success, and with success came visibility: articles in the major newspapers, mentions in art magazines, even a televised report. Predictably, the news didn't take long to reach the Bank of London. Two months later, on the show's opening night in London, two brawny members of Scotland Yard interrupted the party, accusing the couple of breaking British counterfeiting and forgery laws.

Three months after that, London's famous Old Bailey court became a gallery for the accused couple's defense. Before a probably dumbfounded jury, dozens of curators and critics tried to convince the audience that the work was, without a doubt, art. Through the courtroom paraded the names of Duchamp and the Dadaists, theories on ready-mades and conceptual art, pop art, and representation. After six months, the couple was found innocent by a jury that was sick of a man in a wig telling them what to think.

Ironically, the accused woman's letter caught the couple in a full-on economic crisis. For months, Arthur had been afflicted by strange pains that had proved impossible to diagnose. They jumped from one medical exam to another and watched their little savings vanish in pursuit of an undecipherable illness. The letter arrived like a happy memory of those days when they won their battle against the Bank of London. The first to take a stance, as always, was Constanza. Her words were blunt: "See, we've clearly gone down in art history." Arthur, more humble and realistic, suffering from pain, merely replied, "If you say so, but make sure the old lady's not a fraud." That same night, by then a little drunk, he laughed at himself and said, "As if we aren't a couple of old frauds ourselves." He wasn't far off. The couple had lost the media presence they'd won in the trial years before. It had been over three years, in fact, since they'd had a decent show. The letter, then, was like a belated miracle, arriving when no one expected it and only retirement and death were on the horizon. One glass later, the Englishman closed the discussion by speaking, as always, of the weather: "A little Caribbean vacation wouldn't be so bad, especially with this bloody London climate." Constanza didn't even hear him, immersed as she was in thoughts of how this trial would indisputably establish them in art history. That night they laughed as they hadn't in a long time: uproariously.

Two days later, Luis Gerardo Esquilín found the documents and notebooks related to the case scattered across his bed. He would have feared the worst, but then he saw his girlfriend, Mariana, a beautiful mixed-race girl with red curls, emerge from the bathroom. Confused by the strange distance she'd felt from her boyfriend in recent months, the girl had decided to go through his papers. She'd spent the afternoon in the role of jealous girlfriend, searching among the papers for reasons that would explain his aloofness. What she found only served to increase her unease. This, she thought, seemed less like a trial than a debate between pedants. That night, when she saw him, she drove home her observation: "And worst of all, Luisito, is that you're buying it, you're buying into a giant lie from a pretentious old woman." Esquilín didn't know what to say, perhaps because he himself hadn't been able to figure out whether or not it was all a great stunt. In reply, he outlined some legal arguments that not even he understood well, and only managed to bore Mariana.

An hour later, when they were in each other's arms, the girl said that to her, all that contemporary art stuff was just hot air. Two weeks ago, she told him, a friend had invited her to an event at a gallery in Santurce. She'd decided to go, mostly just to socialize, and she hadn't known what to expect. What she'd seen had struck her as incomprehensible and stupid: a dozen dogs walking around an empty gallery. That was the piece. The strange thing, she said, was that people just took it for granted that the thing was worthwhile. "People eat that shit up," she concluded, furious. Then she added, "But you, Luisito, you can't eat that shit, because the courtroom is the courtroom and the law isn't a gallery. You'll realize that soon enough." Esquilín let the comment fall like a silent bomb. He confined himself to quick kisses, tender conversations, the sentimental routine. That night they had sex for the first time in two months, and then the girl fell asleep. He could not, thinking as he was about Mariana's words and what they made patently obvious. For a long time he himself had thought, like her, that contemporary art was a terrible joke, a game for the pretentious. Now he wasn't so sure. He was afraid that the abyss that was starting to separate him from his surroundings would become as conspicuous as it was for his client. He was afraid of getting up one day convinced of some incomprehensible and esoteric ideals. He was afraid, ultimately, of one day winding up among that vanguard of obsessive weirdos that his client seemed determined to recruit, one by one. He was afraid, above all, of becoming an honest but incomprehensible man, shut off in the prison of a private language no one understood. Then the image

of an intellectual with round spectacles rose up before him. He pictured
this Gramsci hidden away in his Italian prison, filling notebooks with theories that would go unread until much later, immersed in a series of obsessions that would nevertheless return him to that monstrous society from
which he'd been expelled. He pictured that man and thought how there
was something almost pleasant about the way private languages imposed
their obsessive worlds. The truly mad thing, he thought, would be for two
crazy people to have the same obsession. In the middle of the night, the
idea struck him as mad, yes, but true. Fifteen minutes later, he was snoring.

5

Around that time, I received some unexpected news. After many days of effort and aggravation, Tancredo had managed to get the newspaper where he worked to choose him as their correspondent for the trial. I was surprised by the news, but I knew Tancredo, and I knew nothing was out of his reach. I myself had considered going at one point, returning to my island and following the twists and turns of this story that was starting to grow like a maze, guided by dark and serpentine forces. Modesty, timidity, or mere indifference had led me to desist. So, when I learned Tancredo would be there, I could only feel glad that my friend would be taking my place. While I was dining in Manhattan with an Italian girl I was getting to know in those days, I could be sure that my friend would be there, in the thick of the trial, representing me one way or another. So when we met for beers at the usual bar the day before his departure and he asked me what I thought about it all, I merely spoke of the strange models old Toledano built in his empty town, and I dropped a nihilist phrase: "Everyone does what they want." I immediately revised my words, adding: "Everyone does what they can." Then Tancredo started talking about the tower, about Sergeant Burgos, whom he planned to meet with soon, and about the various theories he was coming up with. I hardly listened. But I felt an image growing inside me—that of Giovanna sitting in her living room, talking to me of animals that played at camouflage in the jungle.

Two days later Tancredo's first message came, outlining his theory of the tropical baroque. He said that Caribbean art and culture could be figured out quite easily if one understood a fundamental factor: the heat. The tropics were, by definition, entropic: heat led to movement, excess, sweat, baroque mischievousness. Then he went on to talk about the role of the mosquitoes within the tropical cosmology: mosquitoes were the true muses of the Caribbean, invisible but devilish. Where the Greeks had imagined an angel, where Lorca had seen his elf, Tancredo placed the furtive unease provoked by the mosquito. You had only to see, he said, a man doing battle with a mosquito: his movements, insane and excessive, make him look like he's in a trance. I laughed as I read it, imagining my poor fat friend lost in the colonial alleyways, sweating like a pig, dressed in tourist garb in his little sun hat and well-ironed white guayabera. Still, I could only agree with his crazy theories—now that I thought about it, the Caribbean heat was the motor of my tropical joys.

The second message came three days later, written in a less playful tone. In it, Tancredo talked about his meeting with Sergeant Burgos. He described a terribly exhausted man destroyed by the idea, constant and obsessive, that his information had helped to jail a decent woman. The message went on to tell the story of the tower, the twenty-seventh floor, and the stuttering boy, Miguel Rivera. According to Tancredo, Burgos had become obsessed with Rivera's sudden disappearance. Afraid he would return for revenge, Burgos couldn't sleep at night, ate little, spoke even less. He'd become a shadow of the brave man he'd been. When he did sleep, a recurring dream tormented him: in a whirlwind of images, he saw the dark and messianic mural from the boy's room, and he thought he heard the muffled voices of the children he'd seen on the screens of the stutterer's computers. He'd get up sweaty, his heart pounding, sure that Rivera was after him. On nights like that he had no doubt: that boy was the true guilty party when it came to the misfortunes that were plaguing him. Convinced the only way to expel that demon was by confronting him, he spent days wandering around the tower, waiting for his enemy to one day deign to show his face. When nothing happened, he went to a bar, where he surrendered to rum as old boleros played on the jukebox. And that's how he spent his hours, trying to escape the nightmares that stalked him. I read all that and couldn't help thinking how Tancredo didn't belong there. But an immediate rejoinder was inescapable: nor did the defendant belong there, nor the stuttering boy. If there was a story here, it was a disoriented and uncomfortable one of beings who were out of place.

During those months, Tancredo's messages gradually started to build up steam, producing a parallel story to the one I saw on the news. While the TV showed images of the prosecutor, an arrogant man with silvery hair and a false smile, Tancredo meticulously described the routines of the fifty-six families who lived in the tower. When the news scrutinized the last false story the defendant had fabricated, Tancredo described the rituals of the heroin addicts who lived on the tower's upper floors. He had become obsessed with a twilight world that nevertheless obeyed the laws of the most basic everyday life. There, people slept, ate, read, coexisted as in any other place. Somehow Tancredo had managed to get the tower's inhabitants to accept him, to the point where they included him in their private lives and, most important, shared their gossip with him. He told me in the third and fourth messages that he'd made friends with a barber named Gaspar, an old flirt who wore flowered shirts and whose barbershop was one of the tower's main gathering points. There was a very simple reason for that: Gaspar had a TV in his shop. So every other day, when two o'clock rolled around, a bunch of old retirees and one or two young men crowded into the small space to watch the horse races. With all the finesse of the best charlatans, Gaspar claimed to have inside information from a contact at the track. Every morning at noon he made the same call, and after hanging up, he tried to sell the information to the other old men. Two hours later, when they saw their horses lagging behind, they berated the barber and stormed out, prepared to go on with their lives and never again believe the old man's lies. Two days later, they'd repeat the whole scene of disenchantment.

Tancredo understood that few other places could offer so much information about the defendant. Over drinks he made friends with some retired jockeys, and he used those friendships to gain entrance into the lazy group that gathered every two days, like clockwork, in the shop. At first they treated him as just a well-informed gringo. They accepted him, in a fashion, thanks only to the tips he brought straight from the track. Gaspar in particular looked at him suspiciously, knowing that the fat gringo could take away half his business overnight. If the barber put up with him, it was more out of curiosity than anything else. He was intrigued by Tancredo's story, his interest in the tower, his sun hat. Then, unexpectedly, he started to like him. He nicknamed Tancredo "Cano," started to offer him coffee, introduced him to friends. He made room for him, so to speak, in the tower's singular world. That's how Tancredo started to find out what people said about Luxembourg: he listened silently to rumors about a possible romance with Rivera, about her unexpected arrival to the tower at the start of the decade, about the letters she occasionally mailed abroad. Nothing out of the ordinary: common stories that he'd already heard in his conversations with the sergeant. One day, however, he picked up on a detail that caught his attention: one of the old men mentioned that the gringa—as they called her—had gone every day to work in a little café. For almost a decade, said the old man, they'd seen her go down the stairs with her notebook in hand, headed for a café called La Esperanza. When Tancredo asked what she did there, no one could answer. "The same crazy stuff she did upstairs," replied Gaspar.

That afternoon Tancredo refused the coffee the old man offered him three times, and he took his leave from the shop earlier than usual. He went down the three floors separating the barbershop from the street, and was about to leave when he saw Burgos wandering around the ground floor with a desperate and insomniac face. He thought about greeting him, but decided there would be time for that later. Mornings, he thought, always belong to the sleepless. He greeted the guard at the door, and when he crossed the street he asked in a small funeral parlor where he could find La Esperanza. An elderly man with white hair gave him directions, but not before warning him: "If I were you, with that gringo look of yours, I wouldn't go in there. It's dangerous." Tancredo smiled, pleased. He left the funeral home, crossed two streets full of rubble, and after ten minutes he saw, at the end of a street teeming with stray dogs, a small establishment whose sign read: L ESP RANZA. Keeping watch at the entrance, an old black man, skinny as a giraffe, smirked at him. Tancredo gritted his teeth and went in.

La Esperanza was a dump. Tancredo understood that immediately, as soon as he saw the two young men who hissed at him from the corner. One had a dark bandana tied around his head, and the other, sitting on a small wooden chair, seemed not to care that a silver revolver peeked out above his belt, completely visible. They couldn't have been more than sixteen. Tancredo immediately understood the warning he'd been given, but he wasn't intimidated. He'd spend the mid-nineties in New Orleans, where he'd been to similar bars, in even worse situations. He knew how to handle himself. So when he heard another hiss, he raised his arms in a gesture of peace and clarified what he figured the two boys were worried about: he wasn't a cop, just a dumb reporter who worked for a very small paper. The boys made some quick joke, showed him the gun that he'd already seen—seeming to want to annoy him more than scare him—and when they saw he didn't waver, they asked his name. "My name is Tancredo, but in the tower they call me Cano," he replied. "Cano? Like that guy there?" asked the boy with the bandana, holding back a smile. Tancredo looked where he was pointing and saw half a dozen photos of a fat albino man wearing sunglasses that made him look blind. Then he learned that the origin of his nickname was a local musician, pale and fat like him, probably also sweaty. "A salsa singer," the boys said in unison, and he could only burst out laughing. To his surprise, the boys also saw the humor in the matter. More relaxed now, they asked him if he wanted to buy something. Tancredo explained his case: he told them of his friendship with Gaspar and the people in the tower, about his job as a journalist for a U.S. paper, the rumor he'd heard that the defendant had spent her afternoons there, in that café. "So it's the crazy old lady's story you're interested in? Well, hell," said the kid with the pistol. Then he gave a loud cry. The sound was unintelligible to Tancredo but it must have been a name, since a few seconds later, a massive man dressed in an apron and a white cap opened the door to what must have been the kitchen. "This gringo wants to talk about the crazy lady." Without beating around the bush, a little annoyed at the interruption, the man asked if anyone wanted coffee. Three minutes later, sitting across from Tancredo with two mugs on the table between them, he started out by noting the coincidence: Viviana Luxembourg had also liked her coffee with a little milk. She'd ordered one every day, almost without interruption, for the past eight years, up until the day she was arrested.

That afternoon, while behind him customers entered, paid, and left with small packages, they talked about so many things that Tancredo, in his enthusiasm, wasn't sure what it was exactly that made him feel he was on the verge of a revelation. Later, thinking back on the conversation, he managed only to reconstruct the gringa's tedious routine. She had come into the café one afternoon, and returned every day thereafter. Every day it was the same: she ordered a coffee with milk and then began to read. Then, when she finished the first coffee, she'd ask for the domino set and spend a good half hour playing with it, configuring small towers and shapes, compositions that led nowhere. With a second cup of coffee before her, she would start to write in the same notebooks as always, in a microscopic and fragile handwriting that was like a private language. At four o'clock, she went back to reading. "Who knows what books she read. We didn't care. She didn't bother anyone, we didn't bother her. We figured she was loony," the cook said. Tempted more by curiosity than anything, Tancredo had asked if the defendant had ever bought drugs. The man didn't seem to like the question, but he still answered, "Never, but sometimes, all the things she said, it seemed like she was on something." Then he'd gone on to tell a story that the gringa had told him as a joke but that he hadn't found at all funny, although it had remained etched in his mind like a riddle. The joke, as he told it to Tancredo, was about a writer of traditional detective novels who spent his whole life railing against experimental novelists, but when he died left behind an indecipherable work that drove the critics crazy, a piece that everyone tried to read in classic registers but that ended up defeating them every time. An experimental work, Tancredo understood, that turned a life into a simple postmortem joke. The idea, bizarre but strangely inspiring, that a whole life could be the prologue to a posthumous joke may have been what made him feel as though the moment of revelation was approaching.

"Can you explain what that joke's all about?" asked the man. Tancredo, perhaps in solidarity, perhaps out of simple condescension, told him that it didn't make any sense to him either, that it was surely just madness. Then he asked a final question of the cook, who was now flanked by the two boys. He asked whether, during those years, they had ever asked the defendant why she'd decided to settle in Puerto Rico. During recent months the press had speculated a lot: from the most obvious hypothesis about the local climate, to conspiracy theories that posited the island as the center of operations for a broader criminal network. The man replied that in truth, he had no idea. The few times they'd talked about the island, it seemed to matter very little to her. Although, he added, she spoke perfect Spanish, a very neutral Spanish, as if she didn't come from anywhere or as if she were trying to hide her origins. Then he seemed to recall a detail. He said that during the first year after she came to the tower, the gringa seemed obsessed with a specific event: the death, on March 22, 1978, of the famous tightrope walker Karl Wallenda. The distinguished patriarch of the world's most famous family of trapeze artists had fallen to his death that day, victim of an unexpected storm that hit while he was walking the tightrope between two buildings in El Condado, the island's most well-known tourist area. The gringa, the man went on, seeming to search his memory, didn't talk about anything else in those days: she wanted to know the specific details, the local reaction, even hear the voice of the commentator who had been narrating the stunt. She spent long hours in the afternoon sketching identical drawings depicting the moment when his feet began to fail him, sketches of initial instability. Tancredo recognized the anecdote, he knew the story of Wallenda's fall, but he didn't know it had happened on the island. Listening to the story he thought, for a brief moment, that perhaps Gaspar and the old men in the barbershop were right: maybe the accused woman's whims really did spring from an inexhaustible font of madness. The expression on the face of one of the boys interrupted his moment of doubt. "Hey, don't we have one of those drawings around here somewhere?" asked the boy. Then the man got up from his chair, and after a few minutes, during which the only sounds came from drawers opening and closing, he came back from the kitchen with a drawing in hand. When Tancredo saw the series of drawings the man put before him, he felt a sharp and unexpected pain in his stomach, as if all this were some child's cruel joke. He saw dozens of sketches in miniature. He looked at the first steps, sure and light, that gave way then to the first hesitations, then to a curved figure and then again—in a truly painful sequence—the tightrope walker's free fall. Then he saw that the sequence of caricatures was not linear but cyclical, and that in the final boxes, the little figure that represented Wallenda returned to stand on the tightrope, to start his ordeal all over again. It made him think of the flipbooks that used to fascinate him when he was a boy, whose pages showed an animated scene: a figure throwing a basketball, a Mickey Mouse jumping on a trampoline, the frustrated attack of a rhinoceros. He even remembered one little book that showed the scene of a kiss. The childhood memory didn't bring him any happiness or nostalgia; it only served to highlight the accused woman's strange cruelty. "She was something crazy," one of the boys repeated, and Tancredo merely agreed with a short nod. Five minutes later he was out of the café and headed back to the little hostel where he was staying during those weeks.

The hostel was called El Balcón del Mar, but it had no view of the sea. It was located in the university area of Río Piedras, a setting more urban than beachy. He was surrounded by a strange mixture of student bohemia and local color that, in his third letter, he referred to as "a delicious hive." That night he couldn't sleep and went out barhopping. At one point, among the kids' conversations, he heard a phrase that struck him as macabre but precise, appropriate for what he'd seen that day: "Hell is an incomprehensible sarcasm." The phrase, vague as it was, calmed him. As long as words for the world's malaise still existed, the world was viable. He fell asleep within the hour, the jukebox rhythms still echoing over his alcoholic exhaustion, convinced that he understood the defendant.

In his seventh letter, Tancredo told me about the image that plagued him throughout that night. Halfway between sleep and drunkenness, floating in the air like a half-drawn dream, a calendar date stood out. The numbers themselves were fuzzy, but in that swamp where awareness and oblivion struggled, he knew clearly that it was the date of Wallenda's fall. "Even though I don't remember it now," wrote Tancredo, "it had to have been March 22, 1978, because ever since that night I can't think about that date without feeling overwhelmed." Then he went on to describe the way his mind—always hyperactive and sometimes antic—had come to associate the date with the moment Toledano's family had disappeared. Unable to accept what he felt was clear evidence, I pictured the strange models old Toledano was building in a distant town and struggled inside over whether or not to tell Tancredo the man's full story, beyond the bits and pieces I'd let slip in our conversations; I was convinced that for the first time my friend's madness would carry him to the necessary conclusion. The urge for silence won out. Instead, I took out Giovanna's file and rummaged through her notes like a retired detective, remembering her quick movements as she smoked, and toying all the while with that jade elephant that somehow brought me closer to her. Well into the night, the conclusion came to me: even farces have their consequences.

6

Ten days before the trial began, while reading one of the notebooks, Luis Gerardo Esquilín came across a loose paper crumpled up among the other pages, the faded ink almost illegible. He was surprised to see that it was written in a different color and on a different kind of paper, but he did recognize the defendant's haughty, minuscule handwriting. Without thinking much about it, he copied on his computer the string of names and notes that appeared on the paper:

> Baudelaire, Flaubert, Wilde, Joyce, Pound, Brecht, Burroughs, Nabokov, Brodsky, Onetti, Pasolini, Bernhard. In each of those cases, literature before a judge. There is also a dispute there, in literature, between art and law. Always remember young Kafka, who at twenty-seven wrote in his diary: "We are outside of the law, no one knows it and yet everyone treats us accordingly." Always remember Kafka, the great launcher of impossible parables.

Beneath the entry he recognized a series of drawings. On more than one occasion he had come across similar doodles among his client's writings, but he still didn't know exactly what they were meant to depict. He did have a few hypotheses: he thought the figure could be a stealthy walker, a private detective, or a Russian gymnast. When he showed it to Mariana one afternoon, her response was immediate: it was a little man dancing on his toes. This time, though, Esquilín found a date under the drawings: March 22, 1978. The date caught his attention, perhaps because it reminded him that his younger brother's birthday was one day later, on March 23. He opened his computer and searched for the most important events of that day. He found little: the birth of a renowned marathon runner, the ending of an Asian war, some events that involved then president Jimmy Carter. When he was about to give up, he found an article that struck him as more relevant: the death of Karl Wallenda, which had occurred on the island on Wednesday, March 22, 1978. He spent the next hour collecting information about the Wallendas, about the patriarch's death and his family's stubborn but vaguely poetic decision to continue risking everything on the tightrope. He remembered having heard the story before, from his mother, but even so he found the anecdote singular. It seemed odd that someone like Wallenda, as experienced as he supposedly was—a man who had even walked a tightrope over Niagara Falls—had died crossing between nearby buildings. He told himself that if this were a detective novel, the story would start there, to then weave a transatlantic conspiracy around Wallenda's death. Then, he said to himself, it would be a matter of connecting the threads of this story, watching it cross the decades until his own arrival: he, the lawyer Esquilín, would be the one to solve the secret crime. He thought that if one day he ever wrote that story, he even had just the right title: *The Wallenda Conspiracy*. The idea made him burst out laughing.

These notions didn't come to Esquilín out of nowhere. They were based on a rumor that was starting to spread through the media: that the defendant was merely the visible face of a much broader network. Virgina Mc-Callister, said the tabloids, was one member of a broad activist collective, the visible face of an anonymous network that was just beginning to show itself. It wasn't, thought Esquilín at first, such a crazy idea; in those days, anonymous networks of hackers were becoming more common: invisible activists, cybernetic collectives. Even the most conservative American media outlets warned of an army of traitors led by the ex-model. When he finally dared to discuss the subject with the defendant herself, Esquilín was met with a great peal of laughter. "Poor guys, they clearly don't understand anything All art is already a collective act." Feeling himself defeated again, humiliated for his weak theoretical understanding, he spent the next days planning his reply. Three days later, when he found the Wallenda doodles in the defendant's notebook, he felt tempted to hand over his idea about the conspiracy to the press. He laughed at the thought that he would be reenacting the defendant's own crime: he would bring the reporters to that bristling border where reality and fiction mix together.

Three days later, wearing a suit and tie, he made his first visit to the tower. He was surprised by that social microcosm where even misery seemed to have its appointed place. He went down hallways teeming with grimy, cheerful children, until he reached the defendant's old apartment. On several occasions he'd tried to find out why his client had decided to live there, in that underworld where not even the police dared to tread, but he'd received no answer, either from the notebooks or in his conversations with the woman who claimed to be Viviana Luxembourg. Nor did he find a clear reply that afternoon, when he went into that apartment, now perfectly empty. It's true, though, that once he was in the building he saw that this world was much more normal than he'd imagined: normal kids, typical apartments, old people who whiled away their hours just as they would anywhere else. A perfectly normal world that obeyed, nevertheless, a logic of its own. Sweating through his shirt, he felt a strange calm as he passed through the space the defendant had occupied for almost a decade. The space where she had schemed. He found it larger than he'd imagined, better lit, airy, and welcoming. Exhausted, defeated by the heat, he loosened his tie and went over to the window. The urban panorama of roofs and streets, the concrete maze that opened up before him, made him think that his relationship to the case was like a painted landscape, a wide, colorful landscape where the artist swears she has hidden an image, but before which one could stand for hours without finding the slightest hint of that secret figure. The defendant's trick, he thought, had been to place herself at the exact point where her crime became wide and omnipresent as the city itself. To place herself at the precise point where the image of the crime started to be confused with the landscape of the law, with its most genteel heart.

He went back to his apartment without asking any questions or interrogating any witnesses, unable to admit to himself that something was starting to eat away at his conscience: the feeling that he was standing before a strange image whose meaning fled at the same speed he tried to catch it. He spent that afternoon lying in bed, looking at the ceiling with a child's mischievous expression, searching for shapes in the sea of irregularities woven into the concrete. Then he remembered the game he used to play when he was a boy: every night, unable to give in to sleep, he imagined drawing maps and constellations on that false sky. He found islands, white archipelagos lost in vast seas, small continents, worlds that made him feel protected by a network of secret meanings. That afternoon, defeated by the heat and the humidity, he realized that his confusion came from a mistake in his perspective: for over three months he had sought the key to the case in his client's psychology, when really it would be found somewhere else. Then he remembered the defendant's phrase: "All art is already a collective act." He thought back to those words and felt that they hid a much larger story in which the trial he was so caught up in was just the tip of the iceberg, Overwhelmed and sweaty, he fell deeply asleep before he could deduce where it would all lead. He woke up five hours later, unable to tell if it was day or night, if it was still today or if tomorrow had already come.

7

That same afternoon, while Esquilín was sleeping, Tancredo went to the tower to find Sergeant Burgos, planning to ask some questions about his encounter with Miguel Rivera. He wanted to corroborate a hypothesis that had come to him in his sleep: that Rivera was the true author of the whole mad project of fake news stories. He was surprised not to find him prowling around the lower floors. Nor did he find him higher up. In the barbershop, Gaspar confirmed his worst fears: Burgos had been seen drunk, rambling around the top floors among the heroin addicts. Then he'd disappeared. Worried about his new friend, Tancredo headed to the police station and learned that, after a month of odd behavior, the sergeant had quit his job. Tancredo was about to leave when a secretary, unable to keep quiet, whistled to get his attention. Then she told him, with a furtiveness that struck Tancredo as odd, something she claimed to be the only one to know. Two days after he quit, Burgos had boarded a plane for New York. Tancredo tried to ask if she knew what he was doing there, if he had friends or family. The woman just replied that everyone on the island had someone there. Then she said goodbye and went back to her office.

That afternoon Tancredo mulled over Burgos's disappearance. First the stutterer, then Burgos. Before long he had a clear idea: it was all part of a longer series, a great chain of sudden disappearances that hid, without a doubt, the true story of the crime. Sitting in a nearby café, he imagined a great exodus to the north, a tremendous progression of sleepwalkers setting off in the opposite direction from the one in the defendant's notebooks. A great pilgrimage in which the Caribbean seeks to disappear into a diffuse north. He tried to shrug off the weight of the image by doodling a picture. Ten minutes later, when the waitress came to pick up his empty mug, she found, sketched on the napkin, an impressively detailed drawing that looked like a great march of penguins toward the sea. Thinking the drawing would make her son laugh, she saved the napkin.

That night, hours later, I received a message from Tancredo. A message that started out by relating the latest events, Burgos's disappearance and the growing media coverage of the trial, but then took on a strange tone—

strange for Tancredo, at least. I had always thought that irony and theory served as shields to defend himself from the hostility of a cannibal world, and that his system worked pretty well for him. The somber, shaken tone of his latest message made me feel that wasn't true: it seemed like reality was finally starting to infiltrate his theories. He told me he spent nights thinking about Burgos, Giovanna, me—all those who, he said, had fallen prey to Virginia McCallister's madness. He spoke of a great conspiracy that originated not in a human mind but in a cosmic figure that grew steadily. I recalled my first months with Giovanna, months of exhaustion and delirium, and understood why my friend was starting to rave. Too much rum, too much heat, too many theories. I thought again of that scene I'd recovered years earlier: my father taking me to the vivarium, those afternoons when I stood before the glass and waited for a seemingly invisible animal to awaken, before I suddenly understood that the creature was precisely the landscape in which I was searching for it. Those animals, I thought, devoured the landscape just as Virginia McCallister seemed to devour any story that tried to neutralize her. I thought about Giovanna, about old Toledano, I thought about Tancredo, about the hours I had lost trying to find the pattern behind Giovanna's project. I told myself that Tancredo was right: it wasn't clear just what was unfurling before our eyes, which story was becoming visible and which was hiding, where we might find the legible pattern behind the enormous web being woven by an elderly model in a Caribbean jail. Tragedy or farce? I felt a sudden shiver and thought that for some stories, the old categories aren't enough.

8

In the days leading up to the trial, the tabloids' conspiracy theories took off, with claims of invisible networks and anonymous collectives. Two prestigious writers, one Chilean and one Californian, wanted to write profiles of the model-cum-artist, and whispers even spread that a U.S. movie producer was preparing a film about her life. Also during those days, perhaps thinking that it was all a staging of the eternal division between art and life, between art and society, a group of Norwegian artists calling themselves Konsept began a social media campaign to defend this artist who, according to them, was recovering the vital avant-gardism of Duchamp.

Everyone wanted a piece of her story.

There was no lack, either, of speculation about her mental state: the word *bipolar* was mentioned, as were dissociative identity disorder, Alzheimer's, and dementia. A newspaper from South Florida mentioned a less well-known illness: a strange disease called noncontinuous dementia, in which the patient, though fully self-aware, is unable to comprehend her life as a continuous present. For Luis Gerardo Esquilín, the matter of the defendant's identity had become an obsession. He found her oddly determined in her refusal to talk about her past, her family, that journey they'd taken in 1976. Often, during his long conversations with her, he'd tried to convince her that she would avoid prison only if she explained to him just how Virginia McCallister had become Viviana Luxembourg. His client refused to answer, and Esquilín was again convinced that his strategy was misguided: solitude and prison could matter little to a woman who seemed determined to devote her life to art and contemplation. Esquilín thought of the notes he had found in her notebooks, about Ustica, the solitude in which Antonio Gramsci had outlined his political theories. He became convinced that there was no way out. He, an obscure supporting actor, had no choice but to accept his auxiliary position with dignity and pride.

Sometimes, during the sweltering afternoons of the tropical summer, lost among his papers, Esquilín felt boredom closing in on him from all sides. He seemed to be sinking deeper into the world conjured by a phrase he'd found in the margins of one of the notebooks: "If sleep is the apogee of physical relaxation, boredom is the apogee of mental relaxation. Boredom is the dream bird that hatches the egg of experience. A rustling in the leaves drives him away." Written like that, without a name or a source, without much relation to the nearest phrases, the sentences had seemed arbitrary at first. Still, something made him copy it into his own notebook. After a few months, perhaps imitating the process of incubation they suggested, the words became a sort of talisman that the lawyer carried with him everywhere. He just had to wait, give in to boredom as one surrenders to solitude. One day the egg of experience would be incubated and the truth of the case would be revealed, exact, buoyant, and weightless, like a dream one rises from happy and forgetful. One day he would fall asleep, and when he woke up the case would be just a distant, half-forgotten nightmare, a whisper of what could have been his greatest glory. Every day, when six in the morning rolled around, the alarm went off and Luis Gerardo Esquilín again faced the proof that night only erases the slightest of sins. There was nothing for it then but to brush his teeth, return to the notebooks, and keep going.

Tancredo, on the other hand, also obsessive, bored, and sleepless, felt lost amid a clutter of talismans and clues. He spent his afternoons collecting all the material that had been published on the defendant: local and foreign articles, TV reports, rumors and speculation. Nothing was excluded from that archive: the photos documenting the young model's rise at the start of the fifties, her first movie appearances, the brief mentions of her gradual political radicalization, her entire career, until he reached the final photos that showed her wearing a cream-colored prison jumpsuit, aged but still elegant and beautiful. He spent hours watching black-and-white movies she'd starred in, thinking about how the world and its people had changed, convinced that within those movies, in the gestures and laughter, was hidden the solution to the strange enigma that would occupy so many people years later. He found nothing but the image of fame and glamour regarding themselves in the mirror: the flirtation typical of the cinema of the era, the easy dialogues and precise stagings. Everything fell into place, everything seemed to be according to fashion. In those moments he found it impossible to think that this woman would one day come to live in the tower, toiling away like a monk.

Still, he didn't give up. Though he didn't know the whole story like I did, he tried to put together the pieces, both political and personal, as if it were all a giant jigsaw puzzle that only revealed his own confusion. Meanwhile, he turned in breezy columns to the newspaper that employed him, articles that only summed up the general feeling among the public, drawing from the old men he visited at Gaspar's barbershop, some conversation he'd had with Burgos before his inexplicable flight, anecdotes he heard from university students in the bars near his hotel. Still, Tancredo being Tancredo, every article ended with a crazy theory that he managed to slip in among trivial details: on the nature of art, its eternal battle with the law and with beauty, or about the island's role in a great continental conspiracy. He would publish an article and the next day, at eleven in the morning, after a quick round of local bookstores, he would hop on the bus that an hour later would drop him off three blocks from the tower. Once there, he took three turns around the lower floors, looking for signs of the disappeared Sergeant Burgos or the enigmatic Miguel Rivera, knowing he would end up in Gaspar's barbershop, savoring the tedium with half a dozen retirees. Hours later, when he tired of their conversations, he shyly took his leave and again walked the five blocks full of rubble and dogs between the tower and La Esperanza. Once at the café, already under the the locals' protection, he imitated the defendant's ritual to a T, ordering a coffee with milk and starting to read. From his disparate readings—books on history, literature, and art theory, but also on quantum mechanics, topology, and even comics—he extracted quotes that he included in the messages he sent me in the evening. Then, once the caffeine's effect had waned, he asked for the set of dominoes and spent the next hour making figures, little towers and mazes, quincunxes and marine forms that he copied from an old catalog of natural history he'd stolen from me before he left for the island. Swearing to himself that he would follow the ritual just as he'd heard it described, he played until boredom got the better of him. Then, finally ready for thought and reflection, he ordered another coffee with milk and started writing: minimal notes, random thoughts, the kind of crazy aphorisms that can come from an agile mind unafraid of the absurd. He even tried to imitate the defendant's minuscule handwriting.

He tried to find, through vulgar imitation, the exact place where two souls commune. He was trying, so to speak, to become Viviana Luxembourg. To understand her motives, her actions, her tics and manias. The idea wasn't his: he'd read an art book that talked about a Uruguayan, an unusual artist of noncreativity, who'd spent the last twenty years of his life perfecting his copies of a single Van Gogh painting in an attempt to understand exactly what the Dutch artist felt as he painted those flowers. Every afternoon, unable to understand the defendant, Tancredo remembered the Uruguayan's failed project, and a cold, deep pain swelled in his chest, forcing him to leave.

The more messages I received from Tancredo, the more I was convinced that our roles were being reversed, and now he was the one going deeper and deeper into the madness of William Howard, the drunk gringo Tancredo had met in the Caribbean, the one who was convinced that islands could be collected like stamps or coins. I feared Tancredo was moving deeper into a borderless world, where the limits of humor threatened to blur with those of terror. Tragedy or farce? The question was repeated again with nightmare insistence, while the first day of the trial grew inexorably closer. I thought about Giovanna and repeated to myself that patience was the trick: someday the joke would break out of its shell and show its mocking face.

In the margins of a tedious discussion of *Brancusi v. United States*, Esquilín found a quote that caught his attention. It said: "To do nothing at all is the most difficult thing in the world, the most difficult and the most intellectual." This time a source was given, one Oscar Wilde, whose name he vaguely remembered from his high school English classes. He'd read very little back then and worked even less, so most likely he hadn't even read the book in question. A second hungover memory surfaced: he remembered having seen the name mentioned in the list of literary court cases that the defendant had mentioned. He spent the next half hour searching through the dozens of open documents on his computer, until he finally found the quote in a document he'd titled "Random thoughts."

There was the name, lost among so many others that likewise sounded vaguely familiar but whose works, to his embarrassment, he'd never read: "Baudelaire, Flaubert, Wilde, Joyce, Pound, Brecht, Burroughs, Nabokov, Brodsky, Onetti, Pasolini, Bernhard. In each of those cases, literature before a judge." Reading Wilde's phrase again, Esquilín told himself that maybe this was what the defendant was after: a final dwelling where she could sit down to do nothing, a private monastery in which to chisel boredom into intellect. He thought of Wilde, of Gramsci, and what came to his mind was something he'd heard about years before on TV: a Buddhist monk who had spent the last fifteen years of his life meditating and waiting for that final instant when his spirit would express itself in a perfect gesture. A minimal gesture, a kind of swimmer's stroke, in which a whole life would be concentrated. Perhaps, Esquilín thought, Virginia McCallister had imagined her life as a pure effort that was leading to a final gesture, a judgment that would redeem her not only in the public's eyes but also in her own. To do nothing, and then do it all. Or better yet, he thought, to do it all, give everything, and have it all lead to a marvelous nothing. To reach, at the end of life, a marvelous oasis of boredom where she could sit and pronounce a final word. An irrefutable truth brought his speculations to a halt: the date of the trial was approaching, and she still wouldn't admit her real name. It was time to get to work.

9

The trial had been scheduled to start on July 15. Three days before, the foreign journalists decided to get together for a few drinks, perhaps thinking that the trial would be long and they should make some friends. Or maybe they were only hoping to share information. When it came time to choose the venue, someone commented that no one knew the island better than Tancredo. He chose an outdoor bar full of bohemian students, on a corner of the university city where the local intelligentsia convened to the pulse of music and rum. Accustomed as they were to the tourist areas, the other journalists found the suggestion dangerous and exotic, a satisfactory serving of adventure before the arduous days of work that awaited them.

That night they saw a face of the city very different from the one they'd experienced around their hotels. Here they found little of the shrill splendor of the lobbies full of women in high heels and salsa orchestras playing for tourists. They felt a different panorama opening up before them, an authenticity that had little to do with the folkloric costumes of the servers who waited on them in the traditional eateries of the old colonial city, or with the countless restaurants that claimed to have invented the piña colada. Here, authenticity was an atmospheric murmur, an entropy different from any other chaos. It was, as Tancredo said, a delicious hive where a multiplicity of voices, shouts, and laughter accumulated, ultimately weaving a great filigree full of life. In one corner of the bar, surrounded by empty beer cans, a group of locals danced to the beat of an old jukebox. Songs by Ismael Rivera and Héctor Lavoe, salsa rhythms that very few of the reporters knew but that still made them feel strange heartache and brief joy. Captivated, they watched the dancers turn. They commented on everything, described it all.

Observing the scene, Tancredo thought that aside from the color of their skin, their overly flowery clothes and their unmistakable accents, it was their gaze that ultimately betrayed their irrefutable foreignness: tourism was, more than anything, a way of looking. Description, he thought, was the worst trap of the costumbristas. If they wanted to go deeper into that world of which he already felt a part, they had to break through the anthropological barrier. He disappeared through a little door between two murals, and when they next saw him, he was carrying a generous round of Cuba libres. After that came a second and a third. By the fourth, Tancredo could sense tongues loosening, and the gossip started to flow. That was how he learned the rumors circulating among the journalists. Rumors about a possible romance between the defendant and a local youth, about the real reasons behind her trip to Latin America in the mid-seventies, about her possible ties to certain Peruvian radical leftist groups. Between one drink and the next there were also jokes about Esquilín, his horn-rimmed glasses and his look of a defenseless little novice. But it wasn't only his appearance that seemed to earn the journalists' mockery. There were also rumors about the witnesses the defense was preparing: an Italian journalist claimed to have information saying that they were to call none other than Yoko Ono, whom, she said, the defendant had met on a spiritual trip to the eastern Amazon. It would be a circus of celebrities, they said. A clown parade orchestrated by a demented old woman. With every Cuba libre, the laughter and speculation grew. A French reporter even said he had sources claiming Yoav Toledano was still alive. The other journalists denied that possibility: according to them, Toledano and the little girl had died a long time ago, on that fateful journey they knew so little about.

Tancredo let them talk, half an ear on their alcoholic speculations and the rest of his attention on the dozens of young girls coming in and out of the bar. That night, however, it wasn't beauty that caught his interest, but the silhouette of a skinny drunk he'd seen around the bar circuit before. Always cheerful, always drunk, he was eternally open to starting up conversations with the young patrons. Until then, perhaps because of his thinness, perhaps because of the backpack he seemed to always carry, Tancredo had thought this was just one more eccentric student, but that night, when the man passed by the journalists' table and smiled, he realized this was no youth. His graying hair gave him away, his missing teeth, his wrinkled smile: the marks of a passionate life. He watched him disappear into the crowd and told himself that someday he would talk to that mysterious man.

He didn't have to wait long for his chance. When he went in search of another drink, he found the man belly up to the bar, fairly tipsy, trying to explain the plot of his new novel to the barman. You've got to be kidding me, Tancredo thought. The guy's a writer. Before he could decide if it was really a surprise or not, he felt a hand clap his back and heard the man address him: "Man, I feel like I've seen you before. You look like you want to hear about my novel." Before Tancredo could utter a word, the man began to narrate, in impressive detail, the project that had occupied him for years. Convinced that this discourse would be more interesting than his colleagues' conversation, Tancredo bought the man a drink, and, after making a toast to island women, the author went on with his diatribe. At their table, his colleagues alternated gossip with drinks, in a sequence that would soon carry them to the dance floor.

The writer called himself Juan Denis, and according to him, the novel, as understood since Cervantes, was an outdated artifact. No one cared anymore about the adventures of senile old men. He downed his drink in one gulp, ordered another, and went on: no one cared anymore about one man's experience. *Any* man. Or woman, or transvestite, whatever, he said. The novel was about to enter a new phase: an inhuman phase, as he liked to call it, in which human experience mattered little. "Just think," he said, "the human being has only existed for two hundred thousand years, while the universe has been around for over fourteen billion. And the novel's ambition shrinks even more when it narrates from the perspective of one life. Thirty, forty years, sometimes a day: the novel's scale has shrunk until it's disappeared." Denis's idea was to return the novel to the scale of the stars: to write novels of multiple layers, novels that could be read the way you read the passage of time on the surface of rocks. "*Hermano*, have you ever been to the Grand Canyon?" he asked. Tancredo gave a slight nod of assent. "Then you know what I'm talking about: the idea is to make a novel as badass as that. An empty novel, full of dust and air, a geological novel that depicts in an instant the monumental passage of time. An archival novel, that's what it is," he finally blurted out, seeming not to care whether his interlocutor understood what he was saying or not.

Tancredo felt a strange complicity. Drunkenness, he thought, meant feeling the world's energy as a great embrace. He liked the man's theory, the way with just a snap of the fingers Denis dispensed with centuries of tradition and empiricism, betting on a greater epic, cold but strangely moving. He was about to issue a critique when Denis, a new drink in hand, his voice shaking and stammering more and more, interrupted him again. He wanted to tell him more about his project. Something "badass," he repeated, intermingling profanity with all his conceptual jargon. He said that for years he'd been planning a novel about the history of fire: a novel where fire was the true protagonist, a novel that would start with the chemical equation of combustion and then spread over all the continents and all the ages, a novel that would cross history like a field in flames. He had spent years excited about the idea but unable to carry it out. He was lacking the form. "Form": he repeated it three times, showing his yellowing teeth each time, stinking of rum, and then he explained how two weeks before, after a weeklong binge, he had found the solution. Talking with a retired physics professor, he had learned that in different parts of the world there were sometimes underground fires so voracious that humans could do little to quench them. Some of them had been burning for more than a thousand years. Denis spoke with a singular emotion, with joy that verged on euphoria and that many would call the ravings of your typical alcoholic. Listening to him, Tancredo understood that anyone else would have shown him less patience. He'd seen it with his own eyes: how night after night the students were bored or scared by the delirium of that unlikely genius. He also knew that, ultimately, what this happy drunk was really after was a patron who would go on paying for his drinks. It mattered little: theories were always worth more than drinks, and this one had made him think of the small town where Yoav Toledano was hiding. A pang, cold as déjà vu, immediately pierced his back. The very idea that this man could know the details of the case, including that secret that supposedly only Tancredo and I knew, brought on an intense terror. He tried to talk about it, ask the writer if he knew about Toledano's small town, but when he finally got his question out, it was met with an unequivocal response: "Enough with the theories, let's find some ass. The girls are pretty around here, aren't they? What do you say, gringo?" Denis gave him a slap on the back that resembled a hug, and with a fresh beer in hand he disappeared among the dozens of students now filling the place. Tancredo didn't know what to do. He felt that paranoia was winning out, forcing him to find connections everywhere, linking signs no one else seemed to see. He ordered another Cuba libre and told himself that this was the true joy of thought: the implosion of the universe in a theory equally gorgeous and mad.

When he went back to the table where he'd left his colleagues, they weren't there. He found them a few minutes later, dancing happily near the jukebox. Among them, eliciting delighted laughter, Juan Denis was contorting his thin body with the clumsy flexibility of a puppet. Farther on, in a corner a little apart from the group, the Frenchman was dancing with a beautiful young local. He looked for the Jewish journalist from New York he had a crush on, but he saw to his sad surprise that she was kissing a local reporter. Love wasn't his thing. Half an hour was all it had taken to turn a civilized conversation into a happy, alcohol-fueled bacchanal. Still intrigued by what he'd heard, that geological and chemical story, he considered approaching Denis again. But one glance was enough to convince him that little remained of the writer, entirely replaced now by the drunk. Then he had one last Cuba libre, listened to some kids recite poetry to a drumbeat, and walked back to his hotel.

When he got there, he sat down at his computer and searched the internet for information on Juan Denis. He found very little, which made him think the drunk man had made it all up. No Puerto Rican writer used that name. Still, he liked the idea: the most innovative literature, the most avant-garde, was written by an unknown author who had invented it as a simple solution to a personal alcohol shortage. Perhaps, he thought, the ideas didn't come from Denis. But he couldn't find any mention of a novel on underground fires, or any geological novels. Just a mention of the concept of *longue durée* as it appeared in the writings of the French historian Fernand Braudel. In his internet drifting, Tancredo ended up at an article about a literary movement that argued for noncreativity and plagiarism. He read about Kenneth Goldsmith, who championed the disappearance of the genius as an archetypal figure of the writer, and who sought instead to replace it with a more modern figure: the programmer. Since the invention of the internet, he wrote, the world had filled up with texts. The modern artistic gesture, then, was not writing more, but learning to negotiate the monumental quantity of existing texts. The article included examples of texts produced under this new proposal: a typed reproduction of *On the*

Road; a lawyer who had presented her legal reports as poems; a writer who spent his days in the British Library copying the first verses of every English translation of Dante's *Divine Comedy*; a printed version—in the form of a nine-hundred-page book—of a single copy of *The New York Times*. One poet had even transcribed the forensic reports of certain illustrious deaths, like John F. Kennedy's and Marilyn Monroe's. The avant-garde, however, was not without risk. The article ended by noting that more than one of these writers had had problems with the law; recently, Borges's widow had sued a Spanish writer who had tried to rewrite one of her husband's lesser-known books as a comedy.

Tancredo found it all fascinating. There were, he said to himself, ways of understanding the defendant, of understanding what was at stake in the trial. Then he decided to forget about the case. He thought again about Juan Denis, that magnificent alcoholic with his impossible novels. He wondered if the man had somewhere to sleep that night, if he had some faithful friend who would help him get home. He fell asleep himself a few minutes later. The next morning, while everyone in court was preparing for the trial, Tancredo got up early, walked a few blocks to the bookstore he frequented, and asked about a local author named Juan Denis. The confused bookseller said he'd never heard of him.

10

The night before the trial started, Luis Gerardo Esquilín couldn't sleep—plagued not by anxiety but by an idea that hounded him. He was afraid that in his eagerness to fulfill every one of the defendant's wishes, he'd forgotten the other story: the one that traced not just her identity as an artist but her identity as a flesh-and-blood person. It pained him to have left unexplored the family photos and the trip his client claimed not to remember. On more than one occasion, in the story she had given the examining judge, the defendant had managed to omit that fragment from her life, sometimes claiming amnesia and other times simply refusing to admit that she had lived during that time. With the trial's start just hours away, Esquilín felt he had become his client's puppet, the first pawn she would sacrifice in a game that would go on for years.

An email he received that very morning had only deepened his fears. It was from none other than Alexis Burgos, whose name he recognized from the police statements that had led to his client's capture. He remembered the details only vaguely, but he knew it was Burgos who had glimpsed McCallister's photo book, and Burgos who, confused by the discrepancy between the names, had started to unravel the enigma. In his first weeks as her defense lawyer, he'd tried more than once to get in touch with the man, but every time the reply had been that Burgos was out, Burgos was sick, Burgos didn't work there anymore. Knowing the man had left his position, he wasn't surprised to see that the sergeant was up north, writing from New York—although the logic he gave for the move, which he claimed to have undertaken to combat his insomnia and depression, struck Esquilín as strange: he could think of few places less relaxing. He didn't linger over the question. The lines he read next seemed to be written precisely to confirm the anxiety that had been eating away at him since the early-morning hours.

Reading Burgos's missive, Esquilín had the feeling he had accidentally wandered into a tornado, at the center of which was a deeply confused and tired man. He missed the old days, when you had to only look at an envelope to know where your interlocutor was writing from. Emails, he thought, dissipate the sender's voice through ambiguous zones. He had the strange feeling that the voice that addressed him was the voice of labyrinthine New York itself, into which the sergeant had disappeared. It was a cold and tired voice that scrambled chronology and introduced without preamble many topics Esquilín knew nothing about: a stammering boy named Miguel Rivera, an immense mural on which human history was sketched like a great divine nightmare, a screen crowded with young faces that Burgos said he'd briefly glimpsed. Burgos refused to pass judgment in his message. He merely listed a series of events that seemed to be strangely related. He mentioned the faces, then the mountain of enlightened children that the defendant had talked about on his first visit, and how she'd emphasized that what she was telling was an epic story about the end times. Finally, the email mentioned the text that Burgos claimed to have found in the stutterer's empty room: a story without an ending, its laborious rhetorical twists only leading to other false endings in an infinite chain of detours that reminded Esquilín of Rube Goldberg machines. The memory of those machines made him think that maybe this whole enigma was about something very simple: nothing but a chain of tired men trying to impute meaning to a madwoman's ravings. Burgos closed the message by admitting that he was drinking more than usual, and that he was writing from a profound exhaustion. Looking at the many typos that marred the email, Esquilín realized that the trial was one day away, and he didn't even know whether he could believe his client or not.

That night he was unable to sleep, convinced he'd forgotten something fundamental. He got out of bed on tiptoe, trying not to wake Mariana, sat down at his desk, and spent the next half hour online, looking for the latest articles about the case. He saw photos of the defendant, the classic before and after pictures, the opposing photos of the actress and the accused woman, Virginia McCallister and Viviana Luxembourg. He felt a little disconcerted to see his name mentioned in more than one article, but he told himself that there was no time for distractions; he had to work. He looked for the papers he'd prepared for his presentations, and after a first reading, he told himself he had fulfilled his responsibility to the utmost; he'd carried his client's logic to the limits of reason. He returned to bed telling himself that the show was ready, but Burgos's email returned to cloud his conscience. Esquilín was sure that his knowledge of the notebooks, of which the police had given him copies, was better than anyone else's. He could cite almost from memory the cases and annotations that populated the 174 notebooks that composed *Art on Trial*. Of the other 73 notebooks, he realized then, he knew very little.

Desperate, he got up again, went to the photocopies he'd made of the notebooks, and quickly found the first installment of the second project. On the cover he read, in uppercase letters, the title: *THE GREAT SOUTH*. Poetic title, surprising title, a good title, he thought. Then he dove into the notebooks, which he had already looked through on several occasions, but from which he felt strangely removed. The first time he read through them, he thought they were a previous project, belonging to the defendant's esoteric phase. For the back burner, he'd thought. Hours from the trial, however, it all seemed to take on new relevance.

Among the many notable quotations, he found one that seemed to point toward a community of the disappeared, a story that made him think of Sergeant Burgos's opaque voice as he described an infinite and useless text that disappeared within itself:

B. Traven, Hart Crane, Ambrose Bierce, Arthur Cravan: to disappear in the fearful South. To turn disappearance into the work itself. Antonin Artaud, Malcolm Lowry, William Burroughs, Jack Kerouac: disappear into the infernos and return, like Dante, to tell the story. The only true artwork is disappearance itself.

Esquilín, who knew his client's rhetorical strategies better than anyone, immediately recognized the structure of the argument. Again, he thought, with the list of names. As if each arbitrary series suggested a theory of the cosmos. He thought about going back to bed, but curiosity won out as always. He searched for information about the life of B. Traven, the first name on the list. The initial thing that surprised him was the photo at the top of the Wikipedia page, a double image where the writer appeared in profile and head-on, his pose and face reminiscent of a mug shot. The lively mustache, the serious frown, all topped by a plaid beret, made him think that the man was laughing at the camera. That man, he thought, had the face of a dog, one of those good and loyal dogs that are mocking us deep down. It seemed like a joke, the opening to one of those ironic postmodern movies he and his girlfriend occasionally liked to watch. The story he read next didn't let him down. It was a complex tale of disappearances and anonymities, a transatlantic picaresque that he found strikingly similar to his client's. A carnivalesque game of masks that made him think that history was a great circus put on by a troupe of nutty artists.

Between 1925 and 1960, almost twenty books had been published by one B. Traven, an enigmatic author who claimed to live in Mexico but of whom little was known. Books of adventure mixed with anarchist ideas, books about wild native Mexico and capitalist exploitation, books published directly in Germany to favorable reviews. All by an author who had built his life as a maze of knotted identities.

From the austere peace of his small house on the outskirts of Acapulco, B. Traven managed to keep his anonymity intact for years, until the success of his novels attracted the attention of the press and the public. One afternoon, reading one of those books, a writer and journalist named Erich Mühsam thought he recognized in Traven's style the turns of phrase used by Ret Marut, an old colleague from his years as an anarchist leader of the fleeting Bavarian Soviet Republic, in which, from April 7 to May 1, 1919, German socialists had placed their most lofty hopes. His friend, it was rumored, had spent the years before the revolution acting on the most remote stages of small German towns. He had debuted in the theaters of distant Idar, then moved on to those of Ansbach, Suhl, and Danzig, until he finally landed in Berlin. The strange thing was that, according to Mühsam, Ret Marut had been arrested and executed after the fall of the Bavarian Soviet Republic, on May 1, 1919.

A possible explanation arose years later, when Will Wyatt and Robert Robinson, two documentarians from the BBC interested in uncovering the Traven enigma, consulted the records of the U.S. State Department and Great Britain's Ministry of Foreign Relations. They found something very interesting: after he escaped execution, Marut had reached Canada, only to be turned away and sent to the United Kingdom, where he was imprisoned in Brixton as a foreigner without a residence permit on November 30,

1923. When he was interrogated by British police, Marut confessed to being Hermann Otto Albert Maximilian Feige, born in the city of Świebodzin on February 23, 1882. According to Polish national records, after his brief military service, Otto Feige had vanished. The documentarians managed to follow his tracks, confirming that during the summer of 1906, a certain Otto Feige briefly acted as head of the ironworkers' union of Gelsenkirchen. Following his artistic leanings, he would set off for Berlin in the fall of 1907, using the name Ret Marut.

In the middle of the night, totally wrapped up in the story he was reading, Esquilín thought it all—the anarchism, the multiple identities, the misleading moves—fit perfectly with Viviana Luxembourg's profile. Every clue seemed to hide a story, even the names. When he read that Marut was an anagram of *traum*, the German word for "sleep," and also of *turma* ("herd" in Romanian, "accident" in Finnish, and "horde" in Latin), he wondered if perhaps "Luxembourg" also hid something else, some linguistic twist that would bring it closer to the Norwegian word for "troop" or the Danish word for "plague." When he tried to find more information, he learned only that if a country bears your last name, the name disappears behind the country's history. Then he explored another detail that had caught his attention: the fact that many of B. Traven's novels, especially the ones from the apparently famous series of "Jungle Novels," explored the inhuman and exploitative conditions the natives suffered in the state of Chiapas, where they were forced to work the mahogany forests in concentration camps called *monterías*. Esquilín recognized Chiapas, mainly from stories of the Zapatistas, and remembered the masked face of Subcomandante Marcos, that great anonymous cowboy who, when he was a boy, had led him to believe that Mexico was a Latin American version of the old west. He remembered that when he was a child, the subcomandante's image had revived the figure of the superhero: a masked, nameless man planning a new world from the jungle. He remembered how one day, when he was nine or ten and his parents had a table full of guests who asked him what he'd like to be when he grew up, he'd surprised them all by replying that he wanted to be like that masked Robin Hood who lived in Chiapas. He remembered how they had all laughed and how later, at bedtime, his mother had come to his room and told him that the man was no Robin Hood, and Chiapas was no place for decent boys like him. Suddenly the image came to him clearly: he imagined Viviana Luxembourg deep in the Chiapas jungle, conversing with the subcomandante about art, revolution, politics, and anonymity. He understood then that his client's lists were a desperate attempt to become part of a story. Beneath those lists was a woman's determination to earn a place in the great history of anonymity.

Traven's story, however, didn't end in a Brixton jail. His arrival in Mexico, his surreptitious transformation into B. Traven, and his establishment as one of the most acclaimed and translated novelists of the time still required an explanation. As often happens, one was found by people who weren't looking for it. After the commercial success of Traven's book *The Treasure of the Sierra Madre*, published in English by Knopf in 1935, Warner Bros. acquired the film rights and hired John Huston to direct. Huston started to exchange letters with Traven, and they agreed to meet at the Hotel Bamer in Mexico City. Predictably, Traven never showed. Instead he sent a translator named Hal Croves, who presented a notarized document authorizing him as the writer's representative. Croves would appear again months later at a meeting in Acapulco, and would be present throughout filming, imposing his opinion on several occasions, which led many of Huston's collaborators to think that this gaunt and taciturn man was, in fact, B. Traven himself. The movie's three Oscars in 1948 were enough to make the writer a subject of public discussion. Warner Bros., understanding the commercial potential of the aura Traven's persona was starting to take on, even started the rumor that there was a reward of five thousand dollars for anyone who found the real B. Traven.

A Mexican journalist named Luis Spota, following clues from the Bank of Mexico, came upon a posada on the outskirts of Acapulco where a man who gave his name as Traven Torsvan lived. The neighbors called him "el gringo" and said he'd been born in Chicago. Indeed, according to his papers, Torsvan had been born on March 5, 1890, in Chicago, had crossed the border into Ciudad Juárez in 1914, and had obtained his Mexican ID in 1930. Spota realized it was all a lie. He bribed the mailman and confirmed his suspicions: month after month, Torsvan received checks made out to B. Traven. Sure that he had enough information to incriminate him, he showed up one day at the posada, and face-to-face with that man who claimed to be Traven Torsvan, he presented his discoveries. The man emphatically denied being Hal Croves or B. Traven. Three days later, on August 7, 1948, Spota published his great discovery in the weekly journal *Mañana*. Two days later, Torsvan disappeared.

They called him "el gringo." Just like my gringa, thought Esquilín as he poured himself another cup of coffee. He tried to imagine the posada in Acapulco, where that man who had been so many—first Otto Feige, then Ret Marut, then disappearing into the names Hal Croves, B. Traven, and Traven Torsvan—had finally decided to be himself. He imagined it pleasant but plagued by flies, hot and well arranged for boredom. He imagined it a bit like the tower where his client had hidden out without hiding for nearly ten years. Places where one can disappear under a false name, he thought. He took a sip of coffee and reread the quote that had led him to Traven's story:

> B. Traven, Hart Crane, Ambrose Bierce, Arthur Cravan: to disappear in the fearful South. To turn disappearance into the work itself. Antonin Artaud, Malcolm Lowry, William Burroughs, Jack Kerouac: disappear among the infernos and return, like Dante, to tell the story. The only true artwork is disappearance itself.

Convinced that his client saw herself in that long tradition of anonymity and invisibility, Esquilín picked up a pen and got ready to write the name Viviana Luxembourg in front of Traven's, when he was assaulted by doubt: Which group did she belong to? Those who had disappeared, or those who'd returned to tell their stories? Then he felt that the defendant had planned this whole thing in an attempt to jump from one list to the other. He laughed—it was like pure religion. The death and resurrection of a messianic Marilyn Monroe.

———

Like all stories, B. Traven's ends in death. On March 26, 1969, in Mexico City, Hal Croves died. In an improvised press conference, his widow, Rosa Elena Luján, confirmed his death and revealed that his real name was Traven Torsvan Croves. According to her, he'd been born on May 3, 1890, son of a Norwegian father named Burtoon Torsvan and a British mother named Dorothy Croves. Two days later, as specified in his will, his ashes were scattered from a plane flying over the Chiapas jungle.

When he finished reading the story, Esquilín felt that it was all a puzzle whose pieces fit together but formed a disjointed landscape, halfway between countryside and beach. With his wife's help, thought the lawyer, Traven had played a final joke on the experts and the Mexican state. He finished his days as multiple as he'd lived them, having been born in both Świebodzin and in Chicago, surrounded by a dozen names and different personalities. Traven, thought Esquilín, had been many people so he could ultimately become none. He had liked one quote in particular: "The creative person should have no other biography than his works." It's a good quote, he thought. The artist as anonymous, a multiple being. The artist as one who renounces being one, and becomes many. Then he thought about the trial he would face tomorrow. The trial, too, was rather like a delayed joke.

He looked at the computer's clock and found that it was already almost four o'clock. Five hours left until the trial started.

Outside, two drunk young men shouted that Sunday was the new Friday. Esquilín thought how a trial was a staging of the discrepancy between common sense and the world. Or at least a staging of the discrepancy between the pieces that compose the world.

11

The face of the woman entering the courtroom didn't show any trace of her time in prison. Dressed like a dandy in a black suit, white shirt, and dark tie, she seemed utterly immune to her circumstances. Long gone was the fragile princess who had captivated American moviegoers half a century before, the pretty young girl, fragile and lovely. Now she wore an air of aloof maturity, as if, capable actress that she was, she'd spent years planning every detail of the promenade that was now her one last show. Escorted by two police officers, she walked to her bench and sat down without ever turning her eyes to the public or showing any sign of repentance or nervousness. She didn't react to the TV cameras or the flashes that documented each of her steps. Once she was sitting beside her lawyer, she kept her eyes fixed on the judge, as if the whole thing were a conversation between them. Behind her, a wave of whispers rolled from left to right, in accordance with the geometrical logic of the room's arrangement: the general public sat to her left, while to her right, the journalists watched her as though stealing confused glances at a sphinx. "The Beauty of Art Before the Law's Merciless Eyes" read the headline in one of the major papers, hours after the event.

Seated five rows behind the defendant, between a French journalist and a hungover New Yorker, Tancredo felt like what was happening there was actually the opposite: the law was finally being forced to position itself before the inclement eyes of art. There was no madness in the defendant's eyes; quite the contrary, they showed a fearful lucidity that would lead more than one of his colleagues to later declare that the woman appeared bewitched. To his left, among the crowd, he recognized Gaspar. Next to him, some residents of the tower looked happy to be witnessing that televised spectacle. Then he thought he saw, hiding in the crowd, Sergeant Burgos. A second look told him the resemblance was pure fancy. Burgos, or what was left of him, was further away than anyone could imagine. In front of them, the defendant seemed to be calmly awaiting a pronouncement from the judge. The sphinx, thought Tancredo, always waits for the other to speak first.

Beside her, also dressed in a black suit, white shirt, and dark tie, Luis Gerardo Esquilín looked like a tender, childish copy of the defendant. At the sight of him, Tancredo thought that he'd never seen a lawyer so young, so defenseless, such a kid. He looked restless and nervous: he moved his hands a lot, and his face belied an eternal exhaustion. To his right, the burly, gray silhouette of the prosecutor depicted the opposite: the arrogance the law acquires over the years, the gray and decadent curls of mediocrity, the slow, complacent gestures of a man who has confused truth with power. Facing them, the judge, a brown-skinned man with white hair and a broad smile, looked bored as he listened to the clerk read the twenty pages of the prosecutor's report, a truly incomprehensible jumble of legal jargon through which, from time to time, the familiar allegations could occasionally be discerned: the defendant's transgressions and her falsified news, the effects on the stock market. Listening to it all, it occurred to Tancredo that the law was a private jargon invented by the learned to mock the rest of civil society, an incomprehensible and empty language that hid the law's terrible arbitrariness. Looking at the judge's bored face, Tancredo thought that after years of the game, this man seemed to have withdrawn from it. To his right, paying false attention, the jury were like actors in a TV trial: a certain discomfort and agitation seemed to force them to exaggerate their movements, to adopt the artificial poses of supporting actors. Observing the scene, Tancredo wondered whether the defendant might not find it all funny, accustomed as she was to real actors, real theaters.

Three hours later, after pleading not guilty to each of the twelve crimes she was accused of, Virginia McCallister left the courtroom as remote and haughty as when she'd entered. Beside her, the young lawyer appeared happy to have survived his first round. Above them, flying over the long chain of camera flashes, a whisper spread through the audience: this trial would be short and simple. Between the legal jargon, the judge's boredom, and Esquilín's exhaustion throbbed an inarguable truth: the defendant was determined to dig her own grave. She refused to negotiate with the prosecutor, refused to plead insanity, refused to have a dialogue. A real nutjob, commented a French journalist with a half-smile. Tancredo, however, thought it was magnificent: a dialogue between two fools who refused to speak the same language. A dialogue between deaf people, in itself a perfect metaphor for a world where no one understood each other anymore. The defendant, he thought, wanted to make clear not only her own innocence but also her absolute illegibility. Her laws were something else, her traditions as well. That trial would be her final work: casting the world as an orchestra of deaf parrots.

12

The following months passed in a whirlwind, a cloud of last-minute news stories trying hard to offer novelty where there was only a tedious, absurd process. The prosecution was focused on two points: proving that the defendant was in full command of her mental faculties when she committed the acts, and demonstrating that said acts were illegal by means of an exhaustive presentation of three specific cases. Regarding the first objective, the only obstacle they seemed to face was, paradoxically, the tenacity with which the defendant herself boasted to the psychiatrists of her mental health. More than one of the psychiatrists who saw her opined that a person who finds herself in that situation and doesn't doubt her mental state for even a second must be crazy. The rest of their notes confirmed what some people had already guessed: Virginia McCallister suffered from a mental disorder that forced her, on the one hand, to dissociate from her past identity, and on the other, to adopt a new one—the one under which, she said, she had carried out the actions she was being tried for. According to three psychiatrists who saw her, the defendant's case was not a clear-cut amnesia but something more complicated; her change of identity was a decision: she had *decided* to be Viviana Luxembourg. She told the examining judge and would repeat in court that she remembered her American childhood perfectly, her early years in North Carolina, the period of her media ascent, first as a model and later as an actress. She even remembered the first years at Yoav's side, their initial trips to Cuba, a handful of other memories from the time. There was a specific date that marked the break: her memories reached April 15, 1966. The rest, the long period that stretched from then until April 15, 1987, belonged to an absolute oblivion from which she claimed she could salvage nothing. She said she'd gotten up one day without any memory at all of the previous twenty years, convinced that a new life project lay behind a new name: Viviana Luxembourg.

Then the story reemerged. Now under her new name, she remembered having spent almost ten years backpacking around Latin America. A couple of years in Buenos Aires and its provinces as a member of an experimental circus troop built on the tenets of Augusto Boal's Theatre of the Oppressed. That was where she said she'd heard, for the first time, of Jacoby, Costa, and Escari and their anti-happenings. Then she remembered a long stay in Montevideo, of which she primarily recalled the neighbor's cats, the silent dusk, and the sad cries of gruff men. After that came a solitary period in the Atacama Desert. A magnificent time of which she said she remembered reading only one book, a strange volume of almost a thousand pages about Tehuelche rhea-hunting practices in Patagonia. A very odd book, she added—though no one had asked—within whose pages the sense of the desert became sharp and defined as an illusion. She remembered, as well, the aloof irony of the llamas, the aristocratic pose of flamingos on a lake, and the constellated sky of the salt flat where she had finished reading that sublime book. Then she remembered a trip to the north. Years in trucks full of men with rough and violent voices, long conversations on subjects she would later forget, dreams conceived under the open sky. Years of reading during which she crossed Bolivia, Peru, Ecuador, always with a book in hand. As she told it, it was during those years that she started to imagine her artistic project. Years of intellectual euphoria and intense readings, years full of projects and sketches she later erased, convinced that every artist must have a single obsession and just one project. Years in which her very idea of art was reformulated constantly until it was buried behind the terrible intuition that art was nothing but art history. The idea came to her clearly, one summer afternoon of unbearable humidity, as she sat in front of a colonial fort in Cartagena de Indias. Art was nothing but its own story, the story that led to the present moment and that asked for—cried out for—the emergence of the new. That illumination was followed by years of intensive labor, years of notes and readings that would end the day when, floating on the windy waters of Lake Atitlán, the image of the Panajachel volcano finally offered her the missing piece: all art involves judgment. Art was the history of the judgment of art, she thought then. Two days later, she heard a news story on the abandoned tower, and she knew that was where she would set her project into motion. The next day, carrying a very small suitcase, she headed for Puerto Rico with the happy conviction that her years of wandering were finally reaching their end. It was time to sit down and work.

———

Lively, savage, epic—from afar, the picaresque tale of the defendant's life could awaken the enthusiasm of the most blasé reader. The press—always focused on the obvious—jumped all over the description of that journey, mostly trying to bring back some color to a trial that from the start had seemed like a series of expert monologues. The defendant employed all her artistic jargon, and the prosecutor seemed determined to cite as many boring legal documents as possible. The trial had been going on for only three weeks, the witnesses were still to come, the crowd in the courtroom had shrunk, and TV ratings were plummeting. What was left, then? The story of her travels and the gaping abyss between two dates: April 15, 1966, and April 15, 1987. The press tried hard to extract any possible conclusion from a journey that in many ways recalled Che Guevara's mythical travels through southern lands.

To Esquilín, many of the details of her travels didn't fit together. He found it impossible to believe that the defendant had gone unnoticed for so long; it seemed strange that she'd come to the island without a passport identifying her as Virginia McCallister. He found it astounding that so far no one had questioned the most obvious thing: the date of the rupture. What had happened on that April 15, 1966? Esquilín had only needed to read the defendant's file to learn the obvious: on April 15, 1966, in a small New York hospital, Carolyn Toledano was born. He found it odd that neither the date nor the information seemed to catch the attention of the press or the prosecutor. He imagined that the prosecutor must have a different strategy, and that perhaps, with the years, he himself would learn that the law cared little about private lives.

Still, he couldn't shake an intuition. Since the night of Burgos's message, he'd become obsessed with the idea that, hidden among the pages of the second series of notebooks, written in a private code, there was a second, secret story, the weight and pain of which the defendant was trying to bury under the scene of an absurd trial. Every evening as the case progressed, he dedicated several hours to those secondary notebooks that the defendant herself disparaged as meaningless scribbling. He searched for the secret code, analyzed dates, compared trajectories. No one disappears without a reason, he said to himself, thinking of B. Traven and his anarchical pilgrimage to anonymity. No one disappears without a reason, he repeated, while the date—April 15, 1966—blinked on his computer, like the beginning of another story that might have been better to forget.

On one of those nights, as he was paging through one of the notebooks of *The Great South*, he came across a list of places whose names he didn't recognize: Topolobampo, Colônia Cecília, Canudos, Nueva Australia. At first he thought the defendant must have made them up. After giving them a second glance, he thought that maybe they were small towns that she had visited during her long pilgrimage through Latin America, where perhaps she had loved some salt-of-the-earth drunk or local poet. What he found on the following pages, however, gave the lie to his theories.

Written with a copyist's diligence and discipline, organized as precisely as encyclopedia entries, were historical, geographical, and political descriptions of the listed colonies. The towns weren't towns, or even hippie settlements, but small anarchical colonies that a handful of crackpots had built almost two centuries ago during the fever of utopian socialism. A small, five-pointed drawing appeared at the top and bottom of the page, seemingly sketched in a moment of distraction.

Topolobampo (1886–1894). First Mexican colony founded by utopian socialists in the United States, under leadership of Albert Kimsey Owen, the famed civil engineer who would try to finish construction of the Chihuahua–Pacific Railway. He would also attempt a failed project called the Great Southern, which Owen imagined as an interoceanic railway that would start in Norfolk, Virginia, cross all the southern states, and then head into the Tarahumara Mountains in Chihuahua, until it finally reached the bay of Topolobampo. Today, after its failure as a utopian colony, Topolobampo is a port on the Gulf of California, located in the municipality of Ahome in the state of Sinaloa, Mexico. In the old train station you can still see a steel plaque with its original route: Ojinaga–Topolobampo.

Colônia Cecília (1890–1893). Experimental colony founded in 1890 according to anarchist principles. Located in the municipality of Palmeira, in the state of Paraná, led by the Italian journalist and agronomist Giovanni Rossi. Rossi, encouraged by the Brazilian musician Carlos Gomes, went to speak with Dom Pedro II about the possibility of founding a community based on anarchist ideals. After he received a promise of land from the monarch himself, the Brazilian Republic declared its independence, and Rossi's only choice was to buy the very lands he'd been promised. A year later, the colony had almost 250 inhabitants, practitioners of free love. Poverty and the inability to efficiently distribute work, however, would end up forcing many of the colonists to set out for new lands. Two years later, in 1892, barely twenty colonists remained.

Canudos (1893–1897). Political-religious colony founded in 1893 in the Brazilian state of Bahía, under the messianic mandate of the preacher Antônio Vicente Mendes Maciel, who would later be better known by the name Antônio Conselheiro. Under his ideological command, a motley crew of social pariahs—including freed slaves, indigenous people, cangaçeiros, and farmers stripped of their lands—managed to build a community of around thirty thousand inhabitants, and were even able to wage war against the newly formed Republic of Brazil. Its independent and communist nature, along with the monarchist ties of some of its members, forced the Republic to declare war on Antônio Conselheiro and his followers. The national army's first three invasions were bravely fought off by the villagers, but they were conquered in the fourth, when the settlement was burned to the ground. Today the region is underwater as a result of the construction of the Cocorobó dam, by means of which the state intended to bring water to a region battered by drought. When the water level is low, the ruins of the old cathedral poke up above the surface.

Nueva Australia (1893–1894). Paraguayan colony founded under the pretexts of utopian socialism and directed by William Lane, a prominent figure within the Australian worker's movement. Following Lane's ideas, the colony was governed under certain basic precepts: a mixture of communist ideals with policies of racial

separation and abstention from alcohol that eventually brought
the colony to the verge of dissolution. In 1894 two hundred new
colonists arrived, but the colony collapsed soon after, when fifty-
eight members, including Lane himself, decided to flee and form a
new colony they called Cosme, thirty-eight miles south of Nueva
Australia. William Lane would die more than twenty years later,
converted into a defender of the ultra-right wing, writing conservative newspaper columns under a series of pseudonyms.

As he read the entries, Esquilín imagined a ghost town where dozens
of white men walked slowly by, singing sad songs. He thought of William
Lane at the end of his days, now a recalcitrant right-winger. He thought
that a name as dazzling as Giovanni Rossi didn't belong in the Brazilian
jungle. He thought of the underwater ruins of Canudos, which struck him
as the perfect symbol for the great catastrophe that was modern history.
This old gal, he thought, likes her temples in ruins. He remembered the
strange acoustics of the churches of his childhood, the way the preachers'
voices turned to echoes, and the boredom that washed over him when
the homily began. He was distracted by the sound of the phone, but he
told himself there was no need to answer. He reread the passage that his
client had underlined in blue pen, the part about the Great Southern, that
immense railway Owen had dreamed up in a delirium of modernity. He
printed a map of the American continent and tried to follow the train's
imaginary route through southern lands. From east to west, as if doing
battle against the sun. Again, the shrill ring of the phone distracted him,
but he promised himself that he wouldn't answer until a third call.

Half an hour later, just when he was starting to realize that there was no
more story beyond the one apparently projected by his own neurosis, he
found himself drawing in the margins of his notebook the five-point figure
he recognized from many of the defendant's notebooks. It looks like a five
in dominoes, he thought, but another look refined his impression. It looks
like the silhouette of a butterfly drawn in points, he corrected himself. He
started to look in the notebooks for an example of the figure, but the
phone rang again. This time he answered. From the other end of the line,

a bartender's hostile voice informed him that María José Pinillos had come into his bar sloppy drunk, aggressive, and shouting. A young man had gone to the bathroom minutes later and found her lying in her own vomit. When they asked her who she knew on the island, she'd handed them a slip of paper with the lawyer's name and phone number.

Esquilín confirmed that he knew her, then put on a shirt and headed out. Half an hour later, he encountered a lamentable scene: a sloshed woman trumpeting the destruction of history and the end of days.

13

When she entered Bar 413 and ordered the first rum, María José Pinillos had gone two months without alcohol and had been on the island for three days. She flew from Miami on the same plane as Marcelo Collado and Guillermo Porras, although none of them had any way of knowing that the others were also involved with the defendant. When they arrived, all three took their places in the taxi line, but they didn't speak. Pinillos, who was first in line, asked the taxi to drop her off at the address the lawyer had given her, 205 Calle Luna. The old town, quaint and touristy with its cobblestone streets and pastel-painted houses, reminded her of the years she'd spent living in Antigua, Guatemala, when she was young; that was where, in front of the beautiful San Francisco church, she had burned a dozen sacred statues and landed in jail. Putting an end to beauty, she thought, is no easy thing. Three minutes later, in her room on Calle Luna, she opened her suitcase and took out the only book she'd brought—an old volume of poems by César Vallejo. She read two pages of the book and wrote down the first ideas that came to her, then she took out a pen and drove it hard into her left leg. Then she returned to her notebook to record once again her reasoning for this ritual: "Alcoholism is the desire for self-destruction. Driving the point of a pen into my leg is a homeopathic remedy for this desire that will end up annihilating me."

That night, after cleaning the dot of blood that the pen had drawn, she went out to walk along the cobbled streets. She saw drunk young people and lost gringos, dark streets and clubs spilling music, narrow alleyways with small bars that two months ago would have tempted her to perdition. She kept walking until the temptation passed. After a while, tired, she sat down in a plaza. She took out the Vallejo book and started to read a poem whose title, "Epístola a los transeúntes," seemed appropriate for the situation:

Epistle to the Pedestrians

I resume my rabbit day
my night of an elephant in repose.
And to myself I say:

This is my immensity in the raw, in bucketfuls,
this is my delightful weight
that looked under me for a bird;
this is my arm
that on its own refused to be a wing;
these are my scriptures
these are my alarmed balls.
Lugubrious isle will illuminate me continental
while City Hall leans on my intimate collapse
and the assembly closes my parade in spears.

She read the poem a few times out loud and pictured an Italian street, where a small man with an imposing mustache embraces a horse that has just been whipped. Then she returned to the lines: "This is my immensity in the raw, in bucketfuls, this is my delightful weight." She thought of Giacometti's sculptures of spectral walking men, the elegant fragility of horses, the contours of fire that she found so seductive. Afraid of being taken for a crazy woman, she looked around again. There wasn't much to see: a family crossing the plaza, two boys riding skateboards, a giant totem pole statue that struck her as excessive. "Lugubrious isle will illuminate me continental," she read again. How strange the sober world could sometimes be, intoxication always just around the corner. How strange islands could be, always hidden within themselves. Only then did she think—for the first time since she'd arrived—of the defendant. She remembered the woman whose letter had meant salvation, and thought that everything was starting to make sense. They were both, unconsciously, trying to redeem a past full of ashes. Both of them were struggling with a cursed inheritance. When she looked around again, the boys on skateboards and the family had all disappeared. She thought about buying a drink, but Vallejo came to her rescue again.

Two days later, when Esquilín finally managed to make his way through the crowd of punk kids crammed into the 413, he found Pinillos in the midst of a diatribe against the gods. "Fucking Vallejo let me down," she babbled. Esquilín thought this Vallejo must be a former lover, some old and painful loss. Or a current, abusive lover, he thought when he saw the dozen bloody red dots that punctuated the drunk woman's left thigh. While she rambled on, he brought her a glass of water, wiped up the vomit, and apologized to the bartender. Once she was cleaned up, he patted her hair and said, "Easy now, let's go home." Only then did he see the book of poems under her and realize that Vallejo was just a poet. He asked the bartender to put the book into the artist's bag and got ready to walk her to the car.

Once María José Pinillos was asleep on his sofa, Luis Gerardo Esquilín, now stinking of rum and vomit, gave in to his curiosity. He opened the artist's purse, took out the book of poems, and started to read, when a dozen loose pages fell from the book. Filled with shame, cowardly but nosy, the young lawyer closed the door to his room and sat down to steal a look.

At first he thought they were just a series of photographs of mountainous landscapes, spaces that were green but empty. Each photograph was captioned with a series of names that sounded indigenous: Pexlá, Cocop, Ilom, Vicalamá, Cajixay, Amajchel, Jakbentab, Xix, Chemal, Xexocom. Farther down, toward the end, he found a title and a name: *Scorched Earth*, Óscar Farfán. Then he noticed that on the back of the last page, copied in pen, there was a quote written in an incomprehensible language:

> Tuyab'e 1982 kat uluq'a Chaxi'chalanaje' tukukoome' anikitza katchanaj tuvldestacamentoe' tu xemak, Perla tetz tx'avul. Kat ulitz'esachanaj uq'aku kab'ale' tulkatq'ab'i vatulchanaj katojveto' jaq'tze'. Kat tze'kajayil, kuchikoje' katitz'ok chanaj, katiyatz'chanaj talaku txokob'e, askat itz'esajchanaj q'oksam. Kat atinchanaj tukukoome' oxval okajval ch'ich', katchit itxakchanaj kajayil uq'aq'etze'. Unb'ie' Kul tetzik akunb'ale' ukab'ale' vekat tze'i (Nicolás Cobo Raymundo).

He made no attempt to translate. He turned back to the photographs and began to sense a certain absence becoming evident in them as he looked closer. He contemplated the way the weeds grew over that absence with the heavy lethargy of grass overtaking abandoned cemeteries. Then he remembered having read something about scorched earth in the notebooks of *The Great South*. Online, he read:

> The policy of burned or scorched earth is a military tactic consisting of destroying absolutely everything that could be of use to the enemy when an army advances or withdraws across a territory. The historical origin of the term "scorched earth" surely comes from the practice of burning grain fields during wars and conflicts in antiquity. However, it is not limited at all to harvests or provisions, but rather includes any sort of refuge, transport, or supply belonging to the enemy.

Below, two historical examples caught his attention. The first linked the tactic of scorched earth with the military strategies of General William Sherman and his famous March to the Sea. The second clarified the relation between Pinillos and his client: the scorched-earth policy had been used mercilessly by military forces during the Guatemalan civil war. Drawing no further conclusions about the connection, Esquilín flipped through the photographs again. Empty photos, images of mountain weeds, photos where history became a great mausoleum, to be devoured by nature and oblivion. He opened the door, returned the book and papers to the bag, turned off the lights, and lay down to sleep.

When he woke up the next day, he found the artist reading beside the window.

"Why you?" he asked. "Why do you think she chose you, out of all the radical artists—why you, precisely?"

María José Pinillos sipped her coffee before answering, unequivocally, "Because my family history is also full of fire."

That afternoon, after appearing in court, Esquilín visited the apartment shared by three other witnesses. He asked them the same question.

Marcelo Collado, hungover after a night on the town, redolent of marijuana and alcohol, thought Esquilín knew something he didn't. When he realized the lawyer was not going to spill any secrets, he answered, "How should I know? Maybe because no one else has written about the role of law in the writings of Macedonio Fernández. What do I know? Maybe she got up one day, saw my face on some academic portal, and thought a guy with a face like mine would go along with her dumb game." Esquilín's silence only intensified his fears, and Collado started in on a tirade against law and the system, against governments and capital.

"Easy, Collado," said Esquilín. "Truth is, I think the old lady's madder than a goat."

The Venezuelan finally took a breath. "Still," he said. "What this world needs is more madmen like Macedonio." He poured himself a glass of pear juice, turned up the volume on the radio, and sank back into his reading.

Guillermo Porras, on the other hand, shy and insecure, thought the question was an attempt to call his credentials into doubt. He had asked himself that same question more than once. Why that strange honor for someone like him, who had decided to retire from art before even starting? Unable to find an answer, he mentioned his studies at the Rhode Island School of Design, his coursework on the history of conceptual art, the names of his most distinguished professors. He didn't find the confirmation he was seeking in the lawyer's eyes. He asked permission to light a cigarette, and only then, as billows of smoke wafted around his fragile frame, did he finally let himself talk about his thesis on monetary mutilation and art history, about the imaginary artist and his mural of U.S. dollars.

He was about to recite his grade point average and his résumé when Esquilín stopped him: "I already know everything you're telling me. What I'm asking is, do you think there's some personal reason why my client thought to recruit you in particular, and not others?"

Porras held his cigarette in midair. He had confronted the trial as a professional, as cold and objective as the letters the defendant had sent him. The idea that a personal story could be the reason he was summoned struck him as remote and daring. "To tell you the truth, *mae*, I hadn't even thought to look at it from that perspective," he said as he took another drag.

Esquilín showed him the part of the file that mentioned how the last information they had on the defendant before the trial was her November 23, 1976, ticket from JFK to San José, Costa Rica. Surprised, Guillermo

Porras said that Viviana Luxembourg had never once mentioned any such trip to the land of the *ticos*.

Then the three of them sat down to organize their strategy. Halfway through the meeting, Esquilín commented on the absence of Arthur Chamberlain, who should have also been staying in the apartment. Then Collado remembered a letter they'd found when they arrived at the apartment. It was addressed to the lawyer and sent by a certain Constanza Saavedra. Esquilín, recognizing Chamberlain's wife's name, hurried to open and read the letter.

Saavedra wrote that after several medical tests, Chamberlain had been diagnosed with a neuromuscular disease—but the diagnosis had come too late. After giving a speech at a gala in honor of a group of young artists, Chamberlain had suffered a grand mal seizure that had left him paralyzed from the neck down. That was two months ago. Chamberlain had been in physical therapy since then, and it was starting to show positive results. He could move his hands a little, he could take a few steps. He could, in sum, dream of someday painting once again with the frightful exactitude of before. Saavedra closed her letter by expressing the sadness they felt at not participating in the great trial, and wishing them all the best in what was to come. She included one of Chamberlain's drawings.

It was true: the degree of detail he achieved was striking. It looked exactly like a dollar.

Near seven in the evening, they finished their preparations. Complaining about how light the local beer was, Porras took out three cold ones and they toasted to the madness of Viviana Luxembourg. Then, when Collado started to roll the first joint, Esquilín excused himself. He had to meet with the final witness, Gregory Agins. Porras swore he'd read something by the man, though he didn't remember the title exactly. Collado swore he'd never heard of the retired professor.

Esquilín packed up his things and left just as the Venezuelan was taking the first hit. After crossing two streets teeming with cats, he reached the corner where Gregory Agins was staying. From the second-floor balcony, a man with a disheveled appearance and clear-framed glasses greeted him as if he'd been waiting for years.

Face-to-face with the man, Esquilín thought that he could well be the defendant's lover. He carried his years with the shabby ease that comes only with risk and a life well lived, that balance of experience and care that only comes to a man who has nothing to lose. For a brief second he thought he was looking at the disappeared Yoav Toledano, but he knew that was impossible. Esquilín tried to remember how old the man was, and decided he had to be over sixty but under seventy. Agins, in perfect, Mexican-shaded Spanish, invited him in. Without asking, he set a cup of green tea in front of the lawyer.

They spent the next two hours discussing the case, trying to cross the impossible bridge that separated theory and law, while between them, serpentine and restless, a golden cat kept watch. When it climbed up onto the table without the slightest murmur from Agins, he understood that the cat was no stray but another visitor from California. Gregory Agins called it Wittgenstein. All cats, said the old man, are much like philosophers, skeptical and silent, gruff and distant thinkers. Esquilín merely nodded, while he thought maybe this was why he preferred his animals dumber, more loyal, and oafish: he was a dog person. An unexpected doubt suddenly disturbed him. In his relationship with the defendant, was he a cat or a dog?

Two hours later, defeated by the old man's intellectual intensity, he knew that his mind could go no further. They had discussed judicial precedent that existed around the subject: the case of Michelangelo and the Council of Trent, when the artist was forced to admit that the nudes in his portrayal of the Last Judgment were not worthy of the Sistine Chapel; Paolo Veronese facing the Venetian inquisitors, trying to explain why, in his representation of the Last Supper, Jesus Christ was accompanied by two turbaned Turks, a man bleeding from his nose, and a dwarf with a parrot. Over cups of green tea, with the cat snaking around them, they discussed the famous article on *Brancusi v. United States* that had consecrated Agins's intellectual career, and the 1955 destruction of the *Portrait of Winston Spencer Churchill* at the hands of his wife, Clementine. Esquilín couldn't help thinking of María José Pinillos when he imagined that scene. What would she be doing right now? Reading poetry, or walking drunkenly down the streets of Santurce? What did it really mean to be an iconoclast, if not that one was willing to self-immolate?

Agins's intellectual speed left Esquilín no time to speculate. When he returned to himself, the Californian had already moved on to a new case. The lawyer, in search of a way out, asked the old man the same question he'd put to Pinillos, Collado, and Porras: Why do you think that, out of everyone, Viviana Luxembourg chose you in particular?

Gregory Agins leaned forward in his chair, thoughtful, before giving the same reply as the others: a timid "I don't know." Then he seemed to rethink his response.

Agins mentioned his political adventures during the seventies, with a special emphasis on his participation in the socialist commune Los Muchis in the Arizona desert. Los Muchis: Esquilín thought he'd heard the name before, most likely in the defendant's notebooks.

"Maybe we're united by a political commitment, a certain interest in alternative societies, alternative histories," noted Agins. Then he told a long story: the story of the commune at the edge of the desert, a story that the young lawyer found heroic, even though ultimately it was little more than a plagiarized utopia.

The story started on the mountainous campus of the University of California, Santa Cruz, during the spring of 1972, and it ended on the edge of the Arizona desert in the summer of 1975. It began with a redheaded woman who interrupted her friends one day to suggest a spontaneous trip to Mexico, the Mexico of Jack Kerouac, Neal Cassady, the Mexico of the beatniks and the peerless heroin addict William Burroughs—to the Mexico of that little group of gringo poets her friends loved, and about whom she, despite not having read their work herself, knew every story. It ended three years later, when the penultimate member of the group, high as could be on peyote, asked young Gregory Agins to tie him to a horse—a ritual begun by Antonin Artaud, another poète maudit, on the plains of another desert and under the watchful eyes of other Indians.

Between the young redhead's first innocent suggestion and the penultimate man's madness was an incredible chain of events and experiences that made Esquilín think he hadn't lived enough. He had never even left the island, not even to visit his father's family in the Dominican Republic. He had certainly not set foot in that furious Mexico Agins spoke of between peals of laughter, a Mexico where a drunk named Burroughs murdered his wife in a William Tell act gone horribly wrong, and later said that otherwise he never would have become a writer; a Mexico where crazy old Artaud got high and finally disappeared among Indians and peyote. Gregory Agins and his friends went there twenty years later to see what remained of the site where the avant-garde had reached its apotheosis, only to find an empty corner with a small sign that read: MONTERREY 122. That was where the same brave redheaded girl, when she read about Albert Owen's Socialist colonies, suggested founding a colony of their own, fueled by sex and alcohol. An anarchist colony, not on the outskirts of Sinaloa, as Owen had wanted, but in the desert itself, as an homage to that demented Frenchman her friends talked about so much.

The redhead—whose name was Alexandra Walesi—had an idea that was no less brilliant for its simplicity: all avant-garde art, according to her, was the strategic copy of a previous avant-garde. There was no such thing as originality, only the pleasure of repetition. And so, they would be the first avant-garde artists to boast of their plagiarism. And just like that, as Agins told it, they began to prepare for a utopian community that blended the ideals of all their old idols: Albert K. Owen and Antonin Artaud, the beatniks and Herman Hesse, the pill and Che Guevara. The friends strolled through Plaza Garibaldi dreaming of their anarchist commune, vowing not to return to Santa Cruz for a long while. All they were missing was a name.

Gregory Agins, who had also been reading about Owen's utopian projects, suggested Los Muchis, a variation on Los Mochis, the name of the notorious Sinaloan colony.

Over the following weeks, running on alcohol and hallucinogens, they dedicated themselves to building models of their colony. One afternoon, high and walking through the Hotel Casino de la Selva, between murals by

Meza and Siqueiros, they decided that the colony needed a precise shape, a geometry that would tell the stars that they were there to stay. Agins proposed the famous rhodonea curve, discovered by Luigi Guido Grandi around 1725. Walesi imagined a city drawn as the Seed of Life, a figure she said symbolized the seven days of creation. Then a fragile blond girl with a timid voice mentioned that she had heard once about a secret society of Hollywood hippies who tried to build a commune in a Latin American jungle in the shape of a five-pointed figure. According to her, the figure was called a quincunx, and it was said to be the building block of all other natural forms.

Esquilín thought immediately of the five-pointed doodle that he had started to absentmindedly draw in his own notebooks. Ever polite, he waited for the old man to finish his story, and then asked if Agins could draw a map of Los Muchis. As soon as he confirmed it had the same shape as his doodles, he gathered his things, excused himself, and left.

Once he got home, he looked for his notebooks and confirmed what he already knew: the five-point symbol was the same. He remembered copying it from one of the defendant's notebooks, but he didn't know exactly which one. He found many entries online about the quincunx, the name for which he found even stranger in Spanish: *quincunce*. He learned that it took its name from Roman currency. He read the story of a seventeenth-century British writer named Thomas Browne, who had proposed a theory where art and nature coincide, linked by the basic shape of the quincunx. This Thomas Browne was an irremediably young man with a pair of enormous, melancholy eyes that made Esquilín wonder how he himself looked to the jury. He tried to distract himself with thoughts about old Agins, Pinillos and her scorched earth, the defendant's Latin American pilgrimage. Now that, he told himself aloud, was life. He, on the other hand, always so concerned with reputation, wasn't brave enough to leave it all behind and set off in search of adventure.

Or maybe he was, he thought as he gazed at a dozen representations of quincunxes on the screen. Perhaps this trial was precisely the moment to play his cards, to get out of the profession, break the mold, defend another kind of law. The image of the tower rose up in his mind. He thought of all the worlds that were hidden in the world, like those alternative societies young Agins and his friends had tried to replicate without much luck. And then he remembered the page he had copied a few days before, with the list of utopian colonies. He was pleased to recognize, at the beginning and end of the page, the quincunx.

He briefly considered the possibility that it was all a big hoax, a prank that the defendant and her witnesses were playing on him and the law, but ultimately decided those considerations would get him nowhere. Then he looked for the information his client had given him about her correspondance with Agins. He found no mention of the anarchist colonies or the five-pointed figure. Tired and confused, he lay down to play with his dog. He again recalled the enigmatic B. Traven and the phrase from his client's notebooks: "The only true artwork is disappearance itself." He thought about Burgos and his message, full of brittle enigmas, and he told himself that everything in his story was conspiring against him.

It didn't matter. He felt unstoppable as he sat down at his work table and drew the five-pointed figure, as if it were a talisman. Then he fell asleep, mulling over a curious fact old Agins had mentioned a few hours earlier: that a Tarahumara tribesman could run for two days straight without a drop of water.

14

Around that time I got an email from Tancredo in which he talked about a man he'd met walking on the beach. The man was scouring the sand with a metal detector, convinced that someday he would find the treasure that would finally pull him out of poverty: a shining Rolex, a lost emerald, a wedding ring someone had decided to leave behind—but all he found was garbage, the remains of tin cans, corkscrews, coins, and other useless scraps. Then the email drifted into disquisitions on William Howard, the great masters of patience, the characteristics of islands, paintings by Hopper; he wrote more about Burgos, the stutterer, the defendant's strange lucidity, Esquilín's trembling hands. Meanwhile, I mentally rewound the scenes of the trial. I pictured the defendant's face and I couldn't help thinking of Giovanna; I saw her whitish hair and remembered how its strange color gestured toward nothingness and anonymity. If there's a story here, I said to myself, it begins with the false color of Giovanna's hair. Then I went back to reading Tancredo's message, toying with the jade elephant. I thought of all the stories my designer friend had told me, and it occurred to me that all of them were about ruins.

15

Two days later, still dwelling on the defendant's secrets, Luis Gerardo Esquilín watched the prosecutor present the first of his three pieces of central evidence. It was a news item that, according to the prosecution, the defendant had managed to insinuate into a small Sevillian paper, intending for it to spread, stealthily, through the mass media. He claimed the defendant's strategy was always the same: first, find some small provincial paper, preferably one with external contributors, where she could place the fake news item, then watch as the story disseminated like a hushed rumor.

According to the prosecution, in the early nineties, Virginia McCallister—hiding behind the name Maribel Martínez—had managed to sneak in an article that associated a new medicine with a pharmaceutical product that had been used in the detention and torture of hundreds of prisoners during the Vietnam War. The article cited a very long list of renowned academics. The defendant's strategy, as the prosecutor explained, was to place her false news items within a network of possible truths that would make it circulate without garnering too much attention. Then, when the news picked up speed, the defendant would send a short note signed with her alias to the first newspaper, apologizing for a series of small mistakes that invalidated her article. The newspaper would publish the letter and issue its own apology, not realizing that the news was already circulating independently.

For the next half hour, both the audience in the courtroom and the one watching on TV observed the absurd voyage of Virginia McCallister's false news through the international press. They saw the article that was initially published by the small Sevillian paper reproduced two days later by a tabloid in Madrid, not without the exaggeration typical of the Spanish press, then in Barcelona, Valencia, Olot, and Bilbao. From Basque country the news leapt to North America, appearing nine days after its initial publication in a small Mexican paper. From there it exploded: in under three days, it appeared in twenty outlets, including three major papers, and it was also reproduced during those days in Costa Rica, Uruguay, and Colombia. Only then, with the news circulating widely, did a short note appear in the Sevillian paper, clarifying that it was all a mix-up, and actually, the medicine had no relationship to military torture. This time the note was signed by a Jaime Melendi, who assured readers that his employee, Maribel Martínez, had been fired for her carelessness. As the prosecutor explained, this was all part of the plan. With that note, the defendant finally set the news free from the laws of truth and kept subsequent investigations from discovering the farce. What the defendant understood very well was that by then, the news had gathered enough momentum that it would oblige readers to look at the pharmaceutical industry through different eyes. The story then crossed the borders to the north and was reproduced by several U.S. papers that seemed to care little that in Seville, the initial paper had printed a second item apologizing for its mistake. Once the U.S. press had been infiltrated, the story seemed omnipresent. It was printed in Croatian and Romanian papers, Asian magazines, and even in a small informative pamphlet produced by a medical association in Mozambique. The damage was done.

Tancredo thought again of the old man with the metal detector in the beach town. He told himself that soon, history would be nothing but a great landfill of informational garbage. Two days later, at Gaspar's barbershop, he said: "Someday there'll be more information junk than world, more garbage than dumps." Gaspar just laughed and told him he was going crazy from that trial. He got up and handed a broom to Tancredo, saying: "If you're so worried about garbage, go on and sweep."

That week, the witnesses were called one by one to the stand, where they tried to reframe the prosecutor's examples as art. Guillermo Porras, trembling and timid, invoked before the jury the works of Belgian artist Francis Alÿs, which he said were an attempt to reclaim the "sociological poetic of the rumor." He cited Alÿs's 1997 piece *The Rumor*, in which the artist spread a false story about a man who left his hotel one day and didn't come back, and made it real. With the help of three members of the Tlayacapan community, Alÿs managed to disseminate the story in such a way that local imagination took care of the rest: inventing the man's face, his age, his story. Three days later, as possible explanations for his mysterious dis-appearance made the rounds, the police even issued a poster with a tenta-tive sketch of the individual. As Porras explained, the piece was all about exploring the methods by which a public truth is constructed.

As we all listened, we couldn't help but think of the game called "tele-phone." Children line up and pass a secret down the line, each whispering into the ear of the next until it reaches the last child, who has the responsi-bility of proclaiming the secret—inevitably distorted—aloud. The logic of Alÿs's work was something we knew very well—we'd discovered it as chil-dren. The young lawyer held up one of the 247 notebooks the defendant had supposedly compiled and read a short excerpt she'd cited from Alÿs: "If somebody were to say something to someone, and that someone were to repeat it to someone else, and that someone were to repeat it to someone else . . . then, at the end of the day, something is being talked about, but the source will have been lost forever." More than one laugh came from the au-dience. If that was art, then the kid's game was as well. The absurdity of the trial was made clear: this woman was on trial for trying to play a child's game at the age of seventy. I think it was at that moment when, for the first time, many people started to see the defendant with compassionate eyes.

She, however, didn't seem to be after any compassion. She seemed deter-mined not to show any emotion. From time to time, when one of her wit-nesses was questioned, she made notes in a small notebook. It became clear that her study was a continual process and that the artwork hadn't ended the day of her arrest. I looked at her and told myself it would take just one call from me to put an end to that whole absurd theater, but some-thing told me that would be a betrayal of Giovanna's memory. I turned off the TV, started to read a random novel, and waited for sleep, sure that the next morning I'd have an email from Tancredo that would do me the favor of imagining all possible endings.

Over the course of that week, the prosecutor posed the same question to each of the witnesses for the defense.

He began with a historical anecdote. On October 23, 2002, a group of Chechen terrorists stormed the Dubrovka Theater, taking as prisoner the more than 850 spectators who'd filled the place that night to watch the musical comedy *Nord-Ost*. In exchange for setting them free, the terrorists were asking for Russian withdrawal from Chechnya and an end to the war. Three days later, on October 26, when Russian military forces filled the theater with toxic gas and entered the theater, they found 138 cadavers: 39 of them terrorists, the rest civilians. Then the prosecutor brought up a short and little-known Russian novel written almost a century earlier, in 1905, by a Bolshevik named Boris Stolypin. *The Theater* told a fictional story that was virtually identical to the one the Russian people would experience a century later: one night, in the middle of a production of *Othello* put on by Konstantin Stanislavsky's company, hundreds of Bolshevik soldiers took over the theater. In Stolypin's novel the events were an allegory of the opening of art to the political realm, a sort of "historical awakening" that had to be understood through the lens of Marxism.

"Who," the prosecutor asked, "can assure us that the horrible events of October 23, 2002, were not influenced by this novel? And, assuming they indeed were, does that tragedy become—as the defense's doubtful argument seems to suggest—an artwork, merely because of its inspiration?" The entire courtroom fell silent as Marcelo Collado searched desperately for a way out. He stammered indecisively before citing three French philosophers on the subject of intention. According to Collado, even if one of the terrorists had read that book, which was unlikely, given how little-known it was, the attack could not be considered in artistic terms; it lacked what the Venezuelan, after one of his philosophers, called "artistic intention."

"Who," the prosecutor countered, "could assure us that the defendant's so-called artistic intention was real, and not a mask behind which to hide her *criminal* intentions?"

Collado, breathing nervously, went back to babbling about incomprehensible theories that did nothing but betray his own confusion to the jury.

Later, Guillermo Porras and Gregory Agins tripped over the same question. Porras, sweating profusely, sought to draw dubious distinctions between the two cases, arguing that the prosecutor's scenario violated the absolute boundary of art by enacting violence against one's neighbor. After the Costa Rican's noble and Christian reply, Agins tried to return to Collado's intuition by suggesting that the more than two hundred notebooks that the defendant had written over the course of her project were irrefutable proof that, in her case, the project had been conceived of as art from the beginning. He closed by saying that for conceptual art, the category under which he said the defendant's project fell, documentation was the fundamental evidence of artistic intention. As examples, one could look at the manifestos of Costa, Escari, and Jacoby, and also the writings of Hélio Oiticica, Sol LeWitt, Mel Bochner, Adrian Piper, Yvonne Rainer, Michael Baldwin, Lee Lozano, Kynaston McShine, Cildo Meireles, Sigmund Bode, Lucy Lippard, Rolf Wedewer, Victor Burgin, and Robert Smithson. The list only further confused the jury. Then, in his hoarse, sonorous voice, he said that he had looked through the photocopies of the notebooks and was convinced that the work belonged within the conceptual tradition he'd just evoked, and was equally sure that in the Chechen case there was no such artistic conception. Art, he declared, was a matter of history and documentation.

When María José Pinillos failed to arrive in time for her testimony, Luis Gerardo Esquilín became desperate and restless. He decided that he had no other option but to move up the presentation of one of his secret weapons.

After an hour's recess, everyone returned to the courtroom to find a long collapsible table had been set up, and on it were arranged some twenty-odd numbered boxes. Solemn and silent, two court employees were removing from the boxes the defendant's famous notebooks.

"Two hundred forty-seven," thundered Esquilín as soon as the final notebook was placed on the table. Two hundred forty-seven reasons to believe that his client had thought through the project's artistic logic from beginning to end. Then, with a conviction he seemed to have only recently gained, he invited the jury to page through the notebooks, and he returned to his seat beside the defendant.

The scene was marked by a certain anachronistic charm: the twelve members of the jury walked deliberately around the table, wearing white gloves as they inspected those notebooks the defendant had accumulated over two decades. Perhaps she had always known that this moment would come someday. Perhaps the newly baptized Viviana Luxembourg had foreseen the inevitable arrival of the digital age and had understood that soon the handwritten archive would come to embody a vanishing form of experience and authority. Certainly, when we saw the pile of notebooks on the table, we were impressed above all by the sheer amount of material. Those notebooks could well have been empty. The important thing was that they were there, they took up space, had a presence.

Tancredo remembered the intuition he'd had some days earlier, that the world was filling up with junk and that someday there would be no more room for it all. The future was a garbage world, an information world, he thought as he listened to the lawyer start speaking again. Esquilín asked whether anyone present found it credible that the defendant had undertaken so many years of theoretical work in pursuit of vulgar, criminal ends. Spending so many years pondering the framework from which to understand her project could only be the work of an artistic imagination.

Then he approached the table, picked up a notebook, and began to read aloud. In the passage, the defendant suggested that all art led to judgment, that all art was, at the end of the day, the staging ground for the discrepancy between the law of the present and the law of the future, between legal language and artistic language.

To Tancredo, the quotation seemed arbitrary and unnecessary. He had the strange sense that the defendant was starting to control the nervous young man's speech and logic. Then he thought about Burgos, about Miguel Rivera, the small drawings of Karl Wallenda that the defendant drew on napkins from La Esperanza. This woman's *intention*, he thought, is to make them all into her little puppets, to reach the end of the story listening only to the echoes of her own voice.

After leaving the courthouse, the lawyer met María José Pinillos at the entrance to his house. Drunk and weepy, the Guatemalan apologized for not having shown up in court. Then she said that all the witnesses had been wrong: the truly brave thing would have been to admit that the terrorist attack, too, was art. Ethics didn't matter. Luis Gerardo Esquilín just looked at her with a mixture of compassion and contempt, the way we all look at the monster we're afraid of becoming.

Disturbed by her boyfriend's long nights of work, afraid the trial was coming between them, Esquilín's girlfriend, Mariana, spent her free mornings nosing around among the papers the lawyer left behind. That was how she discovered his interest in that strange five-pointed figure, in the anarchist colonies, in the theories hidden in the notebooks dedicated to *The Great South*. One day, she found what seemed to be the small sketch of a map in the margin of a random page. Amazed at the level of detail, she searched in her desk drawers for the old magnifying glass her grandmother had given her, and when she finally found it, she was surprised to see that the drawing seemed to be a blueprint of a small city organized according to the geometry of the hermetic quincunx. Some twenty names formed a cloud around the miniature drawing. She sensed that it was something important, but she couldn't decipher exactly how this new piece fit into the jigsaw puzzle that her distant boyfriend was trying to reconstruct. She merely marked the page with a yellow Post-it, in the hopes that Esquilín would find it in the coming days.

She didn't have to wait long. That very night, after leaving María José Pinillos with Porras and Collado, Esquilín returned home and began to consult his papers. He opened to the page marked by Mariana's Post-it, and, accustomed as he was to the defendant's lists and doodles, at first he didn't notice the drawing's importance. Then he understood why Mariana had left her grandmother's old magnifying lens on his work desk. He picked it up and held it over the drawing, and was surprised to find the perfect scale drawing of a city composed of small quincunxes. Unsettled, he closed the notebook, threw the contents of his mug into the sink, and decided he needed a rest. He went into the bedroom and found Mariana asleep with the dog.

He got up six hours later, at dawn, convinced he'd heard a gunshot. He found nothing but his anxious dog clawing at the edge of the bed. Unable to fall back asleep, he got dressed, reheated the pot of coffee from the night before, put the leash on the dog, and went out for a walk. The animal calmed, he went back to the apartment, poured himself another cup of coffee, and then picked up the magnifying lens.

There was the map; the night hadn't changed a thing.

He set aside the magnifying glass and was about to call Agins, when in the cloud of names surrounding the map he recognized that of Maribel Martínez, the pseudonym the defendant had used to sign her first false news item. One by one, then, he copied out the other names on that page. He thought he vaguely recognized some of them, but he didn't know from where. Then he did call Agins to describe his newest discovery, sure the old man would have more clues, but he was surprised to hear that throughout their correspondence, the defendant had never mentioned the quincunx. He hung up without an explanation and headed for the police archive, where the evidence record was kept. Each one of the names written on the minuscule map corresponded to one of the fictional identities the defendant had used to disseminate her false rumors.

That day, the prosecutor presented a second false news item as evidence, this time related to an American oil company in the Middle East and its relationship with certain ultra-right-wing groups in Australia. Attributed to a Jeremy James, the article appeared in a Guatemalan newspaper, where it began its pilgrimage through southern lands before taking the leap to the United States. Once it infiltrated the U.S. media, it was reproduced around the world. The same logic, the same blueprint, the same crime. Luis Gerardo Esquilín sat next to his client, silent, showing no sign of his suspicions. No one could imagine that an image was eating away at him: the map of the colony in miniature, and along with it, the list of names that no doubt included Jeremy James. No one could detect a thing, not even the slightest disquiet, perhaps because not even he knew exactly what he felt.

When the session was over, Luis Gerardo Esquilín asked to meet with his client alone. He found Virginia McCallister as calm as ever, satisfied with how the trial was going, with the witnesses' testimonies, the lawyer's arguments. They discussed their final strategies, the possibilities that remained to them. He again had the feeling that the defendant cared little about the actual result of the trial, the years she could spend in jail, a slow death behind bars. She seemed to be making a different play.

Restless and sweaty, he opened his briefcase, searched among his papers until he found the one he wanted, and placed it on the table. There was the real evidence: the photocopy of the small map and the list of names. On a separate paper, he drew a small quincunx and asked:

"What does this shape mean?"

At first he thought he could see a tremor in the defendant's eyes, but her voice emerged terribly collected and serene:

"Nothing."

Esquilín thought about telling her he knew the whole story, about Pinillos's scorched earth and Agins's anarchist colonies, the whole underground story the defendant seemed to be hiding, but the attempt suddenly seemed futile. The old bag can rot in jail, he told himself furiously. He stashed the papers, stammered some insult in English, and left the room without a goodbye.

17

Since her arrival on the island, María José Pinillos had not tired of claiming that the only reason she'd agreed to be a witness in that absurd trial was that she wanted to see the infamous tower where the defendant had lived. Knowing that the end of the trial was approaching, the Guatemalan's complaints had multiplied, and now she added an impossible promise: if someone would take her to the tower, she wouldn't consume another drop of alcohol. Overwhelmed by work, exasperated by Pinillos's immature entreaties, Esquilín had managed to put off the request for weeks. But when he got home the day he confronted the defendant, he soon tossed aside his work papers and told his girlfriend he was fed up with the trial. He dialed the number of the mobile phone Porras had bought for Pinillos, and promised her that he would show her around the tower. When he went to pick her up the next day, he found her sitting in a plaza full of pigeons, reading Vallejo and smoking an electronic cigarette. Seeing her like that, anyone would have thought she was a soul at peace.

Pinillos's first impression when she saw the tower was that it was a modern building even in its incompleteness. Any Guatemalan would have been happy living there, but its luxury was stunted. She liked its atmosphere of precarious modernity, the musical whisper of its ruinous hallways, the labyrinthine feeling of being in a world that followed its own rules. They were ready to start the climb to the defendant's old apartment when a whistle caught their attention. It was a man with a lively mustache whom Esquilín rushed to greet. In his office, with the noise of the horse races in the background, Pinillos—a little bored and tired—watched as Esquilín and the man talked about the trial, about the defendant and the tower. According to this man, things were stacked in the defendant's favor. How could someone be put on trial for such a silly thing? How could someone conceive of a simple game of telephone as a crime? Esquilín tried to change the subject, saying that the cards had been dealt and it would all be over very soon. Still, the man returned to the subject, this time recounting the defendant's strange routine: her extreme hermeticism, her visits to La Esperanza café, the sketches she used to draw on any paper napkin she had at hand. Then, when he finally got bored with the subject, he went over to the radio, turned up the volume, and said goodbye, adding, "Your gringo sidekick is around here somewhere."

Esquilín was stupefied. He didn't know what gringo the guard was referring to; as far as he knew, he had no sidekicks. And then, as Pinillos disappeared down the hallway, he started to ask around. An old man in a flowered shirt told him that the gringo had left for La Esperanza half an hour ago. Not much caring where Pinillos had gotten to, the lawyer followed the old man's directions to the café. Ten minutes later, disgusted by the crowd of mangy dogs he met along the way, he finally saw the sign; trepidatious, he took a step inside. Two boys looked at him defiantly, and across from them he saw a fat man with blond hair who was playing with a domino set.

"Gringo," he said. The two boys rose anxiously from their seats, ready to tell him off. A brief gesture from the fat man—a gesture that struck the lawyer as particularly Latin—seemed to save him.

Cornered by the lawyer, who seemed to have aged ten years in a couple of months, Tancredo explained everything: his job as a journalist, his attempts to copy the defendant's strange routine. Incredulous, sure that Tancredo was part of the conspiracy growing behind his back, Esquilín asked to see the napkin drawings that the old man had mentioned. Neither of them could contain their laughter as they looked at the old napkins where, every afternoon, the defendant had sketched the same comic strip of Wallenda walking the tightrope.

They sat down to talk. According to Tancredo, after three months of imitating the defendant's routine, he'd only managed to confirm what he already knew: you couldn't copy a life. They talked about the tower, old Gaspar and the barbershop, the building's upper floors, and Sergeant Burgos. Tancredo was surprised to hear that Esquilín had gotten a message from his old friend, a message in which, as the young lawyer explained, the policeman mentioned a stutterer named Miguel Rivera, as well as a mural and a strange mountain where children were kings. Tired of keeping secrets, Esquilín confided in his new acquaintance the details of his latest discoveries: the anarchist colonies in the shape of the quincunx, the defendant's interest in scorched earth, the map drawn in miniature. Feeling a sense of déjà vu, Tancredo remembered a conversation he'd had with Burgos two weeks before he disappeared, when Burgos had talked about the correlation between the defendant's stories and those of the stutterer. According to Burgos, the afternoon when they'd discovered the defendant, she had mentioned a false article about a strange mountain inhabited by enlightened children, the same mountain that Miguel Rivera would mention mockingly two days later. That repetition still hounded Burgos long after, every time he remembered the series of young faces he had seen on the stutterer's computers the day of his unexpected visit. Tancredo said he had tried to follow up on that detail but that it hadn't led anywhere; he ordered two beers and they spent the next hour in a simple game of dominoes. In the end, they both swore to follow that clue until they found out where it led.

18

"If one thing is clear in this story," Tancredo would write me a week later, "it's that meaning always comes too early or too late, never on time."

Two days after meeting with the lawyer in La Esperanza, Tancredo watched as the prosecutor presented his final piece of evidence. Soon he recognized the story as the one that the defendant, in an attempt to explain her art, had mentioned to Burgos that first afternoon: he recognized the mention of an anarchist colony in Latin American lands, the supposed participation of a person who later would be an upper executive of a U.S. company, the strange role that children played in that colony. He even came to suspect, very briefly, that Esquilín himself had passed on the story to the prosecutor as a secret form of revenge on his client, but what he heard next made him think that it was, rather, the defendant's final trick.

The story had been published in a small newspaper in Costa Rica just two weeks before the defendant was detained. The piece seemed to fit the typical profile of articles the defendant had infiltrated into the press: the same process of circulation, the same strategy of insertion, the same absurd pilgrimage through the media.

Then the prosecutor explained that the article was attributed to Marie Sherman, a clear alias of Virginia's, whose middle name was Marie and whose mother's maiden name was Sherman, as the state archive confirmed. Just as the defendant had inscribed a quota of reality on the news item by leaving traces of her old name, the article itself was not entirely false. It was, even, in a certain sense, true. There was a record of such an anarchist colony, it was known that the future businessman had participated in it; there were even rumors about the unusual role that children had played in the colony. Unable to process so much information at once, we all watched the prosecutor call the defendant to testify.

We watched her climb up onto the stand with her usual elegance, answer question after question with the same aloofness as always. Until—to our shock—we were witness to how, bit by bit, the prosecutor managed to chip away her layers of coldness and indifference. We all watched as he presented her with a simple date—April 15, 1966—before asking if it reminded her of anything special. When she replied what we all already knew, namely, that the date signaled the beginning of her twenty-year amnesia, he repeated the question and added, "Isn't this also the birthday of someone special?" After her shaken silence, we heard him press further: "Isn't this the birthday of your daughter, Carolyn Toledano?" It was then that we felt that the varnish had finally worn down, leaving exposed the throbbing, nervous face of the mother we'd all seen in the family photos, the human face of that woman who'd spent nearly thirty years searching for anonymity.

The prosecutor called for his last piece of evidence to be brought in. Two men dressed in black entered carrying a large poster that they placed in front of the defendant and facing the jury. At first, as it was turned away from us, no one—not the spectators in the courtroom or the TV viewers at home—could see what it was.

The prosecutor asked if the defendant recognized the image. Finally stripped of her theories, she started to tremble, and then burst into tears. I think no one present in that room will ever be able to forget those tears. No one will forget the defendant's broken, weepy voice as she confirmed that she recognized the image, or the stubborn coldness with which the prosecutor, glimpsing his triumph, merely took the poster in hand and showed it to the jury, then the viewing public.

It was a family photo like any other, a photo that wouldn't have seemed particularly noteworthy were it not for the indigenous little boy standing between the girl and her mother; on the boy's face, we could all see the tattooed shape of a quincunx. This photograph, the prosecutor concluded, had been taken during the first months of 1977 by Yoav Toledano, the defendant's disappeared husband, during their stay in the infamous anarchist colony. Once the defendant had recovered, the prosecutor went on with his interrogation, but it mattered little. No one would forget the sight of her weeping over the image that had finally forced her to confront the past she'd tried so hard to escape.

That day, as I watched the image zoom in on the photograph again, I thought about how everyone would remember it as a painful but abstract picture of a family pushed to the limit by passion. I, on the other hand, was doomed to remember it as a private story, a past that led directly to the face I recognized in the photo I now saw incessantly on-screen. Giovanna. I looked at the picture again and imagined her in her living room, telling stories of insects and jungles, of the tropical journey that in the end would fill her with opaque silences. Then I remembered the photos I'd seen in old Toledano's workshop, and I asked myself where this story would end. That day I received another message from Tancredo, a single line: "Tragedy or farce?"

19

Three days later, when the sentencing hearing began, the prosecutor returned to what happened the day he confronted the defendant with the photo. He alleged that this was clearly a woman fully aware of her actions, who had found in art the perfect way to evade responsibility. According to him, knowing that she would soon be caught, Virginia McCallister had prepared those notebooks as a final escape route, hoping to receive from the jury a compassion she didn't deserve. The tears had made it clear that behind the lies was hidden a real story whose consequences the defendant refused to accept. Art, like life, he added, has repercussions. It was up to the law to regulate the consequences. One could put a lie into circulation, but one could not live a life under a lie, he said. He left it to the jury whether they wanted to imagine for their children a world where art was more important than family.

Convinced that his work was done, Luis Gerardo Esquilín merely summarized the arguments he had outlined throughout the trial. Then, in a voice that gave him away as a finally matured man, cynical and disbelieving, he cited B. Traven's line he'd so admired: "The creative person should have no other biography than his works." He repeated the phrase in his own Spanish translation: "El artista es aquel que no ostenta más biografía que sus obras." If anyone should speak, he concluded, it was the defendant, and he gave the floor to her.

The face of the woman who walked to the stand that day bore no trace of the emotional calamity she'd suffered when confronted with that family photograph. Her fortitude recovered, she took the stand with her customary elegance, as though the previous session had been nothing but a nightmare. If we hadn't all witnessed, just three days before, the devastating sight of her moral collapse, no one would have imagined that this blond, blue-eyed woman was keeping a secret. Still, the damage was done: we'd seen her cry, and the memory of her collapse helped us intuit the cracks, deep and quavering, in a speech that to all appearances was as flawless and infallible as a medieval castle.

She started by talking about the temporal discrepancy between art and law. How could it be that artistic discourse was more advanced than legal discourse? How could we accept that what in the world of art was seen as absolutely valid was seen by the law as a criminal gesture? How should we think about this discrepancy between the discourses that made up the world? Then we listened to her talk about the speeds of the world, about the slowness of the law in catching up to art, about the separation of the world into thousands of private languages. According to her, contemporary society ran the risk of catastrophically repeating the ancient myth of Babel, the dissemination of the divine language into millions of private ones, specialized and incomprehensible. Art was the route of possible return to unified language and a real political community.

Before the stupefied gazes of the audience, the jury, and the judge, she went on to read a list of almost four hundred names, a list that included many of the artists who had had to confront the dictates of the law. She read the list in a monotone, as though emphasizing that there was no escape from this story whose memory she now salvaged as a kind of homage.

Then, without asking for compassion or understanding of any sort, Virginia McCallister walked to the defense's bench and sat down next to her lawyer. Luis Gerardo Esquilín had listened to it all, but all he could think about was the family photo he'd seen three days before.

20

In this story, thought Tancredo as he entered the tower, there are too many loose ends, too many orphan narratives: Burgos's pilgrimage north, the stutterer's enigmatic disappearance, the arbitrary doodles of Wallenda, the incomplete story of Esquilín's discoveries. Then he corrected himself: all stories were necessarily incomplete, any story was covered by secrets in the end.

He'd gone to the tower to say goodbye. He spent the early-afternoon hours in Gaspar's barbershop, and when it came time to leave, he announced that he wouldn't be back. Then he walked to La Esperanza, ordered a coffee with milk, and started to read. He spent half an hour reading a book about marine algae and then, when exhaustion started to weasel in, he asked for the set of dominoes. He played for half an hour, and only then, when he saw that nothing new was happening, no revelation was appearing, he told the two boys of his departure. Ten minutes later, carrying a photograph of Cano, the old salsa singer, he looked at the tower and thought about going in one last time, but an unexpected sight held him back. On the stairs that led to the tower's entrance, he recognized María José Pinillos. She was dressed as a clown; it seemed that alcohol had finally won out. He handed her ten dollars, and thought again about the man who spent his days at the beach with a metal detector, looking for lost treasure.

In one of the defendant's notebooks, Esquilín found a paragraph that struck him as pertinent to the situation. There, among eschatological reflections, the defendant mentioned an anecdote that the lawyer thought was strangely illuminating, even though precisely what interested him was its lack of conclusion.

In the year 1646, a Jew by the name of Sabbatai Zevi, born in the city of İzmir, proclaimed himself the Messiah and prophesied that the end of days would come two years later, in 1648. The year came; the end didn't. The strange thing about the story was, instead of outing him as a mere impostor, it was precisely his failure that made him famous. From then on, he was seen in public plazas, showered in honors, proclaiming himself the Messiah—unable, though, to predict the true end. A man living after the end of times, thought the lawyer.

How, then, to conclude? Perhaps, thought Tancredo, it was best to confine oneself to the pleasure of objective, brief facts. On September 17, after four hours of deliberation, Virginia McCallister, also known as Viviana Luxembourg, was sentenced to twenty years in prison, pending any new charges. The defendant didn't cry when she heard the sentence.

Letter to Luis Gerardo Esquilín, Esquire

(Viviana Luxembourg / Virginia McCallister, January 24, 2012)

Today, out my tiny window, I saw a flock of birds cut through the faultless blue of the sky, and in their inaccessible shapes I thought I saw an image of my own freedom. There were so many of them, all identical in their anonymous jet black, and for a second I thought I saw a possible escape in their aerial games. Then I remembered those years I spent in front of the camera lenses, those days when they all looked at me and I was an image that everyone but me could see. For just an instant, I again felt that strange sensation of being pure image. I can't lie. I must admit that sometimes I liked the freedom of being surface without essence. But then, in the gaps of silence that yawned between the moments of filming, I understood that they—the men, the cameras, the screen—they all thought they possessed me. They believed their rectangles held me prisoner. It was a sad realization. But today I saw the flock of birds break the tedium of the blue afternoon and I laughed, thinking how those people didn't know I never felt as free as in the moments when, though only for a second, I managed to become pure image, just a mask, a being capable of constantly shifting form, changing personalities like names. And then, when I heard the sound of the now-distant birds, when I heard their warble reaching me from somewhere else, someplace outside my field of vision that belonged to fantasy and desire, I thought of Yoav. I remembered the photographs Yoav took of me as a teenager—Yoav, who in a way had been the only one to really *see* me, the only one who saw me beyond the frame of the photos printed in the magazines—and I couldn't help but remember the picture he took of me that day in the middle of the jungle. I saw him as he pressed the shutter and I recognized what I felt that afternoon: the sad sensation that his eyes, too, held something of prison and punishment. I imagined him months later, developing those photographs where he would ultimately see me as everyone had seen me until then, within the rectangle of the photographic frame. And I told myself it didn't matter, that I had to be brave. I had to return to the original intuition I'd had when I was young, when, in front of the cameras that tried to imprison me, I'd understood that any photograph was a mere copy, a copy of a copy, and that I, like that image, was free to run and to reproduce without any feeling of guilt. Free to reproduce the way frogs do in ponds, their tadpoles all identical and yet different. Free to be at the same time that woman whose face Yoav depicted, and to be, nevertheless, eternally another, the woman I had always wanted to be, the same one who now was returning to her ambition, and I understood that, though everyone thought it was foolish, my responsibility was to pursue the intuition that had brought me to the jungle, until I reached an end. I thought about things like that, until the sound of the birds was lost in the afternoon silence and there was nothing for me to do but sit down and write you this letter.

There is no god and we are his prophets.

—Cormac McCarthy, *The Road*

1

For moments at a time, in the landscape's populous calm, the only thing that can be heard is the camera as it flashes. For that instant, all that exists is him, the camera, and the impression that will be left to a future he can't see, but on which he has bet it all. For that instant, nothing exists but him and his belief. Him and his future. Then, gradually, bringing him back to the jungle, the sonata of the roiling tropics filters in: the cacophony of birds, the fluttering of uncaged chickens, the snore of a tired native, the hiccup of some drunken Englishman. Still farther off, in a terribly singular and painful space, the sobs of the daughter whose cries he now hears again.

Only then does he take his eye from the camera and look at her.

Just ten years old, she has the heavy gaze of an insomniac and a terrible pallor that makes him think of Nordic latitudes he's never seen. Beside the girl, a forcefully beautiful woman soothes her with a hand he knows well. With her other hand, his wife labors over a small, red leather notebook, the same one in which, ten days earlier, she wrote: "Day 1, The journey begins." Only ten days and already the trip feels long, heavy, routine. Ten days have passed since a rusted-out bus left them on the threshold of what they dare to call a jungle, but that at times seems like nothing more than a giant garbage dump left behind by an absentee god.

He is distracted by the grunting rumble of a pig as it delves into the garbage. And then he takes in the full scene that surrounds him: the couple of drunken Brits to one side finishing off a bottle of gold rum; the atmosphere of lethargy and siesta over which a teeming nature looms, superimposed; the drugged-out German restaging his theatrical monologue for a laughing group of natives. The rest of the pilgrims sporadically dot the scene, resting under small tin roofs where the last drops of water drum a monotonous beat. And beyond, a man with tired eyes and unusual strength returns to his indecipherable prayer. Ten days have passed since this man, in his rough voice and unplaceable accent, promised them that by month's end they would reach the young seer.

2

They call him the apostle. His arms are tattooed with symbols of war, and over a dozen plastic rosaries hang around his neck. His voice is hoarse, withdrawn. His speech is like a delusional monologue, a private and endless prayer to fill the empty hours. *Gringo maldito*, the natives call him behind his back: damned gringo. He refuses to say a word to them. Even so, five of them go everywhere with him. It's rumored that he came in search of drugs and then found out he could never go back. It's rumored that he comes from a moneyed family, and that when he was young, he showed promise in the theater. It's rumored that enlightenment came to him decades ago in the midst of the jungle, beside the immense tree he claims to be guiding them toward. They call him the apostle because that's what he calls himself. They call him the apostle, but sometimes, the pilgrims have the feeling he's nothing but a tour guide, a drugged Virgil for credulous gringos. Still, you only have to look again, or listen to him in his endless prayer, to know that he, at least, believes in everything he has promised. Now, three stinking pigs meander around him in the mud, while farther on, the natives play cards to ride out their boredom. They all wear American brand names and the ironic expressions of unbelievers. They all—natives and pilgrims alike—call him the apostle, because he promises things. Ten days ago, for example, he promised them that in one month's time they will come to an enormous archipelago in the middle of the jungle, and that there, at the foot of a great fallen tree, the seer will show them the way. In his eyes, somewhere between belief and madness, the gamble of a generation is made manifest.

Ten days have passed since they started their journey on foot, five since the little girl started to get sick. The whole time, the jungle has done nothing but contradict their expectations. The naked natives wear T-shirts with rock band logos; in the place of exuberant nature, there are garbage dumps; instead of lawlessness, the state is omnipresent. Everywhere they go they encounter police, solemn border agents who fight their own boredom by assiduously checking travel documents. Far from the paradise they'd dreamed of, the jungle reveals its most modern face—its ruinous, border-town face.

Nevertheless, they well know that nature is there, latent like a sleeping scorpion. They sense it at night, in the utter darkness that envelops them. They hear it, rather than see it, in the whisper of nighttime animals; the fluttering fowl; the croak of the frogs, like nocturnal birds; the murmur of the insects always poised to wage war against the mosquito net. He, however, has been tasked specifically with making nature visible: as a photographer, he is to document the trip. That's his place: halfway between participation and observation, between belief and irony. Only five years earlier, he earned his living taking photos of the most coveted models of New York. Today, he is following a man who has made an impossible promise. He is chasing after a drugged man's invisible dream.

3

In the evenings, when the heat seems to be winning the battle, they sleep. On the third night, the mother dreams. She dreams she is in a house, safe and calm. Outside, the swish of leaves. Raindrops drum on the roof. She dreams that the storm outside slowly grows until it becomes omnipresent. Then she starts to feel afraid. Her family is a distant pull that makes her think she has to go out, into the yard that has become a dark forest full of owls and bears. In the house, in a corner, a man rather like the apostle cuts out newspaper articles to glue to a corkboard. A sound distracts her. A murmuring cry; her daughter is out there, in the storm. She steels herself and ventures toward the door that marks the threshold between inside and out. But there is no outside. There is no nature, only a great void where history loses its mind. And all is placid and terrible at the same time.

She wakes up crying.

Beside her, the sick little girl is sleeping, while from far away her husband asks her what's wrong.

"I dreamed that nature didn't exist."

4

During the day they cross villages lost in the jungle, wrapped in the climbing vines of tedium, where the men watch them go by with utter indifference, their private form of contempt. They cross villages where the peace they all believed they'd find remains only as a ruin. By the third day, they understand that in these forgotten towns, monotony is the rule. Peace is a mother spending hours removing lice from the hair of a dozen sleepy children. They walk with the distinctive steps of seekers. The natives recognize them and, with a mocking gaze, let them pass.

They walk until afternoon finds them in a village where the drunks are jollier and the tedium ebbs away with the arrival of evening. In these villages, they are ushered in with greedy eyes. Then the hustle begins. A policeman gets up from his drunken stupor and asks for their papers. Still, they never bother the apostle. Even in these villages, the apostle seems to radiate an aura that makes him untouchable. They all present their documents, and then he, sacrosanct and age-old, disappears into the village, as the rest of the pilgrims return to their most vulgar pastimes, alcohol or drugs, yoga or prayer, sleep or sex.

And that's how they spend their days until the sun sets, when the apostle emerges from his penance and finally raises his voice in supplication. Usually he is accompanied by an indigenous woman, much younger than him, who feeds the fire's arabesques. And they all gather there around the nighttime fire, waiting for the apostle to pronounce the first words. Sometimes hours can pass as the man refuses to say a word, and only the moths fluttering over the fire can be heard. But there they stay, united by an obscure belief, gathered around the fire of an unknown passion. They make a bizarre group. Here a high European, there an American with a shaved head, beside him a Central European woman with long braids who smiles when she sees the natives go by, a young girl whose face bears the signs of tired illusion. Frayed shirts, painted faces, plastic rosaries, and candles lit to honor saints. Credulous hippies gathering to imagine a different world as evening falls over an insomniac country. And there, among the stinking pigs and third-world garbage, there *they* are: an everyday family lost in the labyrinth of belief, lost in an immense jungle, waiting for the prayers of a man whose arms are tattooed with an incomplete story of cataclysm and fire, of an enormous tree in a false landscape. They believe. And that belief drives them to wait a little longer.

There they are, a model family—deluxe, straight out of a magazine. They've managed to shake off fame, but they haven't been able to get rid of the other, much more primitive layer that is beauty. And as the pilgrims congregate before the fire, the family shines like stars in an opaque constellation. A beautiful family, a model family, surrounded by a crepuscular world.

When the apostle starts to talk, he begins by looking at them. He lets out a light word and leaves it hanging in the air, and his eyes land on that girl with chestnut hair and dark eyes who now coughs again, leaning behind her mother. She is deeply shy. The girl has her mother's fragile elegance, her father's hushed conviction. Watching the child try to hide behind her mother, looking at her as if speaking only to her, the apostle begins his sermon. His naked torso facing the flames, the fire lighting up that impressive tattooed trunk, he speaks of a final jungle storm, a last whirlwind that will reduce everything to a single point. He speaks of endings, and he cites sacred scriptures with a fluency far removed from his usual reticence. He finally takes his gaze from the girl, and with his eyes fixed on the fire, he speaks of islands and horizons, of underground worlds and millenary disasters. Then he returns to his prayer and the pilgrims around him listen, immersed in a belief that seems to devour everything in its path. He speaks of the great fallen tree and the small seer, and his face takes on an unusual expressiveness, an awful joy that holds madness. Then the indigenous woman who has spent the afternoon with him brings a little bottle, and he drinks. After a few minutes his eyes become flexible, and his gaze is lost beyond the fire. He starts to laugh then, a great peal of laughter that rings out in the night. The pilgrims begin to laugh as well, without reason or direction, while the night grows, fearful, cold, and distant, around the ten-year-old girl, who coughs again, like she's interrupting a party.

5

Her father, meanwhile, stares into the fire. As the apostle returns to his monologue, the father observes the furious swirls that leap from the bonfire and thinks of his childhood. He remembers being in the backyard of his house, between two olive trees, a magnifying glass in hand, focusing solar energy on the surface of an old newspaper. At first it was only light, a circle that shrank to a mere dot, where, happy and brief, the first flames would start to dance. Then the paper would wither and very soon there would be nothing but ashes and the flare of satisfaction in a mischievous boy.

The father remembers the distant afternoon when he and his friends were playing and set a fire, accidentally burning his mother's kitchen. Suddenly he's invaded by the intuition that the origin of photography is in fire. He snaps a photo. He thinks of the light and the flash, but also of that singular process that carries us from a simple equation to the phenomenon he now has in front of him, and he tells himself that the world is full of impossible translations, misunderstood languages. He thinks of the summer afternoon, years ago, when he swore to someday reach the edge of the world called Tierra del Fuego. He remembers how everything back then seemed possible, distant, epic. He's left that open future far behind, along with the Haifa sunsets and his mother's rough voice. Still further behind is the unstoppable will of that boy who sat in his provincial corner and imagined the world as an open horizon just waiting for him and his thirst for adventure. More than twenty years have passed since he swore to reach the end of the world, and he still hasn't done it. Listening to the apostle's hallucinatory sermon, he intuits that he will not manage it now, either. Much as this man talks of endings and fires, of lands looking always to the south, they won't reach the true south that he'd imagined and longed for as a teenager. He's surrounded, he realizes, by a tribe of obsessives who will throw themselves into the fire for this apostle. He looks at the fire, looks at his wife, and thinks that if he is here, it's for her. She believes, because she has fire in her blood.

If he is here, it is for her, old Sherman's distant heir, seeking to atone for a sin by repeating a journey.

6

Halfway through the journey, one of the pilgrims recognizes her.

"Aren't you that actress?"

Assuming the first of the many masks that she will wear over the decades to come, the mother merely frowns:

"I don't know who you mean."

And the pilgrim accepts it, not so much because she believes the response, but because she understands that everyone is here to forget, to leave aside an undesirable past and begin a new life. Over the years the question will repeat, and on each occasion the answer will be the same.

7

Their trek, of course, is not the only one, much less the first. They find the remains of previous journeys all around. In each new village they're reminded of the fact that their pilgrimage is not unique and that others have come before them. Ungrateful men who left everything behind to venture out into the jungle, tired people who one day decided to follow a story that maybe they didn't even believe in.

There are traces everywhere: the shirts adorning the natives' chests, and the plastic refuse they find between villages, in the atmosphere of false expectation that hangs over their crossing. This invisible presence makes them think they have arrived too late, that the pilgrimage could have been sincere only if it had been made ten years ago, when conviction still throbbed intact over history's fire. In every one of their gestures they sense a forgotten repetition. They soothe themselves by saying it's only déjà vu, a tired illusion that in no way stains the authenticity of their journey.

One rainy day, after five hours of arduous walking, they come upon a small shack in the middle of the jungle. Zinc roof, structure made of wood and straw, a hair's breadth from collapse. The open door leaves the interior exposed. There, among old newspapers, a white man, prematurely aged, lies on a pile of rags with a pen in his hand, reading a book that the mother recognizes: the complete works of Heinrich von Kleist in the original German. The pen is very small and so is the book, which makes the man seem huge, a Visigoth warrior lost in the jungle. He's surrounded by empty liquor bottles. And the old man never pauses his reading; he merely lets them know, with a measured gesture, that they can pass.

Something in the scene—perhaps the apostle's melancholic slowness as he stops in front of the shack, or the way he seems to emerge from his perpetual prayer—makes them think he recognizes the old man. He gives no greeting, however, just exhibits a certain deference, seeming to delegate his authority, if briefly. The journey's true goal could well have been to make it to that place. And then the old man begins to speak, very slowly, as if it had been years since his last human interaction. He speaks in a very correct German, as if hallucinating a Bavarian winter.

———

They let him speak, let his tongue loosen. No one thinks his words hold meaning, no one trusts his narrative power. They think to themselves that they could well turn into him, wizened old men lost in reverie. They let him speak, not just out of pity but out of a much deeper fear: that, in fact, he is what they are now, already. Perhaps at the end of history there is only a withered old man narrating a tale no one understands, a story as fragile and elegant as an old horse. That's why they let him speak. To find out how the story they're now living, without understanding, will end.

Hours later they'll learn from the only German in the group that all those stammered words did form a story. Florian, a young actor who reenacts old tragedies for the enjoyment of the natives, will reconstruct it for them just as the old man told it.

It is the story of a French duke from the seventeenth century who decides to spend his entire fortune on a grandiose but simple project: he will build a magnificent mansion in the middle of the jungle, then sit in a humble shack and watch its gradual decay, its slow walk toward ruin.

Accompanied by the best architects, he spends his days drawing up the perfect design for that magnificent monument, that future ruin. While around him the money flows in ships loaded down with gold and slaves, while the continent trembles in the fear of new wars, the image of his ruinous palace in the jungle brings the duke satisfaction and joy. Soon he understands that this is no mere project: his construction becomes, as years pass, an allegory of all possible architecture. All architecture, the duke comes to believe, becomes the image of a future that was not, a future ruined by a present always striving to imagine new possibilities. The idea consumes him. He spends his days thinking about its variations while the ideal of the project is depleted at the same feverish rate as his own fortune. He will die poor, terribly alone, besieged by the countless models of an impossible project he will never carry out.

———

They think of the old man they've just seen. The ancient newspapers, his worn face, the solitude of his eternal reading. Their whole journey is a bit like an empty pilgrimage that is gradually drained by its own senselessness. A long, slow walk toward a void, led by another lost madman who doesn't understand that his time has already passed.

In the afternoons, when the fever goes down and she is herself again, the little girl pesters her mother.

"Mom, Mom," she says while her mother writes. "If I close my eyes, I'm invisible."

Then she closes her eyes again in an attempt to prove that her theories are true.

"Can you see me?"

She goes on, but to little effect. In silence, the mother goes on writing, diligent and obsessive.

In her free hours, the mother sits down to read. While her husband teaches some bored native to play chess, while her sickly daughter coughs beside her, the mother continues the review of anarchism that has brought her to this corner of the world. She will, she tells herself, reach the end of the world carrying the books of this idealism that refuses to give way, even when everything indicates it should.

She has made note of three groups in her notebook: the Lazarists in the south of Tuscany, the Andalusian anarchists, and the Sicilian peasants. Farther down, she has outlined the story of their precursors, the Taborites and the Anabaptists. Then, in her unmistakable handwriting, she finished writing the hypothesis that has brought her here, the conjecture that the apostle repeats again and again, as if turning it into truth:

> The end belongs to the south. Unquestionable: look at Davide Lazzaretti, the messiah of Mount Amiata, look at the Andalusian laborers, look at Piana dei Greci. Even if the northerners deny it, there's nothing else: hope lies in the south. They were wrong, though, to look for the south in Europe. Aguirre knew it well, and my forebear crazy old Sherman knew, the true south is in America.

Farther down she has written a list of dates: 1820, 1837, 1860, 1866, culminating with the day when the apostle has promised they'll reach the seer. During the nights, while she's asleep, her husband reads the pages she has written and wonders if deep down she believes, or if she is secretly trembling behind this fiction.

Five days later, when the path starts to become more rarefied, long and repetitive like a dream, they find another lost traveler, this time at the edge of a gorge. They find him there between a giant rock and the purest emptiness, high and apparently in a trance. A lost vestige of another, now-forgotten pilgrimage. But where the German had told a story of the impasses of architectural ambition, this man has a frenetic monologue on an imagined American genealogy. There is room for everyone in his whirlwind story: Christopher Columbus and Baron Alexander von Humboldt, Hernán Cortés and Moctezuma, the natives of Cipango and the fearful Aguirre. American history comes to a stop there, scrambled by the man's belief that he's descended from Jefferson but also from the first Incan, from Washington but also La Malinche, from Joan of Arc but also from Evita.

The apostle sends two of the pilgrims to tie the man up. Once he is immobilized, the apostle halts his monologue with a simple question: "What is your name and where are you from?"

"My name is Maximiliano Cienfuegos and I come from the whore who birthed you."

He says it with contempt and arrogance, and he follows up by hocking a great gob of phlegm at the apostle's feet. Motionless, his anger reflected in his light eyes, he looks like the enormous caimans they've seen at the edge of the river—tired but still hunting. Then his diatribe starts up again, this time directed against an entire system, against capitalism and the omnipresent and terrible north, against capital and markets, against himself. The apostle gives the order to continue their journey. And they keep walking, willing to refuse everything in order to reach the end they long for, while behind them Maximiliano's voice becomes more distant and fearsome, a vestige of the dread that is growing into a great nightmare that includes them all. The little girl, sick, weak, and scared, turns her head for one last look at an image she will never forget.

11

That night, the mother dreams again. She dreams about the man they've just seen, but he's skinny and pale, sickly like her daughter sleeping next to her. She meets him in the middle of a plain, and he's obsessed with the construction of an impossible machine. She approaches him, trembling, and tells him how he'd told them all the history of America as if it were a dumping ground of names. And in the dream the man is different, a peaceful and sober version of himself, a kind of gaucho who pauses his work to tell her another story, about an archipelago that extends to the south. And the mother looks around, and then she sees that the plain isn't a plain, but a constellation of islands separated by small rivers all flowing toward the luminous, warm south. In the center she sees this sickly gringo lost among the islands, and now he repeats the word that so intrigues and pleases her: *archipelago*.

She wakes up to the sound of water dripping inside the shack. Her husband sleeps peacefully beside her, his arms around the little girl, who seems sicker all the time. "Only a few more days," she tells herself. Around her she sees the other pilgrims sleeping, along with the three natives who act as their guides. Outside, framed by the doorway of that minuscule shack, she makes out the sleepless silhouette of the apostle in front of the fire. She looks back at her daughter and repeats: "Only a few more days, no need to worry." Then she sees the image from her dream again, with total clarity. She sees a multitude of islands without center or end, adrift in the eyes of a man who doesn't sleep, a man who refuses to sleep.

12

Two days later the father gets up and sees his daughter reading her mother's notebook. He wonders what the girl will think of her mother's annotations. What will she think when she sees those sketches of millenarian megalomania, her mother's totalizing zeal? He lets her read, thinking perhaps it's better that way. Let the girl read and decide for herself if her mother's theories make sense. We all, he tells himself, have to grow up with a familial madness, our parents' private ravings. We all have to face, at some point, the legacy of a generation that was only fumbling around in the dark.

13

There's a story underneath history, says the apostle, a universal story that proceeds at a geological, inhuman pace. He speaks in the style of a sermon, but with a scientific shading that disconcerts as much as it comforts the pilgrims. He says: There is the time of man and the time of the gods. Then there's the time of the earth. This story is written at the speed of underground currents, written on the rocks and the bark of trees. It is a history of gradual destruction that finally rises to the surface. One day a man gets up and sees smoke rising from the earth: that is the other story.

Then, as if his personal story were blocking his way, he stops. He scrunches up his face, and, staring off in the distance, he tells the story of the fires.

There's a boy and a town. An American boy exploring with his friend one day when they come across a cave. Plumes of smoke waft from its mouth, but this does not deter them. A common boy with reddish hair and pale skin, timid but reckless, he follows his friend into the cave, only to watch as he is devoured by the earth. The boy runs to the precipice that his companion didn't see, but it's too late, the child is gone. After that, the boy grows up full of an inner rage that he doesn't entirely comprehend. In the story, the boy grows up as plumes of smoke start to appear throughout the town, he grows up with a fury contained like the fire spreading under the earth. His first girlfriend's parents decide to abandon the town and take her with them; his own cousin decides to move; slowly, slowly, the town empties out of people and fills up with smoke. His father, still unemployed, refuses to leave the town where he himself was raised. The boy grows up furious, but doesn't know where the rage comes from.

One day he dreams that he is in the middle of an immense forest. He thinks he hears, amid the roar of a great fire, a child's voice giving him directions. That day he tells himself that if he ever leaves town, it will be to find that boy and that forest.

In the story there is a town that one day stops being a town. It becomes something else: a ruin, emptiness, nostalgia. It survives as a ghost. In the story the town is slowly covered by fields, until all that remains is a cemetery in the middle of the prairie, smoke plumes all around. Lost tourists and the occasional journalist come to question the last ornery holdouts refusing to leave. The town burns down slow as a cigar, until only ashes remain. The town wakes up at its own funeral and recognizes itself in each of the mourners' gestures. In that town, among the mourners, there's a boy, and that boy refuses to think that everything is mere coincidence. He rejects the thought that the fire is simple coincidence. At sixteen years old, the boy tattoos a flame on his chest and swears on the town that is no more that he won't leave until he discovers the secret reason why everything is conspiring to keep him from dying in the place that saw his birth.

In the story, the years pass slowly, following a geological tempo unrestrained by the calendar. Time passes in a great plume of smoke. The caterpillar town finds itself light and crepuscular as a moth. Time passes in the apostle's story, but it hardly matters, since behind human time spreads the awful shadow of that other time, before which human chronology curls into a ball and disappears. Everything passes until one day the boy reads a news article that pulls him from his solitude: other towns also have fires, underground flames that for years, decades, centuries, have been burning in discreet silence.

His town is not alone. From the famous Burning Mountain in Australia to the German Brennender Berg, from the steppes of Xinjiang to the Canadian Smoking Hills, the list appears to him like a gesture of solidarity. Some of these fires have been active over a thousand years, a detail that terrifies him. Suddenly he intuits that the false solidity of the ground hides a subterranean history, with conflicts and resolutions, passion and sadness, rhythms and routines. A geological story like the underworld of Greek mythology, of ancient Hades and diligent Charon. But something doesn't fit. The story is not myth; it is real, hard, fleeting but tangible like fire.

That afternoon he runs through town like he did as a child. He runs with a new eagerness, and he feels growing under his feet the power of history, unknown and fearful, that nevertheless relieves him of the burden of believing he is alone. He runs until he reaches the cemetery and sees the smoke rising up, and he tells himself that the story doesn't end there.

From that day on his belief in the universal, subterranean story grows. Like the emergence of the fires, this story is dictated by far-off reverberations. He starts to alternate reading with the business of life, marijuana with medieval philosophy, cocaine with Renaissance treatises on natural history. He buys a bulletin board and tacks up a map of the world, where he marks the fires and the dates when they emerged, convinced that he'll be able to find the logic behind those sporadic appearances. The boy becomes a man who spends his hours in books and marijuana, observing the constellation that blooms on the wall of his room. He decides to buy three German shepherds, enormous dogs that follow him everywhere and lend him a mountain-man air. He lets his hair grow long, paints his nails black, starts to hang out with the goths in a nearby town. He slowly becomes a weirdo, with theories no one understands, consumed by a terrible fury. Even so, he reads, philosophers and mathematicians, scholastics and physicists, expecting something like an answer. The language of the future, he says to himself, will be the product of an prodigious blend of science and art, history and philosophy.

But all he finds in his books is an inverted image of his own will, a world of private fantasies, traced by a causal logic only he understands. Spurred on by the cups of coffee he drinks one after another, he imagines that the map he's tracing on his wall holds an internal dynamic, a political and historical sense. He writes equations in search of the formula that would explain the map of catastrophes. Cocooned by the paranoia that will mark him for years, he imagines that it's all a conspiracy. He becomes politicized, in his own way. He starts to travel, he goes to all the political marches that happen in New York, New Jersey, Boston, and Philadelphia. Always with his three giant dogs, alone or with friends as strange as he is, always dressed in black, always spouting an incomprehensible discourse.

Politics is different for him than for other people. He is uninterested in elections or current events. His commitment is to those great historical manifestations that he senses beneath the day-to-day. His political history, so to speak, started with the big bang and continues to the present in a game of correspondences only he understands. Politics, for him, is a private code, but he finds the key in a U.S. history book. Among dozens of irrelevant facts, a name leaps out: William Tecumseh Sherman.

First of all, the name surprises him: Tecumseh. It sounds prehistoric, mythical, ancient. It sounds like fire. Then, there's the story: the father, a successful lawyer from Ohio, dead when the future general is only nine years old. The mother, without an inheritance, must support eleven children. The young general-to-be goes to live with a neighbor, the lawyer Thomas Ewing, a distinguished member of the Whig Party who would one day be the first secretary of the interior. It is an American story wrapped in a family tragedy that will be repeated years later when, in the midst of the Civil War, General Sherman receives a telegram informing him that his son is deathly ill. Little Willy dies days later in a Memphis hospital, consumed by typhoid. The young son is dead at the same age the general was when he lost his own father. The rest of the story, he thinks, is shrouded in the pain of that loss. General Sherman's famous southward march, the merciless burning of Atlanta, the "total war" that made his name, the fearful fires: everything is stained by that decisive initial loss.

He reads the story of how, once Atlanta was taken, that man with drooping shoulders and an anxious gait ordered his soldiers to burn it all, the houses and the livestock, the trains and the churches. He reads of a scene he will never forget: while a terrible cloud of smoke rose above the city, the general ordered the band of the Massachusetts Thirty-Third Battalion to play one final song. He reads about Sherman's scorched-earth strategy, and suddenly he believes he has the key to the whole matter, the key to that natural history of destruction he has mapped in his living room. The history he has been searching for found its most perfect incarnation in General Sherman.

In the following weeks, he thinks endlessly about Sherman's March to the Sea. He's attracted by the image of a battalion of men willing to leave everything for an ideal that perhaps they don't even believe in. He finally decides to name his three dogs. The first is William; the second, Sherman; the third, no doubt his favorite, gets the name Tecumseh, the leader of the

Shawnee tribe. He draws the trajectory of the Union forces on the map, their passage through Atlanta and then farther south, until one day, high as can be, with a clarity he won't achieve again for many years, he sees that the fires, like the general, move slowly but gloriously southward.

Then come months of great concentration, months in which the boy does nothing but accumulate information: about General Sherman, about total war, about the South, about the scorched-earth strategy. He fills notebooks. He traces parallel narratives and conjures up possible connections, and even starts to imagine a political conspiracy. He stores up the names of mining companies, oil companies, names of political leaders. But nothing gives him the final image. He thinks he has found the direction of the story, but he's missing its body. Frustrated, he surrenders to alcohol. His dogs watch as he drinks bottle after bottle of cheap bourbon and rereads the information in front of him. He gives up, even though he tries to tell himself that his hero never gave up, even when his son died in the middle of the war.

They are lost years, years when the young man tries to forget. They're years of opioids that leave him sprawled on the sofa, lost in a fragile calm that the dogs make sure, from time to time, to interrupt. His father dies, his friends go looking for work in other mining towns. His peers get married, graduate from college, stop painting their nails black. They're the first years of the hippie era, of Vietnam, years that foreshadow the coming student protests and the progressive politicization of old Sherman's country. For him, however, they are years that pass wrapped in a soft fog, a stupor that hides a deep disquiet.

One day, he wakes up to his dogs barking. On the living room TV he sees a great flame. Soon he understands the more macabre truth: what he sees, what he then can hardly believe he is seeing, is a man burning himself in the middle of the street. That day, the news replays the scene over and over: Thích Quảng Đức a seventy-six-year-old Vietnamese Buddhist monk, burning himself alive. He remembers Sherman's great march, the underground fires, the map of the world forgotten behind him, and he tells himself it's time to return. He tells himself that this is the sign he was waiting for. He remembers his dream: a burning forest, and in the middle of it, the voice of a child calling to him.

He gives himself over to searching for that voice he thinks he's heard, a voice that he now believes must come from the South, Sherman's ruined South. He spends afternoons at the library among books of history and geography, convinced that there he will find the boy he has heard in dreams. The image of the burning monk has reawakened in him that feeling of dread that he had the day he understood his town would end up becoming a ruinous heap. Many of his friends, now in other towns, are called in those years to participate in the war. Not him. He's spent the war's first years embalmed in alcohol, overlooking the draft notices. He doesn't intend to change now. Vietnam: the name sounds decisive and distant, befitting the contempt he feels for a country that has forgotten its people.

In red Profile notebooks, he develops a series of notes that he decides to call *A Brief History of Destruction*. It is a natural history of fire. Destruction, for him, constitutes a politics. He writes the only way he knows how: cutting and pasting anecdotes from different books, writing commentaries around them in the style of old natural histories. He catalogs, stores, writes, until one day, looking through some newspapers, he comes across an article with the headline "A Prophet Child in the Southern Jungle." Without a second thought, he cuts it out and sticks it in his notebook. He doesn't need to read it to know that for him it promises the beginning of another march. It's the middle of the night, but he goes out for a walk with his three dogs, certain that the article will know how to wait for him.

He opens a bottle of bourbon as he walks, traversing the ruinous silhouettes of that town that is no longer. Driven by a fateful will, he crosses the spaces of what once was—the church, the barren town hall, the old school. He goes on walking until he enters the nearest town, feeling oddly light. He leaves his dogs at the entrance to a bar. Inside, three women look at him, ready to get down to business. They approach and he asks them how much, and when he hears the amount he chooses two, a skinny redhead who talks nonstop and a newly arrived Italian who speaks almost no English. He downs one last bourbon and lets the women lead him into a room with a classic decor, in the middle of which is an unmade bed. Strangely lucid, he asks only if he can choose the music. So he turns off the insufferable Elvis song on the jukebox and puts on something that the girls didn't even know was in the catalog, music with strong, deep chords, dark and chilling, music that portends his own fury and longing as he penetrates them that night, the fury of a man using sex as a cure for a suffocating memory, a man who knows he is close to the truth he's been searching for but refuses to look it in the face. They watch him close his eyes, and for a moment they fear he is deathly ill. This man, they think, fucks like someone with nothing to lose, like with a man who has decided to laugh in the face of death and surrender to one last pleasure, dark and remote.

Three hours later, he is roused by the barking of his dogs. Beside him, naked and sweaty, the two women lie in a half embrace. He finishes his whiskey, gets dressed, collects his dogs, and retraces his steps. Stripped of desire, he finally feels prepared to face what is coming. The buildings lit by the first light of dawn, he again sees what's left of the church, the rubble of what was once the town hall, his school, and finally the silhouette of his house. And he goes inside and finds, open on the table, his notebook with the newspaper clipping, which includes a photograph, distant and a little blurry, of a boy with indigenous features, his arms raised toward the sky.

He learns that he has spent three years looking in the wrong place. He never thought that the south and the forest could be so far away, much farther than Alabama, in a world whose language he doesn't understand. He knows little of the lands that stretch out south of the Rio Grande, little of their language, less of their people; he knows almost nothing about the country that holds the jungle where, the article says, in the midst of a great felling of trees, a boy has heard a sacred voice.

A very young boy, he realizes, looking at the photograph. Just a child, who swears he has heard a voice that told him the end was near, and would arrive in a tornado of fire. A boy without parents, orphaned in the jungle, he has apparently convinced dozens of people that the end is coming in the shape of giant tongues of fire that will devour the trees.

In the story there is a journey. A very long journey taken by a boy who believes he has finally understood. A voyage in which that boy, now a man, is determined to reach the south. An odyssey that gradually stretches out, from motel to motel, train station to train station, that grows in leaps and bounds, like the man's conviction. He sees up close things he never expected to see: a black man dying in the middle of the street, desolate landscapes and magnificent ones, a prostitute crying in an alley, an enormous bear eating red fish as they fall over a waterfall, a Mexican worker falling exhausted at his feet and pleading for help, a blind man playing the accordion, a ten-year-old boy spitting up blood, landscapes ablaze and in ruins, men collapsing in the sun, men leaving for war and returning from it dead, a dog barking at the sky, a turquoise-colored horizon under which a long line of tired people files northward while he insists, stubbornly, on making his way to the south.

In the story there are churches and pastors, biblical stories that feed his theories. He hears sermons that teach him, for the first time, the value of the voice, of oral histories, that sow in him the belief that his true role will be that of an apostle, of spreading the word of that boy who dreams of the end of the world in a distant jungle. In the Protestant churches of the south, in black communities that look at him with confusion and a spark of contempt, he finally learns to speak. Prisoner of an inner fury, a man who had always preferred to keep quiet, whom many relatives had believed mute, he now learns the value of the homily. He dedicates himself to practicing speeches that one day he will recite before a church of his own—deep and dark, he imagines, like the jungle itself. He practices, learns, memorizes, until one day, feeling he is ready, he packs his things and tells himself the time has come to set off on his true journey. He walks, first westward to California, and then southward, to that unknown region that intimidates and seduces him. Though he cannot speak Spanish, he crosses the border without looking back.

The rest of the story proceeds like a dream. A months-long crossing over a continent that trickles down through serpentine lands. He rides in trucks full of chickens, trips on hallucinogenic drugs, has unexpected meetings and detours. Months that pass like a dream, without a clear path, floating on a current that guides him blindly until it deposits him, on a day he will never forget, in a jungle where, some say, the tree and the boy he has dreamed of can be found. The rest is history, says the apostle, but under that history there's another story.

There's a story beneath history, the apostle concludes. And though he hasn't mentioned any names, all the pilgrims believe he is that boy who became that man; the apostle is the product of that story and its excesses. They believe they understand him a little, even when his voice once again becomes a pastor's, as he commences one of his high-flying sermons that they're starting to find tiresome. Even then, the pilgrims remember the story of the boy and the burning town, and they know they are looking at a man trapped in mute fury within a story that holds him like a straitjacket.

14

Listening to that story of underground fires and deep histories, the father remembers the biography of Nadar, the years the photographer spent in the Parisian catacombs. The images that made him lose sleep years ago rise to the surface. He remembers a picture of Nadar himself in the catacombs, sitting in front of an illegible epitaph, surrounded by bottles like a drunk. He remembers the image of a man carrying a load of bones on his back—a thin, pale man who was not even a man but a wax statue that the photographer had created as a model: back then, a single photo took hours. When he read that book long ago, the idea that Nadar—the first photographer to depict Paris from the sky, the inventor of the aerial photograph—had decided to descend into the Parisian underground had made him wander, indecisive and unsettled, for hours. He tells himself that if he makes it out of this jungle alive, he will find one of the apostle's burning towns, and he will dedicate himself to photographing the underground fires. He'll sit down to watch time pass, to find a true escape.

15

Three days later, at the edge of a river, they come upon the cadaverous trunk of an immense mahogany tree. On its bark, delicate as handwriting, the tunnels of termites trace the map of a funeral march. It isn't the tree the apostle has told them of, but even so, they're fascinated by that miniature epic on its bark, the way the termites inscribe on the jungle's skin a secret text only they understand. The apostle is the first to stop in front of the tree; he kisses it, then lets the other pilgrims approach. One by one they carry out a private ceremony. The tree is upright, elegant even in its own funeral procession, defeated by an enemy that ate away at its insides. The little girl approaches fearfully until she can see the termite paths from up close. Sick though she is, she will never forget the image of those tunnels made by tiny creatures capable of conquering a giant. To her, the termites will mean the possibility of a world beneath the world, an underworld where powers are shifted and size is no longer important.

The father, too, will begin to ignore the sublime landscapes, the swelling rivers and the mahogany trees, to focus his lens instead on those landscapes hidden on the tropical floor. The majestic waterfalls and sublime volcanic peaks will give way to a subterranean world, a humble atlas that his lens will find hidden in any corner. While the apostle speaks, father and daughter search the surface of the visible for traces of the other reality that pulses within, secret, silent, and fearsome.

16

One day they reach a town full of luxuries. They haven't seen anything like it on their trek. Five red jeeps stop them. Two natives with tattooed arms carrying machine guns ask for their documents and look them over until they're distracted by a distant whistle. A sweaty, shirtless fat man, a white local toasted by the sun, signals to his men that the apostle's people are welcome. A murmur of fear runs through the group, and it only grows when the apostle gives the fat man an effusive greeting. They have reached this place wrapped in an aura of unreality, of distance, lightness, of dreams, but now their eyes are opened. Two men keep silent watch over them from a nearby shack. Farther along, a group of men moves boxes with an urgency they haven't witnessed in these latitudes. Finally, the pilgrims sense, reality is catching up with them. This stubbornly real village lies beyond the apostle's hallucinatory speeches. They see it all clearly: the hustle of soldiers loading trucks, the men in the shack who seem to be mocking them, and they understand, for the first time, that their journey is secondary to another reality of trucks and machine guns, of cynical and greedy men.

After a few minutes the apostle returns, accompanied by the fat local. They've never seen him like this before, cheerful and chatty, friendly. Almost a regular guy. In the two men's laughter they think they hear the complicity of years. The fat man speaks. At the back of the encampment, he says, they will find five roomy shacks where they can sleep and bathe. He tells them they have nothing to fear. Today they will be guests of honor; they will have food in abundance. This village isn't like the others; here there is food and conviction, food and work. His voice has the timbre of a power different from the apostle's. An earthly power, unbelieving and mocking, which suits him perfectly. They see how the men acquiesce to him, fearful. And they understand that it is also their lot to accept without question, to walk with their heads down, feigning disinterest, until they reach the promised shacks. This is the sinister face of the jungle where they thought they'd find salvation. This is the human and vulgar side of their unfinished journey, and the apostle's laugh continues, dragging lies down into the village, intertwined with the fat man's guffaw.

A small bamboo door opens into the shack: an immense room with seven mattresses, seven mosquito nets around them, and five small windows that look out onto a yard where a dirty dog harasses flapping chickens. A wooden table and a wooden floor. And a small, seemingly magical electric light hanging from the ceiling.

Since the pilgrimage began, they've encountered almost no electricity in the villages. They remember with amazement the life they've left behind. That terribly normal life, full of mundane dangers, reemerges with the insistence of the radio murmuring in a nearby lean-to. In that hum of voices they think they distinguish the weather report, sporting results, the most recent changes in the Catholic Church. They remember that they're only fifteen days away from the bus that left them at the brink of the jungle, just two weeks in a sleep from which they now begin to awake, hollow-eyed and stinking. They are tired, no doubt about it. But within the exhaustion, like a hornet, buzzes the feeling—which no one dares to articulate—that they have been ushered into a conspiracy.

A Polish girl, skinny and careworn, with tattooed arms and a light spirit, cuts the tension by telling a story. It's the first time they've heard her voice, airy and shy. She tells of how Alexander von Humboldt came upon a singular man while crossing Venezuela in search of electric eels. In the middle of the plain, he discovered a magnificent electrical machine with cylindrical disks, electrometers, and batteries, all well assembled, a machine as complex as those he'd seen in Europe, or maybe more. Humboldt asked after the gadget's owner, and some lounging plainsmen pointed him toward a simple cabin where a fat man with an impressive mustache was drinking coffee. His name was Carlos del Pozo, and he claimed to have built the machine based on what he'd read in *Traité* by Sigaud de la Fond and Benjamin Franklin's *Memoirs*. A plainsman all his life, he had never left that vast territory, never traveled to Europe or the north. Humboldt spent the afternoon with that marvelous man, fascinated by the fact that in those vast solitudes, where the names of Volta and Galvani seemed to be unknown, a common man had built an exact version of the Electric Machine that had set the Europeans dreaming. The next day, Humboldt left at dusk and a twilight settled once more over the southern plain and over that lonely genius named Carlos del Pozo.

After the Polish girl's story, the atmosphere in the shack is left heavy with half-formed dreams and impossible conjectures. Lying on their seaweed mattresses, protected by mosquito nets, the pilgrims feel that this isolated town is a reminder of their own old world. Better, they tell themselves, to give in to their exhaustion and leave off all these stories.

And the little girl has been watching as they all collapse into bed. For her, the Polish girl's story has brought on a peculiar anxiety. She remembers the greasy face of the fat man who received them, and in a brief flash she imagines that he must be the very same Carlos del Pozo. Caught by curiosity, concentrating her remaining energy, she pulls away from her sleeping mother, passes by her snoring father, and when she opens the door she again hears the murmur of the village. She hears a labored muttering, the vulgar shouts of a foreman disciplining a group of natives. Farther on, surrounded by five mestiza women passing around half a dozen bottles of beer, she sees the fat man talking with the apostle. A fist of blue iron hits her body when she sees the scene, and she runs through the village in search of an escape. She feels fear and happiness all at once as she loses herself in the jungle, dodging mahogany trees and ferns, muddy rocks and thorny plants, in search of the river, the hiss of which seems to grow until it's everywhere. She passes men and women who look at her pale skin in surprise, she hears voices she doesn't understand, but nothing stops her. She chases that whisper of river and only stops when she's right next to it. She sees its furious waters and then, sensing that it marks an invisible border, a white line like sleep, she hears a voice behind her. When she turns, she's looking right into the face of that man she thought she'd left behind.

The face of the man before her holds tenderness and compassion, a rocky hardness over which a subtle kindness grows like a wild vine. Now that she is finally seeing him from close up, far away from the nightly rituals, she thinks she sees his real face for the first time. Seen up close, the apostle's face takes on a provincial sweetness, a touch of childhood and innocence. He seems like someone else: a younger man, simpler, closer, far removed from the apocalyptic figure of his sermons, from the figure that drove her to flee.

"Where are you going, my dear?" he asks her in English.

And in his voice she briefly finds a home.

Then the apostle gestures to a branch and says, "Do you see him? Do you see the little animal?"

And she looks at the branch without seeing anything but that: a jungle branch. But after a while, the girl thinks she can distinguish an animal movement among the leaves. Then she sees it: a little creature playing an imitation game, an animal made of sticks camouflaged among the branches, halfway between death and life. She immediately feels that she herself is like a little creature playing hide-and-seek in the middle of the jungle, playing a game of masks. A sick animal whiling away the hours. She feels this but doesn't understand it, and then she hears the apostle's voice.

"*Es la mantis religiosa,*" he tells her, returning to that language she is just starting to intuit. And she sits looking at the animal with the peculiar name. After a few minutes, a small insect lands on a nearby branch, and the mantis, in a sudden leap, devours it greedily. Startled, she turns in fear, expecting to find the apostle's embrace, but she finds only her worried mother, weeping, scolding her for running away. She is left thinking then about the disappearance of that man, whom she will see with different eyes from now on.

That night she doesn't sleep. Again and again, she's assaulted by images of the creature that appeared among the branches, the awful scene of depredation, the apostle's voice behind her, her mother's sudden appearance. She relives what she's seen, growing convinced that the whole matter has been nothing but a hallucination and that tomorrow, reality will go back to what it's always been: the visible backdrop. She thinks about that little creature with the prayerful name, and in her mind it all mixes together and grows confused: the apostle's voice, his sincere face, her mother's arms, the mantis's leap. And suddenly the girl senses that the world is more than the visible, that small animals lie in wait for their moment to leap out, that there are asymmetrical and invisible worlds. She's reached ten years of age without fears, without ghosts and spirits, but a brief scene in the jungle has been enough to resuscitate an unconscious dread. Behind everything there is something else, she tells herself, the possibility of a world behind the world. She is learning a fundamental lesson: there is nothing more treacherous than peace.

18

Stormy days. Endless rain and thunder. The murmur of the apostle's prayers, and beyond him, an indigenous woman who spends all day carving small figures of a saint. Between attacks of coughing and feverish hallucinations, the little girl peers at her, perplexed. She observes the woman's caution as she palpates the wood in search of the perfect starting point. This repeated gesture becomes central to the girl's universe. Everything seems to be sustained in it, just as the old myths rest on Sisyphus's stubborn determination to carry out an impossible task.

The father watches the scene too: every figure the woman carves is exactly the same. The saint has indigenous features, and in his palms, reaching toward the sky, a small bird perches. Curious, impressed, the father picks up a couple of the little figures and confirms that there are almost no differences. He remembers the story a Mexican friend told him about a painter who spent his life creating various views of the same volcano. After ten years the old man had made more than two thousand sketches and paintings of that incipient volcano. Those who met him during that time said that he had a lucid madness etched into his face, like a disguise he'd put on one day and never taken off. Those who met him in his later period, when he was living as a bum in an abandoned hotel in Cuernavaca, said that he had the precise lucidity of the great obsessives. In the afternoons, in the monotony of the rain, the father tells himself life should be like the stubborn repetition of an empty gesture, the unconditional deliverance of a lie.

They spend two days empty like peace itself, stormy days heavy with the vague sense that soon something will happen. A few times, the apostle sets his prayer aside and spends a couple of hours in the world of mortals; he sits down to listen to the stories the pilgrims tell. He interrupts very little, and when he does his voice sounds different, softer and more sincere, like a light breeze. The little girl thinks she sees the man she saw at the river's edge, a normal, tender man who sometimes sits down to play chess with her father in the afternoons. Yet he is the same man who, on other days, gets drunk with the fat man; the same man about whom rumors start to spread among the pilgrims. It's said that the whole pilgrimage is nothing but a way to hide his dirty dealings; that he owes the fat man money; that he's been seen lying with an indigenous man; that there is no seer, no tree; that he's nothing but a drug addict who's given up, a link in a long chain that now, inevitably, includes them.

Sometimes, they even forget his title. They start to call him "the gringo," like the natives do. Then the rumor starts to spread that the gringo could be a secret agent. As that rumor grows, so does the fear of being mixed up in other people's plans, of being pawns in a game whose logic escapes them. They are willing to participate in the end of history, to believe in a seer with apocalyptic revelations, but they are horrified by the idea—everyday, vulgar, real—that they are caught up in a network of illegal commerce. For the pilgrims, anxiously looking for a new world, there could be nothing worse. Some of them want to end the whole thing, turn back and live in blind belief, rather than find themselves lowered to the level of a fat, drunk drug trafficker. To distract themselves from rumor, in the afternoons of rain and gale, they sit down to tell stories beside the attentive shadow of the woman carving saints.

19

A storm blowing over the story like a great kite. A great catastrophe, the mother says to herself, that gives birth to nature itself, a kind of nature that is the result of catastrophe instead of its opposite. An enormous dumping ground of small, ruinous stories over which grows the moss of a time to come. In her mind, dreams, stories, and memory grow confused. She remembers the cabin lost in the rain forest, and the man inside, old and withered, writing an encyclopedia, unaware of the approaching storm.

The mother refuses to face the obvious: that they are in a village of mundane evil, guests of a man who earns his living through wicked means. She refuses to see the trucks that drive in and out of the village.

On the third day they awaken to peace. Rays of sunlight, tangled in the mosquito nets, are the first sign that the downpour is over. What remains is a slight hangover of storm, interrupted by the clamor of trucks again flooding the village. The father looks for the saint carver but sees only a few little statues she has left behind, saints that must not have met her standards of perfection. He gives one to the little girl, who is in better spirits, free of fever and unusually energetic.

Disconcerted, the girl says, "Look, it's a statue of the apostle."

Suddenly he sees it all through her eyes, sees the monstrous logic they've caught her up in, sees her there holding an idol of the man who, arguably, is causing her illness, and he feels furious. Furious at himself, and when that becomes too unbearable, furious at the apostle. The father looks around for the apostle with an eye to revenge. He looks for him everywhere, until he realizes he simply isn't there.

Their leader is gone. They look for him in the town, at the fat man's house, around the river, but find nothing. They imagine the worst: desertion or death. They imagine him floating downriver, his body the fat man's final message; among the wild branches, bitten by some viper; poisoned by a furious pilgrim. They think they would rather he be dead than to have cut and run like a coward when they're halfway to their destination, with no way of getting out of that shithole town.

Seven hours later they find him in the village, in a monumental fight with the fat man, which they try unsuccessfully to decipher. They all know it's time for them to go. Three hours later, one of the fat man's trucks leaves them at a cabin in the middle of the jungle, full of spiders and snake eggs. In one corner, a native sleeping off his booze seems to be having a nightmare. They will rest there, too, and depart at dawn. A week, the apostle says, another week of walking and they will reach the seer. And though they say nothing, they feel dread at the thought that in seven days they'll reach that place that inspired them to leave everything behind. They are hounded by the image of the fat man and the real, vulgar village they just left. They promised to leave history behind, but history—sweaty and common—is coming for them. One week, they tell themselves.

21

That day, to distract the pilgrims, the German actor performs the play
with which he sometimes entertains the natives. It is from the seventeenth
century, written in an old German none of them understand, but to which
they surrender, intrigued. It reminds them of silent cinema and mime,
the paradoxical fragility of horses' legs, and the silence of monks. It is a
monologue of a stammering voice that trips over itself again and again,
a very old play behind which they sense a modern awareness. And they
laugh, because there is a great deal of comedy in the play, and comedy is
what they want. Comedy is what they need to dispel the grotesque image
of another laugh in a nearby village.

Dark nights follow, static and silent, in which the father distracts the daughter by telling her stories about the constellations. The girl, again feeling tired and weak, just listens to her father's allegories; every constellation holds a new story, another myth, a new way of muffling the fear and bringing some familiarity to the world that now surrounds her like a nightmare. The shy little girl intuits that behind all those words hides a crouching, deep-seated horror, but she is shielded by her faith that her father will tell her stories until there are no more stories to tell.

And the thing her father doesn't know is this: she likes the night, its darkness and silence. In the night, everything is possibility, universes lay coiled. She entertains herself by cataloging the murmurs that she hears: the croak of the frogs, the grunting of pigs, the hiss of the rain, the cicadas' whir, the tired steps of an anteater, the buzz of a lost hornet, the incessant rushing swell of a nearby river. She is disturbed by the thought that if she paid close enough attention, one day she would be able to distinguish, among all those sounds, the termites' military tread, the punctual steps of ants, the lethal drag of the snake, the tarantula's mortal dance.

At nightfall on the river's edge she has seen the red, expectant eyes of insomniac caimans, eyes that remind her of the apostle's deep and tired gaze.

Then she feels a little afraid.

She's seen him at night. While the others are asleep, he moves away from the group and sits out in the open on nights of rain, exposed and alone, his torso bare and his head down. Static and magical like the insect he showed her in the jungle, a creature halfway between vegetable and animal, between death and life. "*Mantis religiosa*," he called it, in that language she's only starting to understand. She thinks of the nights, when everyone gets up to watch the others sleeping.

They don't know that she knows. That she sees everyone wake up in the early morning, contemplating the scene with worried eyes. Like a little jungle animal she likes to feel unseen, to be invisible and motionless as she keeps watch. She's seen them all in their nocturnal tasks. She's seen her mother write her dreams in the notebook she carries with her everywhere; she's seen her father rise in the morning to watch her sleep; she's seen the apostle wander through the night sunk deep in his insomniac prayer. She's seen the drunk British man who spies on her mother's body as soon as she's asleep, the German who tosses nervously in search of a sleep that won't come, the California girl who, every night at three o'clock, looks around like she's searching for her family. She's seen them all, immersed in their dreams and their fears, awake in a seemingly endless vigil. Her gaze has tripped up, uncomprehending, against a couple of men entwined like vines. The odd feeling has come over her that if she could stay terribly still, like the little insect she saw, everything would go back to normal and one day she would wake up at home.

Throughout the long walks that make up their days, her parents have tried to explain the reason for the trip. Only one thing has become clear to her: they all want to see more, to see better, with the same desperate insomnia with which at night they look for the dawn. Her parents have told her that at the end of the road there's a boy, very young and much like her, and that he's also very wise. He is a child like her who woke up one day and saw a different world, and now he is waiting to tell them what he's seen. They have talked to her about underground stories and ancient fires, which strike her as pure fantasy—and that should interest her, at her age, but for some reason it all leaves her cold. Whenever she thinks of that boy, she imagines him pale and tired, a prisoner of his visions. Then a shiver runs over her body and she feels a deep sadness for that boy and for all children, but also for her parents. They all want to see. But she is determined to become invisible.

23

As soon as the father says "The end," she always asks the same question:

"And after the end?"

Her father hugs her, warms her up. Then he tells her another story and everything is okay again. But he keeps thinking about the question she has asked him.

"And after the end?"

24

Arduous days of long walks and little rest. A week, the apostle said, and they follow him. Days of crossing furious rivers full of trees and garbage. Lush, dark jungle. They cross through small villages where they start to recognize signs: natives who use the same rosaries as the apostle, light the same candles, wear the same jewelry. The people in those villages also seem to recognize them, but still, no one stops them. They feel they've been there before; they feel they have forgotten something. But they tell themselves that it's only a week. The father refuses to take pictures; he is thinking constantly about the apostle's story of fire, of old Sherman marching his men southward. Carrying the sick little girl, the father fights to shake off his disquiet at his wife's passion for their absurd pilgrimage. When this is all over, he reminds himself, he will find a mining town and dedicate his days to photographing the underground. The problem, though, is that the days pass, the walks grow longer, and the promised land doesn't appear.

Instead, scattered haphazardly through the jungle, there are small plots of land marked off with barbed wire, weird plantations of green plants whose fruits, which resemble squash, the natives eat to get high. Drugged natives become a common sight deep in the jungle, sometimes alone and melancholic, other times celebrating uproariously. Rushed, never stopping but always alert, they cross those small delirious scenes as if it were all a play, or a dream. One day, at the edge of a river, they find a native proclaiming a hurried speech, tangled up in a language they don't understand. He is a very short man, totally naked, with purple feet and crossed eyes. He stops his speech as soon as he sees them, and in a very poor Spanish, spitting more than speaking, he tells them they will not find what they're after, that the land was stolen from his grandfather, that the man guiding them is known for his lies. They tell themselves that his accusations are all the product of the drug. He wades into the river and returns to his prayer, and they go on with their walk.

One morning, they see a propeller plane cross the sky. A sign that they're close, some of them think. Two hours later, they cross a small village in ruins. Recently burned, sacked, and incinerated. Beyond a scorched mansion is an enormous garden with flowers of all colors, exquisitely arranged, small trees that are clearly foreign, a diminutive fountain. Someone, it would seem, left the house not long ago. They find the scene odd, but they don't ask any questions. If they've understood one thing, it's that their lot is to accept. They watch as the apostle stops in front of the garden, crosses himself, and enters the house.

And they do the same.

They think of all they've left behind. Among the ruins, they discover reliquaries alongside an enormous photo of an old colonel; a room full of maps of the jungle and dozens of small, intact statues like the ones they saw in the fat man's village; a library partially eaten by termites, where the pilgrims sit down among the ruins to read.

Some of the books are of particular interest: the seventeen volumes of Strabo's *Geography*, the five volumes of Baron Alexander von Humboldt's *Cosmos*, the five letters Columbus sent to the kings after his second voyage. Travel almanacs, natural history catalogs, books that classify the world into arbitrary and beautiful categories. On the same shelf as an old German encyclopedia, the mother finds a *History of the Wars of Independence* interspersed with clippings from current magazines, photos of actors and actresses, the shell of a strange insect. She reads horrible numerical records that plot deaths like the coordinates of stars. She gets caught up in reading about the Realist Army, which makes her think of the opposing force, an Anti-Realist Army committed to the destruction of realism. Laughing, she thinks that if she ever had to take part in a war, she would take the side of the anti-real avant-garde, in determined battle against reality.

Lost amid the broken shelves, the father finds a book for the little girl, written by someone who seems to be an apprentice of Jules Verne. It tells of a very long journey, one with a diffuse and ambiguous chronology, but in which the world appears complete, round, and navigable. There is a captain and a war, a catastrophe and a shipwreck; there is a flight and then long years of travel—London, Seville, Tangiers, New York, Calcutta, Havana, San José—in a voyage that then stretches southward, culminating in a long crossing. The protagonist, a Belgian sailor, travels across the South American wilderness. Thousands and thousands of words are devoted to the years the Belgian spends in Patagonia hunting rhea alongside Tehuelche natives. The story puts the girl to sleep, but it gives the father the unsettling feeling he is in a world with no way out. The Belgian marches with the Tehuelche over the Patagonian plains, while the Indians hunt the rhea by dint of patience, forcing their prey to walk themselves to a slow death.

The father isn't clear on whether the end of the book is a joke, a crock of nonsense, or simply a printing error. He keeps thinking about the Tehuelches' nights out in the open, the desert mirages, the final days of the rhea on the Patagonian plains. He tells himself that endings should not be an abrupt break or an absolute resolution, not even the proposal of an open horizon, but a point one reaches in exhaustion.

Beside him, immersed in a book, his wife is smoking.

Endings, he says to himself, should be like a cigarette that burns down, little by little, until there is nothing more than a small stub burning your fingers. He imagines the long southward walk of the Tehuelche, and at the end of it the land he himself had chased for so many years, Tierra del Fuego. The surest thing is that the Indians will never reach the rhea, just as Achilles never reached the tortoise and his wife will never fully consume her cigarette. Defeated by exhaustion, the Indians will watch as the herd of rhea they're following moves farther away against the metallic backdrop of the plain, marching south.

He doesn't finish the book. He refuses to finish it, immersed as he is in the infinite image of that great animal march, taking slow southward steps.

That night they camp in the garden, the jungle all around them. For the first time in a while, they remember the reason for their journey. They came in search of a garden, only to find the ruins of a jungle that no longer existed. Around them, the nocturnal sounds remind them there are only a few days left. They hear two more planes cross the sky, they notice sounds that strike them as vaguely human, sounds that make them think perhaps they're in an ambush. They sleep little. They let the hours pass, hours that, lacking clocks or measurements, are lost in the darkness.

Earlier that day, amid the singed ruins of the mansion, they saw a giant clock. An old grandfather clock that escaped the destruction. They had a perplexed feeling of displacement. They've spent twenty-seven days ensconced in a different time, a lunar time, and they remember one of the apostle's first instructions: leave time behind. As they camp in the garden, they feel the density of time surrounding them, geological, heavy as that unusable clock. Sleepless, they think they hear the tolling of five bells; nervous, they tell themselves that madness is near.

Of all of them, perhaps the mother is the liveliest. She writes a new page:

> Power is expressed only in the capacity for destruction. One should think of destruction itself as a political category. Aesthetic as well. The creator creates by destroying. The politician creates a new world among the ruins. One should think of that initial relationship between art and politics, that initial violence that erupts as soon as the painter decides to mark the canvas with the first brushstroke. Think of the violence of the first line, the first stroke, the first verse. An initial violence that does not spill blood but rather opens spaces. A new world emerging from the flames like the Greeks imagined, a new world that comes from a violence full of mercy and passion like the gods imagined. One must think of that act of destruction as the very basis of all possible politics, as the very possibility of making the foundations tremble. To write a natural history of destruction as if it were a treatise on aesthetics.

At night, while she sleeps, the father reads her entries with a terror that cuts to the bone. They make him think she is not the woman he once loved. He looks at her sleeping and thinks that at least she is sleeping, while he merely counts the hours of his insomnia.

The mother dreams again. She dreams she is in the middle of a war against the Realist Army. Halfway through the dream, she understands that it's all a great mix-up. The battle's stage is not the wide southern plains, but a museum with a mysterious name. The museum is empty and long, and in its main hall an enormous map stretches across the floor, where a man resembling the apostle is walking. As he walks he spills something, a sort of paint that turns into flames that run over the map's surface. The man produces a flaming map as onlookers applaud. And in the dream she is there, clapping for a man she believes in, telling herself that the art of the future must be an undertaking against the world and against the world's representation, a stifled cry in the middle of the ocean, heard only by the seaweed and fish. In the dream the fire devours the entire map and then, slowly, the artist. And she sees herself clapping, her wild applause bordering on hysteria, convinced that she is seeing her future.

25

They set off at dawn the next morning, leaving behind the garden, the house, and the incinerated village. They feel that something is lying in wait for them, that they're caught up in an invisible trap. They see small shacks, recently abandoned, with yards separated by wire and sprouting patches of the hallucinogenic gourds. They come across drawings on the rocks of public figures and movie superstars, cinema icons and politicians painted in color. They find, painted on an enormous rock, the image of Marilyn Monroe, and next to her, Simón Bolívar. A hundred yards farther down, they run into a drugged native, singing happily.

They walk faster.

They cross a small ravine and then a field of ferns, where they find a reddish rock with another drawing, this time of a Spanish colonel next to Audrey Hepburn. In the coming hours they will see many of these odd pairings. Some, like the father, will laugh. Some, following the apostle, will ignore them. Some, like the mother, will try to find meaning in them. Some, like the girl, will merely remain bewildered.

No answer will come.

At noon they see a small mountain rise up, and along with it they hear the sound of a crowd. They hear its raucous approach, and then over the peak they see the first child's mask appear.

With the sun high overhead, they find themselves ambushed by an army of a hundred children who come running down the mountain, their faces covered with white masks, their bodies brown, and their feet agile. They come running down waving a giant purple flag with a drawing of a white tree, and the pilgrims withdraw, startled. The apostle, however, is unfazed. He walks through the battalion, greeting them, fussing over them as if they were his own children, a herd of faceless offspring. The pilgrims watch and imitate him. The children crowd around and touch the pilgrims' faces, hands, and arms, laughing behind identical masks. In the jungle nights, many of them heard a nocturnal whisper and imagined a native uprising. Never, though, did they think the revolt would be the laughter of a pack of kids.

In the midst of this bizarre procession, the little girl forgets her illness for a moment. She has been the only child in the group, and now childhood is all around her. More than the age or number of the children, more than the unfamiliar language they speak, she is interested in their masks. She touches them the same way the children paw at her arms. When she was little she played with masks, and these aren't so different: they are plastic masks like the ones at birthday parties, with a smile drawn on the face. She is the one to ask: And where did these masks come from? None of the pilgrims can answer her. They think they've reached the depths of the jungle, but at every step they take, modernity seems to play another card. They think they've reached an origin outside of time, but an army of children reminds them that the jungle wears plastic. And they keep walking up the slope, climbing the mountain from which the children descended. When they reach the top, the view clears, and they think they see what they've been looking for. They see a flooded plain between two mountains, small islands interrupting its surface, and they remember the apostle's words. They remember how that man who now walks surrounded by children has spoken of a great city etched onto an archipelago.

What the pilgrims see then, or think they see, seems beyond belief:

On an enormous plain nestled between two plateaus, hundreds of little islands seem to float. Among them, weaving seams into the landscape, small water channels draw onto the vast green carpet the unforgettable image of a great archipelago of islands. Each island, in turn, houses a small temple. Hundreds of temples dot the plain, all identical, all facing eastward. It looks like a city of temples rising up from the rain forest, a city that grows in a spiral until it reaches a central island, where the pilgrims think they see an enormous main temple, with five towers and many gardens.

In the canals they see hundreds of small boats, and in those boats are hundreds of men moving slowly through the island city. The pilgrims have reached this place only to be reminded that they're not the first—they are latecomers. A crowd of diminutive human figures moves around below. They see children moving through the canals. Children like the ones who now surround them, dark and small, an army of children like the ones who now take them by the hand and prepare to guide them down. Exhausted, they believe they have finally found the end of their journey.

The apostle welcomes them by announcing the seer's latest prophecy. In two days, this city will be the epicenter of an earthquake.

What follows that vision, the frenetic whirlwind of events that come after the apostle's pronouncement, becomes visible only in retrospect. In the ensuing forty-eight hours, the father sees a cruel circus, but the other pilgrims see a miracle: where he sees the grievous exploitation of hundreds of minors, forced by a handful of white men to work the earth, the others see an army of enlightened children. Where the pilgrims see utopia, he can distinguish the acts of a play put on for credulous eyes. Where the others see a diminutive seer, he sees a child lost amid his own lies. Where the others see resolution, he sees a farce that has spread like an epidemic. It's in that second look that the city shows itself in all its cruel truth: he believes he sees that the temples are actually small factories full of tired and sweaty children, and that the imperial archipelago is merely the outline of an atrocious world whose facade hides the worst kind of abuses. He's supposed to be photographing a utopian city, but all Yoav Toledano can focus on is the happiness and bewilderment of knowing that it will all be over soon. He has come to the edge of the jungle only to find that at the end of a journey, the traveler merely finds his own desire reflected back at him.

So he's not surprised when, at the prophesied day and hour, nothing happens—no earthquake, no fire, no grand finale. It is time to dismantle the fantasy, take the girl to the hospital, return to the life they left behind a decade before: watching TV, eating french fries. He is surprised, though, to see that in spite of the prophecy's failure, the pilgrims rally around the young seer in frenetic excitement. He has reached the end of the journey expecting the moment of disenchantment, only to learn that defeat unleashes fanaticism.

When his wife asks him to take a picture of their daughter next to the young seer, for the first time, he feels not only sorrow, not even hatred, but a mixture of despair and impotence that makes him throw the camera to the ground. If he picks it up then and takes the photo it's not because he's changed his mind, but because he thinks that perhaps, in a distant future, the picture will at least be evidence of the void at the end of the journey. But the second he snaps the photo he knows better. He knows that he'll find in it neither horror nor passion, only a rough, empty portrait: the face of a lost boy deep in a role, and, beside him, the pale, confused, and sickly face of his own daughter, the immediate reflection of his own confusion and distress. As he takes the picture, he understands that the moment has come; it's time to leave.

That day, while his wife is listening to the seer, he takes his sick daughter and escapes. If anyone asked him later, he wouldn't be able to describe the route that brought him back through the jungle to the fat man's town. He wouldn't know how to describe the animal instinct that guided him. But no one will ask. After leaving the girl in the village's small hospital, he looks over an atlas until he finds, among the dozens of coal towns that punctuate the Pennsylvania map, the one adjacent to the ghost town the apostle has mentioned. If the fires ever decide to continue their march, they shall find him there. He kisses the little girl, leaves her a children's book, and sets off, telling himself he will return as soon as he's able to break free from the madness he has just seen.

Fragment #317

(*The Great South*, Viviana Luxembourg)

I wish I could write these lines in a secret code. In a private language that only she and I would understand, my daughter and I. After all, isn't that what life is—a long series of shapeless events ending in a figure in the sand that only two people can decipher? I saw what the others didn't see, maybe because I never wanted to see what supposedly was there. Yoav didn't see anything. I only had to look into his eyes to know he didn't see what I did. All I had to do was listen to him breathe and I knew that all those years behind the camera had blinded him to the scene of injustice that we finally saw there. Seeing is believing, said my grandmother. But to see is also to know what one wants to believe. Yoav thinks I believed it all. He doesn't realize, doesn't want to realize, that I understood the farce of it all. I felt the sadness of seeing that boy exploited by a white man who had convinced him to act out that pantomime for all of us, in exchange for God knows how many coins. Seeing is understanding what's at stake. I saw what others didn't, maybe because they, in their selfishness, sought in that scene the reality they wanted. All of them, even Yoav, wanted to find a salvation that didn't exist, and they couldn't comprehend that in its place was a story of disenchantment and violence. They saw the boy, and behind him they saw nothing. They didn't see the long line of children, past and future—black, indigenous, mixed—who were trying to survive in a world that expelled them from the start. They were searching for the end of the world, but didn't know how to see it when it was right in front of them. I saw what the others didn't. And I knew I couldn't leave, that my story was there and that time had ended up separating Yoav and me, those two youngsters who broke with social expectations and crossed an invisible border. Everyone sees what they want to see, said my grandmother. I saw the scorched earth of my great-grandfather Sherman, and in it, I saw a reflection I'll never forget, the lands that would be razed years later by Efraín Ríos Montt's armies. I saw a child lost in a cyclone of history, acting out in a cruel historical play that obeyed no laws: not those of farce or of tragedy or of comedy. I saw what others didn't see and I knew immediately that Yoav wouldn't understand, precisely because only two people could. She and I. My daughter and I. I saw and I knew right away that my daughter would also see, even if years had to pass before she did. One day she would think back and she'd understand what I saw: the long chain of injustices that ended in mockery at the edge of the world, leaving a wake of disenchantment behind. I knew someday she would understand that behind that child there were many others. I knew she would understand my faithfulness to that vision, even if it was already too late, and that someday she would take it as her own. I felt an enormous joy at the realization. The joy of knowing that something would forever unite us, a secret language that only she and I would speak, from which her father had unfortunately been exiled. I knew that someday she would see the drawing in the wet sand of history, and, comprehending it, she would forgive me. That day, I believe, is today. And I repeat: I wish I could have written this letter in a secret language, in the secret language written by the tides and understood only by the pariahs of history, she and I, my daughter and I. You and I.

The absolutely useless is what I'm interested
in revealing. It leads to nothing, that which
has never led anywhere. Perhaps to brief
exchanges within tunnel passages, leaps between
attempted archetypal images. But the attempted
transcendence of all of this is irrelevant. Just
a dark fume that reports. Nothing.

—Lorenzo García Vega

Two years ago, in the middle of a terrible, snowy winter, when I had finally set aside that enigmatic family's story, something brought it to mind again. Perhaps it was the long periods of snow and immobility, perhaps the feeling of exile that came over me with every winter. Looking out at the piles of snow in front of my house, I kept thinking about writing it all as a story, as if it had been a simple fiction. But then I remembered Tancredo's question—tragedy or farce?—and my path was blocked by the impossibility of finding the right tone, and I was forced back. The story called for a chameleonic genre somewhere between the two, neither tragedy nor farce. My inability to translate my thought into writing left me, again and again, prostrate before the paper, motionless and unable to write a word. Then I would make a cup of black coffee to drink while I paged through the old notes and photographs from the ruinous archive of that once-happy family. Storytelling, in cases like that, was finding a way home. But I hadn't gone home in over twenty years.

A couple of months later, at the end of May 2014—when I was still searching for the right tone and spent afternoons venturing futile beginnings—the news came out that Subcomandante Marcos had made an early-morning speech in the community of La Realidad, Chiapas, announcing the end of the person named Marcos and his replacement by Subcomandante Galeano. That night, I remember reading and rereading Marcos's goodbye message. Like all his dispatches, it was poetic, full of intensity and passion; it began, "These will be my last words in public before I cease to exist." That method of rhetorical disappearance made me think about Giovanna, old Toledano, Virginia McCallister, all those people who seemed determined to find the limits of the art of disappearance. I thought almost fifteen years back, to the corkboard collage of Giovanna's attempt to appropriate a reality that was foreign to her. I remembered how at the time I'd looked at her with condescension, seeing her as meddling in matters she didn't understand, and I couldn't help feeling remorse. Then I went on reading Marcos's message as it outlined a poetics of anonymity much clearer than what I or any of my colleagues could have given: "Our authorities, our commanders, then said to us: 'They can only see those who are as small as they are. Let's make someone as small as they are, so that they can see him, and through him, they can see us.' Thus began a complex maneuver of distraction, a terrible and wonderful magic trick, a malicious move from the indigenous wisdom challenging one of the bastions of modernity: the media. And so began the construction of the character named 'Marcos.'" Giovanna had gotten it right, even though our project hadn't gone anywhere. Some part of her understood the strange magic trick that was Marcos, and she was determined to comprehend him according to his own rules. Then I copied out some lines that seemed enlightening, and that I felt limned the narrative tone I'd sought unsuccessfully for so long: "Perhaps at the start, or as these words unfold, the sensation will grow in your heart that something is out of place, that something doesn't quite fit, as if you were missing one or various pieces that would help make sense of the puzzle that is about to be revealed to you. As if indeed what is missing is still pending." The tone I was after, I thought, was one that gestured, not without joy, toward the eternally absent puzzle piece. I thought about the last night I'd spent with Giovanna, the jigsaw puzzle we'd left half-completed, the conversation we'd never finished.

The subcomandante's pronouncement ended with a categorical condemnation: "So here we are, mocking death in Realidad." If someday I manage to write this family's story, I told myself, it could be summed up as a long joke told to laugh in the face of death.

Two weeks later, on June 11, a small contemporary art gallery in Puerto Rico announced that it would be opening a posthumous show of the work of the deceased fashion designer Giovanna Luxembourg. The news was accompanied by a detail that struck me as significant: the designer had left precise instructions that the exhibit should appear exactly seven years after her death, along with specifications as to the venue, the organization of the pieces, and the texts that would accompany them. She had essentially curated her own posthumous show. To say that I felt betrayed would be a lie. I felt a strange sense of unease, a kind of déjà vu that I couldn't shake off until, a week later, I received a personalized invitation. It was a small envelope with nothing but Giovanna's signature on the flap. Opening it, I found the invitation elegant but generic, except for a detail that made me smile—a quincunx marked on the bottom of the page.

That night I dreamed that I was walking through the empty halls of an enormous museum, sure that I was late, and as I rushed along I looked for Giovanna, but couldn't find her anywhere. I was convinced that this mausoleum-like building *was* the exposition: the museum looking at it-self. I woke up sweating, the dream still alive. Something about it made me remember the anecdote about the theft of the *Mona Lisa*, how in the weeks after the robbery, thousands of curious people crowded into the halls of the Louvre to see the empty space where, up until a few weeks ago, they would have found the painting. I kept thinking about museums, about empty spaces and mausoleums, the way certain things only become visible when they disappear, until the image of Giovanna interrupted my thoughts and forced me to face reality. She seemed determined to make me to go home. I spent hours awake, thinking about Marcos's sudden disap-pearance and the old photographer's great journey, the final scene of Vir-ginia McCallister facing justice, and the last memories I had of Giovanna, until early morning came and I fell deeply asleep. Five hours later, when I finally got up, I bought a ticket.

Eight days later a plane carried me back to the land I had left more than twenty years before. I heard the roar of the plane taking off while to my left, too close to my ear, a girl scarfed down a hamburger. Mine was the opposite of Ulysses's epic homecoming. My return, I thought as I saw the clouds rise up, would have no Penelope or Telemachus; it was a vulgar re-turn to a home that had given me everything, but that, after twenty years had passed, threatened to become a merciless mirror. Not even the dogs would recognize me, I feared.

Four hours later I saw a postcard image that I had forgotten: the old walled city, and around it, the sea. Framed by the window, the image was stripped of nostalgia. I recognized the outline of the great lagoon, some government buildings; even the plane's trajectory as it landed was familiar.

I was returning full of nerves, afraid of not recognizing myself in the old poses, of seeming irredeemably foreign, of losing myself among the people. Of all beginnings, I thought as we approached the landing strip, the most difficult is the one occasioned by a return. Of all the objects of desire, the most seductive and fearsome is one's own identity.

I pretty much stopped thinking after that.

I listened to the flight attendant as she welcomed us, and I let my attention drift to a conversation between two old ladies who reminded me of my distant grandmother. I let myself be guided by the rhythms of the memories that only reappear when you believe them forgotten.

And maybe it was an attempt at evasion that I planned my arrival to coincide with the exhibition's opening day. That way, I wouldn't have time to surrender to reflection. My plan worked, at first. The plane landed at four, and at four-thirty I took a taxi to Old San Juan, well aware that I would have to be ready to leave for the opening at seven. While I looked out the window at the scene, familiar but altered by hotels and highways, signs and people, my mind was caught up negotiating—with a secretary's precision—the succession of events that would have to occur for me to be ready at the appropriate hour: half an hour in the taxi, fifteen minutes to check in, half an hour to unpack and shower, half an hour to walk to the gallery. Beneath that everyday arithmetic, however, memory was preparing its ambush. Even as I refused to give in to remembering, my past was laying its traps for me.

Days later I would remember an Algerian poet's line describing his nation as background noise, a sensation of place more than a series of memories. But that afternoon I thought I was safe from memory and the past, until the taxi took a right and the sea finally appeared, right on time. Only then, before that view so often seen and forgotten, I felt the blow of a battalion of confused memories, and a strange joy. I relived, in an instant, the hours that had passed since my departure, and my island returned to me with the same happy intensity of recognizing a forgotten melody. I couldn't help smiling, and the taxi driver took the opening to start up a conversation:

"The ocean's nice, huh? Say, where you from? Venezuela?"

That was all it took to return me to a place of touristic anonymity. I responded with a curt affirmation, afraid of being outed as an unrecognizable native. Then I was silent, while I watched unfurl before me the cobbled streets and colonial buildings, the tourist city that still keeps its secrets. Ten minutes later, when the taxi finally stopped in front of a small house that had been converted into a hostel, I paid without any more conversation. I recognized, just across from the hostel, an old bar I'd frequented as a teenager.

The exhibition was held in an old building that had once been—as the kid working its impressive wooden front door told me—the house of a slave-owning marquis. As I went in I thought of the many bags of gold that at some point had filled that luminous interior patio, and of the many nights when, in the shadows, men had stood there and negotiated the value of a life. I would have gone on thinking of such things, willing as I was to remain distracted, if it hadn't been for a girl with green eyes and dark hair who, on seeing me enter, called to me by name from a corner full of people. I recognized her immediately as one of Giovanna's helpers, a girl who had been very young back then, and whose face was now starting to show the marks of the passage of time. Time is tattooed on the face, I thought, remembering Giovanna's epigrammatic phrases. Happy to see me, the girl explained that, following the designer's directions, the exposition was made up of four thematic rooms through which I could move as I pleased, without worrying about the order. She tried to start up a conversation then, but another voice, this time calling her name, distracted her, and as she returned to the group I took the chance to slip away through the dozens of people crowding the main patio. I decided to start in the first room to the left, first reading a short quote that adorned one of the immaculate white walls of the inner patio, as an epigraph. I recognized it immediately as one of the many that Giovanna and I had discussed in our conversations. It said:

> I very well remember at the beginning of the war being with Picasso on the boulevard Raspail when the first camouflaged truck passed. It was at night, we had heard of camouflage but we had not yet seen it and Picasso, amazed, looked at it and then cried out, yes it is we who made it, that is cubism.
>
> —GERTRUDE STEIN

Deciding that the best approach would be to escape from the crowd, avoiding recognition and chitchat, I moved into the first room, which had a title that I liked: *Color Theory*. On entering, the amount of material— quotations and pictures, notes and images, even a colorful old coat—made me think of my own archive documenting our long conversation. Today, two years later, when I think of the material spread out over the walls of the slaver's house, I remember one image in particular: a portrait of a boy posing for one of those turn-of-the-century orientalist studies. On his left arm perched an owl that anyone would assume was real if the caption didn't say it was stuffed. I thought the boy looked tired, maybe even anemic. The image was a perfect depiction of insomnia, I thought, and I remembered a photograph of Kafka as a child that I'd seen some-time before. I wondered about the boy's parents; perhaps he was looking at them, just beyond the camera, and they would remain forever in that century in which, over three thousand miles away in the shadows of this old colonial house, slavery was still a reality. That boy, I thought, as I looked at the cracks that fissured the image, was a son of a new century that he was then glimpsing, a time of cameras. The same century Giovanna and I had seen gradually extinguished, leaving behind this strange exhibit now surrounding me.

As I read in the long caption, the boy was named Abbott Handerson Thayer. He'd been born on August 12, 1849, in Boston, and his story was a puzzling mixture of tragedy and heroism. He had spent his childhood years in rural New Hampshire at the foot of Mount Monadnock, whose monumental landscapes had inspired him with a naturist zeal that he had gratified with forays into taxidermy and landscape painting. At fifteen, Abbott had moved to Boston, where he'd met an old painter named Henry D. Morse, who taught him the necessary rudiments to gain acceptance, at eighteen, into the renowned Brooklyn School of Art. There, under the tutelage of the famous Lemuel Wilmarth, he would consummate his career as a naturalist painter, and also meet Kate Bloede, his future wife. Those first happy years were followed by two decades of sadness, marked by three deaths that would leave the painter in a boundless melancholy: first his two children, William Henry and Ralph Waldo, followed by his wife, Kate, after she contracted a pulmonary infection in 1891.

As I took this in, I remembered Marcos's words that I'd read a few days before: "So here we are, mocking death in Realidad," and I thought that that the rest of Thayer's life could be an attempt to forget those three deaths through the art of anonymity and camouflage. After that photo of young Abbott with his taxidermied owl, I found a series of images that made me think of my work in the museum and of Giovanna's interest in animal mimesis, her ability to envision death as the most daring camouflage.

On November 11, 1896, five years after his first wife's death, Abbott Thayer appeared before the annual convention of the American Ornithological Association, prepared to revolutionize the field of evolutionary biology. He claimed to have found an explanation for the nature of color in the animal kingdom: evolutionary protection. Each feather and each shade corresponded to the color that the animal had to take on in a moment of danger, to camouflage itself against the natural background. I was impressed by the list of notables who intervened in the debate that ensued years later, in 1909, after the publication of Thayer's *Concealing-Coloration in the Animal Kingdom*: the philosopher William James, the codiscoverer of evolutionary theory Alfred Russel Wallace, Winston Churchill, and Theodore Roosevelt. Politics, I thought, always tries to follow art.

Farther in, along with a series of sketches and drawings by Thayer himself, I found another interesting detail. Initially imagined as a purely scientific investigation, Thayer's studies on mimicry and coloring had taken a new direction after the start of World War I, when the painter realized that the military could use his theories on color to invent new forms of camouflage.

Whoever managed to make their soldiers invisible would win the war. Alongside that note—which ended by mentioning a fruitless visit

Thayer made to Churchill in the war's early stages—I found an image of a camouflaged British ship. The caption described the events of March 12, 1919, when the Chelsea Arts Club held what they called a Dazzle Ball, for which the guests were asked to wear black-and-white patterns like the ones that were starting to adorn the camouflaged ships of the British marines. I thought of the praying mantis, always dressed in its war attire, imperious and deadly, fearsomely invisible.

The images of that party were followed by a couple of quotes that made me think Giovanna had hidden much of her knowledge from me. Never in our conversations had she spoken of Sir James George Frazer, master of modern anthropology, much less had she cited the paragraph inscribed on the gallery walls under the title *Like Produces Like*. It was the famous quotation in which Frazer distinguishes two modalities of the magical. First, there's the law of similarities, in which an effect resembles its cause; second, the law of contagion, which states that objects that have been in contact continue interacting even when distance is imposed between them.

Our story had something of that magic at a distance. Many years

had passed since the last of our nocturnal meetings, but every one of the words uttered back then seemed to reverberate in the hallways of that colonial mansion. I remembered the panic Giovanna felt at human contact, her peculiar way of avoiding crowds, even in a city that called for collision above all. I kept walking, and in front of me appeared a visual story that the exhibition's curator insisted on referring to, always in French, as the phenomenon of *camoufleurs*. Between the two world wars, a set of artists had emerged who were dedicated to creating camouflages for military use in the national army. According to the curator, the *camoufleurs* started with Abbott Thayer and continued with Lucien-Victor Guirand de Scévola, commander of the famous French Camouflage Section, which, starting in 1915, counted among its ranks artists like André Mare, Jacques Villon, Charles Camoin, Louis Guingot, and Eugène Corbin. Then the names—Paul Klee, Hugh Cott, Franz Marc, John Graham Kerr, Leon Underwood—multiplied with the irresponsible freedom of any series. Meanwhile, piling up alongside them, the various camouflage schools—in addition to France's Camouflage Section, there was the Middle East Command Camouflage Directorate, in Britain, and the Twenty-Fifth Engineers in the United States—gave the impression that here, too, the fate of art had been entangled with that of politics. I thought of Virginia McCallister's notebooks, and the memory of the defendant made me think again of the false white color of Giovanna's dyed hair; she, too, had tried to become anonymous, taking on the colors of that natural background where she already intuited a great historical monster.

Tragedy or farce? I was asking myself again. I remembered something that Virginia McCallister had said during the trial: to understand modern art was to share the artist's obsession. The true question, I thought, was whether obsessions could be shared, whether someday I would come to understand exactly the logic that had led Giovanna to visually trace this fragment of art history. Two little girls ran across the hall and pointed, laughing, toward the old multicolored hunting coat, which had been a gift to Thayer from William James. Tragedy or farce? Perhaps the difference lay in who was telling the story and in how many times it was told. Perhaps, I thought as I watched the girls play hide-and-seek, it was a matter of perspective.

I felt uneasy as I left the room. I finally understood that I didn't know why I'd come, or what I had hoped to find. Perhaps I had only been looking for an excuse to return. I thought about going back to the inner patio, having a drink and socializing, but the remote possibility of finding myself forced to explain my own role in the exhibition pushed me on to the second room instead.

It was a room composed exclusively of cloth and photographs of cloth, reminiscent of Bedouin tents in the Middle East, insulated against the extreme desert temperatures. This room was called *Network Theory*, and it explored the invention, in the middle of the Great War, of a series of nets used to camouflage ground troops from aerial photography. I liked the metaphorical reach of the idea: covering territory with a blanket, a giant butterfly spreading its wings over the world. I thought of two artists I'd heard about whose art consisted of covering historical monuments with huge blankets. I thought of Borges and his story about the map equal in

size to the land itself: a useless map true to size, the remnants of which still exist—according to the story—in the deserts of the West, among animals and beggars.

The inventor of the method was the aforementioned Lucien-Victor Guirand de Scévola, a renowned pastel painter and the director of France's Camouflage Section. In 1918, he had established a system of factories that manufactured nets and employed over nine thousand workers throughout France. In one photo in particular, dozens of women appeared in a tangle of nets that looked like an undergrowth of bushes. The light seemed to filter through with difficulty, and it made me think of the Lebanese bar where the old woman read her outdated newspapers. There's nothing more difficult, I repeated to myself, than sharing an obsession. Then I thought again about the photo of young Abbott Thayer with his stuffed owl, his tiredness and his eyes, and the way men become children again at the end of their lives, or perhaps never stop being children. Adults hidden from themselves, playing hide-and-seek with their pasts, clothing themselves in work and responsibility in a last grasp at anonymity, at forgetting the old photograph, lost among the drawers of the family house, that depicts them as they've always been: children gazing at their innocence. Before I knew it, I'd reached the end of the second room, my mind still on the photo of young Thayer. I was convinced that the exhibit's only reason

for being was to impose an invented order on a project that from the start had been nothing more than a childish whim.

The third room, titled *Skin Theory*, was on the second floor. At the entryway was a quote from Darwin: "Another most conspicuous difference between man and the lower animals is the nakedness of his skin." I heard the echo of my footsteps and I realized I'd finally found myself alone. Perhaps I'd left the rest of the people behind; perhaps I'd lingered long enough that they had all advanced to the final room, earning me this space of silence. Then I realized that this was the room that corresponded to me. I saw, arranged over the walls like a constellation, photographs of dozens of animals that Giovanna and I had talked about on the long nights that closed the last millennium: Brazilian cholas, *Sepia officinalis*, *Phylliidae*, the arctic hare and the sphinx moths. It would be a lie to say I didn't feel happy and proud when I saw that all those hours of work had not been in vain. Something of me had been inscribed on that exhibition from which I'd so far felt somewhat alienated. One detail surprised me: among the photos of animals, I found a series of photographs that depicted Abbott Thayer's late-career fascination with indigenous cultures. According to the curator's text, Thayer had alleged that in these cultures, clothing served the same purpose as camouflage: as a mimetic element, and as protection. The idea that indigenous peoples were closer to the animal world, so clearly absurd and wrong, surprised me, but I didn't linger over it. There were dozens of photographs of indigenous mimesis, interspersed with studies of the practice of tattooing in those cultures. According to Thayer, western cultures had forgotten the mimetic effect of tattoos and dress, preferring instead monochromatic clothing and the simplicity of bare skin. I liked the idea and it made me think again of Giovanna's pale skin and white-blond hair. The paleness of anonymity. A sound distracted me; a small, bald man had come into the room, breaking my precious solitude. Chasing seclusion, or perhaps a slowly arriving intuition, I left that room and went into the next, without caring about its name or reading the information written on the wall.

I was in a very long and somewhat dark hallway lined with more than two dozen masks. Among them, Giovanna had hung a series of quotations in illuminated frames. I walked slowly down the hall that now seemed to grow longer, reading those quotes where countless stories of violence converged: among isolated phrases from General Sherman and from bygone slavers, there were the sayings of runaway slaves, testimonies of indigenous people who had survived the scorched-earth genocide, from children who had seen their parents die in war. I remembered María José Pinillos reading Vallejo, trying to escape her pain through the Peruvian's words, and I returned to that night when I saw Giovanna confront her fears. I saw again her pale fingers playing with the jade elephant and the envelope lying on the table.

I decided to go on walking, to read the quotations scattered before me like the pieces of that jigsaw puzzle we'd left half-finished. Finally, at the end of the hall, flanked by masks, I recognized the photograph that, years before, the prosecutor had presented as the final evidence in the trial of Virginia McCallister. I recognized young Giovanna's tired, sickly face, her mother's dry and determined look, and, between them, the ambiguous face of the child seer. I recognized a quincunx tattoo on that frightened face. A world where words for our discontents still exist, I told myself, is a world that can be redeemed. I looked at the photograph, the three pairs of eyes

staring out at me, and felt sudden vertigo, as though I had reached that invisible border where gazes blend together in a shared pain that has little to
do with tragedies or farces. A pain that abolishes genres, and that encompassed the empty gaze of the reader in the Bowery bar, old Toledano's tired
eyes contemplating the fluttering of orphaned chickens, the tattooed face of
the stutterer and the imaginary William Howard, Giovanna's exhaustion
and the young seer's confusion. I saw us all there, in that great march of
insomniacs. Thinking of the image of young Abbott Handerson Thayer, I

saw us all depicted in that absent gaze, and I decided that Giovanna had brought me here so I would find in that final photo a depiction of that man's life, and in it, a mirror of my own exhaustion. I sensed that someone behind me was opening the door to the hall. Dreading being discovered in my secret knowledge, I left the exhibition. The next day, I was sure, the photo of mother, daughter, and seer would be analyzed in the press.

That night I walked. I crossed the old cobblestone alleyways of the colonial city, feeling unexpectedly light. In a small plaza facing the sea, I came across a group of old men playing dominoes. I sat down to play with them in the tropical heat, and I told them the story of how the Tehuelche Indians had stalked the flightless rhea to death in Patagonia. I finished the story, and when I saw they were all looking at me in shock, I understood that Giovanna had achieved her goal. She had made me into an incomprehensible animal.

Acknowledgments

Literature likes to rave and ramble with a base in what exists. This novel is no exception. In it I imagine a possible world starting from many actual facts: people, quotations, books, theories, and historical events. It would have been impossible to imagine the character of Virginia McCallister without the book *The Trials of Art*, edited by Daniel McClean, and even less possible without the intuitions of Jacoby, Costa, and Escari, whose "media art" inspired the protagonist's conceptual project long before Donald Trump tried to appropriate the term "fake news." Likewise, I wouldn't have been able to imagine my book without the help of *Hide and Seek: Camouflage, Photography, and the Media of Reconnaissance*, by Hanna Rose Shell. Many real characters people these pages: from General William Sherman, whose scorched-earth strategy inspired the book's historical reflections, to Subcomandante Marcos, whose words give hope in what would otherwise be a labyrinth with no way out. Here, reality—and I think the now-Subcomandante Galeano would agree—is an approach toward reflecting on the fictions that structure our political reality. Following that intuition, the book feeds off many others' artistic projects, among which I should mention Óscar Farfán's *Tierra arrasada*; the book *Breviario*, by Juan Carlos Quiñones; and the work of Edward Hopper, Michael Taussig, and Francis Alÿs, without whose sharp fables this book would not be possible. Equally important was the help of Gabriel Piovanetti and Jorge Méndez, whose talent as photographers offset my utter inability to work a camera. I must also thank Gabriela Nouzeilles, whose teachings echo throughout the entire book, as well as my Spanish editors Silvia Sesé, Jorge Herralde, and Ilan Stavans, for their clear-eyed readings, suggestions, and comments. I also want to thank Sandra Pareja at Casanovas & Lynch, Paula Canal and Andrea Montejo at Indent Literary Agency, and Devon Mazzone, Stephen Weil, and the team at Farrar, Straus and Giroux. Finally, I want to acknowledge two very special people without whom this novel simply wouldn't exist: Megan McDowell for making me believe in translation and Julia Ringo for first betting on this book. They have both made it significantly better.

pages ii and 6: Photograph courtesy of the author.

page 40: Subcomandante Marcos in Chiapas, Mexico, 1996. Photograph by José Villa (Creative Commons 3.0 License).

page 294: Abbott Handerson Thayer as a boy, ca. 1861 / Buckingham's Inc., photographer. Abbott Handerson Thayer and Thayer family papers, 1851–1999, bulk 1881–1950. Archives of American Art, Smithsonian Institution.

page 296: Camouflage boat. Photograph from the Bureau of Ships Collection in the U.S. National Archives (Creative Commons 3.0 License).

page 297: Abbott Handerson Thayer, *Stencil Ducks,* study folder for the book *Concealing-Coloration in the Animal Kingdom,* © Smithsonian American Art Museum. Gift of the heirs of Abbott Handerson Thayer.

page 299: Photograph © M. Puttnam, February 26, 1941.

page 300: Women working in a camouflage garment factory, 1917. Imperial War Museum, London.

page 302: Abbott Handerson Thayer, *N. American Indians and Soldiers,* study folder for the book *Concealing Coloration in the Animal Kingdom,* © Smithsonian American Art Museum. Gift of the heirs of Abbott Handerson Thayer.

A NOTE ABOUT THE AUTHOR

Carlos Fonseca was born in San José, Costa Rica, and spent half of his childhood and adolescence in Puerto Rico. At the Guadalajara International Book Fair in 2016, he was named one of the twenty best Latin American writers born in the 1980s, and in 2017 he was included in the Bogotá39 list of the best Latin American writers under forty. He is the author of the novel *Colonel Lágrimas*, and in 2018 he won Costa Rica's National Prize for Literature for his book of essays, *La lucidez del miope*. He teaches at Trinity College Cambridge and lives in London.

A NOTE ABOUT THE TRANSLATOR

Megan McDowell is a Spanish-language literary translator from Kentucky. Her work includes books by Alejandro Zambra, Samanta Schweblin, Mariana Enriquez, and Lina Meruane. Her translations have been published in *The New Yorker*, *Tin House*, *The Paris Review*, *Harper's Magazine*, *McSweeney's*, and *VICE*, among other outlets. She won a 2020 Literature Award from the American Academy of Arts and Letters, and her translations have won the Valle Inclán prize and the English PEN Award for writing in translation, and have been short- and long-listed for the International Booker Prize. She lives in Santiago, Chile.